BASTION
Michael Scott Walton

Punks' Guild Publishing

Copyright © 2025 by Michael Scott Walton

A Punks' Guild Publishing book

Cover art by Travis Walton

Map illustrations by Lucas Walton

All rights reserved.

ISBN 979-8-9997497-0-3 (paperback)

ISBN 979-8-9997497-2-7 (ebook)

For Lace

BASTION'S SPHERE
1 YEAR PRE-NEW ERA (NE)

THE BELT

RUBICON
STATION

AL-HAVINI
STATION

DEIMOS

PHOBOS

BASTION
(MARS)

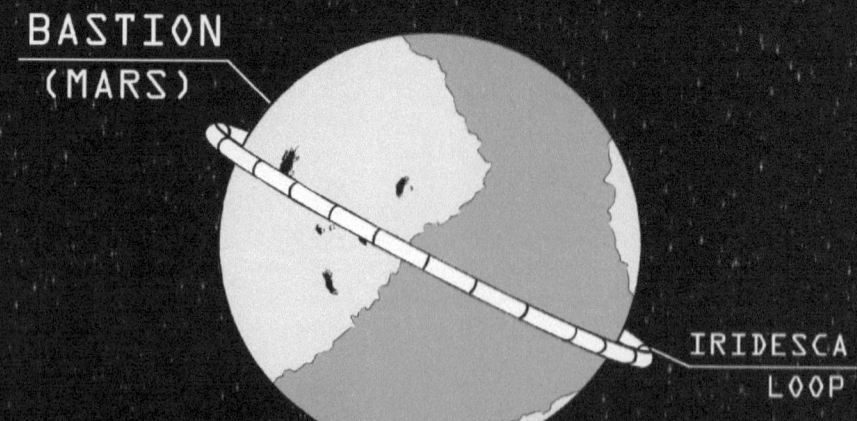

IRIDESCA
LOOP

EARTH'S SPHERE
10 YEARS NEW ERA (NE)

FARSTEAD

SANCTUARY

HORIZON DAWN
STATION

THE INDEPENDENT
COLONIES OF LUNA

EARTH

THE
DANDELION

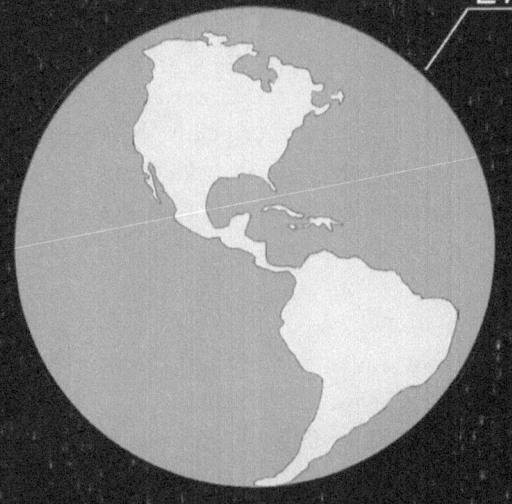

CHAPTER ONE
TORIS

ALISTELLA PAREIDES CALIDAY—MOONBREAKER, TRAITOR, and hero—crouched on her hoverboard as she hurtled between buildings. And, as I'd done for ten years, I chased her.

Alis wore her copper hair in a ponytail that bounced behind her as we flew, her thin white shirt billowing around her and popping out of where she'd tucked it into her brown pocket-padded pants. Her boots, secured to her board by magnets in the soles, were a shade darker than her pants, stained from grease and dirt. On her hands she wore the same fingerless gloves from her time as an Aegis pilot, though she'd torn off the Bastion seal on the top.

She turned her head, loose locks slapping her forehead, and smiled that brilliant smile, greenish-gold eyes flashing with mischief. I bit my lip and bounced my eyebrows up and down. She winked and turned back, then crouched deeper, slapped her heel on the board, and the miniature turbojet beneath burst with energy, rocketing her forward. I did the same, a "Woo!" escaping as the cold air slapped my face.

To our left, setting sunlight shimmered across the crystalline Corcoran Sea, a sheet of glass between the city and the western mountains that separated the body of water from the ocean. On our right, the buildings of Orilla del Angel blurred by, the metal and brick covered in ivy and moss, the Earth reclaiming the city, and the city welcoming it. Above the city hung helium-filled blimps, cut off in the center, where huge fan blades spun, generating energy that traveled back down to the city through thin cables. Out in the water stood giant solar panels in the shape of sunflowers, following the blazing light as it prepared to settle behind the mountains.

We had to hurry.

Alis pressed her back foot down, and her board leaned back, rocketing her higher into the air. I followed as we left behind the skyscrapers and entered the open air. I could see Alis' target: one of the suspended wind generators. From the distance I was used to, I could cover them with my thumb, but they were really the size of a small building. I also couldn't say I was used to the cold. It bit my skin and kissed my hair and clothes with frost. Alis likely wouldn't notice; just one advantage of the augments she'd enjoyed since birth.

As we crested the turbine, Alis swiveled her board so she was flying horizontal, ran her fingertips along the inflated material, then swiveled back to standing, crouched lower, and pressed down on the front of her board. Teeth chattering from the cold and squinting through the sunlight reflecting off the turbine, I rose above the generator, and at the apex, with the whole world spread below, I pressed down on the front of my board and rocketed toward the surface. Gravity took hold, and with my board's turbojet sucking in air, compressing it, and blasting it out the back, Earth ascended toward me, the spires of Orilla glinting in the sunset.

We dropped between the buildings and both pulled up on our boards at the same time, small thrusters on the bottom slowing us down even further until we stopped in midair, still another fifty or so feet above the ground. Any lower and we'd need to practically crawl toward the ground to avoid disrupting the people walking below.

"You cold?" Alis asked, a mischievous smile tugging at her lips but never quite reaching her eyes. She was forcing it, trying to make me feel better, to make herself feel better, to distract herself from what was coming.

Of course, I played along, which didn't take much, since I was still shivering. "Not at all. I think we should guh-get closer to space next time. I really miss it."

Alis scoffed, then leaned closer and kissed me on the cheek. And it dissipated the cold like fog in the sun.

When our eyes locked again, those gold flecks twinkling, I dropped my smile. She mirrored me. "You okay?"

"No," she said with the flash of a sad smile. That sadness had beauty in it, though, like leaves dying in bursts of fiery color.

"It'll be quick," I said, setting my hand on the side of her face and stroking her cheekbone, over a freckle and back to where strands of hair dropped around her ear. "Then it's back home. Back to normal. Back to the dream."

"So does that mean the nightmare is what's actually real?"

"No, that's not what I..." I let out a breath through my nose. I had a special knack for trying to help and doing exactly the opposite. A real gift. Didn't even need augments to be able to do that.

There was the sad smile again. She squeezed my hand then pulled it away. "I know." She looked down the street. "Navi's close, right?"

"Should be, yeah." I stared at Alis a little longer before following her gaze down the street. Orilla del Angel had been a relatively young city, growing on the shores of the Corcoran Sea, even before Bastion used its orbital mass drivers to pummel the southwestern coast of the region once known as "California." That assault had broken the new, modern metropolis, cracking open buildings like eggs.

Rather than abandoning the city or razing the buildings, the remaining citizens saw an opportunity to begin anew, to embrace a society that was then in its infancy. That was when they narrowed roads and installed more walkways and parks, when they covered parking lots with new buildings, much of it housing. Even some of the cracked-open buildings were enhanced rather than simply repaired. A few blocks down, a beautiful arching wooden bridge crossed between holes in two buildings, the broken windows empty and open to the air, the jagged metal covered by wooden frames and colored tarps like sails that covered the open areas. Trees grew along the bridge and in the reclaimed areas of the buildings, roots growing down walls, winding into the ivy that grew there, too, beautiful in its emerald quivering, and a natural insulator to boot. We called that area the Hollows.

"She should be there," I said, nodding to the building on the left side of the bridge. We nudged our hoverboards forward, turbojets whirring beneath our feet.

As we neared the building, we leaned toward a small platform that jutted out into the air, covered by one of the cloth sails. A few other boards were docked there, as well as a sleek white hyperbike—little more than a seat and handlebars on a turbojet engine and lift fans.

We dropped onto the platform and into the shade of the sails. The calm caress of a gentle breeze replaced the biting cold of flying. Above, the sails snapped and rolled in the wind, the sunlight filtering through them into oranges and blues and purples. Below the sails and in the remnants of the building, people gathered. Smoke billowed out from a sizzling streetcart around which eager patrons waited. Groups talked around tables or played cards, and others stood at stalls, bartering and trading. A group of children ran by, their laughter ringing against the hollow walls.

We jerked our right heels to the side to disengage the magnets holding our boots to the hoverboards. We left the boards in marked slots on the platform and stepped off, passing the streetcart. I took a big whiff of the grilling vegetables and pita bread. Alis closed her eyes and took a deep breath, too. Then she reached back and took my hand.

We wound past tables, smiling at a few people I recognized. The bald guy throwing me a pained smile was one of my childhood math teachers, Mr. Meridot. And he was clearly losing that game of poker. They may not have been betting with money, but that only barely lessened the pain of loss. At a table behind him was Laurendale Nixon, their white hair long on one side and shaved on the other, in a fierce debate with a friend I didn't recognize. We went on a few dates in high school but got distant once we deployed in the War.

At the back of the room, standing at a stall, was Avinavi Li'kai Orius. She wore her black hair in a tight braid down her back and was dressed in fitted black pants and a billowy sky-blue shirt. It was a popular style those days, but it always reminded me of old pirates. I guess that was part of the point, though, in this Era of Reclamation, reclaiming the styles and beauties and creativity of Old Earth eras for the new world. I guess, for whatever reason, pirate style stuck.

I snuck up behind Navi, who was chatting with someone standing behind the stall, and poked her in the ribs. She jerked and spun, jaw tight, eyes just slightly wide, anything but amused. "Toris," she said through gritted teeth. Her eyes darted toward Alis, but she didn't otherwise acknowledge her. That little intentional action poked me somewhere under the ribs, churning my stomach with an odd cocktail of frustration, sadness, and a whisper of doubt. But that cocktail bubbled away to an aching pain when Alis squeezed my hand and walked away to browse some of the other stalls.

"Is it really so hard?" I asked, trying to keep my voice down. "Is it really so hard to just show a modicum of decency? She's been here longer than half the people in this room. But you wouldn't treat them so coldly."

"Half the people in this room didn't shatter a moon and kill under Bastion's banner, did they?"

"Half the people in this room didn't abandon their home and help win the war, either, *did they*?" I took a step closer. "Ten years. She's been part of this community for ten years. She's grown to tolerate your behavior, because that's who she is. Because she understands the complicated feelings you have for her. The least you could do is give her the same grace. She has to deal with enough." More venom than I intended snuck into that last phrase.

Navi stared at me with green eyes that mirrored my own, and I saw some of the fight leave her as her features softened. When she did that, when the stress wrinkles smoothed out, I saw the little girl who'd watched with me as tungsten rods thrown from starships burned through the atmosphere like divine punishment. The little girl who'd held my even smaller hand and pulled me closer. The little girl who'd laughed as we ran through the dry, crackling grass, trying to stay out of the searing heat of the experimental orbital mirrors. The young woman who shed a rare tear and held onto my hand a little longer than usual when I finally decided to get off my ass and do something about Bastion.

"What did you need?" I asked, doing some softening of my own. "We need to get out there before..."

"Yeah, I know," Navi said, reaching into the satchel slung over her shoulder. "It's just some insurance, if things get rough." She pulled out a thin, silver, metal bar that curved just slightly. "Put it on her temple and it should short out the mindjack."

I stared at the thing balanced on her fingertips, not ready to take it. "Something that shorts out a brain implant doesn't sound very safe."

"Safer than the alternative," Navi said, and I couldn't quite find the words to disagree with her. I had a few scars that wouldn't help my case there. Sighing with impatience, Navi slid the bar into my pocket. "Vic made it. She said it should just knock her unconscious. That's it. It'll...it'll protect both of you. Promise me you'll at least try it."

I looked into those worried eyes again. Navi carried enough on her shoulders without having to worry about me. Earth communities didn't really have leaders anymore, at least in terms of formal authority and heads of institutions, but there would always be those who stood taller, who helped more, gave more, and that was Navi for the community of Orilla.

"If it comes to it, yes. I'll use it."

"Thank you," Navi said, patting me on the cheek a couple times, the last more of a light slap. "Fly safe. Come see me when you're back, okay? Vic says she may have a lead on a specialist."

"From Babylon?" I responded, hesitant to stock any hope in yet another dead end, especially from one of the last capitalist cities on the planet, which was only becoming greedier in its death throes.

"No," said Navi. "From Farstead."

Despite my hesitation, hope bloomed warm in my chest. "Tell Vic thank you. I'll see you...after."

I found Alis at a stall, leaning over a collection of bottled paints, hands clasped behind her back. She straightened when I got closer and smiled.

"So she gave you a brain taser? Did you solve it?"

I grimaced. "Oh, that was a bad one." Navi could whisper all she wanted, but it wouldn't do much to prevent Alis' augmented hearing from catching it. "I won't use it, don't worry."

Her smile dropped, and she became even more serious than Navi. "Yes. You will."

***

We hurtled through the trees, the white and silvers of the buildings earlier replaced by the greens and browns of what had once been a "national park" centuries before, back when humanity at least pretended to care about nature and set aside protected areas.

It had taken too long, but they'd finally learned.

Much of the park, once called Yosemite, had been cut down to fuel the expanding industries of the twenty-first and twenty-second centuries. But regrowing the forest had been a top priority when the Pioneers left Earth and founded Bastion on Mars, taking their poison and exploitation with them.

Alis and I were going deep into the wild, past even where those of Old Earth had ravaged the forest. The further from Orilla, the better.

I looked west, to where the light was chasing the horizon. Then I glanced up through my goggles toward Alis, standing leisurely on her hoverboard as if she weren't hurtling through the air at over a hundred miles an hour. She looked fine, but that could change at any moment.

After another half hour of flying and winding past hillsides and cliffs, our destination came into view: a ridge that looked into a forested valley, gray snow-capped mountains on either side. The setting sunlight glittered on a waterfall a few miles away. On that ridge was a small wooden cabin.

We pulled up on our boards and circled around the cabin, descending until we were level with the ground and only a few inches from the grass, then hopped onto the earth. My head swam for a moment, the valley swaying from side to side. Flying that fast for that long without any assistance or containment always messed with me, but Alis of course walked like she'd just been on a leisurely stroll. I, on the other hand, stumbled like a drunk for a few steps before I planted my feet until the world steadied itself.

Alis put her hands on her hips and stared out over the valley. Her torso rose and fell with a great sigh. So many things danced on the tip of my tongue, ready to fly, and my heart ached knowing that none of them would help. I knew every thought going through her head. They were the same thoughts that came and went every two years, every cycle. *How long will we have to do this? What if I don't return this time? What if I hurt someone?*

What if someone else dies?

What if it's Toris?

We'd had enough repeated conversations that she held her tongue, too. She hadn't demanded that I stayed behind for at least the past two cycles, knowing it was a lost cause. One cycle, she'd tried leaving without me, the night before we were prepared to leave. The note she left behind was as useless at preventing me from following as the words I ached to say.

So instead of saying anything, I walked up behind her—only stumbling once—and wrapped my arms around her waist before setting my chin on her shoulder. "I'm here. I'll be here the whole time. And I love you, despite the Wolf."

Alis sighed again, this one shorter and softer. "Despite the Wolf," she repeated, and she sounded anything but comforted.

I squeezed her waist once and kissed her cheek. "I'll get us set up." If she noticed my shaking hands, she didn't say anything. But ten years of this, and as hard as I tried to focus solely on Alis, the threat of imminent danger was a stimulus my body couldn't ignore.

As a meager distraction, I got to work preparing the cabin for the following couple of days. I lifted a thick lever on the side of the cabin and two panels popped open. Miniature versions of the floating wind generators hanging above Orilla drifted into the air, connected to the side of the cabin by cables. They rose until they hung fifty feet above the roof. Next, I turned a dial that would route power from the field of smaller sunflower solar panels and their batteries into the cabin.

I rounded the corner and stepped inside. The cabin was small, nothing more than a small kitchen and frayed-rug-covered living area, complete with couch and table, and an adjoining bedroom. I flicked a switch and lights sparked to life, shining on the dust motes, then took a breath of the musty air. Covering my mouth and nose from the dust, I threw up the corner of the rug and opened the trapdoor beneath. The lights below flickered, taking the already-eerie room to a more fitting horror-story setting. This room was empty except for chains on the back wall, bolted to stone.

There, all alone, I let a tear fall.

Alis was outside, sitting on the ridge, knees pressed up against her chest and arms around her knees. I sat beside her in the soft grass and stared out at the valley. A small flock of birds fluttered from the forest toward the gray mountains. It would have been idyllic, if not for the circumstance. Then again, that could have been a metaphor for everything. This new world would have been a utopia, if not for everything we'd lost, if not for the inescapable fear that maybe the Solar Gulf War wasn't really over. Maybe it was just a matter of time before another rod came hurtling through the atmosphere, or an Aegis itself landed in Orilla, cracking our haven and breaking the last of our hopes.

"We should chain me up now," Alis said. "Or you can use the thing Navi gave you."

"Maybe we won't need either this time. You went almost a whole day last cycle. I think you can resist it. Then this'll just be a nice vacation." Even as I said it, I cringed a little. I knew my attempt at encouragement wouldn't land. But I had to try something.

Alis looked over, gave me a sad smile, then looked up at the sky. Yeah, didn't land.

I followed her gaze to the heavens. With the sun nearly set, the stars were coming out. One shined brighter than the rest, and it had an orange tinge to it. Mars. When I was a kid, the "star" bulged around its center from the Iridesca Loop, the planet's magnetic field generator. But no longer. Now the planet had looked as it did for centuries. As it should.

Thinking that did little to smother the guilt I felt at every thought of the Loop.

Without turning my head, I looked at Alis out of the corner of my eye.

"It's weird," Alis said, staring at Mars. "I hate everything about that place. But every time I see it, I can't help but feel a...longing. Or maybe it's just grief. Sometimes I wonder if I could show them, if they could just see what we've built, see the joy and fulfillment, if they'd come around." She let out a breath through her nose. "But that's the desperate little girl that I somehow can't get to shut up. Some subconscious drive for their approval."

"Older sibling syndrome," I said, and she snorted. "You never know. Their society isn't sustainable. It has to fall apart someday, just like it did on Earth. Bringing the problems to a new planet just draws out the inevitable. Maybe you haven't walked them down the streets of Orilla, but you planted the seed. They know where to look for the path, and it'll be there waiting for them when they're ready."

She turned to me and I to her. The light reflected off the gold flecks in her eyes as she smiled. That time, it wasn't sad.

"I love you," I said.

"I lo—"

The rest of the words decayed into a breath. Alis' pupils dilated. Her jaw went slack, and her head listed to one side.

Mars hung directly overhead.

"Eh, shit," I said.

Then she attacked.

CHAPTER TWO

TORIS

ALIS GRABBED A CLOD of dirt and flung it in my eyes. I instinctively jerked backward, eyes burning. Her hands clamped around my throat, and she shoved me to the ground, squeezing with her augmented strength. It took only seconds for my head to start feeling lighter. The Wolf always went straight for the kill.

Clawing at her arms did no good, so—already praying for forgiveness—I reached in my pocket for the device Navi gave me. I wouldn't be able to reach her head to short out the malfunctioning mindjack, but it'd likely give her a good shock.

After fumbling around the cold metal, I found a switch and flicked it as everything around started to fuzz. Then I slapped the device against her thigh.

Her hands went rigid and vibrated, and I rolled away, swiping the dirt out of my burning eyes. Alis was already on her feet and running for me, hate in her eyes and a snarl to her lips.

I dropped into a low squat, planting my feet.

But that didn't much matter when she immediately swiped her leg out and swept my feet out from under me. I hit the ground—hard—and rolled out of the way just as she dove in a tackle. She carried her momentum into a handspring that sent her sailing into the air before she landed gracefully, then burst after me again. I huffed in a breath—it really wasn't easy fighting someone whose endurance and lung capacity was exponentially greater than yours—and lifted my left arm to block a swing from Alis' right fist. The impact sent a shock of pain up my arm and into my shoulder, but it was enough to deflect the punch. Cringing from what I was about to do, I swung my right shin into the side of Alis' left knee. She cried out and collapsed onto all fours. Augmented or not, she was still human, and the injury she'd sustained during the war had only become more vulnerable in the past ten years.

"Sorry," I muttered, reaching to place the device on Alis' head. But then her hand darted out and she punched me right where it counts. Pain knifed up into my stomach, and I fell backwards, emitting something between a cry and a squeal. I swear I somehow felt that pain all the way up to my head, and I resisted the urge to throw up. Through my squinting eyes, I saw Alis limping toward me. She reached down and wrenched one of the small sunflower-shaped solar panels out of the ground, holding it by the stalk. The aesthetic choice to build solar panels that way was suddenly far less appealing when the triangular petals looked a lot like knife blades.

The Wolf always went straight for the kill.

I scrambled backward and to my feet, my back to the wall of the cabin. To my left were the cables where the floating wind generators connected to the building. Below those lay our hoverboards. The fact that Alis hadn't gone for those reconfirmed a hypothesis I'd formed a few cycles before: whatever was happening to bring out the Wolf, it wasn't about survival, nor about escaping. It was about hurting me. Killing me.

She also hadn't gone for the device Navi had given me, which confirmed another hypothesis: the Wolf somehow either lacked Alis' memory or lacked rationality and strategic capability. Because Alistella Pareides Caliday was a trained fighter, a soldier, the Moonbreaker herself, and she could have immediately—and easily—removed that threat to her from my possession if she put even an ounce of effort behind it. Instead, the Wolf had gone right for my throat.

Why did all these thoughts run through my head as Alis was stalking toward me, shoulders back, with a weapon in her hand? It happened almost every time. The brain jumps through some interesting hoops when someone you love is trying to kill you.

I couldn't best her, even if I kept kicking at that bad knee. She'd adapt and watch out for that, now. But if I could trap her, subdue her, maybe I could get the moment I needed to put the device on her head. It was the last thing I wanted to do, but it was becoming increasingly clear that it was either that or get skewered by a solar sunflower petal.

The Wolf snarled and swung her sunflower just as I dodged to one side and spun around her, kicking my hoverboard toward her in a way that looked like I was trying to put a barrier between us. But I had an idea. The Wolf wasn't Alis. And I could use that.

Then the Wolf just stepped over the board toward me. So much for Plan A. Plan B would hurt more.

I crouched as the Wolf stalked toward me, sunflower gripped like a dagger. Then I sprang forward. For just an instant, the Wolf hesitated, clearly not expecting me to directly attack Alis. That gave me a moment to slam into her, not nearly enough to topple her, but enough to make her stumble.

And enough to get me close enough that the Wolf stabbed me in the side.

Pain exploded beneath my ribs as the sharp petal, accelerated by Alis' augmented strength, punctured my skin and the muscle beneath. I cried out and pulled away. The Wolf jerked to follow, to stab me again, but they were rooted in place.

"Ha!" I exclaimed, which somehow sparked even greater pain in my stab wound, causing my celebration to deteriorate into a cringing "ow."

Alis was standing on my hoverboard, her magnetic boots secured to the board. But since it was *my* board and coded to the magnets in my boots, the board itself wouldn't start up. Fortunately, magnets were magnets, and those were strong enough to hold a rider even if they were hanging upside down, say, a thousand feet in the air as they flew above a wind turbine.

The Wolf could disengage the magnets by swiping their heel to the left, but the Wolf didn't know that. Only Alis did. So, instead, they thrashed, the snarl in their face deepening with rage. They flung the solar sunflower to the side and bent over, trying to pry up their feet with their hands. Even with all that modified strength, magnetism won out.

After a little more thrashing and a lot more pulling, the Wolf stood up straight and stared me down, an animal in a trap.

The injury in my side pulsed with pain as blood pumped from the wound. I needed to get it wrapped. Soon.

I walked around the Wolf, wary of getting within reach of those hands. They jerked, trying to turn, but the hoverboard was heavy enough that they didn't turn very quickly.

"I'm sorry, sweetheart," I said. Then I set Navi's device behind Alis' ear, as close as I could to where the malfunctioning mindjack sat implanted in her brain.

Alis spasmed—no, Alis didn't feel anything...

The Wolf spasmed, then their head dropped forward, limbs hanging limp at their side.

I reached out to touch Alis' shoulder, to hold her, but my fingers hung in the air an inch from her. They were shaking.

And then they fell.

***

Alis lay on the bed below the cabin, the manacles around her wrists and ankles connected by thick chains to the stone wall behind her.

I sat at the other end of the room, back against the wall, staring at her unconscious form. She looked like she was sleeping, not like she was lying unconscious because I shocked the computer implanted in her brain. Had it hurt? Was it hurting now? Was I going to cause permanent damage? Navi may have assured me that there wasn't any great risk, but she'd never accepted Alis, and I always wondered how far that distrust would one day go.

But all of the indicators said that Alis was fine. After I'd chained her up, I'd checked her vitals, and those all appeared to be regular. I hadn't thought to bring something that could check her brain activity, but I could do that back in Orilla when the cycle had run its course.

Waiting was still painful, though. I couldn't bring myself to leave her—I rarely could during a cycle; usually only to sleep or eat—even after the Wolf had just tried to kill me. I'd flicked the switch off the device to at least make sure it wasn't sending a continuous current into Alis' brain. Now I waited for her to wake, even if that meant waking up as the thrashing and snarling Wolf.

I cringed as the pain in my side twinged. I'd wrapped my stomach and side in bandages and kept the bloody shirt off. That injury would become a new scar to add to my collection. It wasn't the worst I'd received—a few cycles before, one of the chains had broken and the Wolf got me across the cheek, narrowly missing my eye. That'd been—

"Nh," Alis grunted, the chains clinking together as she shifted in her bed.

I sprang to my feet and slid to her side, dropping back to my knees. "Alis, is that you? Are you all right?"

She squeezed her eyes tighter, teeth grinding in a grimace. "My head," she grunted. But even those couple words were music to my ears.

"I'm sorry," I said, reaching up and stroking her hair, moving my fingers around the device. "I'll take it—"

Alis' hand shot up, and she grabbed my wrist. She tried to open her eyes but then squeezed them closed again. "No. Keep it there. 'Til the cycle's over. Just in case."

"I...okay."

"Are you okay? Did I...hurt you?"

"No, you didn't—"

She sighed, and I'm sure I would have seen her roll her eyes if they hadn't been closed. "Did the Wolf hurt you?"

16

"Nothing some bandages and painkillers can't fix. I promise." I squeezed her hand.

Alis cringed again, and it took so much self-control to not rip the device off her head and destroy it, even if it wasn't currently shocking her. "Earlier this time," she said.

"Yeah, by a few hours, at least."

"Why?"

"I don't know. Could just be the relative rotation. Something that places Bastion at a clearer alignment to us."

She shook her head. "Getting worse. Earlier every cycle."

I took a deep breath, held it for a moment, then let it out slowly. Alis was convinced that she was deteriorating, slowly devolving into the permanent Wolf. I wasn't so convinced.

"I'll check the orbital data," I said. "The rotations. There's gotta be an explanation."

"Yeah, there is," she said, and Alis' eyes opened enough that I could see the emerald green and gold flecks of her iris. "I'm broken, and I'm just going to keep cracking until I shatter." She shook her head. "And I won't let you get hurt when I do."

"You won't. The Wolf isn't—"

"Toris, it's—"

"No." That came off sharper than I intended. "No," I repeated more softly. "We'll find a cure. We'll end the cycles, I promise. We just might have to...speed up the process."

Alis gave me a sad smile and squeezed my hand. She knew as well as I did that the odds weren't looking good. The mindjack that was malfunctioning and causing the Wolf to emerge was implanted directly into Alis' brain. Removing it, even at the hands of the best surgeons on the planet, would kill her. That wasn't a shortfall of the technology, it was intentional design by the scientists of Bastion, though of course most who received the implant were completely unaware. Just as unaware of what Bastion could do to them through that mindjack.

"Maybe this is the key," Alis said, gesturing up to the device. "Something that can detect when the mindjack tries to activate and shorts it out."

"And knocks you unconscious every time? We can do better than that."

"I'm unconscious anyway, or at least unaware. May as well make sure I'm not hurting anyone at the same time. It'd be little different than coming up here every time the cycle gets near."

"Did you see anything while you were under?"

"Olli," she said, swallowing. "So if something can knock me out to keep those memories from bleeding in, I'll take it."

I frowned but nodded. "It's an idea. Let's talk to Vic when we get back. We can...ow. Alis. That...oh." Alis had started squeezing my hand so tight my fingers were going numb. Her pupils had dilated, and her smile slowly twisted into a snarl. I grasped the Wolf's wrist with my free hand and pulled my fingers from her grip. Those hateful eyes followed me as I stood up and backed away toward the ladder. Only when I turned and climbed up to the main level did I hear the Wolf start thrashing, slapping the chains against the side of the bed. It yelled out in Alis' voice, but with a guttural edge.

At the top of the ladder, I closed the trapdoor. Then I stood and stared out the window, hands on my hips and tears in my eyes. As hard as I tried to deny it, I knew Alis was deteriorating, each cycle earlier and more aggressive. We'd been hunting for a cure for years, but we had to do more.

Outside, hanging in the black night, mocking me, was the orange eye of Mars.

CHAPTER THREE

ALIS

(Twelve-and-a-half years earlier)

THE ORANGE AND BLUE marble of Mars hung below the viewport. Olympus Mons, the tallest mountain in the solar system, stood sentinel over green-grass and red-rock plains, white snow capping its peak. To the southeast rose the Tharsis Montes, three squatter mountains that emptied their waters into the Capri Chasma River, which flowed eventually into the shimmering Mar Borealis ocean. To the northwest of Olympus Mons, climbing onto its slopes, were the towers of Bastion, humankind's greatest achievement. The city that represented the resilience and determination of the brightest minds and strongest hearts. Surrounding the planet was a silver ring, the Iridesca Loop, Mars' artificial magnetic field generator, a shield against the sun's brutality.

"Stop fidgeting."

I looked down and to my left—which wasn't so easy with the armor plating protecting my neck. Crouched there on the metal catwalk was Lanitea Aurora Caliday, my sister. Her black hair was tied back into a long ponytail, freckles dappling the tan skin of her nose and cheeks, a wrench held between her teeth. She attached the maroon metal plating she'd been repairing to my shin.

"Try that," she said, voice muffled by the wrench in her mouth.

I moved my lower leg back and forth at the knee. "Feels good. Thanks."

Teah stood and gripped one of my shoulderplates, then pulled a screwdriver from the belt at her waist and secured the plate. When she was finished, she slapped my shoulder. "Stay in your cockpit this time and you won't have so many reasons to thank me. I did adjust your sync port so you won't get such a jolt next time you eject."

I turned, still surprised by how light this latest version of armor was. "Sometimes it feels good to punch terrorists with my real fists." That didn't even get a smile out of her. "You okay?"

Teah took the wrench from between her teeth and stuck it into her toolbelt, then fixed the grease-stained cream-colored shirt that had come untucked from her black pants. She looked down at her feet, which told me she was going to lie before she did. "Yep."

"Teah."

She sighed and straightened, looking me in the eyes. "I failed my sync test. Again. They won't let me retake it. Said it's not something you can just 'practice' for."

"I'm sorry, T." That had to be the fourth time she'd taken the test. At least. I wouldn't put it past Teah to hide more attempts. "Did they explain what went wrong?"

Teah pulled away and shook her head. "Only that the Aegis kept rejecting my 'jack. They said it could be for any number of reasons."

I looked past where Teah stood on the catwalk to my own Aegis, the titanic, fifty-foot mech that waited for me to take it into battle. It was humanoid in shape, with arms and legs that were slightly longer than the average human. Its head was long, too, and narrow, with no facial features, just smooth maroon metal with glowing lines of blue light running down the right and left thirds of the faceplate. Mounted to the shoulderplates were cannons, and an arsenal of other weapons lay beneath the armor. The catwalk we stood on led to a trapezoidal opening in the side of the Aegis' torso, where its upper ribcage would be. Piloting that mech in the name of Bastion, in defense of home and heritage, was an honor, one that Teah had chased for years.

"There are other ways to serve," I said, knowing it wouldn't solve all her problems. It definitely didn't; she wouldn't meet my eyes again and just stared out the viewport, down at Bastion, at our home. "They're proud of you, too."

"Pft," Teah scoffed. And, to be fair, I didn't have much evidence to follow up my assurance. Teah wasn't childish enough to be jealous of her older sister's accomplishments, nor was I vain enough to draw her envy. But utility to the nation, service to the cause, was always the expectation of our family growing up. Father had been part of one of the many crews who completed the terraforming of Mars. He quite literally helped build humanity's new home, and he bore the infirmities to show for it. Mother had worked in the asteroid Belt for one of Bastion's most lucrative enterprises, ensuring the continued prosperity of the young civilization. They'd served their nation, they sacrificed for the future of humanity, and they expected their children to do the same. I had. And, as far as I believed, so had Teah. But it wasn't enough for her, especially after Mom's death.

"It's one path," I said, slapping her on the shoulder. "Think of all the fail...dead ends that the Pioneers encountered. If they'd continued down those paths, we wouldn't be here. Humanity would still be rotting away on Earth. You just need to find the right path."

Teah sniffed and finally met my eyes. "And you need to get going. Phobos isn't going to secure itself."

I held her gaze for a moment longer, then nodded and sent a mental command to my mindjack. Metal slithered from my suit and over my head, covering my face completely. A HUD lit up within the mask, showing me my environment as clearly as if the faceplate was up. The only thing separating the view from reality were the several notifications dinging for my attention in the top-right of the screen.

"This one's for you, T." I said, lifting my fist. Teah bumped it, then we slid our fists down each other's forearms.

"Have fun," she said, then walked away down the catwalk and out of the launch bay.

I waited until the door slid shut behind her, then turned, rolled my neck back and forth, and entered my Aegis. After stepping through a small airlock, both the thick outer door and the inner airlock door slammed shut. The Aegis' cockpit was simple, dominated by a reclining seat surrounded by instruments and screens. I grabbed two bars and heaved myself into the seat, settling down. When I was in position, a cord snaked out from the seat and plugged into a port at the base of my helm. A jolt ran through my head as the Aegis synced with my mindjack.

I flicked a switch on my right side and activated my comms. "This is the *Sanguine Lycan*, booting up."

Screens above me showed the Lycan's systems—all green—as well as our battlecruiser's flight path toward Mars' moon, Phobos. Below the bolder flightpath was a flashing dotted line that connected the starship to the moon. That was my trajectory.

I pressed another button and restraints slid out from the seat, latching onto various points in my armor.

"*Confirmed,* Sanguine Lycan," came a voice from command. "*All systems are green. Priming for launch.*"

The Aegis jerked as a giant arm slid the huge mech into its launch tube.

"*How are we feeling today, Caliday?*" That voice was Vice Admiral Ecker. I could picture him standing on the bridge, one arm behind his back, the other holding onto the collar of his coat.

"Feeling grateful to serve as sentinel and sword, sir," I said, the traditional phrase so natural coming out for the thousandth time that I barely registered saying it.

"*Very good. These extremists are a rot. Not so different than the rot that eroded the foundations of the Earth and forced our ancestors to brave the journey here. Their riots are dangerous, but their ideas more so. If we have the chance to remove both, you do that.*"

"Understood, sir."

"*We have intelligence that they're primarily holed up in Stickney's southern dome. You'll have to be quick; they've threatened to compromise the remainder of the city if their demands aren't met, and if the attack on the starport is any indication, they have the means to do so.*"

"Quick and clean, sir," I said. "Do we have the targets' 'jacks tagged?"

Vice Admiral Ecker was silent for a moment as I pressed in a bulky button near my left hand. A *clunk* echoed through the Aegis as the charging cables and fuel lines detached and the ports closed.

"*We've tagged them to the best of our ability. But it's safe to assume that anyone remaining with them is also compromised, whether we've caught them committing a crime or not. We can't rely wholly on the tagging. Rot, Caliday. Rot spreads fast.*"

"Understood...sir." My stomach churned and I shifted in my seat, suddenly uncomfortable. Pre-launch nerves. That was it.

"*Very good. As always, thank you for your service. Good luck, Caliday.*"

"Thank you."

"*You're cleared for launch. Godspeed. Bridge, out.*"

The line died, and I took a deep breath, held it, then let it out slowly, my helmet taking the carbon dioxide I expelled and circulating it back through the suit as it pumped more oxygen into the tiny space.

I sent a mental command, as simple as thinking a limb into movement, to my mindjack. Through its sync to my armor, and the Aegis beyond that, the jack switched the camera feed inside my helmet. At first, it was only darkness, with the occasional blinking yellow light. I was seeing through the cameras in my Aegis' face, staring at the wall of the launch tube.

"*Sanguine Lycan,*" said a computer's voice in my ear. "Launching in three." I gripped the handles on the side of my seat. "Two." Magnets engaged in my seat, holding my armor there as an additional precaution to the restraints. "One."

I held my breath. I closed my eyes.

"Launch."

The magnets and belts strained as the Aegis rocketed out of the launch tube. I opened my eyes as green lights whizzed by so fast they became a single line. Then the wall of the tube disappeared and I squinted into the light reflected off Mars. The blue of the Mar Borealis stared back at me, the result of comets and asteroids caught and dropped onto the planet. A miracle of humankind's ingenuity.

But the Borealis wasn't my goal. It was time to get to work.

With another mental command through my 'jack, thrusters fired on the side of my Aegis, spinning me so I was facing my target: Mars' largest moon, Phobos. It was an ugly irregularity compared to Earth's smooth, gray Luna. Tan and gray, pocked with damage, and deformed by an especially large crater that dominated almost half the moon. Stickney Crater. And on the crater's northern edge was Stickney, a small colony of domed structures.

The stubborn determination of humanity had stretched even to that arid rock, with Stickney growing from an observation station during Mars' terraforming to a proper colony. Now, as Bastion grew and thrived, those who didn't work hard enough to live in the city—and who decided to avoid the city's growing underworld—moved to Phobos' domes. Over time, the colonies had become a petri dish for the very rot Vice Admiral Ecker referred to: challenges to Bastion's authority and prosperity, and even to the philosophical underpinnings of the entire society, the pillars of capitalism, order, and security. Several weeks before, extremists had destroyed several points of critical infrastructure at Phobos' small spaceport, crippling trade and commerce between the planet and the moon. In the end, those actions would only hurt the civilians of Phobos, though the extremists would certainly manipulate those consequences in their favor.

I wouldn't give them the chance. I was the consequence they couldn't manipulate, the pillar of Bastion come to crush them.

The flight path on my HUD flashed green as my thrusters brought me into alignment. With a thought, I killed the thrusters, then engaged the rockets inside the lower back and thighs of my Aegis. Gravity slammed me deeper into my seat as I blasted toward the moon.

I left Mars behind and passed over the silver Iridesca Loop. My system beeped as I passed outside the magnetic field. There was little point to the notification; my Aegis' armor would protect me from radiation and debris. After all, the armor was originally designed during the Belt Rush, when drones were proving inefficient and the signals weren't sharp enough for the control that corporations needed to mine the precious metals found there. When the Aegis proved their utility in the Belt, the natural next step was to put them to use maintaining the peace and security of humanity's new home. Could a smaller special-ops squad have been sent in to handle these terrorists at Stickney? Of course. But I was a symbol. I was the power of Bastion for all to see, for all to fear and respect. We didn't need to deal in the dark. We wanted these extremists to fall for all to see.

As I flew closer to Phobos, Stickney rotated into view, little more than pebbles that glinted in the sunlight. I cut back the power to my rockets, but my flight path changed from green to orange, indicating that I was still likely to overshoot the moon. To slow down, I engaged thrusters on the front of my suit, and slowly my path slid back into the green.

Phobos came up fast, and the colony of Stickney grew, a cluster of domes on the rocky surface. Through the glass, I could see the green of trees between squat buildings. On the northwestern edge of the colony was the blackened husk of the spaceport, all of the docks and launch pads blown into complete disuse. Frustration bubbled in my chest. How absolutely ungrateful. How totally arrogant. These terrorists weren't sending any message other than utter disregard for the wellbeing of their neighbors. Reports claimed that the extremists were the descendants of Pioneers, that they were native to Mars, but we had our suspicions that they were more likely invaders from Earth, another futile volley in the ongoing Solar Gulf War.

Either way, rot was rot, and I was there to burn it away.

My thrusters pivoted me perpendicular to the moon's surface and with a quick burst slammed me down in the ruins of the spaceport. Dust and debris blasted in a corona around me, bouncing off the nearest of Stickney's domes, which towered just a few more feet taller than my Aegis. In the reflection of the glass I could see my maroon armor, the blue light of the lines framing my helm eerie in the dusty darkness.

I'd landed in the crater of one of the old landing pads, a few broken cranes beside me. To my right, the husk of a shattered starship lay in the wreckage, the stylized half-circle, half-eagle's-wing of Bastion charred beneath its bridge. Apparently the terrorists had blown the ship's reactor as part of the attack, no doubt an attempt at metaphor.

I flicked a switch near my right hand, which would allow me to speak directly to the mindjacks implanted into every citizen of Stickney. Unless, of course, they were Earther terrorists.

"*Citizens of Stickney,*" I said, my voice also projected from speakers on the outside of the *Sanguine Lycan*. "*This is Commander Alistella Pareides Caliday. I am here to liberate you from the fear that's crippled your colony. To the terrorists who perpetrated this horror, surrender now. And to the citizens of Stickney, help me protect you. Stand up for our people and for justice. Stand with me."*

While I waited, I expanded the reach of my mindjack, scanning the colony. The authority afforded by my position allowed me to see every other mindjack signal within those domes. I saw most of them as blue dots within a holographic map of Stickney. Some of the jacks, however, shined red, with an especially dense cluster in the southernmost dome, right where Ecker said they would be.

I could disembark from the Aegis and hunt down the terrorists myself, but I didn't want to risk innocents getting swept up into this or caught in a crossfire if the criminals decided to resist arrest.

Plus, justice meant giving people—even criminals—the chance to make restitution themselves. I was here to give them the opportunity. I genuinely hoped they took it.

Inside Stickney, the red dots weren't moving, the criminals staying put. I knew they heard me; my broadcast didn't just come out of the Aegis' absurdly loud speakers, but I'd tapped into the colony's system as well.

I waited. No movement.

"This is your final warning," I broadcasted. *"Surrender now. Your cowardice has harmed enough people. You destroyed your own means of escape. If you come with me, I can assure you a humane end. If you don't, I can assure you that the squad that comes to remove you will be far less merciful."* My backup stood armed and ready aboard the *Fang*, Ecker's battlecruiser. I'd lead them into the colony if necessary.

Another ten minutes, but no movement. The entire colony was eerily still, in fact. A held breath. Like they were waiting, too.

Then, finally, a handful of shapes moved in the nearest dome. They weren't marked red.

I dismissed the map of the colony and switched to my outer cameras, still staring at the dome and my dark reflection. After a few more moments, there was a hiss of air as one of the colony's airlocks opened, spilling white light onto the ruined spaceport. Five individuals in gray spacesuits stepped out of the door and onto the concrete walkway.

I tensed, telling my Aegis' systems to scan for weapons, unconventional explosives, anything. They were clean. Maybe they'd found a way to bypass my sensors?

"Stay back," I warned.

But they didn't approach. They lined up beside each other, blocking the still-open entrance to their colony. Then they reached out, clasped hands, and stared up at me.

For a moment, I just stared. A billow of blackened dust rolled over their feet. These people were standing in the wreckage of an attack that crippled their own home, defiant to my demands for justice? And what a pointless defiance it was. Their height barely reached the ankles of my Aegis.

I tapped into their mindjacks in addition to speaking through the armor: "*You would protect killers? You would harbor those who crippled your colony?*"

They stared up at me for a moment, then came the crackle of their speech: "*Our worth is not determined by our industry. By our output. We are not crippled. Without the exploitation of Bastion, we are thriving.*"

Ecker was right. Rot. These were the very ideas that sparked the Solar Gulf War between Mars and Earth. That, and who could lay claim to the bounty of the asteroid belt.

"*Regardless of your philosophies, these terrorists killed innocent citizens of Bastion. They robbed mothers and fathers of their children. Justice must be served.*"

"*Far less lives were lost than those Bastion has taken. Where was their justice?*"

I hesitated. That wasn't the same, was it? Was that really all they intended? Justice?

No. It wasn't the same. "*Whatever your grievances with us, no Bastionite directly harmed any of your people, as your people harmed ours.*"

"*Are we not your people as well?*"

My breath caught, finding no words to carry. I hadn't intended to speak that way, to distinguish between the two. They'd caught me there. But I could use that. "*Citizens of Bastion serve the needs of the greater whole. Citizens of Bastion do not kill others because of complaints about working conditions. There are proper legal channels to voice those grievances. We are a society of law and order. So I would ask you that question: Are you our people? Are you with Bastion?*"

In a response that couldn't have been planned, more Stickney citizens stepped outside the colony, dressed in spacesuits, and joined hands in three more lines behind their companions. My 'jack was counting thirty of them, all of them still glowing blue. None of these were the criminals; they were still hiding. Cowards.

"*Are you here to help us?*" asked the Stickney spokesperson. I scanned their mindjack, wondering if they were one of the colony's leaders, a governor or representative. But no, her name was Monalua Hailey Cruzino. Her identification image showed bright green eyes and short black hair. She worked in the colony as a teacher, of children, specifically. "*I would think,*" Monalua continued, "*if we were your people, if you had any concern for the people of this colony, you'd be sending in humanitarian ships, not battleships. Food and water, not an Aegis.*"

"I...that aid will come. Justice comes first."

Monalua chuckled into her microphone. A sad, defeated laugh that devolved into a sigh. "Of course it does."

This was ridiculous. This woman was asking for aid when they wouldn't need aid if their own people hadn't blown up their spaceport. What ingratitude. What arrogance. They wanted to separate themselves from the stability of Bastion society, and yet they had to rely on it.

"I am not here to debate," I said. "That's for the courts. Surrender the criminals. Now."

Monalua didn't immediately respond, but her and her people, still holding hands, drew in closer to each other. "We don't condone the means our brothers and sisters used. We mourn the lives that were lost. Allow us to deliver the justice they deserve. They—"

"CALIDAY!"

I jerked in my seat.

"Yes, Vice Admiral?" I asked through clenched teeth.

"Why are you still listening to this drivel?" Of course they'd been tapped in to my communications feed. "Shut them up and get them out of the way. The Sentinels squad is preparing to launch. Do your job. Give them a clear path."

"Sir," I said, double-checking that I'd muted the connection to Monalua and the rest of Stickney. "They aren't armed. They're not our criminals. They're just...protesters. Annoying protesters, but they don't support what the terrorists did."

Ecker sighed, and I could practically see him pinching the bridge of his nose. "What did I tell you about rot, Caliday? Do you think it started with the terrorists? They're the consequence, the result, the tree that fell and crushed a house, buried a family. No, the rot starts in the roots, with people like her. Like all of them. They're lost, which means the whole colony is likely lost. If we don't stop the rot now, if we let it spread beyond the colony—and we should pray to God that it hasn't already—then what's next? A direct attack on the city? On a station? Do you feel comfortable letting people like this go, knowing what that rot could do to your family?" He paused. "I really don't need to explain myself to you. You follow my orders and remove them, however you need to. Do you want to feel better about it? Here." A wave of red washed over my sensors as every citizen of Stickney was marked as red. My stomach twisted. "Does that ease your conscience? Do I need to help you visualize the threat like a child? Get the job done, Commander. Now."

I stared out at the colony, at Monalua and her people behind her, at the burnt ruins of the spaceport. I looked at the Bastion starship, blown to pieces, along with its crew. And I imagined that same Bastion seal burning on the flag flapping in Father's yard.

There was more at stake here than just a colony, than just a spaceport. Ecker was right. This rot was dangerous, and we couldn't let it spread any further. We couldn't trust Monalua to handle the criminals. Maybe she'd inspired the attack herself. She was a teacher; maybe she'd been indoctrinating these terrorists for years.

With a thought through my mindjack, the lights running down the side of my Aegis' helmet and down its arms and torso turned from blue to bright red. "*Citizens of Stickney,*" I said, projecting my voice into every mindjack in the colony as well as through my Aegis' speakers at their highest volume. "*Surrender the terrorists now, or you will all be under arrest. Resist arrest and you will be forcibly taken into custody or incapacitated under suspicion of aiding and abetting terrorism. Monalua Hailey Cruzino and company, you are under arrest for obstructing Bastion authority and sheltering convicted terrorists. Get on the ground, now.*"

Some of the protesters hesitated, looking from left to right at their companions. A handful let go of their neighbors' hands and dropped to their knees, putting their hands behind their heads. But the majority of them stood defiant, heads pointed toward me.

"*We will no longer be crushed beneath Bastion's boot,*" Monalua said. "*If you want to keep doing it, you'll have to do it literally, with the entire system watching. We stand together.*"

I cut off my link to Stickney and isolated my connection with Ecker and the *Fang*. "Sir—"

"*No one's watching, Caliday,*" Ecker responded. "*We've cut off all signals coming from the entire moon and have wiped any recordings of your arrival. The* Sanguine Lycan *never came to Phobos.*"

I reconnected with Stickney, ignoring the knot in my stomach. "*Very well. If you stand together, every citizen of Stickney is now under arrest. The colony will be locked down as you are all processed. Cooperate, and maybe you'll see your families again. Resist, and you'll learn what the boot actually feels like.*" With a signal through my mindjack, I sealed all the exits around Stickney. It wasn't as if they had anywhere to go. I was standing in the wreckage of their only means of escape.

That got the rest of the protesters to kneel, other than Monalua and a citizen beside her. Inside the colony, I could see the people finally moving, scrambling to check the doors only to learn that they were truly locked in. It was a flood of red, surging against the walls of the colony like waves. There was a problem with Ecker's illustration: I could no longer tell where the actual terrorists were. They could be moving to do more damage, and we'd never know. Maybe Ecker still had a bead on them.

"On your knees, Cruzino." I said, leaning my Aegis forward so my faceplate was looking directly down at her. She just stared back with callous disrespect. Bastion built the colony she clearly thought she was so brave in protecting. Bastion gave her a home, a livelihood. Patriots died to build this new society in the stars, and now people like Monalua wanted to bring us all back to the dregs of Earth.

And I was on dusty, dark Phobos to ensure that didn't happen.

"KNEES!" I shouted, at the same time activating a thruster near my shoulder. The burst blasted all of the protesters back, slamming them into the side of their colony. They slid down to the ground, several knocked unconscious, and a few—yes, even Monalua—on their hands and knees. A command through my 'jack released a swarm of black bird-shaped drones from beneath the outer plates covering the back of my Aegis. They followed the tagged mindjack signals, split in half, then wrapped themselves around the wrists and ankles of the protesters. Another command drew the drones together so the prisoners were in a circle, bonds held close together by magnetic force. Monalua's head swayed, but she fought to stare up at me, her defiance strong even on her knees, even bound.

"Sanguine Lycan *to the* Fang. *Prisoners are prepared for transport. Proceeding to arrest the remaining terrorists. Please send additional—"*

A white flash exploded at the edge of my vision before it felt like the moon itself slammed into my side. My Aegis flew into the air, launching me away from the ruined spaceport and slamming into the dusty rock before sliding another half-mile to a stop. My systems flickered, vision flashing between the outer-camera view and the inside of my cockpit. My left arm and ribs burned. Whatever had hit me hadn't broken through the armor into the cockpit, but the mindjack's connection to the Aegis had a strange effect where its pilots felt a measure of pain as if the armor was our own body.

The flickering vision slowly eased up and the cameras stabilized, many of the systems repairing themselves. I groaned and turned toward where the attack had come from—and stared right down the barrel of an anti-starcraft cannon. The giant gun still smoked, a cloud of dust and soot hanging between us, disturbed by its blast.

"Sssssss" It was Ecker, trying to reach me through the damaged communications equipment. "Sanguine Ly-ly-lycan. *Do you copy?*"

"C...copy," I stammered out. "ASC. Northwest edge of the colony. It—"

"Yes, we see it. We had all the colony's defenses offline and protected. Someone hacked in. We're preparing to launch a volley. We'll melt the entire colony off the moon, and the rot with it. Vacate the area—"

"Sir," I interrupted, cringing as I waited for the Vice Admiral to yell at me for that, but he remained silent. "Let me handle it. They've initiated combat; with permission, I'd like to finish it."

A pause, then: *"Break that moon, Caliday."*

I took a breath, shook the ache out of my head, and shut down all my Aegis' exterior lights. Hopefully the terrorists would think they'd done critical damage. I should have had another ten seconds before the cannon was cooled down, adjusted, and prepared to fire again. While lying on my back, I primed the thrusters on my back, mental finger on the trigger. In the corner of my vision, light blossomed as the cannon prepared to fire again.

Stickney had brought this on itself. Monalua and her protesters must have only feigned peace while their hacker prepared to strike me down, to attack Bastion once more.

This rot was poisonous, and I would burn it away.

Seconds before the cannon fired, I ignited my thrusters at full power, blasting me away from the ground with such force that I cracked the very stone. As I sailed into the air, arms spread wide like a dancer mid-flip, the cannon's round flashed by beneath me. Once it had, I ignited the thrusters in my Aegis' boots and in the low gravity rocketed over the red-and-gray ground and the blackened spaceport in almost an instant.

While still upside-down, I wrapped my Aegis' arms around the barrel of the cannon, planted my feet, then pushed off while launching the thrusters on my back. The cannon fired in my arms, sending vibrations through my cockpit, and the heat from it even permeated several layers of protection. But I was unscathed, and the armor around the suit's arms was only superficially damaged.

Hydraulics whirred in the suit as I landed and pulled the cannon's barrel toward me, forcing it back further than it was designed to go. For a moment I thought the Aegis' strength may fail me, but then the metal of the cannon gave way and the barrel bent backward toward me. I wrapped my hands around the base of the barrel and lasers in the *Lycan*'s palms burned through the metal until it came free. I hefted the barrel over my shoulder, launched into the air with a brief burst from my thrusters, then fired the thrusters pointing up from my shoulders, sending me hurtling down as I slammed the barrel like a spear into the cannon. It puckered under the force, metal shearing before an explosion blossomed, pushing me backward a few meters.

I stood there, staring at the burning wreckage, heavy breaths hissing through clenched teeth as the adrenaline settled down. That would teach those terrorists to try and take me down. To fire at an Aegis of Bastion.

I called a diagnostic of the armor up into my vision. The right side of the Aegis shined green, save the arm, which glowed yellow from the heat damage it took when the cannon fired the third time. But the left side flashed red, with the torso an especially dangerous maroon. The shot had nearly penetrated the armor. For a moment, I switched from the view outside the Aegis to the view inside my cockpit. The white lights had shut off, replaced by flashing red warning lights. To my left, the cockpit wall was cracked and sparking in several spots. That was...that was much closer than I'd thought. My Aegis had never taken such a direct hit. And it wouldn't be able to take another.

I switched back to my external view, where the flames of the destroyed cannon flashed and snapped. Hopefully whatever terrorist had hacked it was somewhere beneath all that rubble.

But that wouldn't be Stickney's only anti-starcraft cannon. Bastion would have installed several during initial colonization to fight off pirates and other opportunists. With a quick thought, I armed my own cannon, which had been secured on my armor's back. It swiveled up its track and locked into place on my shoulder, a hum filling my hearing as it charged up.

I scanned the area, but none of the other cannons had left their underground chambers. In fact, the entire scene was eerily still. Even the colonists had stopped...

Stickney was aflame.

The closest dome had been blown open, the glass shattered and oxygen venting out along with churning fire and smoke. Only a single mindjack signal shined red within that dome. But as I watched, it flashed then faded. Even Monalua's signal was gone, buried beneath wreckage at the base of the dome.

What had...

Oh.

The cannon. When I'd forced it over and up, I'd forced it to fire on the colony. On the colon*ists*. Space colonies were fragile. All it took was a single breach to...

I...

It wasn't my fault. I hadn't pulled the trigger. I was defending myself. Defending Bastion. I was trying to defend the people of the colony, but they'd rejected it.

Those justifications rang true. They'd certainly hold up in the investigation that would certainly follow.

So why did the pit in my stomach just feel like it kept boring deeper?

"*Sanguine Lycan* to *Fang*," I said, trying to keep my voice steady. "Please send medical crew. Prisoners from...remaining dome will require medical attention."

"*Are you all right, soldier?*" Ecker asked.

I didn't respond.

"*Caliday?*"

"Yes. Sir."

The Vice Admiral chuckled. "*You took my orders literally, didn't you, Moon-breaker? Cracked the stone and broke open that shithole like an egg. Well done, Caliday. The terrorists will think twice before striking Bastion again.*"

Or I'd just given them even greater reason to.

I stared into the fire, feeling deeply that I'd just sparked one of another kind.

CHAPTER FOUR

TORIS

A WEEK AFTER THE Wolf's cycle ended, I prepared for spaceflight.

Morning sunlight beamed through the open windows, illuminating floating motes of dust. Outside our home, the floral solar panels opened their petals and turned to face the sun. The smell of last night's rain still lingered in the air, and I took a deep breath of it as I buttoned up my pants. It was a simple room; beside me and underneath a window was our bed, sheets and comforter a crumpled mess. Behind me was a small closet and on my other side a dresser. Ahead was the hallway that led to the rest of our small home on the outskirts of Orilla del Angel. A warm contrast to the cabin we'd spent the cycle in.

"Wait," Alis said, padding over the wooden floor in her fuzzy socks, hair up in a barely contained bun and still in her pajama shorts and tank top. She looked at my side, where the injury from the Wolf had scabbed over. She leaned closer. "I think you're good."

"You've said that for a week," I said with a smile as Alis straightened, put her hands on her hips, and cocked her head as her eyebrows pressed together with concern. "I'm fine. Really. How's your head?"

Alis shrugged, bun bobbing, even more strands abandoning its hold. "Fine. Less every day."

I stared at her for a moment, biting at the inside of my lip, wondering if I should push further. I hadn't had to use the shock device any more during the cycle, but even after the Wolf had retreated as Mars and Earth's paths diverged, Alis was squinting in pain and rubbing her temples. She didn't seem to have suffered any other memory loss or other brain damage, but that did little to ease my concern.

"Could you at least rest another day? You don't—" Alis cut me off by stepping close and putting her hand on my cheek. As always, my breath caught. The morning light made her strawberry-copper hair shine and caught the gold in her eyes. She'd just brushed her teeth, so I could smell the mint on her breath mixed with the comfortable scent of sleep in the room.

"You had no choice," Alis said as I leaned my head into her hand and closed my eyes. "I'm here. I'm safe. I'm me. You over-worry when you feel guilty, and you need to be focused today. You need to come back safe to me." In her eyes I almost caught the shimmer of tears. Alis had lost so much, she perpetually was on the edge, where one more loss would push her over.

I leaned in and pressed my lips against hers, grabbing her waist and pulling her closer. The tense worry in both of our muscles melted away as we caved into each other. I squeezed Alis tight, then pulled away, my hands still on her waist. "I'll be safe. And I'll have Kuma with me."

Alis scoffed as she squeezed my arms, then pulled away, opened a dresser drawer, and started rifling through her clothes. "That doesn't make me feel better. I admire that you volunteer for this every time, but...I agree with your sister on this one. There are bigger problems to handle here without bringing in more refugees. There's room on Luna, or in some of the stations." She pulled out some pants, closed the drawer, and turned to me. "But most importantly, it doesn't have to be you putting yourself in danger every time to bring them here."

I waved my hand in dismissal before turning around to grab my black and blue-trimmed flight jumpsuit out of the closet. "There's no danger. We're picking them up from Farstead. And this is more than just a refugee run. Vic thinks there's a mindjack specialist among them. A bioengineer. They may be able to give us more answers."

Alis was replacing her pajama shorts with pants. She chuckled when I made a point of staring at her legs as if I were frozen in place. In truth, there wasn't much acting necessary. "Just because there aren't starfighters or battleships trying to shoot you down doesn't mean it's not dangerous. You've got a target—"

"No one knows about that," I interrupted, more sharply than I intended. That was always the case with this conversation: guilt tended to exhibit itself in symptoms of defensiveness. "I'm just another degenerate pilot to them. Not worth the effort."

Alis stared at me, then sighed out of her nose and pulled off her shirt while I looked away and stepped into my jumpsuit. I shoved my arms into it but didn't zip it up. That thing got way too hot way too fast, and I'd have enough time to heat up while Kuma and I rode the Dandelion Seed into orbit.

"You were dangerous," I said, and it didn't sound as sweet as I'd meant it in my head. I stepped closer to her and took her arm after she'd slid it into her shirt. "And you were the greatest thing to ever happen to me. Those people want something better. They want change. It's worth the risk. And if there's even a chance there's someone who can help us figure out the Wolf? Find a cure? I'll take that risk, too."

She looked from eye to eye, and again I could see that paranoia. I needed to be more understanding of that. "I understand all that," Alis said. "And I appreciate it. All I'm saying is that it doesn't have to be *you* running the refugees back every time, and that you need to realize, whether you think you're in the clear or not, that you are in danger. Bastion's pride is chronic, it's a rot that won't let go, and from pride comes vengeance, whether you're the intended target, or whether they just want to hurt every 'degenerate pilot' they can." She gently nudged me away so she could finish getting ready. "You're *my* degenerate."

I chuckled. "And honored to be so. I'm sorry, I'll be more careful. I'll be more wary. And I'll stop volunteering so frequently for these flights. As long as you stop volunteering every time for the duties that no one else wants to do. You don't have to do that every time, either."

"Toris, it's some cleaning shifts and repair jobs."

"Repairing sewer machines," I said. "All I'm saying is you don't have to be the first to sign up for the duties nobody wants. We're supposed to share those responsibilities, even the shitty ones. That's the point of the Compact. You talk to me about guilt, but Alis, you paid your price. You don't have to keep paying it."

She looked at me with a firmness that made me feel like I was a gust of wind asking a continent to budge. "I do."

I nodded, knowing when there was little use pushing further. "Well, try to enjoy yourself while I'm gone, too. I'm sure Navi would love the company."

"Ha! Yeah, we'll go watch old rom-coms and braid each other's hair." She wrapped her arms around me and we pulled each other into a tight embrace. "I love you. Fly safe. Please," she said, her voice muffled into my shoulder, the warmth of her breath almost making me shiver.

"I love you, too." She kissed me, longer this time. Her gravity threatened to hold me there, stronger than any rocket engine could escape, so I squeezed her and pulled away. Then I grabbed my backpack off the bed, saluted her, winked, and walked down the hall. She stood there, arms folded, wearing a smile that looked more sad than happy. When I stepped outside and closed the door to our home, I felt like I'd left a part of me in there with her.

But there were duties to be done, new family to welcome to their new life. Their new home.

And a lead to chase, one that hopefully wouldn't be another dead end. One that would lead us to the end of the Wolf.

I pulled my hoverboard out of its charging port on the side of the house. A breeze blew over the tall grasses surrounding the building, bringing with it the scent of flowers, and a hint of the tomatoes that were almost ripe-red in our vegetable garden. A cracked, overgrown road ran in front of the house, the remnant of an old neighborhood, one that had been mostly destroyed during the Bastion mass driver attack that leveled much of the region and created the Corcoran Sea. I could barely see our neighbors' home, its patched roof just visible over the tall grasses between us. In front of the house, on the other side of the street, the ground sloped, covered in a blanket of the same tall grasses and punctuated by trees. Over the trees and miles of fields and buildings, the edges of the community of Orilla del Angel, was the glitter of the Corcoran Sea. At its shore was my destination, a silver sliver at the end of the green.

After one last look at the house, I stepped onto the hoverboard. It hummed and rose into the air just above the roof of our home, then I leaned forward and rocketed away from the hillside, foliage turning into a blur below. I passed over fields of sweet rice and vegetables, orchards of fruit and even a hillside winery. That food would sustain the people of Orilla del Angel, with the surplus going to other nearby communities, traded for their own unique foods and goods. I wished that Alis would have volunteered for a shift tending to the crops or harvesting for once. But she always had to take what others wouldn't. Part of it was out of selflessness, and part of it was out of self-punishment. She'd done it for nine-and-a-half years, ever since I brought her to Orilla. I'd tried every argument to get her to see that she'd done enough, that she'd done enough before she'd set foot on Earth, that our society no longer functioned around what was owed or earned. Clearly, I'd had little success. At least she finally ate the food the community grew. I'd literally gotten on my knees at one point to help her overcome that one.

I pushed the nose of my hoverboard down and gradually descended, following the slope of the hill toward the sea. At its edge, that silver sliver came into focus: a sleek train suspended above its track, its design reminiscent of a dolphin. I decelerated as I came closer to the station, scanning the—

Blinding light caught my eye, causing me to swerve. That inertia got me into a spin that forced me to crouch and wrench my board up to get control again, just as the bright light hit me again. This time, I shielded my eye and peeked underneath my hand as the ground came up to me. Just as the light hit me again, nearly sending me falling off my board, I found the source: Murakuma Acalar Hakekoa.

Kuma stood beside the station steps, a small mirror in his hand, directing sunlight right at me. He wore that stupid, mischievous smile behind his short black beard, his hair pulled back into a braid. Woven lines and geometric patterns made up a tattoo sleeve on his left arm and continued onto his chest, disappearing beneath his loose-fit blue shirt. He was taller and broader than me, but didn't need any augments for that, just strong Pacific Islander and Southeast-Asian ancestry.

Beside him, rolling her eyes at Kuma's antics, was Navi. I was pretty sure I knew why she was there, and I'd rather take sunlight in the eye than have this conversation with her again.

"Please, blind me," I said as I approached them, board under my arm, "so I don't have to watch you sprint from the shower to your quarters."

"Who's making you watch?" Kuma said before tilting his head to Navi. "I find towels wasteful. Just trying to do my part."

She rolled her eyes again.

"Here to see us off, sis?" I asked, sliding my board into a charging port beside the elevated platform. "That's so nice."

"I'm here to help with a shipment that came up from the coast. An actual duty, a responsibility that helps the community."

I clenched my jaw and looked at Kuma, who just widened his eyes a little. Alis' concern, I could understand. Navi's obstinate attitude just pissed me off. And how she'd treated Alis before her cycle didn't help, either. I couldn't help but try to beat her at her own game, best her using her own appeals.

"What a coincidence that you happened to volunteer for that knowing we were heading out this morning," I said with mock appreciation. Then I dropped that for a more serious tone. "Just because a duty isn't included in the charter doesn't mean it's not legitimate. Isn't conforming to that just a step toward a system that restricts us doing what we feel is right?"

"Oh, please, that's—"

"And you seem to forget that our 'community' extends beyond Orilla. We're helping our community because those desperate, poor, starving, exploited people *are* our community. And maybe we'll help our community here by bringing back people we need, people with experience and knowledge that helps us all."

Navi paused before responding, narrowing her eyes in a way that told me she'd at least conceded that I'd made some good points. "However noble you make it sound, it's nothing but naive. You can bring back ten good people and one

Bastion loyalist, and you'll harm many more than you help. Even the ones you think are innocent have Bastion in their blood. We don't need that illness to spread here."

"You're generalizing, again, Navi," I said as I zipped up my jumpsuit. "That's the kind of thinking that led to the End. You know that."

Out of the corner of my eye, I could tell Navi was staring at me. Then she looked down and sighed. "You and your fallacies. Just because it's a generalization doesn't mean it's not worth consideration. Maybe it is generalizing, but keeping a wall up that keeps everybody out is worth avoiding the risk of letting in the next world-ender." She stepped close to me, most of the argumentative tension gone from her face. "I know Vic said there may be a lead, but that doesn't mean you have to bring more people back. Why do you keep doing it? Do you think you have some debt to them? You two don't owe them for—"

"No," I said, eyes darting to Kuma, who looked away, teeth working beneath his beard. "It's not that."

"Okay. Is it for Alis? Does she keep asking you to do it?"

"Why do you say it like that? Like she's some kind of spy, trying to bring her people in. People need the help, so we help them."

"Other pilots would volunteer," she said. "Why do *you* have to do it? When you could stay here with Alis, when you could make a difference here."

"Navi, we make these flights only twice a year. I fulfill my duties..." I trailed off, shaking my head. "You know what, I don't need to explain anything to you. Come on, Kuma." I adjusted my pack on my shoulder and stepped up onto the platform. Kuma followed, stepping around Navi.

"Toris."

I stopped just before the open train doors but didn't turn toward her.

"Be safe. Please."

I looked back just long enough to say, "I will."

"I've got his back," Kuma said, punching me in the back of my shoulder. "And everything else."

Without waiting for a response from Navi, I stepped onto the train. When we found our seats, I glanced out the window. She was still standing there, arms folded again, but less out of defiance and more like she was trying to shrink, hunching into her arms. She looked out past the train, toward the sea, with a mix of worry and sadness that reminded me so much of Mom.

She stood there until the train lurched and started rolling down the track, then she turned away and walked back toward Orilla.

***

As the train began decelerating, the outside, which had been a blur for the past forty-five minutes, coalesced once more into solid shapes. And the Dandelion came into view.

The Dandelion was a cluster of space elevators anchored to giant ships in the Pacific Ocean. Traditional rocket launches dumped too many chemicals into the atmosphere, especially as the rate of space travel accelerated. So, following the Belt Rush and increased access to the asteroid belt, some early pioneers of Earth's blooming new society parked a handful of the big rocks in geostationary orbit, used them as counterweights tethered to those ships in the Pacific with giant cables, and then employed those cables to carry ships and passengers to the orbital asteroids. They'd carved out the asteroids to act as spaceports, which ships could launch from without any detriment to Earth's environment.

As our train came around the final bend on the peninsula that separated the lighter crystal of Corcoran Sea from the deeper blue of the Pacific Ocean, we could see the nearest Stalk, the one-meter wide graphene composite tether that stretched from the planetside terminal to the orbital starport. From that distance, it was a thin black line that could have been a trick of the light if you didn't know that little line was one of the greatest feats of human ingenuity. The space elevator was an old concept, a dream of science-fiction novels, but Earth's wealthiest had brought that vision to life shortly before they started abandoning the planet altogether in what would come to be known as the Exodus Era. During the Solar Gulf War, extremists had destroyed that elevator, seeing it as a symbol of the oppression we were all fighting to leave in the ashes of history.

But at the end of the Solar Gulf War, when we'd pushed back Bastion's fleet and its continent-cracking mass drivers, and it was safe, the best engineers, physicists, and other brilliant minds went to work. The Dandelion was a symbol of its own, much like that first elevator, but in every different way. It was a symbol of the reborn Earth's resilience, proof that we weren't just the detritus of humanity that Bastion liked to pretend we were. We could build like Bastion, but better. It was also a symbol of our new principles, our society's dedication to becoming better stewards of the planet, and doing that all while still maintaining our status as an advanced civilization, one that could still participate in interstellar trade and relations without damaging our planet or exploiting its people.

Kuma had his nose nearly pressed against the glass, staring up at the Stalk as our train lurched to a stop and the doors hissed open. We both peeled ourselves away from the view and stepped onto the platform. Cool ocean wind washed over us, and I took a deep breath of the salty air. The platform dropped right down to a pier that stretched over the water. Docked beside the pier was a small white ship, solar sail retracted against its mast, an aesthetic blend of ancient galleons and more modern passenger boats. We walked the pier, through a scanner, and up the ramp onto the ship. Inside, we found a seat and settled in once more.

There's a lot of sitting when it comes to flying. More than flying, really. Not my favorite part.

But after a few more passengers boarded, also bound for the Dandelion, the boat left the dock, the solar sail unfurled and caught that morning sunlight, and we were off.

"I didn't ask," Kuma said, leaning forward and resting his elbows on his knees as he lowered his voice, "how was the last cycle?"

I shook my head. "It's getting worse. It used to be that she'd only turn when Mars was in perfect alignment, sometimes even only when Bastion was facing toward Earth. But it gets hours earlier every time. We used to have a day or two at the cabin before she turned. This time we didn't even make it past sunset. And...I don't know...maybe it's in my head, but I feel like the Wolf is getting more aggressive. Navi found something that shorted out the mindjack, but Alis is still getting headaches from that. So it's not a solution."

Kuma nodded along as I talked. Then he shrugged and leaned back into his chair. "Maybe this group will be the one. I trust Vic."

I'd been saying that for almost ten years. "Maybe."

Kuma settled back in his chair and folded his arms, looking out the window at the ocean. "What if you didn't worry so much about the mindjack and focused on the signal? Because it's gotta be a signal, right? Why else would she...why would the 'jack mess with her head only when Mars was aligned? Maybe some part of it's still connected to the Bastion network."

"I mean, yeah, that's one of Alis' predictions, too. She thinks what triggers the Wolf is a kind of leftover signal, something caught in the network and stuck there from when she...broke free."

"Then couldn't you just jam the signal? Or bounce it back somehow? It's just waves, like any other." He shrugged. "Keep them from getting to the receiver."

"Jamming." I sighed. "We tried that only a few years in, when Alis first had the theory. Vic thinks it may not be a wavelength signal, but quantum entanglement. That would also explain the odd behavior. Bastion messing with science they don't fully understand but putting it in people's heads anyway."

Kuma frowned. "Guess the temptation to surveil and control your population is too tempting. Risk-reward and all that." He leaned across the narrow aisle and slapped my knee. "But there's always a solution. Just gotta find the person with it. So, like I said, maybe this is the batch."

I nodded and looked out the window. Blue water rushed by, clear skies above. In the distance, a huge, boxy ship caught the sunlight. It was an automated cleanup craft, one of many that worked to undo the damage humanity had done to the oceans.

"Risk-reward," I said, then turned back to Kuma, who had his head cocked, listening. "Are we being too risky, bringing all these people back?"

He scoffed, and I turned back toward him. "You gotta stop letting Navi get in your head. You want to talk about risk? Bastion wouldn't risk another war with Earth. We showed them how vulnerable their little science experiment is. You want to talk about a nuclear deterrent? How's the sun for a nuclear deterrent?" He shrugged again. "Mass-driver deterrent in this case, I guess."

"You don't feel like we...owe them anything?"

Kuma paused, clearly wondering if I was joking. When he could tell I wasn't, he asked, "Owe them for what?"

I swallowed the lump in my throat that formed before I could even say the word. "Iridesca," I said it in almost a whisper, as if anyone on that boat would really know what happened that day.

Kuma leaned forward, at least on the same page about being discreet. "We don't owe them shit, and you know that. We're not helping them because they're Bastards, we're helping them because they're people, because they're human beings who've been under Bastion's boot and suffered the consequences for too long, and they've decided to do something about it. You said it to Navi yourself; we're helping them because they're our neighbors, too. And to find Alis' cure." He smacked me on the knee again, this time with the back of his hand. "Come on, ignore her. She's always guilt-tripped you. If you had listened to her ten years ago, eleven years ago, you'd have never met Alis, and you'd never have become a hero. A *hero*, Tor."

I shook my head, the words making my skin crawl. "I'm not." I had to move on from that subject. Already the memories were threatening to come back. The plasma rifle shots. The screaming. "And are you just a saint? Ten years is a long time. You're still just doing this out of the goodness of your heart?"

"You trying to get rid of me?" he asked, cocking his head and smiling. "I do it for the same reason I've always done it, brother. The more people we help, the stronger we are. The more people we take away from Bastion, the weaker they are. And even more than that," he patted a chest pocket on his jumpsuit, "Mele would want me to help them."

I gave him a smile that let more of my pity slip through than I'm sure he wanted to see. "Yeah, she would." I could still see Kuma's little girl running around, giggle bouncing off the walls like sunshine, black hair in a braid like her dad's. It'd been twelve years since Bastion took her life. It had broken Kuma, broken his marriage, and it'd borne something dark inside him, something I knew I only saw the tip of, the rest of it hidden deep inside.

"Then let's go make Mele proud," I said, holding out my hand across the aisle.

"And get Alis cured." Kuma grasped my forearm and I grabbed his.

A half-hour later, the boat slowed down as the solar sail retracted and the electric motor took them the rest of the way to the Stalk. We disembarked the boat, squinting in the bright sunlight, the rays feeling markedly more intense that close to the equator, where the centrifugal force acting on the elevator and its tether was strongest.

The base of the Stalk was a simple dome building. The meter-wide tether rose out of the top and climbed and climbed and climbed, gradually curving with the curvature of the Earth. Every time I looked at the Stalk, my brain tried to make sense of it, waited for it to fall down into the sea despite understanding, at least at a fundamental level, the physics of it all. But no, the rotation of the planet, combined with Earth's gravity and the centrifugal force pulling the tether outward *and* upward, kept the Stalk as taut as if a god were holding tight the other end.

We disembarked with only two other passengers; the rest would take the solar sailer to a different Stalk in the Dandelion. After all, the elevator could only take four at a time. Inside the dome's small lobby, volunteers on duty checked us in, verified we were who we said we were (though I'd seen at least one of these volunteers on several other flights), and pointed us to our reserved lockers in a room to the right of the lobby.

I opened my locker to the worn blue pressure suit that waited there. Stuck to the inside of the locker was a picture of Alis, laughing as I chased her outside the cabin. That had been before only her second or third cycle. Beside me, Kuma touched a picture of Mele in his own locker. Her black hair stuck out at all angles as she smiled as broad as her little cheeks would stretch, showing off the gap where one of her teeth had been.

We donned our pressure suits, grabbed our helmets, kissed our pictures good-bye, and returned to the lobby. The volunteers guided us behind the lobby to the true base of the Stalk. The elevator vehicle was four connected pods that resembled giant pills, except for that flat end that faced the tether. Each pod was eight-feet tall and maybe six feet wide. Not the ideal space you'd want to be confined in for three days, but that's sustainable space travel for you.

The volunteers went through all the standard safety procedures—how to detach from the climber vehicle if necessary, where to find extra oxygen tanks if pressurization failed, that kind of fun stuff—before shaking our hands and wishing us quick good lucks.

Kuma plucked at the backside of his suit. "I forget that this suit gives me a wedgie every. Time."

I smirked and Kuma held out his hand, the one that had just been digging between his cheeks. I stared at it, then with an "oh, right," he held out his other palm, and we clasped forearms again, this time letting go and sliding the backs of our hands up each other's arm until they sailed off above our heads.

"To the stars," I said.

"To the stars, brother."

With a final nod to the volunteers, we stepped into our pods, and they sealed the door—and the many layers of radiation, pressure, and temperature protec-tion—behind us. Each pod was built to carry an individual and featured only a small, slightly inclined bed against the back wall, a small three-by-four-foot bathroom, and a screen for entertainment. A gentle hum vibrated the cabin.

I slid my backpack into some netting secured to one of the walls and strapped myself to the bed. When I was snug, a green light turned on over my door. The volunteers would see that, too, indicating that I was ready for launch.

"*Safe travels, spacefarers,*" said one of the volunteers over the speaker system.

"*Dandelion Seed 4, priming for launch.*"

The vibration intensified, and I closed my eyes.

"*Seed launching in five, four, three—*"

The vibration reached a pitch that was just on the threshold of grating.

"*Two, one.*"

Gravity held onto my stomach as we shot into the air. But it quickly settled back into place as my body adjusted to the acceleration.

Please, I thought, eyes still closed. *Let this be the one.* Gravity may have been slowly releasing its hold, but something in my chest was still pulled downward. I felt it every time I left the world, every time I left Alis. As if the entire planet, as if gravity itself, wasn't concentrated around a molten core, but that woman in her messy ponytail and pajama shorts. The woman I loved and the Wolf I hated.

Let this be the one.

CHAPTER FIVE

TORIS

AFTER ALMOST TWO WEEKS of sailing away from Earth, Farstead grew from a twinkling star to a gray- and red-striped cylinder. While they were too small for us to see, our sensors were picking up ships flowing both to and from the station. As the edge of Earth's territory, the station was a critical center of trade and commerce. It was a middle ground—a middle space?—where those who aligned more with Earth's culture and values could still also engage in commerce without compromising themselves by fully participating in Bastion's exploitative corporatism. If they weren't living on Earth's surface, they weren't held accountable to the Gaia Compact, the social contract we all agreed to after the End.

I rubbed my eyes and sat back in my chair, still waking up after Kuma had called me to the bridge. It was still the middle of ship-night, which we aligned to our typical night in Orilla, but the rest of the system didn't adhere to our circadian rhythms.

The *Harriet*'s bridge was dark, a hologram of Mele twirling in her flowery dress spinning light from where it stood on Kuma's console. A peninsula split Kuma and I, running into the center of the bridge, a holoprojector we used for maps. Through the viewport, I could see the *Harriet*'s forks, like the legs of an H. She'd once been a cargo hauler, and those forks allowed her to push heavier loads, while compartments housed under the forks handled most shipments. Spread like wings from the starboard and port sides of the forks were the ship's solar sails, almost translucent against the night.

"We've already got clearance," Kuma said, pressing a button that pulled in the solar sails, then he throttled back our rocket power even further. When we got closer, he'd kill them completely and maneuver using thrusters and, once in the station, steam bursts. "They said they'll have the refugees in the hangar and ready to board. Didn't sound too thrilled to have us."

I shrugged, unsurprised. It'd been nearly seven years since Bastion officially lifted the restrictions enacted by the Johnston Resolution, but Farstead was understandably still anxious about refugees. After all, they'd been the site of several conflicts during the War, and once or twice in the years before the Resolution faded into the dark pages of history. They preferred the transfers quick and easy, with as little chance for protest and violence as possible.

A night of sleep on the station would have been nice—the *Harriet's* beds weren't exactly built with comfort in mind. But we'd done worse, and I was anxious enough as it was to meet these refugees and find out if one of them could help Alis. At least then, even if I was disappointed, I'd know. Hope was a dangerous thing. It drove me across the stars, but if I let it, its fall could break me. Already I could feel the detritus of so many previous hopes piling up somewhere I hid it all, behind stubborn optimism and sheer desperation. That dam would break one day. With luck, it wouldn't be that day.

We fell in line behind a queue of ships preparing to dock at Farstead. We were only the fourth back. Two of them looked like passenger liners preparing to land in the hangar. The third was a heavy, boxy, cargo transport. That transport had the half-circle, half-eagle's-wing seal of Bastion stamped on its hull. I wondered what they carried, what it cost, not in money but in the very human sweat and blood to produce it.

Those ships soon glided into Farstead's hangar, and we followed. While most pilots had to maintain constant communication while landing inside a station hangar, Kuma and I could do it completely quietly. Mostly quietly, at least. Kuma liked to whistle in time with the thruster bursts he used to direct the *Harriet*. Inside a station hangar like Farstead's, they'd use steam to move the ship, not burning fuel.

As the hangar swallowed us, I blinked at the bright lights after so long in the dark of space. Docks ran down the hangar to the left and right, magnetic clamps holding everything from small personal craft to a couple star-yachts, to long and layered passenger liners. Docked in a line were Bastion-stamped starfighters. Military-class. Ten years and they hadn't changed much. I shook my head—and shook away the uncomfortable memories that rose up when I saw them.

Kuma directed steam bursts from the bow of the *Harriet*, nudging us toward our assigned dock. Then a few bursts from the port side sent us veering to the right, and a burst from the starboard side straightened us out. A more prolonged stream from the prow brought us to a stop. A green light illuminated on the station wall and the magnetic clamps latched onto the hull.

I stood up and cracked my aching lower back. "Let's keep the reactor warm. If we're not wanted, I don't want to push it."

Kuma touched his hologram of Mele and stood, too. "I'll get the fuel. How's our reserve looking?"

As part of the Gaia Compact, we didn't build or contribute to economies on Earth, but we needed a reserve—a savings account, really—to pay for things off the surface. Farstead had to pay to maintain its condition, so it required payment as well. I knew that conditions for workers on Farstead were nowhere near as bad as Bastion, but something still felt wrong as those numbers ticked down.

"Getting low," I said, "but we should be fine to refuel for the return trip. And I promised Alis I'd grab her some of those orange candies she likes, if you could?" Kuma gave me a thumbs up without looking at me. "After that, I don't know. We may need to bring some goods next time."

Kuma chuckled. "I think if there's a next time your sister might sabotage the train herself."

I scoffed, but there wasn't much humor behind it. I would bring back refugees as long as they needed it, but...I knew firsthand the risks of bringing a part of Bastion back to Earth.

Please let this be the one.

When the pressure light above the airlock indicated that the terminal tunnel on the other side was full of oxygen, we disengaged the lock and stepped onto Farstead. Every step through the tunnel was light, too light, the station's artificial gravity at least half as strong as Earth's.

We walked out of the terminal and joined a corridor with other travelers, a group of well-dressed Bastionites heading back to their starliners, a few working-class crewmates in jumpsuits disembarking their cargo ship. They gave us a friendly nod. The Bastionites didn't.

At the end of that corridor, which ended ahead of all the docked ships, was a large waiting area not unlike the Dandelion's starport, full of travelers who had either just disembarked or who had passed through the station's security on the way to their ships. There were shops and food stalls like the Dandelion, too, but the similarities largely ended there. Flashing neon signs flashed above far more expensive and totally wasteful products, like aesthetic body augments or bulky jewelry that looked almost like armor. Patrons tried on golden pauldrons and gauntlets, laughing loudly as their friend struggled to pull a glove over his bulky rings.

Toward one end of that large space, however, was a group that looked as out of place as I felt. Our refugees—one of them held a handwritten sign facing the docks that read *Harriet*. They were a crowd of around twenty, many of them in grease-stained jumpsuits with holes and hasty patches. Others wore street clothes a generation or two out of fashion. A color-faded sweater that was several sizes too big slumped off one girl that couldn't be more than twelve. Another wore a shirt that had only a single sleeve, a fashion on Bastion nearly ten years ago during the war. Alis had a shirt like that.

They carried their wear not only in their clothing, but across their flesh as well. Many of them had scars, some were missing fingers. A few had burn marks, and a couple had limbs wrapped in bandages. As pity for these poor people sank in, frustration rose at an equal pace. Nearly ten years after the Solar Gulf War and nothing had changed in Bastion. Her people's worth was still determined by the labor they offered, their bodies nothing but soft, warm machines to complete tasks. I'd wondered if Bastion would remove its law preventing corporations from using automated machines to complete tasks, but clearly not. The propaganda would say those laws ensured that everyone had a job, that they enabled everyone to play an important part in the future prosperity of their great society. But all it really meant was that the corrupt corporations could take advantage of more people, could exploit them, could force them into the heavy labor that, on Earth, machines would do. And, of course, the same laws that claimed to enable employment did nothing to require the businesses to pay a livable wage. Those kinds of restrictions and regulations were done away with even when that ruling class still lived on Earth, before the Exodus. No, these people sacrificed their bodies and still starved. Still broke.

They were simply the ones who realized that the prosperity they were promised from neon signs across their cities would never be theirs. And it was mine and Kuma's job to guide their way to a new prosperity. A true prosperity.

Could one of them be our lead? I couldn't keep the hope from butterflying in my stomach.

"You got the speech this time?" Kuma asked.

I nodded. "After you get fuel, what do you think about getting them all a bite to eat before we take off?"

He slapped me on the shoulder. "I think you're a big softy and we may not have the money for it, but I'll see what I can do."

"Thanks, brother."

Kuma headed off and I took a deep breath and stepped toward the crowd. As I approached, several of the refugees looked at me and nudged each other. A few shrank back, maybe wondering if I was either a Bastionite or Farstead security, despite me looking like the farthest thing from either.

others. And that you'll fulfill your duties to your community as you so choose, so long as you do contribute. You promise to live in harmony with one another and with the one world in the universe that we were made for. Otherwise, we don't ask or require much of each other. We live our best lives, free. We care for each other. Our worth lies in how we live up to these promises, how we better each others' lives and find purpose and fulfillment in our own. Any questions?"

Rarely did anyone ask questions. It was a lot of information, and they'd sign just about anything to go anywhere they could find food and shelter. But this time, Cixin raised his hand.

I chuckled. "You don't have to raise your hand."

"How do you enforce this?" he asked as he lowered his hand. "Without police, without a military?"

I nodded. "It's a good question. We hold each other accountable. For one, our society has evolved for the vast majority of us to adhere to these values subconsciously. It's in our hearts from birth, taught through our entire lives. When someone violates the Compact, they're generally given chances to change, to grow. If they continue to cause more harm than good for the community, they become exploiters, and we no longer support them. Many communities force those violators to leave, and they need to either make it on their own or find another chance in a new community. It's not a utopia. It's difficult to completely root out greed and pride and selfishness. But we've done our best. It turns out, when people have what they need, and you remove competition from the foundation of society, they're much less likely to envy their neighbor."

Cixin smiled. "It sounds like utopia to me. To all of us. Thank you." He grabbed my hand and shook it again, eyes welling with tears. "Thank you so much. All the money in all the worlds couldn't repay you for what you're giving us."

"I'm not giving you anything. You're just returning home." I paused as they whispered to each other and stood, taking my pause as the end of my ramblings. It was, but...

"I could...I could use something personal, though." They all paused, looking at me, a few dropped their smiles, that deep-rooted trauma at owing a debt wiping away their hope. I instantly regretted saying anything, but I was already stuck with one foot in my mouth. May as well make it two and take the chance. "Someone very dear to me was like you, once. She left Bastion for a better life, too. But...something went wrong with her mindjack. It has very...negative side effects.

51

And no one's been able to help us. Does anyone here happen to be familiar with 'jacks? Could you help me?"

The refugees looked at each other, waiting for someone to step forward.

Cixin did.

"I'm familiar," he said with a somber nod. "More than I'd like to be. It's the primary reason I'm leaving. But for you, for this, I would be honored to help you."

I couldn't help it, I swept that skin-and-bones man into my arms in a great hug, tears now coming to *my* eyes. I was joining them in their hope, even if it was of a different kind.

It was more hope in that instant than I'd felt in years. We could break the cycle. We could kill the Wolf.

I pulled away from Cixin. "Sorry." I sniffed. "Thank you. Thank you so much." I clapped, then reached into my bag and pulled out the thin holo-pad where they'd sign the Gaia Compact. "All right. Let's get you all home."

CHAPTER SIX

ALIS

(Twelve-and-a-half years earlier)

BASTION HIGH COMMAND AWARDED me for Stickney. The Pioneers' Courage Crest, an honor reserved for those who displayed the spirit and bravery of the innovators who'd settled Mars and shaped it into our home.

Then, ever in the pursuit of opportunity, Bastion High Command awarded me with a new mission, deep in the enemy Sphere.

A flickering hologram of Luna hung in the center of the briefing room, its diameter a hundred times greater than Phobos. I stood, arms folded, in my fatigues, Vice Admiral Ecker on the other side of the hexagonal room. Several other officers from the *Fang* listened in. Our shuttle would be ready to take us up to the battlecruiser in a few minutes. Then we'd begin our two-month journey to that moon.

Luna occupied a unique position in the Solar Gulf War. It was technically an independent entity, but it considered itself an ally of Earth's. Throughout the war, boycotts or severe tariffs had limited interaction between Bastion and the moon, but it had remained a significant artery in Bastion's economic system. We couldn't trade directly with Earth, but we still benefited from many of its resources. They may have been trying to hoard those resources, likely hoping to starve us. Fortunately, we controlled the Belt, much to Earth's chagrin, and that gave us the metals we needed to build up our civilization and our military. We could be ideal trade partners. Symbiotic, even. But it was war.

We couldn't conquer Luna, not without further inflaming tensions in the war and creating a new enemy of the only reliable trade partner in Earth's Sphere. Add that to the lives it would take to win the moon's many colonies, and the losses would greatly outweigh the rewards.

"But we can't leave Luna alone," Ecker continued, pacing on his side of the projection table. "We expect retaliation to our response for Phobos, and we simply can't allow them to take our embassies and trade centers. Those are extensions of Bastion, and they're critical not only to our infrastructure, but to this war. It's our foothold in the Sphere." He pinched Luna's hologram and zoomed in on a clustered colony near its south pole, straddling a pair of craters. "This is Mwezi. It's one of the largest colonies on Luna. Yes, it's Swahili for 'moon.' The Mudbrains' creativity certainly dropped off. It is an ideal location for a colony, however, with plentiful ice nearby for water supply and suitable sunlight for solar arrays while the nearby craters supply adequate shade. It's a regular tropical paradise. Which is why it also boasts our largest concentration of operations on the moon. We employ more than half its citizens, and our relationship with the colony is a critical factor in its success. Under the authority of the Johnston Resolution, to ensure the security of Bastion and our interests, we are going to secure Mwezi."

He zoomed in closer, revealing a spaceport at least double the size of Stickney's beside the colony's many domes of various sizes. "The spaceport is most important," Ecker continued. "Commander Caliday, since you've already proven yourself as an expert in securing spaceports, and since the people of Mwezi will certainly be aware of your reputation, you'll lead taking control and holding it. Earth will likely make a stand there. They won't give up any inch of that moon easily."

"What resistance do we expect from Luna's government?" one of Ecker's officers asked. "They may respect our claims on our property, but certainly not the entire colony."

Ecker nodded along, then responded, "We're in talks with their government, and we hope they'll see reason, but we can't wait for their bureaucratic gears to grind when Earth likely won't wait, either."

"Sir, I..." I said, something gnawing at me too deeply not to say something, not after Stickney. "With respect, can you explain more of the logic behind justifying this...mission under the authority of the Johnston Resolution? My understanding was that the law applied only to Bastion and stations in Bastion's Sphere, and even then, it only restricted travel between the Spheres. I understood it as a containment measure." The government had approved the Resolution after my...after Stickney. I hesitated, anxious at being perceived as questioning my superiors. "To contain the rot."

Ecker, who'd been raising a skeptical eyebrow as I spoke, nodded and frowned at my final statement, as if I were a child who got it close, but not quite close enough. "You're right, Commander. It is a matter of containment. But why do we need containment? What's the root motivation?" He swung his hand forward, thumb resting on his forefinger like a politician. "Security. It's our line in the sand, our 'no more.' That line, however, can't be cleanly drawn somewhere in space between our Spheres, not when we have interests on Luna. Not when we have loyal people there. The Johnston Resolution prevents them from traveling home, since we can't risk the rot following them here, so we will bring home to them. As an extension of Bastion, Mwezi is as if it were on Mars' surface. There we'll do what we've done here. We'll secure our people. Protect our trade infrastructure. And we'll root out the rot."

There it was. Exactly what I was afraid he'd say. This wasn't just about protecting Mwezi's spaceport and ensuring terrorists didn't cripple it like at Stickney—that I could understand. And I could understand protecting our people there, many of whom were certainly threatened by Earth-zealous terrorists. But...that close to Earth, whether they were born on Bastion or worked for Bastion, those people could have been brainwashed without realizing it. They could be unaware victims of Earth's propaganda. If that were the case, would Ecker just see them all as a sea of red threats again?

That wasn't the only question I had. The officers seemed satisfied enough with Ecker's response on Luna's government, but I wasn't. What if Earth ships had sailed on Phobos, claiming that it had rights to secure Stickney because it had residents there?

But Phobos wasn't independent, not like Luna. Maybe we were just applying pressure to a situation that they would see our perspective on anyway. We weren't invading, just protecting. Securing. Containing.

Repetition did little to calm my swimming stomach. But I couldn't push the Vice Admiral any further. Not in that moment.

"Understood, sir. Thank you. Please excuse my...ignorance."

Ecker nodded and returned his attention to the hologram. "After Caliday secures the spaceport, our pruners will enter the colony dressed as infantry and flanked by Sentinel squads."

I nodded, suppressing a shiver. "Pruner" was a nickname for special agents who'd grown in number in the several weeks since the signing of the Johnston Resolution. They were enforcers of a different breed, who had superior intelligence on citizens and who "pruned the rot." That usually meant arresting Earth citizens living in or visiting Bastion who stepped out of line in one way or another. Where I'd been sent as God's own hammer to Stickney, a threat of total destruction, the pruners were the surgeon's scalpel, removing strategic targets in the name of protecting the broader population. At that point, I wished pruners had been sent to Stickney instead of me, but that didn't change the fact that something about them made me uncomfortable. I'd met a few, and they were quiet, arrogant, and too proud of those they'd killed rather than arrested.

I...supposed that the military had need of people like that, didn't they? I was the symbol who could get my hands dirty if I needed to. They lived with constantly bloodied hands without attention, without renown, in order to protect Bastion. I had to forgive them their less-than-ideal qualities. For Bastion.

Yeah. For Bastion.

"Our final objective," Ecker says, "is to secure the city. That may take several forms. If we're underestimating the bureaucracy, it could be that the colony's already secure under Bastion leadership by the time we arrive. If not, our military pressure may accelerate that process. However, we don't have time to waste. If that pressure doesn't give us the colony after one month, we exert pressure of a stronger kind. Democracy. Our Bastion-loyal representatives in the colony government will call for an emergency vote. They'll vote to secede from Luna and officially become part of Bastion's Sphere. All the roads lead to securing that colony for our people." He leaned forward on the ringed holoprojector. "For our future."

"And if democracy doesn't work in our favor?" another officer asked.

Ecker leaned back and folded his arms. "Then we'll carve a road of a different kind. We have the legal precedent, and Earth can't afford to stop us. We won't touch the rest of Luna. Only Mwezi. We won't do anything to bring them into the conflict. But the vote will work in our favor." Something resembling a smile twitched in the corners of his mouth.

"The pruners," the first officer said in realization. "They'll be using that month to ensure the people's loyalty. They'll ensure the vote goes in our favor."

"They'll ensure the security of Bastion, as is their duty" Ecker corrected, but the smile was still hiding there. "Our objectives simply have synergy. The people of Mwezi will still make their choice."

The officers nodded along, some of them tapping notes into PalmPros, screens holoprojected into the palms of their hands from bands around their wrists. I stood there, hands clasped behind my back, thumb rubbing a raw line into my own wrist.

"Any further questions?" Ecker asked. When none of the officers responded, Ecker said, "Wonderful. Thank you for your service. The end of this war is in sight. If we can expand our operations, if we can gain this foothold in Earth's Sphere, we can guide this conflict toward a surrender."

That felt like quite the jump from strategy to outcome, but the officers didn't seem to mind. They clapped. I kept rubbing my wrist.

"Report to your shuttles immediately. The *Fang* burns out in six hours." The officers saluted. I did, too, though less crisply than I'm sure Ecker preferred. I spun to follow the others out of the room as Ecker turned off the holoprojector, but before I could step over the threshold and out of the room, Ecker called, "Caliday. Wait a moment."

I stopped and turned again. Ecker grabbed my elbow and squeezed. I fought the urge to cringe and pull away. He'd never shown anything resembling affection prior to Stickney. But now he more frequently treated me like his buddy. Though I knew I was more than likely just his showpiece.

"I've got some good news for you," he held his arm up, gesturing for me to head out of the room. I raised an eyebrow and obeyed, stepping out into the hallway. Floor to ceiling windows on the other side showed the Bastion skyline, its white and silver spires shining in the noonday sun. To the right, the northwest, Olympus Mons loomed.

The hallway was mostly empty, the officers from the briefing heading in a group for the landing pads where their shuttles were waiting.

And to the left of the briefing room was Teah.

She'd cut her black hair to her shoulders, and she wore, of all things, a military uniform.

It was stiff, black, and trimmed in purple. Those colors only belonged to one branch of the military.

I should have smiled. Should have hugged her. Should have at least said her name, but I just stared.

"I know you've been advocating for your sister for some time now," Ecker said. "And she's certainly shown her dedication. All we needed was to find the right path for her. Now you can guide her on her first official mission. Congratulations, Caliday." He gave Teah a quick salute, which she returned. "I have a feeling the two of you will leave quite the legacy. Catch up, then report to your shuttle."

"Yes, sir," we said in unison.

I watched Ecker stride down the hallway for a moment before turning to Teah. She was still standing practically at attention, stiff, chin sticking out, neck stretched. She let her gaze follow the Vice Admiral for a moment before turning to me, a challenge there, a look I'd seen a thousand times, from when she was determined to win a game of tag as kids, to when I told her not to pursue becoming an Aegis pilot. She'd stared at me with that same look, the defiance at something I hadn't even said yet. It was a look Mom had. She'd even shot that expression at Death when it stared her down from the foot of her hospital bed.

That defiance told me that Teah already misunderstood the reaction she was assuming I'd have to her uniform. It was the same emotion she was defensive against when she told me she was taking the sync tests to become an Aegis pilot. I knew the horrors of war, and I didn't want my little sister anywhere near them. Part of my purpose in fighting was so that she wouldn't have to.

"I've been seeing those colors more and more lately," was all I could think to say as I nodded toward the purple trim of her uniform. Why? Who knows.

"Good," Teah said. "If there'd been more of us when you went to Stickney, the colony may still be there." I raised an eyebrow at the accusation in her tone. She'd been different with me since Stickney, quieter, like in that car ride with Father to the awards ceremony, when I really needed my little sister.

I swallowed the defensiveness that rose to meet her tone. "Yeah, I agree. I wish they'd been there."

She blinked, and her expression softened, some of the stiffness releasing, as if she were surprised at my response.

"Is that why you decided to become a pruner?" I asked.

"We're delators," Teah corrected with more offense than pride. The Bastion military had named their shadow operatives after ancient Roman prosecutors and informants. I guess they chose to forget the part where the delator system became as corrupt as the rest of the Roman Empire. "And I'd been taking preliminary exams and training before that." More of the stiffness disappeared as her self-defeat took hold. It had the same effect on my frustration. "I started after I failed the sync test the second time. I wanted a backup."

"Why?" I asked, wishing I'd asked it so much sooner. "Why did you need a backup? You're not any less—"

"I don't think I'm less than you," Teah snapped, the bite echoing down the hall. "It's not all about you. They killed my mom, too." She glared at me, tears brimming in her eyes, and I knew not all of that anger was directed at me. "If I couldn't be a pilot, I would do what the Aegis couldn't. I'd help Bastion from the inside. I'm good at being invisible."

She was right there. Hide and seek became no fun with Teah as we got older, nor was it fun for my Father when she'd run off to avoid his berating. But I knew she didn't just mean she could hide well. This may not have been all about me, but Aegises cast long shadows, and they could render plenty invisible.

I sighed and pulled her into a hug. She resisted at first, then her hands grasped onto my shirt.

"I'm...proud of you. I am. It's just...the thought of you being surrounded by terrorists...Now I'm just gonna picture you inside Stickney every time I think of that nightmare. And you'll be inside Mwezi and..." I pulled away and wiped a tear off my cheek. "Sorry. That mission...messed with me. All of this is messing with me."

Teah nodded. She could tell. Of course she could tell. No one could read me like her. "Then maybe it's a good thing you won't be alone with your thoughts."

"Yeah," I said, summoning a smile. I'd have much rather been alone than worrying about my sister in that colony. Didn't the Vice Admiral see that as a potential problem? "Well," I sniffed, "we shouldn't be late to your first mission, Delator Caliday." I stepped to the side and gestured toward the landing pad. Someone opened a door at the end and the sound of shuttle engines roared through. We needed to hurry.

Teah started walking and I fell into step beside her. "Thank you, Al. I...thanks. I'll watch my back. You just worry about watching yours."

If only she knew how impossible that was.

CHAPTER SEVEN

TORIS

IT WAS THE DAY the Wolf would die.

That's what I hoped, at least. It's what I'd been hoping, dreaming, wishing, since Cixin Alloway Mellowgold joined Kuma and I on our ride down the Dandelion Stalk after disembarking from our return aboard the *Harriet*. Despite both Navi's and Alis' concerns, the flight was smooth, not a Bastion ship in sight. The passengers all behaved themselves, with the only near exception being an older woman who started projectile vomiting halfway through the voyage. That wasn't all too uncommon in that kind of flight, but we quarantined her for the rest of the trip just in case. I think that only made her more sick, but she still made it. They all made it, and the looks on their faces were as satisfying as the first time when Kuma and I called them all to the bridge to watch our approach to Earth.

Once we returned to our bay at the Dandelion's spaceport, most of the passengers, all having signed the Gaia Compact, took shuttles to other ports and Stalks that would then transport them to all the corners of the world. Some had distant relatives here and there, others wanted to return to ancestral homelands, and a few had dreamed of settling down in very specific places, like beneath the boughs of the Sahara Forest or Switzerland's emerald hills. The refugees continually hedged their hopes, a part of them refusing to believe me that no barrier, no wealth ceiling, could keep them from fulfilling their dreams and establishing a home. Suffering under Bastion's Shades for so long would do that to a person. I only saw their new reality actually sink in when we landed at the Dandelion and they didn't need to pay for passage to the other Stalks. They looked at each other, then at me, with mouths hanging open and tears in their eyes. They were home, and they were welcomed like it.

Cixin was the only one who returned to Orilla del Angel with us. We'd talked about Alis' condition several times on the flight back, and I could see the gears turning in his head as he thought through possible solutions. I didn't want to pressure him, though. He'd just left a traumatic experience, and it wasn't easy starting a new life in such an unfamiliar place. So, despite his kind protests, I told him to take a week to acclimate, then he could examine Alis. He grudgingly agreed, clearly feeling like he owed me for the passage from Farstead. I needed to assure him that Earth didn't work like that anymore. Plus, we had plenty of time before the next cycle.

Waiting hadn't been easy, though, and I kept checking the time during my duties throughout the day.

"This shipment's headed to the coast," Alis said, seemingly less distracted than I was. She hunched over a flickering computer screen that read out the other communities in the region that needed food shipments. After reading the specific coordinates, I plugged those into the side of the sleek truck floating above a magnetic road. Most of the vehicle was a long bed filled with round, juicy tomatoes, with a small electric engine compartment at the front. "Next three are headed west," Alis said once the coast-bound truck hummed to life and started on its journey. Two of the next vehicles were loaded with wheat, and one with tomatoes. I had to step behind Alis to input the coordinates, and I kissed her on the cheek and squeezed her waist as I passed. She smiled.

Once those trucks were off, Alis and I locked down the shipment center—a long building that looked like a barn from the outside. Other workers were wrapping up their duties for the day. Laurendale Nixon, white hair tied up in a bun, walked up to us as they scrubbed their hands with a towel. They were wearing a grease-stained jumpsuit.

"Hey Tori, Alis."

I rolled my eyes but smiled at the nickname. "Repair duty today?"

"Yup," they said with a sniff. "Finally got the vineyard water unit repaired. Now it should drizzle on the plants rather than firehose them. Today's the day, isn't it?"

"Yeah!" I exclaimed at the same time that Alis said, "Hopefully."

Laurendale glanced back and forth between us. Then they focused on Alis. "You nervous?"

"Nervous about the procedure or nervous that it won't work? Because yes."

"I mean," I said, "we don't know if it'll be a 'procedure.' He may be able to do something without being invasive. The guy knows his stuff."

Laurendale just looked at me, and Alis looked at Laurendale. Okay, maybe that wasn't the most empathetic thing to say.

"Whatever happens," Laurendale said, "we've got your back. We'll all be waiting for the good news. And if it doesn't work, we'll still keep you," they winked. "Wolf and all."

"Thanks, Laur," Alis said, and pulled Laurendale in for a hug. I sighed and looked out over the fields, where an automated harvesting unit was plucking tomatoes off the plants. In the distance, a watering unit similar to the one Laurendale had repaired was hovering over a cornfield, spraying water over the plants like rain. The city center rose to the right, with the Corcoran Sea glimmering to the left.

"Good luck!" Laurendale shouted with a wave as they joined a group of other workers on a hovercraft headed for the city center. We waved as they pulled away, then headed over to where our hoverboards were docked and charging. I'd pulled mine out of its dock, but Alis was standing still, hand on the upright board, head bowed a little.

"What is it?" I asked, setting my board down. "Did she get in your head?"

"No, *you* got in my head," she said, fire singing the edges of her tone. She looked at me, and there was more sadness and worry in her eyes than anger. "What if it doesn't work, Tor?"

"It'll work," I said, lifting an arm to hold her. But she jerked her shoulder back, which was all I needed to know she didn't want to be touched. "And if it doesn't, we'll find another way."

"What if there isn't another way?" she asked. "What if we're stuck with the Wolf? Could you do that?"

"I...that's not even relevant. Thinking that way isn't going to do us any good. Neither of us wants to live with that. Do you?"

"No, but I may not have a choice. You do. And not just you. Navi and everyone else." Her shoulders slumped inward.

I closed my eyes and took a breath. Alis was more terrified of losing her new family than losing the Wolf. She'd already lost one. And I wasn't doing enough to convince her that we were her family no matter what.

"I'll choose you, always. Despite the Wolf. I've told you that before."

Now it was her turn to close her eyes. "Despite the Wolf," she repeated.

"Why do you keep repeating that?" I asked, some of my guilt transmuting into frustration. "What's wrong with that?"

Alis looked up at me, and I saw the pain in her eyes, creasing her brow and wrinkling her forehead. There was an answer I should have already known, but

I clearly didn't. Something my own fears and frustrations and traumas were keeping me from realizing. Maybe I didn't have that answer, but I had others.

"I. Love. You." I poured my passion into every word. "I am here, and I am yours. No matter what. You won't lose me. You won't lose this family. I promise you. Just like I did on the *Harriet* all those years ago. I've kept that one, haven't I?"

Some of the tension in Alis' face softened, but not completely. "You have. I love you more than you can understand. And I appreciate all you're doing...putting so much into finding a solution."

"That's something you never have to thank me for," I said. "It's like thanking me for eating food or getting a good night's sleep, so much a necessity that it doesn't feel like effort."

Alis smiled, then cringed a little.

"Yeah, that one was bad," I said. "Kuma made me watch some of his romances on the way back from Farstead. Guess they've gotten to my head."

Alis chuckled, and after the tension constricting that conversation, the sound was magical. "Sure, blame it on the show." She finally pulled her hoverboard out of its dock. "Come on, lover boy. We've got an appointment." Then she tossed the board on the ground, hopped on, and zipped out over the fields.

And, as always, I gave chase.

***

Life on Earth was treating Cixin well. His joints and cheekbones were less pronounced, and the bags under his eyes were considerably lighter. Every once in a while, his eyes would still dart nervously to some unknown sound, and he seemed hesitant to smile, as if he were afraid of the happiness he'd found.

"The good news is, your brain is remarkably healthy," Cixin said. He stared at a holo-tablet, the hologram projected between two thin metal bars. On it he read details from Alis' brain scan. She lay on a table, a silver ring around her head. It projected its own hologram, a complete, detailed replica of her beautiful brain. "Healthier than most," Cixin said. "I'm assuming you've been augmented?" Something bitter accented his tone, but I knew it wasn't directed at her, just the privilege and institution those modifications represented.

"Mm hm," Alis said, as uncomfortable discussing it as Cixin was bitter.

"That's probably what saved your life," he said. "De-syncing from an Aegis like you did would fry most people's minds. Bastion isn't kind to those who want to think for themselves."

"Do you still have your 'jack?" Alis asked.

"Of course," Cixin responded. "Like I said, tampering with it would kill most people. We're not all so fortunate."

Alis' jaw flexed. And she stayed quiet.

Cixin swiped something on his tablet and the hologram of Alis' brain swiveled to its right side and zoomed in on the temporal lobe. He tapped his tablet again, and something so small I'd missed it before flashed red: a small circle, implanted directly into Alis' brain. A mindjack. Its surface looked singed.

"Have you had anyone else look at this?" Cixin asked as he zoomed in even closer and rotated the brain back and forth, examining the problem from multiple angles.

"A few," Alis said. "But they were all Earth natives. People have tried to re-verse-engineer mindjacks, but they haven't managed to get it right." She shifted on the bed. "I guess it's hard to fix something you don't totally understand. They could identify the damage, and they confirmed that it was because of the...way I de-synced from the Aegis, but they couldn't really say much else with confidence."

"And the...state change that the malfunction causes, Toris said you call it the 'Wolf'?"

"Yeah," Alis said. "Started more as a dark joke, really, since it comes on whenever Mars and Earth align. Like a—"

"Yeah, werewolf. Yeah. That is interesting. I assumed that your state change is a result of the damage the mindjack is attempting to cause your brain as part of its failsafe. But if that were the case, you would always be this 'Wolf.' But since you only experience the change during planetary alignment, then there must be some kind of phantom signal. Maybe the mindjack's so damaged that the failsafe can't totally activate, and your brain endured its initial burst, so it takes a nudge from Bastion to bring it to life. What was the last signal sent to it?"

"Uh." Alis swallowed. I reached out and grabbed her hand. "It was the Day of Dominance."

Cixin stared at her for a moment, his eyes going wider. "You were at Mwezi. You piloted the *Sanguine Lycan*. You're the Moonbreaker."

Alis stared up at the ceiling and bit at the inside of her bottom lip. There was no question to answer. Nothing to clarify nor to correct. I'd told Alis that she may not want to bring up her participation in the Day of Dominance, because anyone in Bastion, *especially* someone in Cixin's lot, would be very aware of the Moonbreaker. But she insisted that only the truth would give Cixin the context he needed to solve the problem. Of course, she was right. It was right with a risk, though.

Cixin finally looked away from Alis and at his tablet, blinking repeatedly. "I had family on Phobos. A sister."

I almost stood up out of my seat. "She's not—"

"Tor," Alis said, squeezing my hand. Then she turned to Cixin, and, somehow, I tumbled even more deeply in love with her. "I understand if you don't want to help me. I don't deserve your help. I don't deserve what Orilla's given me. I deserve worse than what this mindjack is doing to me. I've said sorry to enough people to learn how hollow of a word it is. But I swear to you that I've lived every day of the past ten years, and I'll live the rest of my life, trying to help more people than I hurt. And I know that won't be enough, but it's all I have to give." She sniffed and a tear rolled down her cheek. She usually kept that pain, that regret, in a sheltered place deep within. I knew how much it hurt her to unseal that vault. "I really will respect whatever you need, Cixin."

Cixin listened, staring at the wall. I thought I saw his jaw quiver a little. My chest practically burned with the breath I was holding, with the effort of resisting jumping to her defense and listing all the ways she'd saved so many more lives, all the ways she was deceived by Bastion. Instead, I just squeezed her hand and rubbed her knuckles with my thumb.

"Bastion made monsters of us all. I know your legacy as the Moonbreaker has been swallowed by the legacy of the traitor. And that makes you a hero. You were there at the Battle of the Loop, weren't you?"

"I was," Alis said, then she turned to me. "But I wasn't the one who—"

I squeezed her hand too hard and vigorously shook my head. She shot me a look and let go of my hand.

"Well," Cixin said. "That all tracks. If you de-synced on the Day of Dominance, that phantom signal could be what's causing your state change."

"Okay, that's something," I said, leaning back in my chair. "We always thought it was just the malfunction itself messing with her head. So what do we do to cut off the signal? Can you just extract the 'jack?"

"Oh, no," Cixin said, shaking his head as intensely as I was a moment before. "No no no. Even if the failsafe is malfunctioning and may not kill her that way, the mindjacks are still physically impossible to remove without causing severe bleeding within the brain."

I sighed. "Assholes."

"The understatement of the era, my friend," Cixin said. "In every way. It's a kind of dark poetry, isn't it? No matter whether we escape, no matter how far we run, we always belong to Bastion. Property, slaves until the end."

I rubbed my face with my hands.

"However," Cixin said, and I froze, staring at him through my fingers, "we may be able to either deactivate the mindjack or, yes, cut off the signal. Turning off the 'jack is more likely to have adverse effects. It's difficult to determine the extent of the damage the initial de-sync and faulty failsafe did to the brain, and therefore it's hard to know what will happen if we attempt to deactivate it. Like I said, property, and Bastion hates giving up property. However, we could create what's called a Faraday Shield to cut off the signal."

"A Faraday Shield?" I asked. "What's that?"

Alis was the one to respond: "It's like a Faraday Cage, but instead of a mesh, it's more like a sheet, a covering, of conductive metal. It blocks signals and electromagnetic fields. We used them in..." she trailed off and swallowed, but held my eyes. I gave her a small smile. She turned to Cixin. "I've seen people try that. After the Day. They'd wear helmets that they said were Faraday Shields. But they didn't work. The signal still got through."

"Yes, it did," Cixin said, "because those shields likely used typical metals, Earth metals. But Bastion's crafty, and the mindjack signals are such a frequency that they penetrate those metals. There's only one metal that signal can't penetrate. And it sure isn't typical."

He didn't even have to say it. The precious metal of Bastion. The foundation of the Pioneers' fortune, and the fortune of their descendants. "Mithril."

Cixin pointed at me and nodded like I'd just gotten an A on his test. "Mithril. If you have Mithril, I should be able to make a Shield."

Alis sighed and sat up, removing the halo from around her head and setting it on the counter beside Cixin. "We don't have Mithril. No one in Orilla has Mithril."

"No one?" Cixin asked, surprised. "I mean, I know Bastion's hoarded it, but I'm surprised you didn't secure some during the War."

"We did," I responded. "But it was quickly bartered or traded away. An economy without money was...awkward for a while, and valuable items, even if they weren't technically currency, started functioning like it. So, like wealth, there's only a few people on the planet who've hoarded it. Many of them used it to secure a home in Bastion." Alis was looking down, gripping the edges of the table she'd been lying on. "Hey, this is good. This is something. This is more than we've ever had."

"But it's not just about finding Mithril," Alis said. "It's like you said, the people who have it won't just give it to us, and they won't trade it for anything less than half of Orilla. They live on the edge of the Compact, and they like the power that privilege gives them. Even then, we wouldn't know where to start looking."

She was mostly right, but not completely.

"Babylon," I said. "There's some in Babylon. And I can get it."

Alis tilted her head. "You don't want to go back there."

I moved off my chair so fast that it slapped against the back wall, took Alis' hand, and sat on the table beside her. She squeezed my hand and smiled, tears glistening in her eyes, all the frustration from the moment before replaced with love. "Do you still need any convincing that I'd go anywhere, that I'd walk the world and search any system for you? I flew to Farstead for ten years and you think I won't go a few hundred miles to get what you need?"

She scooted closer and pressed her forehead against mine. "I love you."

Cixin cleared his throat.

I pulled away, reminded that other people existed in the world, and hopped off the table. Cixin was on his feet, turning off his holotablet and clicking the two metal bars together. I stepped around the examination table and shook his hand. "Thank you so much," I said. "You have no idea how much this means to us. Please let us know if there's anything we can do for you, repair work, take some of your duties, anything."

Cixin smiled and nodded humbly. "I'm more than happy to help. This is why I got into bioengineering in the first place, to help people. Bastion took that from me. As they took so much from you," he nodded to Alis. "You owe me nothing. This is how it should be, correct?"

I shook my head, amazed at the man. "A week on Earth and you understand what we're trying to build more than half the people building it."

Cixin touched his chest and smiled again. "That's very gracious of you. Good luck in Babylon." He started for the exam room door. "Let me know when you're back, and we'll put a muzzle on that Wolf."

***

Alis and I touched our hoverboards down at the Hollows just as the sun was going down. Lights hung across the broken skyscrapers where the food and trading stalls had settled in. Many of the tables were occupied, and they went silent as we stepped off the landing platform. Kuma half-cringed from his seat, one eye nearly closed as he stared at me, waiting to see if this would be yet another disappointment. Laurendale sat a few tables down beside Tallowdane Livamoor, his eyes a little wide in anticipation. Even Navi sat near a back table, hands clasped with Vic, the engineer who'd made the device that shorted out the mindjack and who'd given us the lead to Cixin. Her dark brown hair fell across the shoulders of a bulky jacket and the tank top beneath.

"Geez," Alis said, looking over everyone. "Don't look so excited to see us."

"*Should* we be excited?" Kuma asked, cringing deeper and sinking into his chair.

I swept around Alis and swung my arms wide. "We have a cure!"

The common area exploded with clapping and cheering and whooping. Kuma nearly knocked his table over as he stood up and threw a fist in the air. Mr. Meridot, my old teacher, clapped and gave me a somber smile. Navi let out a breath she'd been holding, and Vic leaned her head back and mouthed a "Finally." Other friends, neighbors, family all joined in. It brought tears to my eyes to see it all. I looked back at Alis, and it was clearly doing the same to her.

"Our new friend from Farstead has a solution," I said as the cheering died down, and I made a point of looking at Navi. "I won't bore you with the details, but all we need is some Mithril."

Some of the smiles froze or faded. Kuma stopped mid-clap, smile devolving into something closer to a cringe.

"Tor," Navi said from the back, but I waved her away.

"I know, I know. But I know where to get some."

Navi's jaw flexed as she clenched her teeth and resisted saying anything. She knew exactly where we'd find that precious metal. And I didn't like going back there any more than she did, but none of that mattered.

"We have a cure!" I exclaimed again, and the response was less enthusiastic. I didn't mind, though. In fact, I just chuckled. "Thank you all for being here. Thank you for supporting us, for welcoming Alis," I made a point of glancing at Navi then, too. "Thank you for being our family. If we still had tabs, I'd say all the drinks are on me." At least that got a few chuckles. "But, please, let's celebrate together. Because this time next week, the Wolf will be dead!" The final cheers were a little louder that time. Kuma even tilted his head back and howled at the darkening sky.

And celebrate we did. Tallowdane poured everyone drinks from the wooden bar they'd built into the back corner of the floor. We laughed and discussed and told stories. Kuma tried to catch Alis up on the plot of *To the Moon*, ever attempting to convince her to watch it. The sunlight faded into the black completely, and the stars twinkled behind the hanging lights and snapping tarps and sheets hanging above the Hollows. At one point, Kuma broke out a guitar and strummed away. Alis took my hand and pulled me to my feet. I sloshed some of my drink on the ground as I tried to set it on the table while Alis dragged me into the open area beyond the tables. I pulled her close and we spun, sashayed, and swept around the circle, navigating around other dancers as if they weren't there.

Cixin joined us all at one point, choosing to sit in one of the back corners. He accepted a drink but never took a sip, staring at the group gathered, at the smiles, at the skyscrapers around us, at the open sky, with mouth hanging open and on the verge of tears, as if he were staring at one of the wonders of the world.

But none of us were as young as we used to be, and the night became quieter. Kuma's frenzied strumming gave way to tranquil picking as he leaned back and closed his eyes, one foot set against the edge of the table. Tallowdane talked with Laurendale, who sat on the bar, empty glass dangling from her fingertips. Mr. Meridot had retired. Vic and Cixin were in deep conversation, throwing out engineering terms and concepts like they were speaking another language. Navi had retired, too, but not before giving me a hug and a kiss on the cheek, and not before gracing Alis with a rare hug as well. She must have finally accepted that with a cure, Alis was going nowhere.

When midnight was just around the corner, Alis and I flew home, smiling as the cool night air washed over us, the stars a dome above us, blotted out occasionally by the cloud of space junk in orbit. Luna hung in a waning crescent, white with the dark domes of colonies webbing its surface.

In the hills rolling down from our home, trees swayed in the moonlight, then the waves of crops and the black pit of the Corcoran Sea. We landed and docked our hoverboards, then entered the quiet, dark house. I went to flick on the light, but Alis set a gentle hand on mine, dragging it down. I turned to her. A shaft of moonlight shined through the window onto her face, over the thin scar on her cheekbone, the strands of hair sticking out from dancing. She took a step closer, grabbing my shirt and pulling until we were pressed together. I swallowed. She smiled.

"Thank you," she whispered, the sound like wind through aspen leaves, like the lapping of waves on the shore. Her breath was warm on my face. "Thank you for never giving up. Now or twelve years ago. Thank you for every day, every encouragement. I." She looked down at my lips then back in my eyes. "Love. You."

I put my hands on her waist and pressed her tighter against me as if I could absorb her, make us as one as I felt we were. "Thank *you* for dealing everyday with my infinite imperfections. Thank you for forgiving me when I fall short. I." I had to swallow again, my mouth dry. Shit, this woman made me a nervous teenager, a mortal at the feet of a goddess. "Love. You."

Then we moved together, not I to her nor her to I but us to each other. We kissed, but that's too small a word. We crashed together, lips to lips, the passion of a supernova and the serenity of night all at once. My heart raced in my chest, desperate to reach hers. The whisper of the wind and trees and the chirping crickets faded, swallowed in a silence that enveloped us as tightly as we held each other.

We shed our clothes in between labored breaths, trading one item for a kiss before tossing away the next, moving in rhythm until I broke the illusion stumbling to pull my sock off. But we just laughed and fell onto the bed, the sheets cool on my skin. I scooted back as Alis prowled over me, hands sinking into the mattress, soft hair brushing my chest and making me shiver. When her face was over mine, she paused, tilting her head and scanning my face, eyes hovering over every detail, though I had no idea what details could be so interesting.

Then she leaned down and kissed me again. Softer, this time. Not like a crash, more like a flutter, a breath, a breeze. She did it again, a flake of manna, a drop of cool rain. Then she fell against me, dropped onto me, running her hand through my hair as the droplets of rain became a downpour, a crash of thunder. And I wrapped my arms around her and became the lightning to meet it.

Chapter Eight
Toris

I KNEW SOMETHING WAS wrong before I opened my eyes.

It was still dark, for one, and it was rare for me to ever wake up before dawn. The feeling was deeper than that, though.

I struggled to open my eyes, blinking away the last grasping threads of sleep. Leaves rustled outside the dark, open window, bringing in the fresh scent of the night and a hint of the salty sea.

Beside me, the bed was empty, Alis' sheets cast away. Maybe that's what had woken me up? I forced myself up onto my elbows to look at the bathroom door, but no light shined through the crack underneath.

"Alis?" I called out, but only the dark silence answered.

I swallowed and licked my dry lips as I threw off the sheets and stood up, feeling suddenly vulnerable in my nakedness, as if something was out there waiting in the dark, watching through the window.

After pulling on a loose, thin white shirt and stumbling into some worn black sweats, I called out for Alis again, to no response. I checked the bathroom, then headed down the hall to the living room. It wasn't all that rare for nightmares or headaches to wake Alis up in the middle of the night. But the living room was empty.

And the front door was open.

It wasn't cast wide all the way, just barely popped inward, which for some reason made me feel even more unsettled. It didn't help that the living room looked disturbed. Our coffee table was knocked askew, and a few books lay on the ground, knocked from their shelf.

I kicked aside the books and threw open the door. Outside, the crescent moon was brighter, shining over the Corcoran Sea in the distance. I looked over at the bench beside our door, where Alis would sometimes go when she really needed a moment of peace. When I saw it was empty, my heart started to race.

"ALIS!" I yelled, my voice echoing out over the hills and fields. A few birds fluttered away, but nothing else.

"Shit, shit, shit," I whispered as I went around the side of the house. Her hoverboard was gone. I ran my hands through my hair and went back down to the road, looking up and down it and to the airspace above, searching for the lights that would blink on her board through the night. In the darkness, they'd be easy to see.

But, of course, the only lights were the stars above, the occasional distant streetlamp, and a few twinkling signs of life up the hill to the northwest in Orilla del Angel's downtown.

Between the dark buildings, however, was some bright light, much brighter than it should have been this late in the night. It could have been the Hollows. Maybe the party was still going. Maybe Alis just needed to get out, and she'd gone back there. The day before had been a big one; I wouldn't blame her if she couldn't sleep.

That justification felt like a far-flung hope, but it was enough to calm me down for the moment as I mounted my hoverboard and took off with such speed that a cloud of dust burst in my wake. I hurtled into the air, above our neighbors and toward downtown, where I wove between buildings, banking so sharply around one corner that I skidded the bottom of my board against the metal of a skyscraper. When I turned another corner, the Hollows came into view, and with it, the sound of shouting voices echoing down the otherwise quiet streets.

I swung up on the landing pad and de-magnetized my boots from the board before I'd even touched the ground, leaving the machine to crash to the metal pad as I jumped off. Alis' board was nowhere to be seen, but other boards were docked there, as well as Vic's hyperbike and a small hovercar Cixin had borrowed to get to the party that night.

Most of the group was still there, crowded near the back of the gathering area, all turned away from me, and some people had returned or joined. There was the back of Navi's head, and beside her were a few others who hadn't been at the party, but whom I recognized from living near the Hollows.

At the sound of my footsteps, Navi turned. Streaks of tears shimmered on her cheeks. I stopped. There was more than sadness on her face. Her jaw was clenched, her nostrils flared, and those expressions only intensified when she looked at me. With her eyes still locked on mine—and others turning to look at me—she moved out of the way.

Cixin Alloway Mellowgold was dead.

Not just dead, ripped apart, his throat torn open in a bloody mess. His mouth hung at a disturbing angle, his eyes still staring at the ceiling. The same eyes that had stared at me with such hope and gratitude at Farstead, that had regarded Alis and I with such kindness as he reignited hope in our hearts.

And I knew, both from the violence of the attack and the anger on Navi's face, exactly who had done it.

The Wolf was loose.

"How do you know." I didn't say it like a question. My own voice sounded distant. "It...the cycle..."

Vic turned away from Cixin. Her lip was bleeding, her black hair disheveled. She'd been here.

"I..." I took a few steps closer to Cixin, and the group parted, some of them shooting me glares or shaking their heads, others with looks of pity. As if I were a child who was finally facing the consequences they'd warned me about all along. "Are you okay?" I asked Vic.

"Yeah," she said, none of Navi's anger in her voice.

"Did she...did it say anything? Before..."

"No. Just ran out of the dark. Didn't even care I was here. I only got hurt because I got in the way. Those augments...hurt."

I nodded, more familiar with that pain than she knew. "This can't be possible," I whispered, unable to take my eyes off Cixin, despite the sight of him churning my stomach. I felt like I had no right to look away. I *was* the child. These were my consequences. Cixin's consequences. "Mars is on the other side of the sun." I swallowed, my mouth dry. "The signal shouldn't be able to reach her. This has never..."

"Cixin was clearly her...its target," Vic said. "It must have perceived him as a threat."

"But it's not...it shouldn't work like that. The Wolf isn't actually sitting in there, waiting to attack. It's the phantom signal, that's what Cixin..." I swallowed some bile that rose to the back of my throat and finally looked at Vic. "And why would it leave me alive? The Wolf always tries to kill me. Always. It's blinded by rage. I never thought it even had the capacity to reason like this." Vic's eyebrows bunched together in what looked like a mixture of pity and concern as my speech picked up speed in desperation to rationalize the tragedy. "I thought it took up all of her brain, that it didn't even have her memories. I thought—"

"You were wrong." Navi's expression lacked all the pity that Vic displayed. "You were wrong. He was wrong. We were all wrong. I was wrong to let this happen in the first place."

"*Let* this happen?" I snapped, my guilt and worry and defensiveness clashing with an ugly friction. "We all know you'd love to rule over all of us, Navi, but you don't. You didn't *let* me do anything. If that's how you want it to be, you can go to Bastion. Alis suffered through your shit for a decade, and..." I trailed off, the anger fizzling out at my own mention of Alis' name. It conjured an image of her, out there, afraid, alone, burdened by guilt heavier than ever before. Not to mention endangered. The Wolf put her in as much harm as it put anyone else. Calmer, even in the face of Navi's growing anger, punctuated by her hard jaw and widening eyes, I continued: "I don't care what you think, as if that wasn't clear enough. Alis is scared. She's alone. She's as much a victim of the Wolf as anyone, more than anyone. We need to—"

"More than Cixin?" Navi asked.

My anger flared up at that, but a look at Cixin doused the flames. I let out a breath, crouched in front of Cixin, and took his hand. He'd shaken that hand so vigorously on Farstead, with such firmness, a strength that reflected his willpower. As always, Navi was wrong about Alis, but Cixin deserved better than for me to forget him in a wash of fury while he lay there.

"I'm so sorry, Cixin," I whispered. This was for him. It wasn't to placate Navi or anyone else watching. It was the least I could do, and it'd still never be enough. "I promised you...I promised you more than this. I hope that, at the very least, these weeks gave you the peace and joy you were looking for. I hope it was the sanctuary you dreamed of beneath the Shades. And I'm so sorry you couldn't enjoy it longer. I know Alis is sorry, too." I squeezed his cool hand. "I swear to you that I'll make this right. You were going to help me kill the Wolf for us. Now I'll do it for you, too."

I stood up and turned away, wiping aside a few tears. "I'll bury him," I said. "Down in the foothills, looking over the sea."

"Then what," Navi said, but her tone was anything but a question. She knew the answer, she just wanted me to say it out loud.

"Did you see which way it went?" I asked, looking only at Vic.

She glanced at Navi before responding: "South. Southeast, maybe? I don't know why it didn't come after me, either. It seemed intent on going somewhere else. Like it only had eyes for that, just like when it..." she looked at Cixin but didn't say anything else.

I nodded and, under the gazes of everyone who'd gathered there, lifted Cixin into my arms. He'd put on a little weight since his time in Orilla, but he was still light. Small. Fragile.

"You don't know where she went," Navi said, following me as I carried Cixin toward the landing pad and his car parked there.

"Where *it* went," I corrected, but didn't say anything else. I didn't need to explain myself to her. I was tired of explaining myself to her.

And, in that moment, I was just *tired*.

The door to Cixin's car popped open as we got near, and I nudged it wider with my foot, then lay Cixin across the backseat.

"Tor."

I shut that door, then I took my hoverboard and placed it on top of the car, engaging a magnet that would hold it there.

Then I stood beside the car, hand still on the board, back to my sister and everyone else watching. A breeze whispered by.

"I'm sorry." I turned back to face Navi. "I know you don't understand. But I'm going to figure out what's going on. I'm going to kill the Wolf. And I'm going to bring Alis home."

"We don't know if Alis is still there," Navi said. "And if you can't remove the mindjack, then she'll always have that connection to Bastion. She'll always be a threat."

I shook my head, more sad than angry. And tired. So tired.

I opened the door to Cixin's car.

"If you leave, if you try to bring her back, you're a threat to the rest of the community, and you're exiled. Find another home to endanger."

I stared at Navi, hoping she'd take it back, hoping she'd remember all we'd endured together, hoping she wouldn't give all that up.

But she just stood there, defiant, arms folded, chin held high, a hint of tears in her eyes.

Without a word, I got in the car, closed the door, and flew away.

In the rearview mirror, Navi finally broke, her head dropping into her hands, Vic putting an arm around her shaking shoulders.

CHAPTER NINE

ALIS

(Twelve years earlier)

ON THE THIRD DAY of the Siege of Mwezi, Earth's military approached Luna.

"They're holding at 350,000 kilometers," I said to Ecker, where he stood on the bridge of the *Fang*. The ships were little more than silver splinters between the moon and Earth. Through my mindjack, I urged my Aegis' cameras to zoom in, and additional information flashed up onto my HUD. It was a small force, only four battleships and a few squadrons of starfighters, with more waiting in the ships' hangars. Parked behind them was a simple light cargo hauler, looking very out of place on the edge of a would-be battlefield. "I'm not seeing a cruiser. Maybe it's running behind?"

"*More likely they lost it,*" Ecker scoffed. "*This is just another indicator that their military is dwindling. We're close to winning this war, Caliday. We may not even need Mwezi at this point.*"

If only that were true, then I could have been back on my way home. Our way home. But no, I was stuck waiting in my armor, the great red symbol of Bastion, while Teah was wandering the streets of the colony, likely rubbing shoulders with the enemy. In fact, her job was to identify the enemy, and all it would take was a single pissed-off Mudbrain to decide to stand up and fight back. I could be by her side, guarding her, but no. I'd been stuck staring at the giant green-and-blue marble in the sky for three days, guarding the colony from nothing but gray dust and trading ships. At least now I had something real to guard it from.

"*They won't risk violating their agreement with Luna,*" Ecker said. "*They have much more to lose than we do. Let them spectate. Let them see Mwezi choose sides. That'll do wonders for their morale.*"

But how long would they watch? Surely Earth had agents inside every colony on Luna, just as we did. They must have known we were attempting to sway the vote. Maybe they had their own measures at play, too. As long as those measures didn't get in Teah's way.

"What are your orders, sir?" I asked, pulling back from Earth's starships and looking up at the Earth. We were facing the massive blue of the Pacific Ocean, shreds of white clouds hovering over the waters, wider and deeper than any ocean back home. On the rim of the Earth, shining with the coming day, were the islands of Australia and Japan and the Asian continent. A crater near the continent belched a cloud of smoke and debris from Bastion's orbital bombardment in response to Stickney.

"Your role is more important than ever, Caliday. Show the Mudbrains that we won't be moved. That we're right where we belong, with our people, and that we won't be intimidated."

That was a long-winded way to say stay put and keep doing what I'd been doing for the past three days. Great. I felt so inspired.

For what must have been the tenth time in those three days, I tried to contact Teah. And for the tenth time, she ignored me. That was the thing with communication devices implanted in your brain; it was impossible to miss a call. She was on a mission, and Ecker surely would have told me to focus on mine, but I wanted to ensure that Earth's forces coming into the picture didn't change anything on the ground for her.

"Caliday," Ecker said, *"the emergency session's begun. The vote...hold."* Ecker's voice went from excited to hard as stone on that final word. I tensed and watched the Earth ships. They held position, no outgoing attempts to hail, no shuttles headed for Mwezi, no weapons heating up. I felt like a gunslinger in one of those ancient western stories. Except my Aegis staring down the barrel of a battleship was anything but equal. More like a revolver versus a nuke.

I turned back to Mwezi, a colony at least ten times the size of little Stickney. These domes were at least a hundred feet tall, dwarfing even my Aegis. I stood in the colony's spaceport, a half-ring of docks and hangars that surrounded one of the city's outer domes. The port had been quiet since we arrived, with only the occasional Bastion-bound cargo ship lifting off. Expanding from the port were tunnels with high-speed maglev tracks inside, connecting Mwezi to Luna's other colonies. Those tracks had remained active. We'd taken to calling this operation the Siege of Mwezi, but all we'd really restricted was trade with Earth, and even that was hard to control when the goods leaving Mwezi could end up on an Earth-bound ship departing another colony. If anything, this was a siege of ideas, of symbols. Where the bureaucracy and the pruners worked in concert to ensure the voice of the people was heard, that the Mudbrains didn't suppress the will of the majority. That the rot didn't spread further.

At least, that's what I'd told myself as I'd stood outside the colony and my stomach twisted as I thought of what Teah was being ordered to do in there.

"*Commander Caliday*," Ecker said, voice sharp and curt. I could hear officers shouting around him. "*We need you inside the colony. Now. Popping starport doors.*"

"What? What's going on? Are we under attack? Where's Teah?" But my only response was the thirty-foot-tall metal doors hissing as the air inside vented into space. Then the doors slid open, spilling light onto the dark moon. I guided my Aegis inside, bending over so my armor's head wasn't hitting the ceiling. It was a loading airlock, a massive space where huge containers—and their crew—could transfer between the colony in the docks. The *Sanguine Lycan* took up the entire space, more like an adult playing in a child's toy than a killer war machine.

My hands shook with anticipation as the airlock pressurized. What was on the other side of that door? A wall of protesters? A cannon aimed at my Aegis' heart? Teah taken prisoner or...

I swallowed. I couldn't think like that.

"What's the situation, sir?" I asked in the calmest voice I could muster.

"*The rot, Calliday. Always the rot. The Mudbrains have taken control of the city center. The vote was illegitimate.*"

Illegitimate? What did that mean? "We lost the vote?" I asked.

"*No, Earth's been at play here longer than we have. Our people are in danger. Bastion's in danger, and we must act quickly.*"

"Where's Teah?"

"*Are you Vice Admiral, Caliday?*" Ecker snapped, so loudly that his voice crackled over the transmission. "*That's what I thought. Get your Aegis to the city center. Now. If you care about your sister, you'll put a stop to this.*"

I couldn't quite tell if that was intended as a threat from Ecker or a jab driven by Earth's threat. Either way, if Teah was in the middle at the city center, that's where I'd be.

The dome ahead was purely industrial, full of cranes, shipping containers, and maglev lines that led out onto the docks and deeper into the colony. Neither my cameras nor my sensors detected anyone, but I wasn't surprised it'd been evacuated. If it came to combat, this dome would have been the first collateral damage. And I'd developed a reputation for collateral damage. I had my Aegis run an instantaneous scan of the dome, which was only a half-mile long, and told it to identify places where I could step without causing damage.

Despite Ecker's boasting on my behalf and his encouragement to embrace my reputation, I'd never managed to be proud of it.

The scan completed and produced an overlay on my HUD where critical infrastructure blinked red and safe, sturdy spaces were marked in green.

I crouched, the armor storing potential energy just like muscle, then sprang forward, using a short thruster burst for added momentum. I sailed over containers and ducked under a crane, planted my foot on an empty concrete pad, and pushed off with another thruster burst, the concrete cracking beneath me.

"*We're tracking you, Caliday,*" Ecker said, his voice far less friendly than it'd been the past few weeks. The show was over. "*Popping cargo doors into Mwezi proper.*"

Ahead was a door similar to the one through which I'd entered the industrial zone. Set beside a maglev line that would carry workers and citizens into the city, the huge door was meant, like its mirror, for cargo transport and transfer.

Fortunately, I didn't have to wait for this door to pressurize. I didn't even wait for it to open all the way as I turned sideways and launched through the door, its edge scraping my Aegis' chest.

Waves of stimuli assaulted my sensors, and I slid to a stop, buckling the concrete beneath me. Sheltered by its dome, Mwezi had grown to look much like any other city, albeit with shorter buildings. While they couldn't quite be considered skyscrapers, some of the buildings ahead in the city center towered above my Aegis at seventy to eighty feet. I stood in another smaller industrial zone that gave way to rings of squat housing units that gradually rose almost like the slopes of a mountain to the colony's center. Tiers of maglev lines ran through the city like veins, and I could see aircraft hovering like insects in the city center. A blue sky projected across the dome, complete with wisps of cloud.

I shut off some of my more sensitive sensors, which tried to feed me information on everything in the observable area, from street maps to individual people to the plants growing on rooftops. Instead, I focused on intel's data on the city center's location. And I ran a scan through mindjacks for Teah's. She didn't show up.

"*Caliday, if you get distracted on more time, I'll come pilot the Lycan myself, and I'll rip you right out of there. Do you understand me? Get moving!*"

Maybe they kept the pruners invisible? Somehow cloaked their mindjack signals? It would—

"*NOW, SOLDIER!*"

"Shit," I hissed, then burst forward, bounding over a maglev line and springing over a ring of boxy housing units. Screams filtered into my cockpit from external mics as Mwezi citizens ran for their homes, a titanic metal monstrosity hurtling over their heads.

And when they looked up at me, I saw Monalua, defiant, unmoving, burned to ash.

I shook my head and focused up when I nearly tripped over a bridge, adjusting at the last minute with a thruster burst that sent me over it. I landed firmly, cracking asphalt, and kept running, hurtling between buildings that gradually grew taller. Soon the buildings rose above the *Sanguine Lycan*, sleek and covered in glass that reflected back my red, lanky shape as I sped between them. The navigation flashing my route on my HUD directed me to turn right at the next street. I twisted at my hips and banked around the corner, crouching low, then pressing my fingertips against the ground and pushing off.

Then I slid to a stop, thrusting bursts out of the front of my armor to shed more speed.

A line of tanks, cannons, and soldiers bristled up at me like a wall of black and silver thorns. I swallowed, seeing Monalua in my mind, then feeling the blast of the anti-starship cannon. Before I could think about how to react, I held up my hands, then slowly lowered them and straightened up. My reflection in the building beside me caught my attention. I was a towering god, smoke sloughing off my armor, the wall of weaponry below almost laughable.

But I wasn't laughing. I was trying not to throw up.

"*Bastion Aegis, designation* Sanguine Lycan, *you are trespassing in this city,*" came a magnified voice through my speakers. "*Under the Treaty of Independent Spheres, your government agreed to keep all military assets outside the colony. The colony of Mwezi has voted to retain its independence. If you take one more step, Bastion is officially declaring war on Luna. Leave Mwezi, now. And leave Luna. We want no part of your war.*"

I took a step backward. Then another.

"*What are you doing, Caliday?*" Ecker shouted through my mindjack, making my skull ache. "*Did I order you to retreat?*"

"Sir," I said, my small voice echoing in the cockpit. "They voted."

"*The rot voted,*" Ecker responded. "*And it's spoiled the entire body. It was an illegitimate vote, and we do not recognize it. You will proceed to the city center. You will finish this mission.*" Then I heard him turn away from his radio and shout, "*Tell them if they refuse to follow my orders, they will be court martialed and jailed for the rest of their lives. This is WAR!"* And I heard a crash as he slammed his fist on something.

I stared down at the line of weapons and soldiers following their orders, protecting their home. Protecting it from an invader. From me.

But...wasn't this my home, too? Wasn't it an arm of Bastion? So...were they the invaders? Were they...

I tried to hail Teah one more time. And one more time, she didn't respond. Was she one of the others refusing to follow orders? One of the ones Ecker was screaming at? Or would she follow him? To prove herself, she might.

I didn't need to prove myself. I already had. I was the Moonbreaker, the Scourer of Stickney, bearer of the Pioneers' Courage Crest. And it all fit about as comfortably as my uniform. Responding to terrorism in a colony on our Sphere was one thing, but this...

This was ridiculous. I was an Aegis Pilot of Bastion. And now I had a chance to make a difference for our world, to secure a foothold, maybe even to set us on the path to ending this war. That would protect our home. That would protect Teah. And Father, too. It would...

I closed my eyes and let a deep breath jet out my nostrils. Even those thoughts sounded like they weren't my own, even if they should have been. They were the thoughts woven through stories and billboards and propaganda and the sneers of Father with his friends. They were the thoughts built by stories told since the Pioneers reshaped Mars and kept Earth from accessing the bounty of the Belt, sparking the Solar Gulf War. The stories that got me to join the military, to secure cities, to ground starships, to remove the rot.

Maybe the rot got to me. Vacuum, spacesuits, and Aegis armor apparently weren't enough to keep that rot out. It started with Monalua, defiant as she stood up for her people.

It ended here, on Luna, in a city I shouldn't have been, facing down an independent people defending their home after they voted to tell us to get the hell out.

"Caliday..." Ecker's tone had an edge sharp enough that he didn't need to say anything else.

"Sir," I said, my voice stronger than it'd been. "We should respect their vote, as we'd expect any power to respect ours. We have an advantage against Earth right now, but if Luna joins their side, couldn't that tip the scales? Shouldn't we—"

"For fuck's sake, Caliday. I knew Stickney shook you, but I really thought you would be stronger. But the rot spreads deep, it seems. And you should know better than anyone that I will burn. The rot. Away."

"I'm sorry, sir. Court martial me if you have to, but I don't think this is what we stand for. This isn't what I swore to do."

I cut off my communications and shut off my radio. Then, hands shaking, I turned on my external speakers. "I'm not going to hurt you, but Bastion forces will—"

One of the Mwezi soldiers turned, swiveling their plasma rifle, and shot their comrade in the head. Then they shot themselves.

The gunshots sparked chaos. The soldiers nearby the scene of their companion's murder spun on each other, clearly unsure who to trust. A few of the soldiers fired at me, likely thinking that I fired those shots, but their attacks were rushed, and most of them missed. A few lanced into my armor, setting off warning lights in the cockpit. I watched the tanks, instincts telling me to reduce them to ash before they could attack, but both of us remained still.

Then one of the tanks turned its cannon on its neighbor and fired through its armor, setting off an explosion that blasted away half of the remaining soldiers. Had Bastion infiltrated Mwezi's forces? Had

Had

Had

Had

Had

I cringed, my head suddenly throbbing with pain. I...

Why did I feel so tired?

Not tired, but...disoriented. Unmoored. Drifting, like I was about to fall asleep or pass out.

Then a blade extended from my Aegis' wrist, ten feet long and wreathed in churning purple plasma.

I hadn't told my armor to do that. Something was wrong. Beyond wrong. I tried to send a command through my mindjack, to retract the blade, but the only response was pain like a knife through my brain. I cried out and jerked forward, everything around me devolving to static for a moment.

When they resolved back into solid screens, I could only watch as my Aegis, my own arm, swept through the Mwezi soldiers, blazing through bodies and cutting through the remaining tank like butter.

My suit's helm retracted just in time for me to vomit into my cockpit.

The acid burning my throat was still nothing compared to the pain in my head. And neither of those held a candle to the aching in my chest, a guilt that I felt hardening into stone in my gut, calcifying into my soul.

And it clearly wouldn't end there.

The same screens that had been projected into my helm's HUD shined in the Aegis' cockpit above me. I lurched forward as the *Sanguine Lycan* launched down the street, propelled by a thruster burst and then its powerful legs, no concern for the infrastructure around it as we smashed through a suspended maglev bridge, sending concrete and metal exploding in every direction.

We banked around a corner, and the wide avenue leading to the city center opened up. Trees lined the center and sides of the road with rows of blue and purple flowers in between them. The buildings on this street were the tallest in the city so far, sleek and shining in the sun filtering through the glass dome far above. At the end of the street and atop a sloping rise was a squat, column-lined building. On my HUD, it flashed green. That was my destination. The seat of power.

And an army stood between me and it.

Multiple lines of soldiers waited, rifles leveled at me. A handful of tanks flanked them, with a single larger machine in the center, double the size of the other tanks. A railgun. It reminded me of alligator jaws, open and ready to chomp. And of all the weapons in that lineup, that alligator was the only thing that could take a bite out of my armor.

Although, at this point, maybe I wanted it to.

I'd killed innocent people. More innocent people.

Unless...I hadn't, had I? Not really. Someone had hacked my armor. No, not just my armor. Every time I tried to use my mindjack, either to stop the Aegis or to contact Teah—even Ecker at this point—my head burned and the 'jack wouldn't respond. Ecker must have hacked it, or someone in shadow ops under his orders.

That must have been what Ecker did to those soldiers, too. If they weren't inside agents, then they must have originally been Bastion citizens, implanted with mindjacks at birth. And Bastion had turned it against them. Against each other.

They'd done the same to me.

I wanted to press the button that would retract the armor's connection from my suit, disconnecting the direct line between my mindjack and the Aegis, but my arm wouldn't move. Instead, my right forefinger flicked open a cover and punched a button. The Aegis vibrated as my shoulder cannon rolled on its track behind my back and settled above its trapezius.

"No, no, no!" I shouted—at least I could still do that. I screamed as I tried to move anything, do anything to get my body to respond. Nothing worked. It was terrifying, a kind of paralysis, but worse, because I could only watch as my own limbs moved on someone else's accord, punching in commands as my mindjack took care of the rest of the calculations. My Aegis' fusion reactor diverted energy to the cannon with a command I could sense leave my mindjack, but that I'd never sent. I could feel the outputs, but not the inputs, wherever they were coming from. It was a new kind of violation, a deep violation that I could never have conceived of.

Because of that violation, the *Sanguine Lycan* was destroying innocent, independent lives in assaults that would surely be spun to maintain the Aegis' symbolism, *my* symbolism, as a defender of Bastion. The spirit of the Pioneers reborn.

Not anymore. They couldn't use me like that, and I felt stupid that I'd allowed it to happen in the first place. I just wanted to serve my family, my world, my home.

I stopped trying to focus on moving. That wasn't getting me anywhere. After all, that entire situation was rooted in my mindjack. I closed my eyes and cringed against the pain as I pushed to access the jack. Each thought, each signal, each neuron firing was like a firework inside my head. I cried out but kept pushing. I was completely locked out, barred from my own mind, my own body.

Scarlet, scarlet, scarlet, I thought as clearly as I could, but the reset code did nothing. Of course, I'd had to share that code with the military when I'd joined in case my mindjack became compromised, so they must have anticipated that.

The vibration inside the cockpit intensified as the cannon neared the completion of its charge. Warning lights flashed as the soldiers fired at my Aegis, but nothing pierced the armor. Another warning flashed on the screens that the railgun was also charging up. Why wasn't whoever was hacking me moving us out of the way? We could easily scale the buildings or thrust over the defenses and fire from a better position.

Unless...they wanted me dead. I was a liability, now. They wanted to control the symbol. I couldn't return home, even to a court martial, and risk destroying that image. I had to die in the line of duty, defending Bastion, burning away the rot that had taken root in Mwezi, that had corrupted and rigged the vote. They'd use me, then throw me away. A railgun that close could take off the top half of my Aegis as easily as I'd cut through that first line of Mwezi's defenses. And I'd deserve it, too.

I felt like I was staring down a tsunami or a wildfire while stuck in quicksand. There was nothing I could do but watch those rails charge and the tungsten-rod ammunition cycle and load into the barrel. To my left, the bar indicating my cannon's charge was nearly at its apex. At the last minute, though, my targeting changed, confirming my worries, and boring a deeper pit into my stomach. No longer was I targeting the defense forces. Now I was targeting the city center.

Teah could be there. If Ecker was using her to influence the vote, she may have been sent to witness it, to make any final prunings.

I screamed, a guttural, primal sound that bounced off the walls of my cockpit as my throat strained to sustain it. At least I could have that, in the end, even if it was useless. Even if...

Wait. I couldn't just scream. I'd removed my helm to vomit—which was really starting to stink. It'd been instinctive, but my suit had responded to that mental signal. I tried it again, commanding my helm to cover my face. It responded, sliding over and the internal screens flashing to life.

How was this working? The suit of all things should have responded to the shadow ops' hacking. It was military hardware. They...

Teah.

She'd been tampering with it, improving it, and that meant improving the programming, too. She said she'd make it easier for me to get out of the cockpit, so maybe she'd done something to isolate the connection to my mindjack. It shouldn't have mattered, but it did.

Teah may have just saved my life.

Through my sync with my suit, I commanded it to vent all the oxygen out of my helm. After flashing a confirmation warning, the air hissed out. Within seconds, I was gasping for breath, lungs clenching. My head started to go light.

And just before I would have passed out, the sharp pain left my head and my body jerked forward. I had control again.

I retracted the helm and drew in a deep breath. Mindjack 101: the brain's survival actions will override 'jack signals. I wasn't sure how long that override would last before Ecker took over again, but I didn't need long.

Back in sync with my Aegis, I fired a burst from my thrusters, shot into the air, and spun. My cannon went off the next second, blazing a giant hole through a building and sending me tumbling backward through the air with its recoil. I slammed into another tower, glass exploding around me. With another mental command, I released the cannon, and it separated from my armor with a *thunk,* sliding back into the wrecked tower behind me. If Ecker got control again, I definitely didn't want him having that.

As if he could have heard my concerns, pain lanced through my head again as the hack came on. Before, I'd had seconds until the paralysis took full effect.

So, with those seconds, I reached behind my head and tore out the sync cord linking my suit—and my brain—to the Aegis.

If I thought the pain was bad before, that was like a match to a bonfire. I cried out and grasped the edges of my seat. Something warm dribbled down my face from my eyes and dripped down onto my armor. I squinted through the pain at the drop. It was almost the same red. Blood. I was bleeding from my eyes.

The blood continued to stream down my face, mixed with tears as I grasped the Aegis' manual controls and...

The Aegis slamming into something brought me back to consciousness. I'd only blacked out for a few seconds, but it was enough. I'd fallen out of the tower and was lying on the street. Warning lights flashed out armor breaches, and on one screen I could see commands flashing by that I wasn't inputting. Ecker was trying to hack the armor through other means.

I had to get out of there.

I released my safety restraints and climbed out of my seat, then collapsed when I tried to get to my feet. My head slammed into the cockpit wall, which didn't at all help.

After a few more shaky steps, I got a hand on the emergency escape lever and wrenched it down. The door unlocked with a low *boom* and slid open, letting blinding light into the dark cockpit. I pulled myself out onto the Aegis' ribs and slid down the back to the wrecked concrete below.

But while I was still at least ten feet from the ground, the Aegis lurched to its feet. I screamed as I tumbled the last of the distance and slammed into the ground, punching the air out of my lungs. It felt like the entire moon shook as the *Sanguine Lycan* took a firm stance and fired rockets from the barrels in its forearms. The rockets exploded across the defenders' line, most of them missing, but one sending a group of soldiers flying backward. That was only a distraction, though, since my maneuver had put the *Lycan* between the defenders and the city center.

While the smoke cleared around the defenders, the Aegis turned, a fifty-foot red god with the glowing lines down its face flickering from damage. I struggled to my knees and scooted behind a chunk of rubble, hiding from its cameras. Ecker would see that I'd popped the emergency hatch. The question was if he cared enough to kill me first.

Evidently, he must have decided he didn't have time, because the *Lycan* dashed toward the city center, raising its arm again as rocket tubes opened on its forearms. I held my breath as I waited for them to launch and—

The only warning I had was a low *whumph* and the dust around me levitating for a moment before the top half of the *Sanguine Lycan* disappeared in an explosion of red metal and shards of railgun ammunition.

The Aegis—*my* Aegis—dropped to its knees, then that bottom half collapsed to the ground. Shouts made their way through my muffled hearing as the Mwezi defenders rushed the armor. I pressed my back against the broken rubble as their boots thumped by and their war machines rumbled down the street.

When they'd passed, I pushed myself to my feet and—after stumbling once—limped into the dark, smoky alley ahead, blood still dripping from my face.

Chapter Ten

Toris

For Cixin, I picked one of the solar flowers beside our home—one that would never wilt, would always turn to the sun. He...his body waited in the hovercar a few feet away. My fingers shook as I disconnected the flower from the power lines. They resisted, and—

"Ah!" I hissed as one of the petals from a neighboring flower sliced the top of my hand.

That pain, that blood, snapped something inside. Fresh ache rippled across my side where the Wolf had stabbed me with a petal just like that. I roared, screaming until my throat burned, and wrenched the flower out of the ground, tearing the cords. Then I hurled the flower over Cixin's car toward the rising sun, cord flying behind it like a tail. I cried out again and slammed my foot down on the flower that had cut me, crushing the metal and glass into the ground.

Another sound escaped, a pitiful moan more than a yell, as tears stung my eyes. Movement in my periphery caught my attention, and I turned toward the window. Our bedroom window. My reflection stared back at me, hunched, back heaving with exerted breaths, spittle dribbling down my chin, my bottom jaw jutting out. I looked less than human.

More like a Wolf.

***

Dawn rimmed the horizon by the time I'd finished digging Cixin's grave. The sky to the east was more white than blue, shadows casting on clouds from the Sierra Nevadas and blanketing most of Orilla. I couldn't look at the city for too long; all I saw was Navi. All I saw was Cixin.

I covered him with a blanket I found in the car, unable to look at his face—or the Wolf's injuries—any longer. He lay covered beside the grave as I dug deeper into the earth. I'd picked a spot not far from mine and Alis' home. I hadn't been able to give Cixin the life on Earth that he'd deserved, so I'd found a place that captured the beauty of the new world. The grave was on a hillside that sloped down toward our fields, where water from rain drones sparkled in the early morning light. Down from the fields was the shimmering Corcoran Sea, which was a metaphor in its own: a scar from the Solar Gulf War that had reclaimed the valley there, but that had become a beautiful landmark that we used to sustain our city. The giant dandelion-shaped solar panels were opening their metal petals to the rising sun. On the other side of the sea was the dark peninsula of the Coastal Range separating the Corcoran from the Pacific Ocean. Above, the levitating wind turbines spun. Beside us, tall grass, flowers, and shrubbery shivered in the breeze. And behind us Orilla del Angel looked down on it all.

It felt colder than usual, though.

I squatted and picked up Cixin once more, then I gently—albeit awkwardly—set him in the grave. I knelt there, hands on my knees, tears rolling down my cheeks as I looked down at his body. He'd escaped Bastion, evaded the many ways he could have died for years, only to die on Earth within weeks.

"I'm sorry," I said to Cixin, the words so pointless that the breath felt like a wasteful contribution of CO_2 to the atmosphere. I stood, picked up the shovel, and dropped the first scoop of dirt on the body. It landed with a thud that made me cringe. Cixin deserved better. I could do better.

"Cixin Alloway Mellowgold. I commend your body to the Earth, to the dust from which we were born, to your home." I paused to take a breath, then I continued digging and continued my...prayer, or the closest thing to a prayer I could muster. Scoop. Drop. *Thud thud thud.* "May the grass grow over your grave, the replacement you deserve to the Shades of Bastion." Scoop. Drop. *Thud thud thud.* "May you be free, unconstrained, unexploited." Scoop. Drop. *Thud thud thud.* "May you be at peace." Scoop. Drop. *Thud thud thud.* "May you uncover the great mysteries of the universe." Scoop. Drop. *Thud thud thud.* "May you..." I hesitated, stabbing the shovel blade into the pile of dirt.

Who was I talking to? Did I really think Cixin was listening? I'd always been...undecided on whether life continued after death. It was a comforting notion, sure. I'd had moments where I thought I'd felt my mom's or dad's presence since they died. Navi had as well, and she was convinced it was their spirits. I was more inclined to accept it as a kind of phantom presence, like a lost limb.

That love was so deep, such a part of me, that some element of that presence remained deep in my subconscious. Either way, whether spirit or subconscious, it was a comforting feeling, followed by the ache of grief. Navi and I both felt that, regardless of our other beliefs.

Still, the world was a strange place, and history had seen enough mysteries uncovered for me to at least consider that more great mysteries remained unsolved. And, like the phantom presence, this prayer wouldn't hurt. If Cixin could hear me, it was the very least I could do. And if it was just for myself, well, then maybe I could have used some comfort, too.

Scoop. Drop. *Thud thud thud.* "May you rest in comfort knowing that no one else will suffer at the hands of the Wolf." Scoop. Drop. *Thud thud thud.* A tear fell with the dirt. "May you rest knowing that you saved lives, in the end. That you will have saved my life—our lives—when this is over. Thank you for that, Cixin." Scoop. Drop. *Thud thud thud.*

With everything said, I dumped the rest of the dirt into the grave until there was a smooth mound. By the end, my muscles were burning and sweat mingled with tears on my face. My legs ached for me to sit down, to rest, just for a moment, but I couldn't. Not while Alis was out there, in danger in the hands of the Wolf.

So I marked the grave with the solar flower I'd picked after my...outburst, and I turned away. I turned away from another Bastionite I couldn't save. Worse than that. Another unfortunate soul who died because of my choices. Because—

No. I couldn't think like that. Not now. I couldn't fall into that spiral. There was no time to climb back out of it.

I stepped onto my hoverboard and flew to the house. Inside, I kicked aside the books that had fallen in the way and headed into our bedroom. I swiped my satchel out of the closet and packed a change of clothes, then I set the satchel on the bed while I changed into a dark-gray shirt and black pants.

As I pulled on my travel boots, I stared at the spot where Alis had lay just hours before. There'd been absolutely no indication that the Wolf was preparing to emerge, and it should have been physically impossible with Mars on the other side of the sun. Had they come up with some kind of transmission innovation in so short a time? That seemed unlikely, but if this was a phantom signal, what other explanation could there be?

One other possibility froze me, hands above my boots: What if it was no phantom? What if someone was actively trying to hack her, even after all this time?

And what if they were coming?

Even more confusing was the fact that the Wolf had left me alone. Vic could have been right in suggesting that the Wolf perceived Cixin as a threat, but threats alone had never been enough to force the Wolf to take control, and it had never shown that kind of sentience before. Its rage had always been focused on me, and I always assumed that was just because I was the closest warm body. Alis had clearly left the house in an erratic manner, but it wasn't nearly as violent as the Wolf moved. Maybe Alis had maintained control for a moment? Maybe it was some kind of hybrid transformation, where the Wolf could access Alis' subconscious, but Alis could exert some control, too?

That couldn't be it. If Alis had any control, she'd never allow Cixin to die.

But if she *did* have any control, she'd leave as soon as she could, afraid that the Wolf would emerge again and hurt more people.

Or the Wolf had left to avoid me, knowing that I now had a way to kill it, even if Cixin was dead. If it had enough access to Alis' subconscious to go after Cixin, it had enough to make a self-preserving decision like that.

I wrenched my boot laces with such frustration that I snapped them.

Tossing the broken lace aside, I stood and grabbed my satchel, then reached into a sock drawer for a card holding some emergency funds. I'd stashed them in case Kuma and I ever needed them on our voyages, or if—God forbid—I ever had to go back to Babylon. Just holding it made me feel like a hypocrite, though. In the end, Navi was right, I'd go against the Compact, against all of it, for Alis.

After grabbing some dried foods, filling my bottle with water, and swiping my solarblade hilt from the dresser, I buckled my satchel shut and slung it over my shoulder. I took one last look at the dark house, holding back more tears as I thought about the beautiful moment we'd shared only hours before. Another moment the Wolf had massacred.

I'd find Alis. She was the priority. And then I'd kill that Wolf. I'd fry it right out of Alis' head. For her. For us. For Cixin.

I locked up the house and grabbed my board, but I hesitated before jumping on it. Where did I even start? Wolfhome in Yosemite? I'd think the Wolf would actively avoid that place; it couldn't have happy associations there. But maybe Alis would flee there? To chain herself up? Vic had said that the Wolf flew southeast, but that didn't mean it didn't turn around.

That seemed unlikely, though. Following animal-like, fear-driven instincts was one thing, but to actively lead us down a false trail took more capacity than I could imagine even this re-emergent Wolf possessing.

As much as I wanted to rush out, backtracking would only lose me more time. I needed more of a lead. And I knew where to start.

I dropped my hoverboard on the ground, stepped on, and took off, leaving our home—and Cixin—behind.

***

I sped over the fields on my hoverboard toward the edge of the city as the sun rose. How long before Navi spread word of my exile? Even just the thought of that plucked my heart. Maybe she only said that in anger. Maybe Alis and I would have a home to return to. It would take a collective vote from the rest of the community. As much as my jabs at her were fueled by frustration, I was right. Navi was no leader. The vast majority of communities had no centralized leader anymore, even if people still tended toward deferring to the authority and judgment of others. Navi's word alone couldn't expel us. I hoped I could rely on the mercy of the good people of Orilla, many of who trusted both Alis and I. But Navi could be persuasive.

I shook my head as I descended toward a squat building in the foothills south of Orilla's downtown. I couldn't worry about that right now. There were too many forces that could push my mind into a dangerous decline. One problem at a time. Find Alis. Kill the Wolf. Then we'd find out if Orilla was still our home. If not, I knew of a nice cabin with a great view and a basement just waiting to be renovated.

The security building had antennae and boxes on its roof, as well as rows of solar panels. A couple small inflated wind turbines levitated above the building, like at our cabin. Critical infrastructure had several power sources, just in case. Decades—even centuries—of network sabotage and electrical infrastructure failures had left our society both very skeptical and very well-prepared.

I leaned my board against the building and flicked open its solar charging ports. I'd likely need a full charge on my journey.

The door was locked. Only those who were on duty to monitor the system would have the key. The night shift would be wrapping up soon. I could wait and sneak in during the shift change, but I didn't have time to wait. And there shouldn't have been anything to worry about from whoever was on duty.

So I knocked.

Three knocks. Pause. Two knocks. Pause. Four knocks.

After a moment, the lock clicked, and the heavy metal door swung open with a loud screech.

"Toris!" Natalitei Khani Alvareza stood on the other side of the threshold, her dark brown hair in a straight line at her shoulders, framing her pale face. Her billowy, open-collared green shirt was half-untucked from her brown pants, and she held a stained cup of coffee in one hand. "You my replacement today?"

All right. That was something. Navi hadn't yet sent the news throughout the city. But she'd likely connect with whoever was assigned to replace Natalitei, even if just to warn them to keep an eye out for the return of the Wolf. I'd likely be an element of that warning, too.

"No, actually," I said, offering as friendly a smile as I could muster. "I just need to check the cameras. Did you...did the system detect anyone leaving the city last night?"

"Yeah," Natali said, turning into the building and gesturing for me to follow. The inside was old, with stained ceiling tiles and wilting linoleum. Like many of the buildings in Orilla, it was in need of renovation, but there were always more pressing needs across the city. We turned a corner under a flickering light and stepped into a large room lined with a combination of old monitors and holoscreens. They displayed every angle of Orilla's border, with little looking at the inside of the city. We weren't big on surveillance, so security was mostly focused on the rare marauders or...exiles. "Someone zipped out of here quick. Maybe 2 a.m.?" She shrugged as I stepped up to the control console. "A little odd but not unheard of. Why?"

"I just need a sec," I said, swallowing and trying to bring some moisture into my dry mouth. "Sorry. You can head out if you need to. I can wait for the next shift."

"Let me help, if I can," she said, looking at me with concern on her face. "It's Alis, isn't it?"

"That obvious, huh?" I asked as I started rewinding the footage from the night before. "What gave it away?"

"Well, you look like you're either gonna set something on fire or start crying."

I shrugged one shoulder. "Yeah, fair enough."

"What happened? You two get in a fight or something?"

"Not exactly." I slid my finger down the console as the camera footage from the night before rewound. I'd selected the cameras facing the south and southeast edges of the city. The sun sank back below the horizon, shrouding the landscape in darkness. So little moved over those hours that the footage could have been frozen, save for a few trees that shifted here and there in the wind. Then, when the time marker flitted past 2:30 in the morning, something streaked across one of the cameras, a line of light that was gone in seconds.

"There!" Natali exclaimed at the same instant. She pointed at the screen, and I was pretty sure her finger was shaking. Too much coffee.

I fast-forwarded at a slower pace until Alis was in the center of the screen. Her back was to me. She still wore the pajama shorts and baggy shirt that she'd worn to bed. Blood stained her right hand and halfway up her forearm.

"Uh..." Natali turned and looked me up and down.

"Not mine," I muttered, my stomach churning. "Are...are there other angles of this zone?"

"Mm hm." The gravity of the situation was finally dragging down her caffeine-fueled excitement.

I moved out of the way so Natali could swipe through to the correct camera. When she found it, she zoomed in, and I covered my mouth as a pained groan escaped.

It wasn't the Wolf, it was Alis. Her face was contorted in a horrified sob, tears streaking her cheeks, her head half turned back toward the city.

Seeing her like that broke my heart. The Wolf must have killed Cixin and either relinquished control or Alis wrested it back. Then, unable to face what she'd done—what the Wolf had done—she'd run.

"Toris...it can't...Mars is..."

"I need to know where she went. Can't we track trajectory?" I'd yet to be on camera duty, so many of the systems were still foreign to me. Natali claimed the duty frequently, though.

"The AI can make some educated guesses," Natali said, tapping some commands on the screen at her fingertips. "They're not perfect, but they're close."

"I'll take anything." It came out as a desperate whisper.

The camera pulled back, and colored lines appeared on the screen, arrows that pointed in a bouquet of directions with Alis as the stem, the origin point. The red arrows indicated low likelihood of trajectory. Yellow for maybe. There weren't any green ones, yet. The arrows overlaid each other as the AI processed.

"It takes some data from orbital satellites, too. There's less of that these days, but it still helps. And the camera can actually detect her movement for at least another ten miles, even if we can't see it, so the AI takes that into account."

"Mm," I said, barely registering her words.

An arrow flashed green, and the AI stopped processing. I wiped the sweat off my hands then zoomed out. As I did, a transparent map overlaid the image to give me a better handle of what that trajectory actually meant.

The green arrow pointed to the one place I hoped she wouldn't go. Not alone.

It pointed to the southern tip of what was once the state of Nevada, to the megacity of Babylon.

I stood up straight, taking my hands off the console.

"Shit," Natali said.

Of course Alis would go there, despite the risks. She had Cixin's blood on her hands; she'd be even more motivated to kill the Wolf than I was, and the mithril there was our only lead.

But if the Wolf emerged and she hurt someone in Babylon, then there'd be more threats to her than the Wolf itself. Especially if they found out she was my partner.

I looked at the clock. Six-thirty. She'd only been gone for four hours, so there was no way she'd have reached the city, yet, especially traveling through the hellscape between us and Babylon. And once she got there, she'd have a much harder time finding her way around. Or, then again, maybe she wouldn't. After all, if there was any place on Earth like Bastion, it was Babylon.

I'd also have the heat against me. Like much of the Earth, those deserts had been subjected to harsh geoengineering by the wealthy opportunists who would become Bastion's Pioneers. The ecosystem was yet to recover in many of those places, making it difficult to traverse. And that didn't even cover the other experiments that went wrong in that area.

All that meant that every moment stressing the details and the risks was a moment wasted.

"Thanks, Natali," I said, turning to leave.

"Uh, sure," she said, still likely trying to process the situation I'd dumped her into.

"Sorry about...all this," I said, feeling like it was the least I could say.

"No problem. I hope you figure this out. Just be careful. I know you have a history with Babylon." She followed me out toward the door. "Does Navi know?"

I paused, hand on the door handle. "Yeah."

Natali patted me on the back, likely reading into the mixed emotions in my response. "I know she has her issues with Alis, and...I'm guessing this isn't helping. But you're not alone. She's been here now longer than a third of us. We've all seen the good she's done. Even Navi. We'll figure this out together."

I gave her a flash of a grateful smile, not wanting her to see that her optimism, however much I truly appreciated it, felt like a prayer into a hurricane at that moment. "Thank you."

She gave me a sad smile back, then turned away toward the main room.

I took a deep breath, closed my eyes, then opened the door—

And stepped right into Kuma.

He yelped, and I jumped backward with a sharp breath.

Then Kuma chuckled, hands on his knees, and shook his head. "Oh, we've been around each other too long, brother."

"How did you know?" I asked, reading where this was going. It wasn't a coincidence he was there. Kuma hated watch duty; he'd rarely volunteer for it, if ever.

"I went by your house. Saw your board was gone. You asked where she went back there, so I figured you didn't know," he shrugged. "So I knew you'd come here, or I could at least track which way you'd gone and try to catch up. Like I said: we know each other too well."

"Yeah, we do," I said, stepping past him without looking him in the eyes. "Which means you know what I'm going to say. You can't come, Kuma."

"And let you go to Babylon alone? I'd be a shit copilot if I let you do that, wouldn't I?"

"It's not just Babylon, it's Alis...it's the Wolf, too. If it's emerging outside the cycle, you can't be near it. You can't get hurt like..." I blinked away the tears that burst to the surface and looked out at the Sierra Nevadas rising to the east, the sun shining over them. Then I turned back to Kuma, his face somewhere between a stubborn scowl and a concerned frown. "I can't..." My jaw quivered, and I took in another breath of the fresh morning air, blinking as a few tears escaped.

"Come here, brother." He stepped forward and wrapped me in a hug, patting me on the back as I returned the embrace with only one arm, the other limp at my side. That comfort cracked the dam, and the tears flooded out, no matter how tightly I squeezed my eyes shut. When Kuma pulled away, I wiped my tears with my sleeve. "If we can skip the back-and-forth now," he continued with a teasing smile, "you weren't thinking of trying to fly there through the middle of the day, were you?"

I cringed and shrugged.

"Of course you were. Pass out before you even get there. Or get burned by the rains. Or eaten by a revenant. Good thing I've got a way to get there safely. But I'm not taking you until you agree to accept me tagging along."

I stared at my old friend, knowing there was no way to convince him to stay in Orilla, whether or not he was bargaining a means to reach Babylon. I'd have done the same for him.

"Deal."

"Good," he said with a satisfied frown and nod. Then he bent down, picked up my board, and slapped me on my shoulder as he stood up straight again. "Let's go catch a Wolf. One last time."

CHAPTER ELEVEN

ALIS

(Twelve years earlier)

I WOKE UP, NOT remembering falling asleep.

The knife in my brain was still there, fading in moments to a dull ache and then exploding as if someone were twisting the blade.

Rough concrete ground against my cheek as I opened my eyes. There wasn't much to see. Smoke and debris filled the alley I was lying in, the end I was facing forking between two other buildings. Cringing against the pain as the blade twisted, I pushed myself to my knees and looked down the alley's other side. The bottom half of the *Sanguine Lycan* smoldered, twisted red metal and cables. The symbol of Bastion, the symbol I'd embodied, reduced to smoke and flame. The irony there was enough to make my head hurt without Vice Admiral Ecker trying to kill me.

It may not have been Ecker directly. He'd clearly been manipulating the connection between me, my Aegis, and his command station on the *Fang*, all of which was facilitated through my mindjack. I'd disconnected from Ecker when I'd broken the sync with my Aegis, but de-syncing in such an abrupt, violent way had caused a problem of its own. Mindjacks were delicate things. And dangerous. It was the price for constant integration between the human mind and the technology that surrounded us. Most of us didn't have to give that price much thought, but I was paying it with interest at that moment.

I stood to my full height and leaned my back against the alley wall, the metal of my armor clanging against the metal of the tower behind me. Slow down. I had to slow down, assess the situation. I was a soldier, even if I no longer had a commander or an Aegis. I was in enemy territory no matter which way I looked at it, considered hostile by both of the warring parties. The defense forces of the Mwezi colony may have taken down my Aegis, but they wouldn't be able to do much against the Bastion forces already in the city, not to mention the reinforcements likely already deploying from the nearby *Fang*. Add that to the support forces from Earth that we'd seen watching us—watching Bastion—and the colony was about to become a hotter battlefield than Luna had ever seen. I wouldn't have been surprised if Ecker elected to nuke the city rather than give it—and its precious economy and infrastructure—to Earth.

That meant I had to get out off that moon. But I couldn't leave without Teah. She was more stubborn than I, so it was possible that she was in the same state I was: resisting Ecker's domination in the face of twisted orders. She would have refused. The pruners wouldn't have gotten into her head.

Teah would still be Teah.

She had to be. In that moment, I wasn't sure which would be worse: that Teah had resisted and was in the same danger as me, or that she hadn't resisted at all, and she was in the City Center, attempting to manipulate Mwezi into ceding full control of its colony to Bastion. Either way, I was in danger of losing my sister.

The main street would be too dangerous, so I stumbled the other way down the alley, walking around chunks of building and shards of smoking metal, then turning toward the City Center and winding between towers. I lost sight of the main road a few times, but after winding eastward again, I'd see it. If I—

I jerked back and slammed my back against the building. A squad of Mwezi defense forces stood at the end of the alley I'd been about to turn down. The length of the alleys was shrinking the closer I came to the City Center as the road on the other side widened to make room for greenery-filled planters and a fountain. I took a breath and looked down at myself. If I was caught in my armor, they'd instantly recognize me as an Aegis pilot. And since there had only been one Aegis trying to destroy their colony, it wouldn't take long to put the pieces together.

Teah had personalized that sync suit for me. Shedding it and leaving it in an alley felt like a sin, a betrayal of all her hard work. Not to mention that hard work had just saved my life, too. Maybe I could be stealthy enough to get to the City Center in the suit, just long enough to find Teah and get off Luna.

I took a deep breath and prepared to dash across the alley, hoping that no one would see the glint of my red armor, but then I cringed and fell back against the wall. There was no way I'd make it into the City Center with the armor on. It'd be surrounded by tighter security after the incident with my Aegis. And we didn't have time for me to be stealthy. This was about Teah. She was more important than the suit she gave me.

After peeking around the corner to make sure the soldiers weren't investigating deeper into the alley, I pressed down on a rounded triangle in the armor below my sternum and the entire breastplate popped loose. I pulled it over my head and set it gently behind a boulder further away from the street. Then I did the same with the gauntlets and leg armor, scattering the pieces among the wreckage. I was gentle about it, making sure the concrete didn't scratch the armor up any more than it already was. When I was done, left standing in the skin-tight black undersuit, I stared at the armor for a moment, feeling like it was something akin to blasphemy to leave it there like that. But I told myself the greater betrayal would be abandoning Teah—or putting both of us at even greater risk—so I wiped away a tear and headed back down the alley.

I felt like I was walking around in my underwear, but I supposed that, combined with my dirty face and disheveled hair, would only aid the appearance I needed to adopt. I was a refugee, now. I had to look the part if I was going to get off Luna.

And so, rather than try to sneak around the defense forces, I stumbled down the alley right toward them, emphasizing my limp a bit.

"Help!" I cried out. "Please!" Speaking twisted the knife in my brain again, so I didn't have to fake the cringe that nearly brought me to my knees. A soldier in white armor ran up and caught me before I fell, putting an arm underneath my armpits and lifting me up. I had a flash of fear, suddenly wondering if they'd somehow recognize me, if they'd been hacked like the other soldiers whom Ecker had forced to fire on their companions. But this soldier only wore a concerned expression on his face.

"You shouldn't be out here," another soldier said from the head of the alley. He had golden stripes on his armor's shoulders. "All citizens have been ordered to evacuate the City Center."

"I..." I cringed again, the pain making me slur my words. "I was in the building that...thing hit. I need to find my sister. She's in...ahhhh," I gasped as the pain speared through my mind. I finished only by pointing up toward the building on the hill, the colony's government center. Tall trees lined the steps leading up to the squat, otherwise unassuming building. Suspended above and beside the building were large holoscreens, all of which were only broadcasting static at that moment. Defense forces had established a perimeter across the street, complete with two more railgun cannons, several tanks, and a few small gunships that buzzed up and down the road.

"If your sister's in there, she's secure," the officer said. "But we can't permit anyone else to pass. Find somewhere else to lie low, or take a tube outside the colony. Some ships are also docking at the spaceport to move refugees. Free of charge." He looked me up and down, scowling, trying to find the pain that was clearly nearly crippling me. "Where are you hurt? We can see if we can help you, but only to get you on your way."

"I...thank you, but I'm fine. I don't have time for treatment. Bastion is..." I nearly actually bit my tongue to keep myself from letting something too close to my identity spill out with my anxious lying. "Isn't Bastion coming? I can't leave my sister behind. I need to get out with her." What else could I say? What would convince them? They had their orders, just like I did. I wouldn't have let anyone through, either. "What if I don't violate the perimeter? What if she comes out here? I know I'm just one person, but...I'm sure you have family. I need to be with my sister. I need to keep her safe."

Something softened in the officer's eyes. He pursed his lips, then said, "That will still violate the perimeter, and we can't make concessions for every individual. Everyone in there has a family that's worried about them, but I assure you, they're safer in there than we are out here." He looked back and forth between my eyes, making me feel like he wasn't done, even though that sounded like a pretty clear "no."

"Okay. Listen." He held up a finger. "And I'm only even considering this because you don't have a shelter to evacuate to. There are security tunnels we use to move troops beneath City Center. We can escort you through—"

The rising hope in my heart froze as the giant screens around the hill flashed from static to a shot inside the building. A woman in a stiff blue uniform with long black hair stood behind a podium. Tiers of representatives stood behind her. Most of them were blurry, especially with the glare from the glass dome high above us. But one person wasn't blurry at all. Teah stood on the second row up, on the left of the uniformed woman. She was unharmed, or at least looked it. How was she there? Had the pruners worked their way so deeply into Mwezi's system that they could really stand with its governing body?

Teah was safe. But was she herself? Was Ecker in her head? I couldn't move. None of the other soldiers did, either, except for the officer, who narrowed his eyes and looked up at the sky, up and down the street. He looked up toward the gunships and said, likely through his mindjack, "Don't get distracted. Check the drones. I want every inch of this city covered. What's the *Fang's* position?" A pause, then: "Maintaining position?" He scowled. "What's their play?"

For some reason, the *Fang* holding position didn't fill me with peace. I turned back to the screen.

"People of Mwezi," the woman said. "The danger has passed. I admire your strength, your resolve, and your faith in us. We've remained neutral in this fight in order to protect our people, our colony. Clearly, the fight has found us instead. However, the assault by the Aegis known as the *Sanguine Lycan* was a ploy. We have concrete evidence that the *Lycan*'s pilot, the Moonbreaker of Phobos, was working under orders from Earth's military, who commanded the Moonbreaker to reinforce her reputation in the ashes of our city, all in an effort to force us to betray our trust in Bastion." My stomach twisted, and I glanced at the soldiers around me, as if they'd suddenly realize I was that very Moonbreaker. When that moment of fear passed, the anger heated up. I watched Teah, but she betrayed none of her emotions.

Ecker hadn't been able to use me in the way he preferred, but of course he had a Plan B. He was using me anyway, as he always had. Had he convinced Teah that I'd really betrayed them? Or had he hacked her, and she'd been unable to break free? I wasn't sure which was worse, but either option made me wish I still had my Aegis so I could tear the *Fang* in half.

"We will not be made into some pawn in this war-game." I scoffed at that, then played it off as a cough. "This despicable move by Earth's leadership has forced our hand. As a result, we have reversed our vote and, for the security of our people and our future, have accepted a *temporary* status as a satellite colony of Bastion. Because of this decision, our people will be safe. We will not directly contribute our people to the war effort, but we will contribute our resources to ensuring that this war ends swiftly, for the benefit of all our Spheres."

My jaw hung open. Ecker had done it again. He'd spun an incident in their favor with me at the center. But this was worse. Much worse. I highly doubted that Mwezi's government pivoted their passionate opinions so quickly. Just like he'd hacked the mindjacks of some of Mwezi's defense forces, his teams may have hacked the mindjacks of these representatives. This was against everything Bastion was supposed to stand for. War or not.

"We will continue to be strong. We will continue to fight back against oppression. We will honor the dream of our settlers, of our families. But we'll do it our way. Thank you for your support. We'll be sharing more details with you shortly, but nothing should change about your day-to-day life. Please standby in your shelters until the lockdown is lifted. The Aegis pilot Alistella Pareides Caliday is still loose, and our defense forces are sweeping the city at this moment to find her." I took a slow step back from the soldiers. The officer I'd been speaking to was looking at the ground, muttering back and forth to someone through his mindjack. "If you see her, alert authorities immediately. Our defense forces have clearance to fire on sight. Until she's caught, she is Mwezi's public enemy number one."

An image of my face popped up on the screen.

Mwezi's leader kept talking, but I was already slowly backing away, watching the soldiers. Most of them continued staring at the screen, likely having not paid enough attention to me to make the connection. But the officer and a few near him—the few nearest me—glanced at each other, then turned back toward me. I stopped moving and looked down, hoping my hair would hide enough of my face to make them think it was all in their head.

Then I heard the unmistakable sound of a handgun being pulled from its holster and the safety clicking off.

"ON THE GROUND, NOW!"

I held up my hands and looked at the officer. He had his handgun trained on me. Every other officer was raising their plasma rifle. Even one of the gunships was tilting to face me.

"Wait, please!" I cried, looking all around me for a way out. Any way out. I couldn't see one. This was stupid. I should have chanced sneaking into the City Center, even if it meant getting shot on sight. It looked like that ending was always going to be inevitable. "Please. That's not true. I didn't take any orders from Earth. My mindjack was—"

"I SAID ON THE GROUND!" the officer shouted, but I could see the confusion pressing his eyebrows together. His jaw twitched.

"Your troops! They fired on each other!" I yelled out. The officer's hand twitched, the grip softening for just an instant. At least I had his attention. "They fired on each other," I repeated in a calmer tone, my hands still held up in surrender. "You probably think they were traitors, too. They weren't. Ecker...Bastion's somehow hacking mindjacks. They hacked mine. They hacked my Aegis. I didn't hurt your people. I want to...I want to help your people. Please." The fact that the officer hadn't yelled at me again was a good sign, so I kept going. "Bastion used me. They betrayed *me*. I can help you. You're not as safe as your leader is making you believe. She may be hacked, too."

The officer stared at me, finger twitching beside the trigger. The other soldiers still had their weapons trained on me, but they kept shooting glances at their officer. They wouldn't fire without orders.

"Quiet," the officer said, jerking his head. That must have been to someone through his mindjack.

"Sir," a soldier beside the officer said. She had a blue stripe on her shoulder, likely a higher rank than the other foot soldiers. "We have orders to fire on sight."

"Cuff her," the officer said. "We'll bring her in. Get more intel from her."

"Bastion could still access her mindjack," the woman said, and I wanted to hiss at her to shut up. "If she's not lying, then they could compromise her again. We lost enough people to her."

"Didn't you hear the Governor?" the soldier said. "We are Bastion now."

I locked eyes with the officer again. There was something soft there. I thought I'd connected with him in some way. Maybe he had a sister, a daughter.

Then something changed in those eyes. They went distant for a moment, and his head tilted to the side. When the focus returned, those eyes were hard.

"You can't run, Caliday," the officer said. Ecker.

I ran.

I spun and dashed for the alley, the closest space with any semblance of cover.

"FIRE!" the officer shouted.

The air exploded with plasma shots, most of them whizzing close enough to whip my hair into my face. One sliced through the outside of my left shoulder, a spray of red and a line of fire that didn't hurt as bad as it should have. Thank God for shock and augments.

Another shot exploded at my feet as I dove into the alley. Footsteps pounded behind as the soldiers gave chase. A blast like thunder cracked the sky open as one of the gunships opened fire. The round slammed into the concrete where I'd been standing just before rounding the alley's corner. The shock wave launched me off my feet and threw me into the side of the building on the other side of the alley, knocking the air out of my lungs.

Coughing in the smoke, dirt, and dust, I pushed myself to my feet and ran. Every step away from City Center hurt almost as much as the wound in my shoulder and the dagger in my brain, but I couldn't get to Teah if I was dead.

Seeing her in that shot, entirely complicit in Ecker's manipulation, I wasn't sure if I had a Teah to get to anyway.

***

The train rolled to a stop. I pulled the hood up on a cloak I'd found on the street and followed the other passengers down the cars and out onto the terminal. Walls of glass looked over the rest of the metal spaceport and toward the gray hills and craters of Luna's surface. The other gates were empty, but as I watched, dust billowed out and a craft touched down, black and bulky, Bastion's seal on its side. A shuttle, likely from the *Fang*.

I followed a few other refugees through the tunnels of the terminal until we reached gate 4. Through the large window above the airlock doors was a starship that must have once been some kind of cargo hauler. I'd seen similar models on our bases back home. Mwezi's spaceport lights shone on its midnight-blue and white-trimmed hull.

As we waited in line to board, I turned toward the other window and the Bastion shuttle a few docks over. Its passengers were disembarking, walking through the tunnel toward the same train I'd just been on. I shivered at how close a call that was.

Then Vice Admiral Ecker stepped past the window.

He started down the tunnel, chin held high, a conqueror. He glanced out the window, and I thought he saw me, but he turned forward.

Then he turned back.

He stopped, then he walked up to the window. I couldn't see the details on his face, but I thought he was smiling. The knife in my head twisted. He tilted his head toward a few soldiers beside him, said something. They followed his gaze out the window, then took off running down the tunnel. Toward us.

I pushed past the others in line, also shoving aside the guilt that came with that, ignoring their growled curses.

A man stood at the open airlock. He had warm brown skin and black, wavy hair, and he wore a jumpsuit with the top half unzipped and hanging down from his waist, leaving a white undershirt beneath. He must have been the pilot, or one of the ship's crew.

"Please," I gasped out. "They're coming. Bastion's coming."

The man's green eyes searched mine, looking at me with none of the frustration that the other refugees were expressing. And none of the recognition I was afraid of following the governor's broadcast. I had a chance here, but not for long.

"You're safe here," he said, his voice gentle. "Bastion isn't known for being smart, but they'd be downright stupid to risk even breathing on this ship."

I took a step closer to him and whispered. "Today, they might. Please."

He searched my eyes for a moment longer, a moment too long, then he nodded and stepped out of the way of the airlock. He looked up at the line of refugees. "All right, everyone! We'll deal with the logistics on-board. Let's go, quick as you can." His voice was still calm, but the change in process, and my disruption, was enough to get the passengers to rush forward. Several of them knocked into me as they stumbled through the airlock tunnel and onto the *Harriet*.

I hurried behind them, jogging through the tunnel and stepping to the side, taking a deep breath of recycled air. The area looked like a repurposed cargo bay, with hooks and tracks still bolted to the floor. But there were also seats filled with passengers in varying states of disarray. Steady vibration hummed through the hull.

The final passengers boarded, and the black-haired man followed. He pulled a switch on a panel beside the airlock, and the door rolled over the opening then locked into place. I leaned over and looked through the airlock window just as Ecker and other Bastion soldiers entered the gate. One of the soldiers shouted. Another pulled a gun from their holster. But Ecker just met my eyes as he gestured for the soldier to lower their gun.

"They're looking for you?" the man asked. "Like *looking* looking for you?"

I nodded, hoping he wouldn't ask why.

He slapped a second button, and another layer of hull plating slid over the airlock door. Then he offered a half-smile, one that only briefly covered the stress straining the lines around his eyes.

"You're safe," he repeated, and I wanted to believe him. "But I'd buckle up." Then he turned and jogged toward the back of the passenger cabin, shouting, "That goes for everyone! Find a seat, and buckle up." Louder, he yelled, "Let's burn, Kuma! New friends on our tail!"

The ship's steady rumbling escalated, and my stomach lurched as the ship pulled up and away from Luna's relatively meager gravitational strength.

I found a seat in between other refugees and clicked into the restraints.

The blade twisted in my head as I leaned back, closed my eyes, and took a deep breath. The *Harriet* shot into the night. Away from Mwezi. Away from my burning Aegis. Away from Teah. Away from so much that I wondered what was left of me for the ship to carry.

Chapter Twelve

Toris

I followed Kuma on my hoverboard toward the edge of the city, where the interstate intersected Orilla's edge before curving alongside the Sierra Nevada mountains. Eventually, it'd turn from the peaks and strike through the Deadlands toward Babylon.

As little as I wanted Kuma to risk his life, he was right. I couldn't cross the Deadlands on my hoverboard alone. The thing could go up to a hundred miles an hour, but that speed would eat through the charge, and it'd likely overheat in the Deadlands, as would I. And that would only happen if the acid rains common to the area didn't get us first.

Plus, as much as I didn't want anyone involved in finding Alis and killing the Wolf—especially not after Cixin—Kuma's presence was reassuring. We'd been through more dangerous circumstances together.

I clenched my shaking hands into fists. I couldn't be stupid enough to get myself killed before I found Alis. And preferably afterward, too.

We dropped our altitude as we came closer to the road. The interstate was far less busy than it would have been in ages past. Most communities stuck to themselves. Without jobs requiring commutes, there was less reason to travel outside of our area. Most of our trade was handled through autonomous vehicles, like the trucks Alis and I had helped fill just a day before. Those AI-driven trucks were most of what I could see on the road.

Near the interstate, however, was a semi-circular cluster of landing pads. Parked on one of the pads was a compact aircraft. Its shape always reminded me of a fish more than a bird, with wings like fins closer to the front of the aircraft than the middle, and giant fans in the centers of those wings for vertical takeoff and landing. The aircraft then tapered from its bulk at the front to a narrower tail with smaller fins and propulsion engines mounted underneath.

We dropped off our hoverboards near the aircraft. "You signed us up for road patrol," I said as Kuma and I walked across the landing pad. "Smart."

"I figured it was the fastest way to the city," Kuma said. "Let's just hurry and take off before Navi realizes what I did and exiles me too."

I couldn't tell if that was a joke or not, so I cringed and said, "Too soon."

"Yeah, way too soon. Sorry, brother."

"Eh, you made it up to me already, with this" I said, nodding to the aircraft. "Seriously, Kuma. Thank you. I was...I *am*..." I clamped my jaw tight as tears rushed to my eyes and anger and fear clashed again, bursting at my seams. "I was stupid to—"

"Oh, I know," he said, cutting me off. I was glad he did.

We approached the aircraft's port side, squinting through the sun reflecting off its white metal hull. As we passed around the cockpit and the wing, a small group of people came into view, waiting near the craft's cabin doors. I counted three. Two standing, bags in hand or on their back, and one sitting on the concrete in the vehicle's shade.

"Oh right," Kuma said. "Requisition said there'd be some passengers."

I nodded. While the primary purpose of these aircraft was to patrol and protect the interstate from that region to Babylon, they were also—as Kuma had aptly mentioned—the fastest means of transportation across the Deadlands. And likely the safest, too. They didn't have space for too many passengers, but if you could sign up for a spot fast enough, you'd have a straight shot to the New Cradle of Civilization.

"Morning!" Kuma called out as we came closer, raising a large hand in hello. The passengers didn't return his level of exuberance, maybe a halfhearted smile here and there. Kuma stopped beside the cabin door, and a holo-panel appeared. He typed in the code he received from the duty requisition, and the cabin door popped open before sliding up into the hull. Kuma stepped aside to allow the passengers to file on.

"Ah!" he said to the passenger at the back of the queue. "We don't get second-time passengers too often. It was my singing that brought you back, wasn't it?"

The poor woman he was talking to had black hair pulled up into a ponytail and a scar on her temple. Kuma was right, I recognized her, too. We'd picked her up on Farstead, in the same group as Cixin. She was the one that'd been scowling at me from beneath her hood. Her mood hadn't much improved during the trip back to Earth; she'd kept to herself. Her brow was certainly less scowl-y this time. In fact, her eyes brightened, and her mouth twitched in an almost-smile.

"That's right," I said, unable to muster Kuma's level of excitement. "Lielana, was it?"

"Lana's fine," she said with a nod, following the rest of the passengers onto the aircraft, clearly not wanting to participate in more conversation.

"Wonderful," Kuma said with a clap. "Everyone get situated and settled. We'll run through our pre-flight checks and get us in the air." Then he turned away, leaned toward me, and in a voice only I could hear said, "We've got us a Wolf to hunt."

Kuma and I stored our hoverboards in the aircraft's rear cargo compartment along with a few of the passengers' larger pieces of luggage. I tossed them into the compartment much less carefully than I should have, than I normally would have in any other situation. I just wanted to get in the air as quickly as possible. With this kind of power, there was even a chance we could catch up to Alis before she reached Babylon.

Once we checked the exterior of the aircraft, we stepped inside the cabin and sealed the door. The cabin was small, with two single rows of four seats in each column against the port and starboard hulls. With nods to the passengers and subtle checks to make sure they were all properly restrained, we stepped into the cockpit and closed the door behind us.

I settled into the co-pilot seat and buckled in. Kuma and I immediately fell into our familiar routine of checking our switches, our gauges, valves, fuel levels, charge levels, weight distribution, and control surfaces. The steady vibration of the craft reminded me of the *Harriet*, and like a lullaby or a sea breeze on a hot day, some of my worries settled. Not entirely—I wasn't sure how I'd sleep until we found Alis and put the Wolf in the ground—but I could catch my breath. I could think a little clearer.

While Kuma wrapped up final preparations for takeoff, I zoomed in and out of a map that displayed our route to Babylon, cycling through different filters for various checks. "Weather's clear most of the way," I said. "We'll hit a strip of storm just before the Glassfields, but nothing awful. Winds'll be blowing radiation right at us, though." I swiped to the last filter, one that displayed recent reports. "May have to be on the lookout for revenants."

"Seriously?" Kuma asked, raising his eyebrows, finger frozen below the switch that would increase the fans' speed and get us airborne.

"Yeah." I scrolled through more reports. "Six sightings this month. Two outright attacks on transports."

"Even dead, they're greedy," Kuma said, shaking his head. "Taking us to the sky." He flicked the switch and the cockpit's vibration picked up intensity. Then we gently lifted off the ground, my gut staying put for a moment before joining us in the air. The ground gradually gave way until we were above the interstate, then Kuma eased us forward and we were off. Toward Babylon. Toward a part of my past I'd hoped that I'd left far behind. But that also meant it was toward Alis. Toward the Wolf. Toward the end of ten years of struggle and the beginning of a better life.

"Thanks again, Kuma, I—"

Kuma held up a finger to cut me off. "If you thank me again, I'm going to land this thing and take you to Navi. No, I'm just kidding, that's too cruel. But I will fly slower. You'd do the same for me. You've done more. I want to help you see an end to this."

"It'll end," I said with a defiant nod as we banked east, following the curve of the interstate through the Sierra Nevadas, the tops of the peaks to our left and right. "It has to. I don't know what I'll..." I trailed off, not wanting to put into words the darkness that surged in as my mind opened that door of possibilities.

"Don't flush yourself down that spiral, brother. Nothing worth your mental energy down there."

"But Cixin...Navi..."

"Navi's looking after the community, and she's looking after you. We solve the Wolf problem, we solve that problem too."

I hoped it'd be that simple.

The silence that fell between us was different from our typical, comfortable one. That silence prickled with so much unsaid. Did Kuma agree with Navi? Did he think we shouldn't have brought Cixin back? Did he think we were endangering the community by bringing back Alis? That seemed unlikely since he was piloting the aircraft to go find her, but it wouldn't be the first time he'd done something for me as my friend that he disagreed with.

Then there was the issue of Babylon adding a layer to that prickly silence. We both knew we shouldn't have been going back there. It was entirely possible that Navi wouldn't have to worry about our exile. Don't exactly need to worry about the damage the dead will do to the community.

But neither of us said anything. Because, at that moment, I didn't care much about the answers to any of those questions, as much as I valued Kuma's perspective. And Kuma knew I was in no state to be pushed, so, like we'd done many times before, we put off the questions. And, slowly, the silence smoothed out as we came toward the foothills of the Sierra Nevadas and looked out over the Deadlands.

The heart of the Deadlands had once been called Death Valley, one of the hottest, most desolate places on the planet. But as humanity poisoned its ecosystem and the precursors to Bastion's Pioneers used the empty land for geoengineering experimentation, the desolation of Death Valley spread, drying up water sources and killing what little life had evolved to survive in the surrounding area. "Death Valley" became too small a name for too large an area.

As we flew out from between the mountain peaks, we could see evidence of the area's legacy. The earth was harsh, cracked desert, hardly even a sagebrush to call it home. To the north, great shelves of desert skewered the sky at odd angles, smashing into each other in a way that looked anything but natural, like a god had taken shards of glass and tossed them down in a pile before transmuting them into stone. They were the Falsas Nevadas, a failure of geoengineering, an attempt to peel up the Earth's crust and shape it to human designs. Their ugliness was dwarfed by the Sierra Nevadas, and the experiment bore no other fruit, despite being attempted in other areas across the world. As far as I knew, it was one experiment that never made its way to the terraforming of Mars.

Smashed near the foot of the Falsas Nevadas, as if a tombstone to that failure, were the twisted remains of a giant orbital mirror. Despite the clear side effects that additional warming would cause an already hot Earth, the wealthy opportunists had used the planet as a test subject for warming Mars. The mirrors were supposed to have covers that would only open over areas of the planet where the heating "wouldn't matter," but, of course, those covers failed. That orbital mirror was one of the first things Earth shot down during the Solar Gulf War, the Deadlands being the best place to let it fall. I could still remember Navi and I running from the oncoming wall of heat the orbital mirror brought as if it were a game, despite our mother's warnings. One day, after a rainstorm, I heard the sizzle of the water evaporating instantly as the mirror passed over.

Then, as if those scars on the horizon weren't enough, ahead of us to the east was a wall of dark clouds. Those weren't typical storm clouds, but another leftover of failed experimentation. These experiments weren't associated with Bastion opportunists, but the kind that eventually founded Babylon. In a misguided attempt to slow global warming, corporations had dumped sulfur dioxide into the atmosphere. While it initially seemed to reflect more sunlight and UV rays back into space, the aerosols damaged the ozone and started cycles of acid rainstorms.

The Deadlands couldn't be more different from Orilla del Angel, a verdant paradise miles from an utter wasteland. The contrast hadn't always been so strong, especially when I was a kid. The long, green grasses that swayed outside my and Alis' home would have been yellow and crunchy most of the year, the breeze warm more than it was welcoming. We'd worked hard following the social changes that started before the Solar Gulf War, reclaiming the land and—more importantly—enabling the Earth to reclaim the land as it should have been. It was a worldwide movement, but some areas, unfortunately, were too damaged, the scars too deep. The Deadlands was one of the largest.

Some didn't think it was a lost cause, but some were stupid. And those someones were the citizens and sponsors of Babylon.

I tore my attention from the scarred land to the cameras on the belly of our aircraft, which watched the road below. As desolate as the Deadlands were, the roads that ran through them had been established long before the area was as dangerous, and they'd remained arteries crucial for trade. Our duty, shared with other communities in the area and Babylon itself, was to ensure that artery flowed smoothly. My screen displayed not only the bird's-eye view of the road, but also fed data sent from the vehicles' computers, everything from the internal temperature (obviously important for transporting food) to engine diagnostics and sensor readouts from their level. If bandits or revenants attacked, their sensors were likely to detect them before our cameras caught them.

"How are we looking?" Kuma asked.

"Clear so far," I said as I scrolled through the data from the vehicles below. "I wonder if Alis hitchhiked on one of these. She couldn't have made it across on her hoverboard before sunrise, especially not past the Glassfields. And she wouldn't let herself get caught in that rain."

"Could be," Kuma said. "She'd be in the city by now if she did."

I nodded. Pros and cons. Part of me had hoped we'd see Alis in the distance, sunlight glinting off her hoverboard, that we'd find her before she ever reached Babylon. At least that way I could get the mithril on my own. I scoffed just at the thought of how that interaction would go.

"What?" Kuma asked.

"Nothing. Just imagining what it'd be like if we caught Alis before she made it to the city and I went on my own."

That made Kuma chuckle, too. "I think you'd see worse than the Wolf if you suggested that."

My mirth slowly died, strangled by the worries, a moment of sunshine through the storm that the clouds quickly smothered.

"As much as you hate it," Kuma said. "Babylon's still safer than the Deadlands."

"Unless they find out who she is."

"True. But she wouldn't let that happen."

"Yeah."

"We'll find her, brother. That's one problem. What's your plan for getting the mithril? Do you think Carivant has it?"

"That's my bet. So at least we'll have a place to start. I just wish that actually made it easier. And that's only if he hasn't sold it."

"Capitalists," Kuma said with a sigh.

"Capitalists," I repeated, shaking my head.

"Do you think Alis will know to look there?"

I shivered at the thought. "I don't think so. I only shared the most shallow details about Babylon. I'm not even sure I ever mentioned Carivant's name. It may take her more time to find the mithril. And that's all assuming that my hunch is right."

"You know her. It's right. She's gonna use that guilt as fuel to fix the problem, just like when we found her. That's good. It means we know her final destination, but we'll get there first."

"That's if we go after the mithril first. I'm tempted to try and find her first instead."

Kuma shook his head. "I get it. But hunting her down will take even longer than infiltrating Carivant's tower. We know where she's going, and she won't be in danger until she gets a target on her back. Hopefully by then the target on us will be sexier to Carivant."

"You're right," I said. "I don't like how much I'm saying those words."

Kuma chuckled, and I did, too. Another ray of sunshine, this one lingering a little longer. Kuma's rationality was once again overcoming my anxious, wild thoughts. Alis was safer than we'd be in that city, so long as the Wolf didn't emerge again. That'd draw not just Carivant's eyes, but those of Babylon's authorities, too, a police force more like a small military. If anything, though, that Wolf was a survivor, and as erratic as the shift was that killed Cixin, it was also over much more quickly than a typical transformation. We had time. We had an upper hand in that chase, even if we were behind.

I looked out at the horizon, at the wall of clouds.

We're coming. Hold on.

***

"Rain," Kuma said as the first few drops pelted the window. I looked up from my diagnostics and sensor readouts.

We were in the wall, now, surrounded by wisps of cloud tinged an odd yellow. I looked back down and swiped through the screens to the weather data. "It's only about thirty miles deep. The plating's holding up all right?"

Kuma glanced at a screen to his left. "For now, yeah."

I swiped back to the belly camera. The wisps of cloud shrouded much of the view, but I could still see the road below, the trucks and containers and the rare smaller personal vehicle.

And something crawling on one of the containers.

I zoomed in with the camera, wondering if it was a trick of the light, but then a column of cloud got in the way. A moment later, a notification beeped on one of the other screens. I swiped over to it. The truck I'd just been looking at detected something on top of it, something heavy enough to set off alerts. Was it a bird? Trying to find shelter in the storm?

Please let it be a bird.

As a precaution, I shut off the belly cameras and sat back, staring ahead.

"Don't look down at the road," I said.

"Ah, great. Revenants?"

I cringed. "Yeah."

Another reminder of unethical experimentation on the glut brought in from the Belt Rush, revenants were the result of quantum teleportation experiments. Test subjects, brought in by the promise of wealth, were supposed to teleport from then-New York to then-San Francisco, but the entanglement failed. And rather than the original quantum information being destroyed, as was theorized, the poor test subjects were left in a state of half-existence, dead by all technical definitions but subsisting in a state of frequent decoherence. They seemed to retain some information from their entanglement, and that information tended to exhibit as fear, rage, and even violence.

"We should probably get them off the cargo, though," Kuma said. "Did it look like it was trying to break in?"

"No, just crawling on it. Like something out of an old horror movie."

Kuma shivered. "Except we created the demons ourselves. There's a plot for you."

"You're right, though. We should..." I trailed off as I caught something out of the corner of my eye. Instinct told me to look, but I didn't. After all, how could I see something right outside our windshield at a few thousand feet? How could I see hair flapping in the wind around an emaciated face, skin flickering to reveal the skull beneath as if it were a faulty hologram?

Trying to convince myself didn't work. I'd still observed it. The revenant disappeared.

"You see that?" Kuma asked.

"Mm hm."

Warning sensors beeped on Kuma's side of the cockpit. He turned them off.

"It could tunnel," I said.

"I know."

"We could pick up thrust, vent some of the heat down below us toward the road if there are more of them," I suggested. "Could make the decoherence severe enough that they don't recover for a while, especially if we hit them before they've been observed. I know we need to protect the road, but we need to protect our passengers first."

Kuma wiped sweat off his forehead. "I didn't know they could jump all the way up here."

"Yeah, they're not a fan of classical mechanics," I said, pushing a light to inform the passengers to make sure they were buckled. I turned my ear toward the cabin, listening for any disturbance. Screams would be a pretty clear sign the revenant tunneled through the hull.

"Yeah, well, classical mechanics and I aren't on the best of terms right now, either," Kuma said. "Where's a black hole when you need one?" He started directing more power to the hydrogen fuel cells at the rear of the aircraft and the engines attached to them. "The acid rain should make them decohere more often, so they shouldn't be too much of a problem for the cargo. We just need to get out of here."

"The one time I'm grateful for acid rain," I said. "Agreed. Punch it."

Kuma pushed the throttle forward, and the Gs pushed us back into our seats. I pressed a button to speak to the passenger cabin. "Hi all, we're accelerating through this acid rain. We'll be out of it in just a few minutes. So please stay seated, stay restrained, and we'll be over the Glassfields and nearly to Babylon."

"Probably should have done that before I hit the gas," Kuma said with a dry chuckle.

I nodded and swiped a few screens over to check the cabin camera. The passengers looked relatively fine. One of them was asleep, another looked calm but was clutching onto the arms of their seat with white knuckles, and Lana was glancing around the cabin, eyebrows scrunched in concern.

"They're good," I said. Then I confirmed that the belly cameras were turned off and closed my own eyes. Kuma was likely setting the autopilot for a moment and doing the same. The revenants could somehow detect the observer that was causing them to decohere, and they'd be attracted to it. For any other predator, that wouldn't be a problem in an aircraft traveling at our speed, but for a quantum half-being that for the most part ignored physical space and distance, it was a problem. So, instead of taking the chance of drawing more revenants by accidentally seeing them, we shut off all the inputs. As for the revenant that I'd seen out of the corner of my eye on the side of the aircraft, hopefully the acceleration combined with the acid rainstorm—which the acceleration would only make feel more severe—would be enough to keep it from cohering on our aircraft.

The console in front of me beeped, but I kept my eyes closed. "Ten miles until we're out of the storm." We'd be safer over the Glassfields, which were protected by multiple barriers that kept revenants out. The monsters tended to keep to the more desolate regions of the Deadlands, anyway. I shivered. Those things—

BEEP BEEP BEEP BEEP BEEP

My eyes snapped open and looked down at the screen. That wasn't a notification signal. That was an alarm. A prompt on the screen read: "Open outer cabin door? CAUTION: Opening outer cabin door at present velocity could result in serious injury." I swiped "No," locking out permissions, and got out of my seat.

"Someone's trying to open the outer door," I said, pressing the button to open the door into the cabin. It didn't respond. I slapped it several more times. It stayed shut.

I spun back to my seat and swiped to the camera footage of the passenger cabin. The screen was static. Sound from the cabin was cut off, too.

I slowly turned to Kuma. He was already looking at me.

"It's in here, isn't it," he whispered.

My screen flashed again. "Permission granted. Warning: Opening outer cabin door. Please stay restrained until the aircraft has come to a complete stop."

"Lock everything down!" Kuma shouted.

"I know! I know!" A total system lockdown would prevent any—

The aircraft jerked, and a roar exploded on the other side of the cockpit door. Someone screamed, then their scream trailed off, carried away in the rushing air.

"We need to land!" I yelled over the sound of the air. "If that thing gets in here while we're in the air..."

Kuma started decelerating and angling us down. I connected to the vehicles below and entered some commands to give us a runway on the road. A moment after the signal went out, the trucks and containers started slowing down or moving out of the center of the wide road.

"How is it messing with our systems?" Kuma shouted, arms shaking as the aircraft bounced against turbulence. "They shouldn't have that kind of finesse."

"You never know what kind of information was transferred through the entanglement before the person was destroyed. And with our luck, we'd attract the smartest revenant in the flock."

"Yeah, sounds right!"

I sat back down and buckled in, despite part of me wanting to break out my solarblade and barrel into the passenger cabin. I wouldn't be able to cut through in time, and I'd likely get sucked out the open door before I could do any good.

Once we landed, I'd do what I could, even if that meant facing down a revenant. Our duty was to get our passengers safely to their destination. I'd never heard of a revenant taking down an aircraft, so we were already going to be the first failure there. We couldn't let anything else happen to those poor people.

And, as terrifying as revenants were, I had experience fighting monsters.

Kuma flew us below the shelf of yellow acid rain clouds. The road stretched out below. A hill dropped down toward plains like obsidian: The Glassfields. We had to land before that, or our chances of survival would be even less than at the hands of the revenant.

Beeps and other alarms lit up the console in front of us. Kuma straightened us out. The road was still clear.

"You've got this, brother," I said, patting Kuma on the arm. "You—"

My screen flashed again. *Engine compartment breached.*

"Ku—"

Something exploded. The world spun, swallowed in black smoke.

And we went down.

Chapter Thirteen

Alis

(Twelve years earlier)

Passengers gasped, a few yelping, as the *Harriet* rocketed away from Mwezi. Looking at a fair few struggling to buckle into their restraints, I wondered how many had ever been on a starship. Most of these people were likely Mwezi natives with no tie to Earth but their ancestry. That wouldn't matter to Bastion, and they knew it.

I closed my eyes and shook my head. I was already thinking about Bastion as if I were outside it, as if I were the "other." As if I weren't dressed in a Bastion undersuit. As if I hadn't been standing guard outside the colony only hours before in a Bastion Aegis. How quickly everything had fallen apart. For me, at least. Manipulating the vote and—if that failed—manipulating the people had clearly been their plan all along. And, again, I was just the symbol to advance their cause.

Our cause?

My cause?

And still, I couldn't escape that symbol. Ecker had turned it against me, proving once again that I was never really in control of anything in the first place.

Wasn't that what I'd signed up for? To give myself to Bastion's...to our, to my...future? I'd sworn an oath to protect our people, to secure our Sphere, and to spark a brighter tomorrow. Those were ideals I'd been taught since I was a child, so ingrained in me that swearing that oath in my stiff uniform felt as natural as breathing. I believed in them. I still did, even as I ran from the people who represented those ideals.

I opened my eyes with a sigh, the Gs letting up their press as the *Harriet*'s acceleration eased. Many of the passengers around me calmed down, prying clutched hands off the arms of their chairs or rubbing the backs of their frightened children. A few rows away from me, a father took the less understanding approach and snapped at his child to stop crying, and I cringed at how much I empathized with that child.

What would my father think? What would they tell him? Certainly what they told everyone else. The broadcast from Mwezi's governor would be broadcast across the Spheres. Maybe it already had. Would he believe them? Did Teah? Or had she contributed to building this narrative all along?

No, she wouldn't have. They'd deceived her, maybe even tried to hack her mindjack, too. She was still down there, maybe vulnerable, maybe in trouble if she'd come to and realized what they'd done to me. How could I get in contact with her? I may have—

A speaker in the passenger cabin crackled before one of the pilot's voices—the one who'd been standing at the airlock—spoke. "Sorry for the bumpy takeoff, everyone. We're currently leaving Luna's orbit and should have some breathing room to regroup shortly. We'll be down with you in a moment to determine our destination together; we want to get you to safety, not just escape this immediate problem. First, though, we need a word with our new friend who had the...uh...entourage following her to the terminal. Could you join us on the bridge, please?"

I almost chuckled at the pilot's politeness. I couldn't have imagined a greater contrast to Vice Admiral Ecker if I'd tried. His attempt at preventing a panic by pointedly eliding that I was being pursued by Bastion soldiers was amusing, too.

I unbuckled my restraints and maneuvered through the passenger cabin, stepping over people's bags and around bulks of families and friends holding each other. At the rear of the passenger cabin was a staircase so steep it was practically a ladder. I climbed it, pausing for a moment as the dagger in my brain twisted once more. If that were any other headache, my modifications would have sped up the recovery. Clearly, something deeper was wrong. Ecker had broken more than just my trust.

The bridge opened up around me at the top of the ladder. Most of the space was dominated by holoscreens and control consoles that wrapped around the edges of the room, protruding out into the bridge's center from the middle of the main console and dividing the pilot from the co-pilot. That protrusion projected a miniature map, which was displaying Luna. A red shape like a dagger in the sky was the *Fang*, hanging outside Luna's orbit. A green triangle was heading in the opposite direction. That must have been us.

A viewport consumed the far bulkhead, from floor to ceiling and wall to wall. Stabbing ahead of the bridge on the other side of the viewport were the sloping forks of the additional cargo containers and the space between used to push larger loads. Beyond that, the void stared back, endless night, pinpricked with stars.

Luna was nowhere to be seen; we were already leaving it behind. Small indicators rotated on the screen, indicating points of interest in the distance, mostly stations. One indicator rotated around a star that stood out amid the rest. It was marked as Jupiter.

On the left sat the man who'd been standing at the airlock, a headset pressing down his black curls. The archaic technology threw me for a second, until my tired brain caught up and remembered that I was on a Mudbrain ship. These pilots didn't have mindjacks. They'd operate everything manually, and they'd need to use outdated technology to communicate.

On the other side of the projected map was another, larger man, black hair cut short and a scraggly beard resting on his upper chest. Geometric tattoos spread down his arm, ending just above his elbow. His skin was a shade warmer than the pilot's, and sitting on his console was a looping hologram of a little girl dancing, her small dress billowing around her, mouth spread in a wide smile.

I wrinkled my nose. The bridge smelled like salty snacks and coffee. And both smelled stale, too.

The pilot finally sensed I was there and swiveled his chair, removing his headset and setting it on the control console.

"All right," he said, reaching past me to press a button on the wall. I jerked more than I should have, instinct taking control. Something about the motion spiked my head pain, and I winced. A door slid down from the ceiling, shutting the bridge off from the cabin below. The co-pilot removed his headset and turned around, too. The pilot leaned against the back of his chair and folded his arms. "Who are you?"

"I'm...a refugee," I stammered. "Like everyone else."

"Bastion brass weren't chasing everyone else," said the co-pilot. "They were chasing you."

I looked between the two men. They both had bags under their eyes. In those eyes and scrunched between those eyebrows was a mixture of emotions. Skepticism. Fear. Sadness. They certainly weren't trying to hide anything, far from the stone-faces I was used to being around.

The pilot sighed then pressed a button below the holomap. He pinched his fingers before spreading them apart again, and the hologram responded, zooming in on the space between us and the *Fang*. Three flashing red triangles sped toward us. Interceptor starfighters. This cargo craft wouldn't be able to outrun them.

"And they're still chasing you," the pilot said. "What makes you so important that they'd devote resources they could be using to secure Mwezi to hunt down a refugee ship?"

I shrugged. The knife in my brain twisted, and I cringed. The pilot raised an eyebrow. "I...I don't know." He cocked his head, and maybe it was the pain, maybe it was my fear, or maybe it was guilt that an entire ship full of innocent, frightened people was in danger because of me. And maybe it was just because I really wasn't in the mood to be questioned by a couple Mudbrains. Whatever the reason, they all melded together into a sharp-edged tone: "Why are you interrogating me like I did something wrong? I'm running from Bastion like everyone else on this ship. Has it occurred to you that they're chasing after all of us, and I just happened to be the last one through the door?"

"Sure," the pilot said with a shrug of his own. "That'd likely have been our first assumption, if we hadn't seen this." He jerked his thumb toward another holoscreen against the starboard wall. It was the governor's broadcast, playing on a loop with the sound off. My picture came up on the screen.

"We know that story's bullshit," the pilot said. "Because the Moonbreaker isn't a spy for Earth."

I swallowed, my mouth dry. Everything seemed to go quiet, the constant rumbling of the engines, the beeps and alerts of the control consoles all around us, all of it faded as I stared at the pilot. My cover was already blown while Mwezi could still see the lights of our burning engines.

"And we know Bastion doesn't give a shit about its own people," the pilot said, "but to brand its great *Sanguine Lycan* as a traitor?" He lifted his chin. "So I'll ask again, and we'd appreciate an answer before we either get shot back down to Luna or launch you out of the airlock. Who. Are. You?"

I looked between the two pilots. The emotions scrawled on their faces had hardened into a deep anger and suspicion I'd seen before. Bastion propagandists and military leaders would have called it the Neanderthal expression of a Mudbrain, the look of primal emotions and a lack of intelligence. But it was the same look I'd seen in many of Bastion's enemies: the defiance of the oppressed.

"I'm Alistella Pareides Caliday, Aegis pilot of the Bastion military's Borealis Fleet. I...I'm not sure what happened. I was ordered to 'guard' Mwezi. I was a deterrent while the city voted to formally become a Bastion satellite. Something went wrong, and my Vice Admiral ordered me into the city."

"And by 'went wrong,'" the co-pilot said, folding his arms, "you mean that you lost the vote." He waved his hand in a circle. "Let's pick it up. Skip the fluff."

"I realized we'd lost the vote, but he'd claimed my sister was in danger. Mwezi's defense forces blockaded me. I refused to fight them, and Ecker tried to...I don't know, take control of my mindjack. At the same time, some of Mwezi's soldiers fired on each other. I desynced from my Aegis, but they took control and used it to break through the defenses. I ejected just before they destroyed the *Lycan*." I cringed, the memory itself twisting the dagger in my mind. "Then I ran. Here. They must have thought I was dead, but that was Vice Admiral Ecker, getting off that shuttle." The pilot took a deep breath and glanced at his co-pilot, who looked at me with his chin tilted up and his lips pursed. "You want to know who I am? I'm not even sure right now. But I'm not a traitor. They're the traitors. To everything we stand...we *should* stand for. But I'm not with Ecker. I'm not a threat to you."

"Except for the fact that three pretty threatening starfighters are bearing down on us," the pilot said. "They won't want to risk your knowledge actually falling into Earth's hands. They made a mess, and they're trying to clean it up. I don't know how they did it, but you and those soldiers aren't the only ones who had their 'jacks hacked. There were incidents across Luna. On a couple stations across the Sphere, too. And there's no way Governor Riobe would have retconned the vote without outside influence. We assumed she was bribed. Threatened. This is a lot worse."

"Toris," the co-pilot said as he looked at the rotating holomap, "they've got weapons warming up."

The pilot—Toris, apparently—stared at the map for a moment before turning to me. His jaw clenched and unclenched. My tongue ached to say more, to defend myself, preserve myself. But I'd said all that mattered for now. This was their ship, and I wasn't going to ask them to put themselves and their passengers at risk for me. I couldn't let more innocents die because of me.

But I also needed to know if Teah was all right. I just couldn't push for any requests at that point. So I waited.

Finally, Toris spoke. "If you think you were ever fighting for any ideals beyond securing greater wealth and power for your elite, then we should start calling you the Mudbrain."

I scowled, hackles rising. "Did you just call me stupid?"

His mouth twitched in almost-amusement. He glanced at his co-pilot. "Not so fun being on the other side, eh, Kuma?"

"Doesn't look like it."

Toris tilted his head as he turned back to me. A hot breath jetted out my nostrils. "I can't convince you to trust me," I said. "And we don't have time for me to try. I can guarantee, though, that I'm...I'm as much a part of Bastion as you are."

The co-pilot, Kuma, scoffed. "Oh, sister, if only saying it made it so."

"I'm not your sister."

"Not by choice, that's for sure."

The holomap beeped. Elsewhere on the control console, a red light flashed, and one of the screens to our left changed, information scrawling across it. Toris glanced at me then looked back at the screen.

"Incoming message," he said, swallowing. "From the *Fang*."

I held up my hands, taking a step forward, desperation—and pain—making me shake. "Please. I...my sister. I went into that city to save my sister. She's still down there. I don't know if they've manipulated her, or if they hacked her mindjack, or if they've done worse. Help me. Help me, and I'll...I'll help you, I'll embody the narrative they're spinning for me. I'll tell you anything." My mouth was running faster than my mind could keep up, fueled by fear. Could I really betray Bastion? My family? My home? Despite everything?

The fact that I didn't have a clear answer made my stomach twist. I didn't have time to deal with that now. I had to survive the next five minutes, and I had to remain free. Teah was my reason and my last resort, my appeal to the Mudbrains' humanity.

Toris stared at me, the lines around his eyes softening a little. Then he turned and flicked a switch, and Vice Admiral Ecker's voice filled the bridge. I shivered, his voice bringing me back to the cockpit of my hacked Aegis, acting of another's accord like a limb out of my control. "*Captain of the starship* Harriet, *this is Vice Admiral Galidon Ecker of Bastion's Borealis Fleet. You are transporting a dangerous extremist, Alistella Pareides Caliday. She's killed citizens of both Bastion's Sphere and the Bastion colony of Mwezi. We request that you relinquish her into our custody to face justice for her crimes.*"

Toris chewed at his bottom lip as he listened, staring down at the floor. Kuma glanced at me. A bead of sweat rolled down my cheek.

"*You'll see three starcraft on your radar. One of them is a shuttle. You will allow the shuttle to dock with your ship and transfer Caliday to us. Comply, and the two fighter escorts will leave you on your way. Resist, and we will assume that you and your passengers are compromised, and we will eliminate the threat that Caliday poses to this Sphere and its neighbors.*"

Toris closed his eyes and took a breath.

"*Starship* Harriet, *please respond. Don't allow Caliday to once more be the reason that innocents die.*"

Toris still had his eyes closed. Kuma watched him, too, lips drawn in a thin line. The holomap flashed red as the Bastion ships entered the *Harriet's* firing zone.

Down below, in the passenger cabin, a baby cried.

I couldn't do it. I stepped forward. "He's right. I won't be—"

Toris held up a finger. I almost coughed on the breath that stopped short.

"This was your commanding officer?" Toris asked.

I nodded.

"Sounds like an asshole. Shouldn't be surprised, I guess." Toris turned and looked at me, his eyes much softer than his tone. Something about that look eased the tension in my chest. He opened his mouth to say something, closed it, and instead said: "You're going to want to strap in." He nodded to a chair to my left, near the back of the cockpit.

I opened my mouth to thank him as I sat down and buckled in, but Toris was already leaning forward and holding down their comms button.

"Vice Admiral Ecker, this is Captain Toristani Arcay Orius and Captain Murakuma Acalar Hakekoa of the starship, *Harriet*. This is an independent starcraft transporting innocent civilians. Firing on this vessel is against interspheric conflict laws. Not that you give a shit about those, but we thought we'd remind you, just for the record." He took his finger off the button and looked at Kuma as he swiped some commands into the screen in front of him. "I'm just saying," he mumbled to Kuma, "I did say—"

"Don't," Kuma held up a finger. "Don't 'I told you so' me right now." He lowered his voice and leaned toward Toris. "The war doesn't determine who it displaces. This is the right thing to do."

Toris shook his head. "If we all die for a Bastionite..." he trailed off as the communication from Ecker dinged in.

"*We appreciate the reminder, Captains. I think the courts will understand the collateral damage given the risks posed by Caliday. This is our final request.*"

Toris tilted his head back toward me, though his seat kept him from meeting my eyes. "He bluffing?"

"He just hacked the mindjacks of Mwezi's government and its military to manipulate a vote in their favor. I'm surprised he's even giving you another chance."

Toris nodded and turned back to Kuma. "In open space we're dead. We're still in Luna's Sphere. We'll veer toward Tranquility, then burn for the border. They may not care at all for the lives on the moon, but I don't think they'll risk firing on other colonies." He grasped a lever and eased it forward, and the rumbling from the ship's engines intensified. "We'll hail the *Dawnbreak*. They won't miss a reason to take on the *Fang*."

Kuma held down a button on his side of the console and spoke, his voice echoing through the ship, "Hey everyone, the fun's not over yet. Please remain fastened in, and we'll have you out of this Sphere in no time." He stared down at a screen, then gave Toris a thumbs-up. "We're good."

On the holomap, the Bastion fighters and its shuttle escort were closing.

A thruster burst from the port side of the *Harriet* pointed us back toward Luna.

The communication channel dinged again before Ecker said, "*Very well. At least these deaths won't be on your consciences for long.*"

The lights in the cabin turned from white to red as the Bastion starfighters launched missiles, flashing on the holomap.

I gripped the edges of my seat.

Toris threw the throttle forward, and the *Harriet* blasted ahead.

Gs slammed me into my seat. I closed my eyes. The dagger twisted.

"Launching chaff!" Kuma shouted. He flicked a switch, and on the holomap between the two pilots, a blurry cloud exploded out the aft of their cargo ship—which was moving with much greater agility than any cargo ship had a right to.

Several of the Bastion missiles twirled in the chaff, confused by the sudden mess of radar signatures. One pair of missiles arced around the cloud, unimpeded.

"Targeting the strays," Kuma said, fingers dancing across his console. Toris was leaning against the direction of our turn, which meant he wasn't new to maneuvers like this. How long had they been avoiding Bastion ships? And why put themselves in danger like this at all? Were they actually soldiers masquerading as philanthropists?

Toris' hard-burn turn brought Earth into sight, the pale blue dot reflecting Sol's sunlight right at us. Through the viewport and fast approaching, much larger than its parent planet, was Luna, domed colonies glinting in the morning light. Mwezi was out of view, but we were fast approaching a much larger colony, Luna's capital city of Tranquility. Where Mwezi and Stickney were a small cluster of domes, Tranquility could have been a postmodern art piece, rings of domes the bases for stalks of metal and glass that rose to spherical structures, almost like trees.

Starcraft buzzed around the city, and all the maglev lanes on the moon started and ended at the colony, the Rome of Luna.

"You're getting a little close," I said, gripping the edges of my seat as we closed in on the highest of Tranquility's globes. "I didn't think Mud—Earthers would use an entire colony as human shields."

"Ha! I'm not even going to think about the irony of a Bastionite, the *Moonbreaker,* talking to us about the ethics of war."

"But she is kind of right," Kuma said as he launched countermeasures at the oncoming missiles. The green lines zipped across the hologram and destroyed the red missiles.

"They're not human shields," Toris snapped, but I did feel like we increased our altitude away from Tranquility a little. "They're deterrents. That's different. We're not holding them hostage. We know Bastion won't fire on them." He swallowed, then said a little more quietly. "Deterrent."

"I don't think you're using that right," Kuma said.

As much as I wouldn't admit it to his face, Toris wasn't wrong. Ecker had manufactured the incident on Mwezi carefully, only to ensure victory and to swing the vote. He'd bought a tenuous, twisted hold on Luna, but damaging any of the other colonies would jeopardize everything he'd risked.

Hence why he was firing missiles at me. My commanding officer was trying to kill me. No negotiation, no second thoughts, no second chances. All because I'd done the right thing.

I'd done the right thing, hadn't I?

As if in cruel response, the knife twisted in my head. Worse than ever, tearing at my gray matter with such ferocity that I cried out and put my head in my hands. I squeezed, trying to use pressure to create some kind of relief, but it only made my skull hurt, too. The starship's bridge faded in and out, like I was slipping between consciousness and the dark. I thought I heard Kuma asking what was wrong, but I didn't have enough control to offer a response.

When the pain reached its peak, and I was sure a blade would burst out of my forehead, I screamed. Then everything went dark.

***

As quickly as I'd lost hold on reality, it snapped back into focus. The pain was still there, but it was less, now, concentrated on one side, around my mindjack.

I opened my eyes. I couldn't have been out long, because we were just passing by Tranquility, one of its globes so close above us that I waited for the *Harriet* to scrape against the glass. Kuma kept glancing back at me, concern pressing his eyebrows together.

"Are you...okay?" he asked.

"She look normal?" said Toris.

"Normal? I just passed out."

"No, you didn't," Kuma said. "You looked like you did at first. Then your head snapped up and you started thrashing around. You looked right at me, looked like you wanted to strangle me. You...I don't know...snarled."

"I told him to zap you," Toris said as he banked the ship around Tranquility and angled us more directly at Earth. I could see the battleships that I'd noted while standing sentry in the *Sanguine Lycan*, white and silver and green slivers against the night. The HUD on the *Harriet's* viewport marked the closest ship as the *Dawnbreak*.

"Zap me?" I shook my head. I didn't thrash around, and I definitely didn't *snarl*. Was Ecker trying to hack me again? Get me to attack the pilots? Or was it something deeper? "It's my mindjack," I said. "I think something happened when I desynced from my Aegis. My head's been killing me ever since." I waved my hand. "A problem for when we're not about to get blown up. Don't worry about me."

Toris pushed a lever forward, and more acceleration pressed me into my seat. "We're out of Tranquility's wake zone," he said. "How far to the border?"

"120,000 kilometers," Kuma said.

"Shit."

Shit was right. That was plenty of time for Bastion's ships to shoot us down, and they'd have a lock on our radar signature, so our countermeasure options were limited. The *Harriet* was clearly outfitted with more than you'd typically find on a cargo transport, but these were Bastion Lion-class starfighters. And their typical transport shuttle's firepower was nothing to sneeze at, either. Bastion put a gun on practically everything.

"We don't need to make it to the border, right?" I asked. "We just need to make it inside the *Dawnbreak's* firing arc. They...Bastion...the ships already fired on us inside Luna's independent Sphere, so they've already violated that neutrality."

"You'd be right if we fired back on the ships," Kuma said. "That'd be self-defense. The *Dawnbreak* would be a warship firing into neutral space."

"I think Luna would forgive that one trespass."

"Depends what they've been fed," Toris said. "And what intel the *Dawnbreak*'s seen. If they all think Bastion is actually tracking down a traitor who killed innocents on Mwezi, Luna may be inclined to let them, and so may the *Dawnbreak*. The battleship may not take the risk."

"Can't you hail them? Tell them I'm here. Tell them what I told you. Tell them I'll...tell them I'll help them."

"Will you?" Toris asked.

The holomap flashed red again as the Bastion ships passed out of Tranquility's wake zone, accelerated, and fired another round of missiles. More this time. The map looked like a swarm of hornets was racing toward the *Harriet*.

"Yes. Yes, I will." I hoped that sounded more confident than I felt. I'd say anything at that point to increase our odds of survival. The officers of the *Dawnbreak* would likely know that, too. But, at that point, being questioned on an Earther ship felt better than floating dead among the debris of the *Harriet*.

"Tor," Kuma said, fingers dancing across his console, "I can't get a lock on all those missiles. There's too many."

"Don't you have guns in your countermeasure artillery?"

"Can't," Toris said.

"What do you mean 'can't?'"

"We're a civilian vessel," Kuma said. "Unless we want to be designated as a warship, which would keep us from doing our job, then we can't have offensive artillery on the ship."

I scoffed. "And you let someone tell you that you can't defend your ship? The people on it? No wonder you're Mud—"

"Don't," Toris snapped. "It's called having principles. Are you sure you don't want us to just drop you off with your friends?"

Frankly, I wasn't sure. I wasn't sure of anything at that moment, but I certainly didn't say that. I didn't say a word.

"That's what I thought," Toris said. "Now, unless you can tell us anything that'll save our collective asses, can we focus on the problem at hand? What are we doing about the missiles, Kuma?" For a pilot vastly outgunned and outnumbered, Toris was remarkably calm. That didn't change the fact that part of me wanted to slap him upside his arrogant head.

"I could launch the hotboxes. That might catch most of them."

"Hotboxes?"

They ignored me.

"We *just* replaced those," Toris sighed. "But since when does the universe reward us for this? Do it." He glanced over at the holomap. "We'll be in their close-range firing arc soon. Hotboxes won't save us then. How far to the border?"

"80,000 kilometers," Kuma said, and Toris swore under his breath again. He let go of the controls and wiped a sweaty hand on his pants. "Launching hotboxes."

A series of deep *clunkclunkclunk*s echoed through the ship and vibrated through my seat. On the other side of the viewport, something—more a cluster of somethings—dropped away from beneath the forks making up the prow of the starship. On the map, those clusters looked like a swarm of other starcraft, zipping away from the *Harriet*.

"Hotbox," I said, connecting the dots. "Cargo containers with an infrared signature. But—"

"And duplicate radar signatures," Kuma said, reading where my skepticism was going. "And small thrusters to get some distance."

I almost opened my mouth to say that wouldn't confuse Bastion missiles, but the holomap proved me wrong, with nearly all the missiles diverting from their path to pursue the hotboxes as we rocketed ahead.

"Smart," I said with an impressed frown.

"Careful," Toris said. "You might accidentally compliment a Mudbrain. Hailing the *Dawnbreak* now. This should be...fun."

"Aren't you with them? Why would—" Kuma's so-so hand wave made me close my mouth.

Toris held down a button beside the one he'd used to connect with the *Fang*. It blinked blue, then a ding rang through the bridge, followed by a calm but edged feminine voice. "*Captains Orius and Murakuma. Why am I not surprised to be hearing from you?*"

"Great to hear your voice, too, Admiral Halgard."

"*My lieutenant told me that was the* Harriet *getting pursued by Bastion starfighters, and I said, 'No, that can't be. Captain Orius would never ignore our blockade—and my orders—and enter newly minted enemy territory.'*"

"Yeah, well," Toris said, actually shrugging. "There's a reason we're not soldiers, I guess. Hey, if we could skip the chastising real quick, we have twenty-seven innocent civilians onboard and have, as you so helpfully pointed out, some angry starships on our tail. Anything you can do to assist?"

Silence for a moment, and I wondered if Toris' insolence had made the admiral hang up. Ecker would have. The utter disrespect made me cringe as if I were smelling something rancid.

Then, Admiral Halgard responded: *"Have they hailed you? Why are those starfighters escorting a shuttle craft? I have a feeling you did something to piss them off."*

Toris didn't immediately answer, and his hand kneaded the bar of the thrust lever in his grip. Kuma looked at him. The captain was deliberating. If Earth knew Bastion had hailed us, he'd open the door to telling them about me, and he may have been wondering the same thing I was: as an Aegis pilot, the Moonbreaker herself, was it any better to be in the Earth military's hands than Bastion's?

"Captain? Didn't get blown up, did you?"

"No," Toris responded, "but thank you for the overflowing concern. They did hail us. They think we have someone important aboard. Someone with information that could compromise them. They wanted them back."

"And, do you?"

"I didn't exactly have time to interview every passenger, Admiral." He paused, then: "And I wouldn't give them up even if I had."

Maybe I didn't want to hit Toris upside his head.

"No, you wouldn't," Halgard said with a sigh. *"I respect that choice, Captain, but that's quite a risk to take for one person. Bastion risked their new foothold on Luna to fire on a civilian vessel in independent space. That person must be important."*

"Frankly, Admiral, importance is never a factor."

A new alarm beeped as the Bastion starfighters entered medium range. They wouldn't need missiles soon. The shuttle looked like it was pulling back, its purpose clearly rejected.

"I know that, Captain. It's why I'm not going to throw you in chains the second we get you out of this mess."

"So that's a yes?"

"Burn hard for the border. I sent a squadron to prepare when we pinged your ship. You took longer than I thought you would to hail. If we still used it, I'd owe my lieutenant some money. I'll give you clearance to board, and we'll get your passengers sorted out. We'll also hail the Fang. *Tell them you're on an official diplomatic mission. Halgard, out."*

"Thank—wait, no!" But the admiral had already disconnected. Kuma looked back at me. If Halgard contacted Ecker, she'd find out who I was.

"We could change course once we reach the border," Kuma suggested, "burn for the Dandelion or Sanctuary."

Toris was kneading the throttle handle again. Then he shook his head. "No. I tried, but I won't risk these people by being in open space longer than we need to. And we'll be surrounded by Halgard's ships. I won't risk one of them stunning the *Harriet* and towing her in. We're lucky she's letting us off the hook this time." Another pause. "Sorry."

"No," I said. "I...thank you."

"Now let's get there without dying," Toris said. The Bastion starfighters were on the edge of their close-range firing arc. The slivers of the *Dawnbreak* and its companion battleships were growing larger, as well as the blue-and-green marble of Earth behind it. Rotating into view was the Dandelion, Earth's cluster of asteroid starports. As inefficient as it was compared to launching from the ground, I had to admire its engineering.

I'd admire it more if we weren't running for our lives.

"Everyone restrained?" Toris asked.

Kuma glanced at a screen. "Yep. All green."

"Good."

Toris pushed the throttle forward one more step, and acceleration pressed me back again, making the knife twist deeper into my head. I bit my lip to stop myself from crying out. An alarm rang out as the Bastion starfighters entered the close-range arc. Halgard's call must have gone poorly, because as soon as they entered the arc, lines of laser fire shot across the dark.

Toris leaned forward, grasping a steering yoke I couldn't see, and the ship pitched downward, maneuvering much more quickly without the weight of all the hotboxes. Judging by the holomap, the lasers looked like they'd all missed, but then a rapid series of alarms went off.

"It's fine," Kuma said. "Just skirted a radiator. They're going for the engines."

"Fan*tastic*," Toris growled as he wrenched the ship to the right, throwing me to the side against my restraints. I heard a few cries in the passenger cabin down below.

The Bastion ships stayed tight on our tail as Toris bobbed and weaved around laser fire. A thin line appeared on the viewport HUD, marking the interspheric border between Earth and Luna. We were still 20,000 kilometers away.

We wouldn't make it.

Toris must have had the same thought, because he pressed the button to connect with the *Dawnbreak* once again.

"*Dawnbreak*, this is the *Harriet*. Any chance you—"

"Harriet, *Admiral Halgard.*" Her voice sounded different. More clipped. Serious, as if a ship of innocents about to be blown up hadn't been serious enough. She must have spoken with Ecker, and she didn't like what she'd heard. I imagined she was in a similar conundrum to Toris and Kuma: risk lives to keep me safe or give me up and risk losing the valuable information I could give them.

My stomach twisted. I'd put a blade in my brain to escape being used by Bastion. Had I given up one master just to stumble into the service of another?

"*My orders stand. Burn for us as fast as you can. Reinforcements are on their way. You are now officially on a diplomatic rendezvous with our ship. That also means you'll follow my orders this time, or I'll stun your ship so badly you'll feel it. Fly directly at us. When I order it, dive.*"

Toris and Kuma glanced at each other, then Toris responded, "Yes, ma'am." Toris brought us up gently so we were on the same ecliptic plane as the *Dawnbreak*, its sliver growing as we approached. Sunlight glinted off a small swarm of Earther starfighters as they shot out of the battleship's hangars. By the time they reached us, we'd be shards in the void.

"Won't flying straight at them risk us—" Alarms blared as more lasers fired. Most of them missed, but I had to squint as one seared through the left fork just outside our viewport. Debris and burning metal vented out into space from the hole, but it wouldn't cause any critical damage. Flying in a straight line, however, would mean that the Bastion ships could line up for a better shot.

"We trust Halgard," Kuma said.

"They'll be in the killzone soon," I said, watching the holomap, where the starfighters were closing into the space where they could more easily hit us with any remaining missiles or plasma rounds. "I thought you all didn't follow orders."

Toris scoffed. "We don't—"

"Harriet," the admiral crackled through, interrupting Toris. "*Dive on five, four, three, two, DIVE!*"

Toris thrust us down at an even more intense angle. The Gs once again twisted the knife in my brain, the edges of my vision going dark.

Then the void above us was rent in two, a white light that seemed to tear through the fabric of the night to reveal the true heavens behind. Warning alarms blared through the bridge, sensors indicating off-the-charts heat radiating against the top of the ship.

An instant after it tore through space, the beam was gone, leaving an afterimage that I'd spend hours trying to blink away. The holomap changed from red to green. The Bastion starships were dust.

"Well, that's sending a message," Kuma said.

"Was that a...particle beam?" I asked, mouth hanging open. Earth shouldn't have had that kind of weaponry. Even Bastion hadn't mastered weaponizing that technology.

Toris didn't answer as he guided us back up to the same plane as the *Dawnbreak* and started easing back on the thrust as we approached. A few minutes later, Earther starfighters shaped like daggers surrounded the *Harriet* to escort us toward their battleship.

I'd seen a few Earther battleships up close, but this looked like a newer model. Its shape initially reminded me of Earth's old aircraft carriers, somewhat flat on top with its belly tapering down multiple decks, but at least ten times the size. On the dorsal of the ship, a shorter series of decks tapered up to an elongated tower at the center that ended around halfway down that longest main deck, which ended in a flat edge. The battleship was silver with emerald accents running its length. For a starship built by a bunch of Mudbrains, it wasn't bad.

Toris guided us alongside our starfighter escorts. I wiped my sweaty hands on my pants. As much as instinct told me to, there was no point in trying to run. I was in enemy territory, now, with nowhere to go. And betraying the limited trust Toris and Kuma had already shown me would be a pretty terrible way to show appreciation for saving my life and risking theirs.

Could I give Admiral Halgard anything significant enough to keep myself alive that wouldn't totally betray my home? Ecker was different. He'd not only used me, he'd betrayed everything we stood for. If I was in a room with that man again, one of us wouldn't make it out alive. But Ecker...he wasn't Bastion. He wasn't my father. He wasn't Teah. He wasn't Mom. He wasn't that defiant symbol of the human spirit. He wasn't the smell of wet Martian dirt, the way sunlight shot its pillars around titanic Olympus Mons. The information in my mind could give Earth's military significant advantages in the war. I couldn't allow myself to be a turning point, to risk the destruction of everything my people had built.

I sighed and leaned my head back against my chair. It was an impossible situation. Either I betrayed Bastion—more than I already had—or I likely risked either life in prison or immediate execution.

A familiar beeping notification rang through the bridge. Kuma looked at Toris, raising an eyebrow. "Is it Halgard?"

"It's the *Fang*."

"Ignore it," Kuma responded.

"No," I said. I unbuckled my restraints and stood up, stepping behind Toris' seat and setting a hand on the holomap projector between the captains. "I'll speak to him."

Toris looked up, searched my eyes for a moment, then shrugged and opened the channel.

"Sir."

"Caliday. The captains allowed you onto their bridge? Mudbrains indeed. Do they know what you did? Do they know how the people of Stickney stood for each other before you broke their moon and wiped out their colony? The blood on your hands may be rotted, but it's still Earther blood."

I resisted looking at either Toris or Kuma, looking instead up at the *Dawnbreak* as it dominated the view outside the glass. We were approaching the portside lower decks, where huge hangar doors were opening, spilling artificial light into space.

"You betrayed everything you stand for," I said, venom dripping from my tone. "Everything we stand for. Everything we're fighting this war for. Independence. Progress. Stability. I'm coming back for my sister, sir, and then I'm going to ensure that High Command knows what you did. What you did at Stickney and Mwezi."

A loud laugh crackled through the speakers. *"You're threatening me? Listen to me, you naive child. You think I'm the architect of Mwezi, but I was only its foreman. Our stability, our independence, our progress comes at a price, Caliday. You clearly aren't willing to pay it, and that makes you as rotten as a Mudbrain. You had so much. I set you up for a future of success. You threw it away. And your sister? You think she'd listen to you?"* He scoffed again.

"I know you hacked her. I know you hacked all of us. I don't know how, but I'll find out, and I'll make sure it never happens again."

"I didn't have to hack Teah. Her unit knew the plan, and she executed it to perfection. She understands the price, Caliday. She understands loyalty. But let me make something clear. Let me give you a lesson in threat. Since you're clearly not motivated by loyalty to Bastion, if you breathe a word to the Mudbrains, your sister will pay the price. Instead, since I'm a reasonable man, I'll look past this. I'll welcome you back—and protect your sister—if you bring something of value back to me from the Dawnbreak. *Sabotaging the ship and its crew would do, too."*

I stared at the control console, fear and hate and anger and betrayal colliding to dam any thought from reaching my tongue.

"*I hope you make the right choice.*"

The signal cut out. Toris and Kuma both looked at me, eyes wide.

"What have I done?" I whispered. And even quieter: "What do I do?"

"Better decide fast," Kuma said, nodding ahead.

We were pulling up to the hangar, between the huge metal doors above and below like dull, shaved-down teeth. Starfighters entered around us, all curving left to where their bays were stacked on each other. Ahead of us were rows of clamps with airlocks between them. Behind the clamps was a glass wall, and on the other side of that stood a squad of armored soldiers, rifles in hand. At their head was a woman in uniform, purple-black hair covered by a sharp admiral's cap. Her hands were clasped behind her back, and while we were still too far away to tell for sure, I could feel her watching me, the enemy, the traitor, the Moonbreaker herself.

Kuma used steam thrusters to orient us parallel to the wall, then he guided us toward the clamps. They secured the *Harriet* with a low *boom* that shook the starship. Below, some passengers cheered, celebrating their safety.

Numb, I returned to my seat, mourning while they cheered.

Chapter Fourteen

Toris

Believe it or not, it wasn't the first time we'd had an engine blown up.

And whether in vacuum or in a gravity well, the same thing happened when engines and their fuel cells exploded: the direction of the blasted force sent the craft into a spin. I'd blacked out the first time it happened, so this time I followed Kuma's lead and leaned my head in the opposite direction of the spin.

Squinting through the discomfort and head pain of the spin, I swiped through analytics on my screen. "Fans are still running! Backup superconductors are good!"

Kuma shook his head. "We're spinning left, right?"

"I think?!"

Kuma threw a switch that killed the portside fan and throttled up the speed of the starboard fan. We lurched, and the spin started slowing down, the Gs letting up enough that the vice on my head gave a little. My hearing came back as some of the cockpit alarms died down while Kuma regained control. At least, as much control as he could wrest from a burning aircraft that may have had a quantum-teleporting monster aboard.

The rest of the pain let up as Kuma fully got us out of the spin. Kuma rotated the fans so they'd continue propelling us forward, albeit much more slowly without the assistance of the engines.

I looked at an alert on my screen. "We're losing power. Dropping altitude."

"Course we are. I'm starting to believe you really are cursed, brother."

As we flew forward, we left the smoke behind, surely trailing a black tail. We were out of the acid rainstorm, which was good for us in one way, but that would make it easier for the revenant to recohere and give someone aboard a chance to perceive it. That was, if anyone was left in the passenger cabin.

I gulped and blinked away the terrified tears that rushed to the surface. Losing a passenger never got easier, despite knowing the risks of the situations we'd flown through. And of all the passengers to lose, one of them may have been another from Farstead. Another like Cixin, who I brought to Earth only to die. Life under the Shades may have been hardly a life at all, but I'd promised them something better.

We left behind the wisps of cloud obscuring our view. Ten or twenty miles away were the Glassfields, rows of solar panels that stretched clear to the horizon, blending together into a black sheet that reflected the sunlight with such intensity that our windshield responded by tinting itself. Above the Glassfields, the air shimmered from the heat mirage. If the Deadlands was hot, it was said walking through the Glassfields was like walking through an oven. Even flying, we'd have had to gain some altitude to keep the heat from baking us inside the craft.

Evidently, that wasn't going to be something we'd have to worry about.

Surrounding the Glassfields was a tall metal and concrete wall, stretching between a natural ridge to the south and the unnatural edge of the Sierras Falsas to the north, meant to keep out both revenants and destructive humans. The interstate dropped into an underground tunnel that ran under the Glassfields and rose again on the other side, just outside Babylon, at the edge of the New Euphrates River.

My stomach lurched as our aircraft dropped, sailing below the top of the Glassfield's wall, leaving an afterimage of the sun's reflection that I tried to blink away.

I checked my restraints to ensure they were still secure, then I pressed the button to speak to the passenger cabin. "We're about to land. Check your restraints and brace!" I released the button, hoping someone was there to hear me. I swiped to the screen that should have displayed the camera feed. Still dead.

We dropped, gravity pulling on us harder than the fans could resist.

"Are we giving the fans full power?" I yelled over the altitude and damage alarms.

"That and then some," Kuma replied. "I think I broke the controls." He rolled his shoulders and shook his head. "Just a routine trip, huh brother?"

Any response was constricted by the tightness in my chest as the ground rose up. Kuma, master of maneuvering, had us level with the dead desert below, but the ground was still a blur, moving fast enough to break us apart, especially in our already-damaged state.

"All right," Kuma said, "this'll be better than nothing!" He reached to his right and rotated the gyroscopic sphere that controlled the fans' positions, and the monitors showed them turning completely vertical, blasting air ahead of them. I jerked forward against my restraints as we slowed down. The ground started to resolve into shapes: crusty sagebrush and cracked, curled earth, like the scales of an old, dessicated dragon.

"Brace!" Kuma called. I grabbed the bar bolted to the bulkhead as Kuma cut the fans' power, and we slammed into the ground. My head snapped forward, something wrenching in my neck. More alarms blared around us as we skidded across the desert floor, the interstate to our right, maybe only twenty or thirty yards away. We started turning, bouncing once over a boulder, before sliding to a stop. Dust and smoke billowed around the outside of the craft.

"Oof," Kuma said. "Not my smoothest landing."

"At least it was more landing than crash," I said, unbuckling my restraints. "Get a distress call out. See if anything's nearby. Babylon can be our last resort, but I'd rather enter the city more quietly than on the tail of this. I'll..." I swallowed. "I'll go check the passengers."

"Hey," Kuma said, grabbing my arm. "There's nothing else we could have done."

I jerked away. "Not helping right now."

I pulled the switch to open the door from the cockpit, and it still didn't work.

I growled under my breath, then slid open a panel concealing a long black handle. With both hands, I gripped the handle and pulled. Nothing. The locks were engaged.

From its place on my belt, I grabbed my solarblade, a tool I'd modified over the years. With a flick of the switch, small magnetic clips popped out of the hilt, stacking on top of each other until they reached the length I'd set. With the tap of another button, a stream of blue-white superheated plasma streamed out of the hilt, following the magnetic field created by the clips. I slid the solarblade between the door and the wall and swiped down, barely feeling the thick lock as the plasma sliced through.

Disengaging and stowing the solarblade, I grabbed the manual handle again. After a moment of burning muscles, the handle started moving, and with it the door. As soon as the pressure seal cracked open, dust and debris billowed into the cockpit. I turned to the side and coughed, closing my eyes. Acrid smoke burned my nostrils, and the heat of the desert rushed in, the air conditioning from the aircraft nothing against the temperature outside, brought in through the void where the door used to be.

Once the door was open enough for me to squeeze through, I brought my arm up to cover my mouth and nose and shouldered inside the passenger cabin. My stomach twisted at the sight of the seat nearest the open door, empty of the passenger who'd been sitting there when we took off. His restraint was torn, blood splashed across the seat. He hadn't been sucked out the door—this wasn't space, the pressure difference wouldn't have been that strong at our speed and altitude—which only meant that the revenant had infiltrated the cabin.

On the other side of the aisle, though, were our other two passengers. The man in the front was passed out, head leaning against the bulkhead, dust turning his black, short-cropped hair white. His chest rose up and down. Breathing.

Behind him sat Lana, and as the dust billowed away from her, I saw she was awake, staring at me with wide eyes, her chest moving so quickly she may have been hyperventilating. I hurried up to her and knelt by her chair. "Are you hurt?" I asked, moving my arm from my mouth.

She just stared at me for a moment, breath jetting out of her nose and moving the dust in whorls around her. Eventually, she shook her head. No injuries, at least on the outside. She'd likely never want to fly in an aircraft again, especially with me at the helm.

"Good," I said. "You're safe. You're going to be okay. We're going to be okay. I'm going to get you out of here," Her wide eyes never left mine. "Just like I got you out of Farstead and away from Bastion. I promise. I'm...I'm so sorry this happened. We're clearly still trying to escape some of Bastion's consequences, too." I moved over to the other passenger and shook him gently. He stirred, bald head rolling around as his eyelids fluttered open. He jerked back as he regained full consciousness, his chest heaving in great breaths of dusty, smoky air before coughing it up again.

"What's your name?"

He wiped some dirt off his face. "Hyrum. Hyrumite Barrowman."

"All right, Hyrum. Are you all right? Sorry. Wrong question. Are you hurt?" I looked around him for any blood, any contusions.

"My neck hurts," he said. "But...not bad for a plane crash, I guess."

"Still a plane landing, technically," Kuma corrected, stepping out of the cockpit. "Just a rough one."

"What..." Lana said, her voice quiet as she looked at the damage around us. "What happened?" Then she coughed, too.

I stood up as Hyrum unbuckled himself and also stood, rolling his neck.

"I'll give you the quick version," I said. I could hold off saying anything, but these people deserved to know the situation we were in. Awareness would keep them safe. And it didn't hurt to teach Lana about her complicated new home. I wished I could have shown Cixin more.

We'll, maybe not more of this.

"The area between Orilla del Angel and Babylon is known as the Deadlands. It's a mess from experiments that Bastion's Pioneers conducted before leaving Earth, and it was practically a hellscape even before that. One of those experiments involved quantum teleportation. It was an unethical failure that left its test subjects medically dead but in a state of limbo where they pop in and out of existence. They ignore typical physical laws of space and distance, and once you perceive one, it targets you." I looked out at the dust billowing past the blown-out door in the side of the aircraft. "They're called revenants. Or flickers."

"Or quantum zombies," Kuma added.

"We saw one on the road below, and it attacked. I've never seen it happen before. Normally the flight conditions make it difficult for the revenant to recohere long enough to cause damage like this."

"It..." Lana swallowed, looking at the hole in the bulkhead. "I think I saw it come through the door. It looked like a person, but...wrong. I saw its...bones."

Kuma nodded. "Sometimes the body doesn't recohere in any logical way, and sometimes it recoheres in parts. They're definitely freaky. Toris and I had one approach our community when we were kids. Still gives me nightmares." He looked around at the damage. "At least I'll have a new nightmare now."

"Did you see it leave?" I asked.

Lana's eyes brimmed with tears, and I instantly regretted asking her to relive that moment, however crucial the information was. "It...cut through his seatbelt." She nodded her head toward the bloody seat. "And it looked like it..." she stopped talking and shook her head. "Then it threw him out the open door, and it disappeared."

I looked out at the desert, chewing on my bottom lip. Lana had observed the revenant, which may have been what caused it to decohere, and that could have marked Lana as a target. Or it was satisfied with its prey, that poor passenger. I didn't even know their name. They could have had a family. Friends. No one deserved to go out like that.

Two deaths in less than a day, and neither should have happened.

"Is it still out there?" Hyrum asked, glancing between me and the desert outside.

I sighed and looked at the two passengers, wishing I could lie. "I don't know. Revenants are unpredictable. Like I said, this one shouldn't have been able to cause the damage it did. So we have to be cautious. Kuma's sent out a distress call, and while we wait, we're going to seal ourselves off, and we're going to cover our eyes. If we don't observe the revenant, it won't bother us. We're going to get you both to Babylon if we have to carry you there."

I stepped past Hyrum and Lana and opened a compartment near the ceiling. Inside were folded blankets. I pulled a few out and dropped them on the ground, then grabbed some speed tape from another compartment. Kuma grabbed the blankets, gathering what I was doing, and carried them to the hole in the bulkhead. Both of us avoided looking out into the desert as the dust and smoke started to clear. Distance didn't matter to a revenant. Even if we'd left it far behind, all we'd need to see was its speck on the sand.

While Kuma held blankets across the hole, I taped them to the bulkhead, blinking as my eyes adjusted to the sudden lack of light. The lights along the aircraft's bulkhead were still functioning, fortunately, but one of them was flickering. At least the air conditioning was still functional. If we lost that, the aircraft would quickly go from shelter to oven.

With a second blanket up, we'd blocked enough of the light. I took a deep breath, the worries about how much this would delay me finding Alis looming in the shadows of my mind. I pushed those worries as far back into that void as I could, guilty for them even crossing my mind when someone had just died and two other passengers were still in mortal danger.

"Will blankets keep it out?" Hyrum asked. "That thing tore through a seatbelt like it was paper." At that mention, Lana squeezed her eyes shut and cringed as if someone had punched her in the arm.

"Quantum's weird," I responded. "They're in a state of half-existence, running on the instincts and emotions left at the time of their death. As long as we don't observe them, the aircraft will be like a...rock or some sagebrush. It won't pay us any mind. It doesn't have the awareness to search for us." Hyrum nodded, still shivering as he stood beside his seat. Lana was still seated in hers, knees up to her chest, black hair falling across her face, drawn to look at the blankets, then turning away rapidly before risking another look moments later. That was the thing with instincts, when you knew something nearby may try to kill you, you couldn't take your eyes off it, even if you needed to.

"But like I said," I continued, "we're going to get you out of this. So try to relax and Kuma and I will find out who's coming to pick us up."

Kuma offered an awkward half-smile, and we ducked back into the cockpit. I pulled the manual handle in the other direction, closing the door behind us.

"What's the damage look like?" I asked, making sure the door was sealed. They didn't need more reasons to worry. "Are we safe to hide in here?"

Kuma stood behind his pilot's chair, swiping through screens set into the bulkhead. "We should be fine. Both engines blew, but the suppression systems took care of the fire and cascading explosions. We've got fluid and fuel leaking out the back, but as long as no one throws a cigarette at it, we should be okay."

"How did the revenant blow the engines?" I asked. "It would have had to be more precise than I've ever heard of a revenant being. It'd have had to recohere in just the right spot. I just told them," I jerked my head toward the door, "these things aren't that intentional."

"Quantum's weird, brother," Kuma said as he swiped through more diagnostic screens. "Maybe one of the test subjects was particularly sharp, and they retained some of that when they went through the experiment? And they've been out here for over a hundred years; maybe some of them are adapting."

"Or it's not a coincidence," I said, folding my arms. "Alis transforms outside of the cycle, with Mars on the other side of the sun, and then we just happen to run into the Super-Revenant?"

Kuma glanced at me with a raised eyebrow. "Conspiracies won't help us get out of this mess. Revenant attacks aren't unheard of, you know that. It's a shitty coincidence, that's all. We should have been more careful, but no one can control revenants."

"Maybe it wasn't actually a revenant that blew the engine," I said. "Maybe it was Carivant. Maybe he found a way to hack the duty records, saw we'd be flying this, and found a way to long-range sabotage it. That—"

"Tor," Kuma said, finger hanging above the screen he was studying. "You need to sleep. You need to get that mithril, find Alis, and get some sleep. Carivant has a lot more to worry about than us. Hopefully he's forgotten we existed, and it'll be a nice surprise when we take his mithril. Focus. Because we've got a problem."

I shook my head then nodded. Kuma was right. We could explore all the reasons when we were safe. Not that we'd be safe in Babylon, but I'd take even that godforsaken city over the godforsaken Deadlands.

"Sure. Yeah. Sorry. What is it?"

"Even with rerouting all the power to the cooling systems, we're going to lose them."

"How long?"

Kuma lifted one shoulder. "Minutes. Maybe a few more if I reroute power from the lighting and a few other systems. The superconductors were damaged in the crash—because of course they were—and the AC is having to work overdrive because of the heat coming through that hole."

"Do it."

Kuma punched in some commands, and the lights went out. Fortunately, the windshield was clear enough, even with its thick coating of dust and dirt, to let in enough light to see.

"Has anyone responded to our distress call?" I asked.

Kuma swiped to another screen, the displays considerably darker than before. "Two. One's four hours out. The second's from Babylon. But they won't come until we pay them a three-thousand dollar fee."

"Three thousand?!" I exclaimed. "Three thousand." I ran my hand through my hair. Capitalists."

"Capitalists," Kuma repeated.

The Gaia Compact demanded that those who remained on Earth didn't exploit people as Babylon did, but as many harsh lessons through history had repeatedly taught, there would always be those who turned inward, who thought in their arrogance that they knew the better path. And so, Babylon existed in a kind of vacuum on Earth. It didn't trade with the other communities, nor abide by any of the other statutes of the Compact, and vice versa, the surrounding communities didn't support the city. They were on their own. But they managed to survive by trading with Luna and even Bastion, both during and after the Solar Gulf War.

"Four hours is too long," I said. "Way too long. That'll put us too far behind Alis. Every minute in that city is a minute she could get found by Carivant or get hurt because of the Wolf. We've lost enough time because of this," I kicked the door, "revenant. And it'll be too long to stay here in the heat. We'll bake."

"Ah, yes," Kuma said, "the us dying part comes second." Then, when I shot him a look: "Sorry, yeah, I get it."

I peeled my shirt off my sweaty skin. The cooling systems were already failing. "We'll have to go for the interstate. Hitch a ride."

Kuma folded his arms and leaned against the bulkhead. "We could reroute the last of the cooling system's power to the systems connecting the ship and the vehicles. Tell them to stop long enough for us to get on one."

I nodded. "We'll have to find one with enough space, which may be tough. And we'll have to get the passcodes to control the vehicle once we're on-board. But it's our best chance."

Kuma stared at me, but through me at the same time, weighing the options.

"Even with a revenant out there?" he asked. "I know four hours is a while, and I know you want to get to Alis as quickly as possible, but we have to think about keeping these people safe, too, Tor."

"I know," I snapped, more sharply than Kuma deserved. "I know," softer, that time. "They're in danger either way, from the revenant or the heat. This close to the Glassfields, we'll get some of that residual heat, too, as if the Deadlands weren't bad enough." Even though I believed that, a twang of guilt plucked at my already-tight gut. Waiting in shelter probably was the safer option, even at risk of the heat. But it was Alis. It was the Wolf. It was Babylon. It was all of it, and I was already fraying. I'd snap completely long before four hours was up.

"Only one of us needs eyes to guide the rest to the highway," I said. "The rest can be blindfolded. That'll help our chances. And that's if the revenant isn't long behind us."

Kuma stared at me a moment longer, then he nodded and turned toward the wall screens. "Rerouting power. Cutting cooling systems."

The hum of the air conditioning cut off, leaving the aircraft completely silent. Wind whistled against the hull outside. Through the layer of dust and dirt on the windshield, I thought I saw a shadow. I looked down, focusing on the screen. I didn't see anything. A trick of the light, the wind.

"You've probably only got two or three minutes," Kuma said.

I scrolled through the vehicles whizzing by on the interstate. Most of their manifests marked them as full to capacity, carrying food from Orilla and other coastal communities across the continent and vice versa. But there was one, coming up from San Diego. Fish, so we'd smell great at the end of the trip, but at least we'd be cool.

"Got one," I said, connecting to the vehicle and pulling it over to the interstate's shoulder. I memorized the truck's passcode and closed the screen. "Let's go share the plan. They'll love it."

Kuma scoffed and pulled the manual handle to the passenger cabin. Lana was standing now, pulling off the sweater she'd been wearing and tying it around her waist. I noticed a few pale scars on her arms. Her black hair was sticking to her sweaty forehead.

"Sorry for the heat," Kuma said. "But we've got a plan. Good news, bad news situation. Bad news is that we can't get another aircraft here before we bake in this oven. But the good news is we have a vehicle waiting on the interstate."

Hyrum's eyes widened. "We have to go out there? With that...thing?"

I held up my hands. "It's only about a hundred yards. We'll run for it, and we'll put blindfolds on all of us but one. Reduce the chances of observing the revenant."

Lana looked between the three of us, jaw slack. "So we die in here, or we die out there?"

"No," I said. "I told you, no one's dying. We don't know if the revenant's even out there anymore." I paused, pushing down the frustration at saying the same thing over and over. I wasn't the only one fraying.

"A hundred yards," Hyrum said, nodding to punctuate every word. "One hundred yards. That's close."

"That's the spirit," Kuma said. He walked toward the rear of the cabin, where another emergency blanket lay. With a knife from his pocket, he cut out three ribbons and passed one to each of us. When I hesitated, he pushed the ribbon toward me. "I love you, brother, but you're already on the edge of losing it. Let me take this one."

I looked at him, teeth clenched, unable to muster an argument. He was right, my tired, stressed mind would be much more likely to search out the revenant just on instinct. Kuma was more focused. More in control. That didn't mean I didn't hate the idea of him being the one at risk. The revenant always went after the one who observed it, who caused it to decohere.

"You've done too much for me today," I said.

"No such thing," he said with a wink. I took the ribbon and, after helping Hyrum tie his own, fastened mine around my eyes, tying it tight enough that nothing slipped through.

"All right," Kuma said, "my little schoolchildren. Join hands." I smiled a little. Leave it to Kuma to lighten a life-and-death moment. I grasped his hand and wiggled my fingers in the air behind me. A smaller hand grabbed onto it. Probably Lana.

"Please don't let go." Definitely Lana.

"Only if you don't let go of me," I said. "I'm sorry this happened. Not exactly what I promised back on Farstead, huh?"

"Ha. No, not exactly. But funny enough, I'd still rather be here."

That should have given me comfort, but I just wondered if Cixin felt the same.

"Taking down the blanket," Kuma said. I heard tape tearing from the bulkhead, and the barest amount of light filtered through my blindfold. Not enough to make out any details, fortunately. Heat washed over us, settling on my skin with an intensity that made my arms prickle.

"Coast looks clear. Let's go. Light jog, children." He started jogging, and I followed his pace, Lana following behind.

"You good, Hyrum?" I called.

"I think I peed a little."

"Friend, you don't want to know how many times I 'peed a little' on an aircraft," Kuma said. "Keep running, you're all getting gold stars." He had to yell above the rumble of the nearby interstate. I nearly stumbled over a rock but saved my footing, my mind spinning at the lack of sensory input, with the stress and exhaustion just adding momentum.

We had to be almost halfway there. We were going to be—

Lana's hand jerked back, and I almost lost her. Hyrum yelled out.

"Don't look!" Kuma yelled, true panic tightening his tone. It was a voice I'd only heard my calm friend take on a few times, all of which when we were about to die. "Hyrum, don't!"

The revenant would have him. He didn't have long. Someone else was about to die.

Unless I did something.

I opened my eyes and turned. If I could cause the revenant to decohere and mark me as its target, I could at the very least distract it until we reached the truck.

But I was too late.

The revenant flickered, once a woman with long brown hair, flowing in the air as if underwater. It clung to Hyrum, two hands wrapped around his neck and legs wrapped around his waist as its head dove in. It partially decohered thanks to my observation, skin flickering to the skull beneath as Hyrum's blood spurted into its mouth. But it had its prey, and satisfying that hunger overrode its defense mechanisms.

"TORIS, TURN AROUND!"

I did. I closed my eyes, tears falling down my cheeks.

Hyrum screamed. Then he stopped. Like a radio cut short. But instead of static, I just heard a squelch and then a splatter.

"Keep running!" Kuma shouted.

Every instinct told me to rip off the blindfold and look back, to see the threat coming at me, but I resisted. Just under the roar of the interstate, I could hear Lana crying behind me. But still she held on.

"Over the barrier, now!" Kuma shouted, slowing down. I reached my hand out and felt concrete, then guided Lana in front of me. She let go of my hand and climbed up. I followed, kicking with my foot until I found the road and hefted myself over. "Passcode!" Kuma shouted.

"TYJ77865!"

A door clicked somewhere in front of me, then hissed open. Cold air blasted me with such surprise that I jerked back.

"Inside. Inside! It's right in front of you. Watch your step!"

I reached both hands out until I felt the edge of the door, then lifted my foot until I felt the floor. I pushed myself in. "Lana! Are you in?"

"I'm in!"

"Kuma!" No response. Just the rumble of the cooling systems around us and the roar of the vehicles outside.

"KUMA!"

"Here, brother."

I heard the door hiss closed, and the heat on my face faded. I pulled off the blindfold. We were surrounded by boxes, the container lit only by dim lights near the ceiling. When I breathed, fog puffed out. Kuma sat against the door, chest heaving. I looked to my right, then my left, and found Lana sitting against a box marked "Swordfish."

"Is it safe?" she asked.

"It's safe," I said.

She pulled down her blindfold. "Is Hyrum...Did he..."

I looked to Kuma, who just shook his head and looked up at the ceiling, blinking away tears.

I slammed my fist down on the floor of the container as the truck accelerated, rejoining the rest of the traffic on the interstate.

Another life I should have protected. Another life I failed. Another life lost because of the Wolf, who set us on this path.

This would be the end of that path. It had to be.

It would end in Babylon.

CHAPTER FIFTEEN

ALIS

(Twelve years earlier)

THERE WASN'T ANY BLOOD in my cell.

Either the Mudbrains were thorough cleaners, or they were far more patient interrogators—and likely less effective—than Bastion's. I heard that we'd...that they'd...that we'd intentionally left blood in the cells when its prisoners were either released or...otherwise disposed of. Bastion was skilled in psychological assault just as much as physical.

Maybe the Mudbrains weren't so adept, or maybe this was psychological priming of a different kind. Lull me into complacency. Make me think they may be gentle, friendly even. And maybe then I'd be more likely to divulge information.

Unfortunately for them, I wasn't even sure what I would do.

I'd faced another temptation to flee before they could restrain me. Hold Toris or Kuma or another hostage and demand a craft to leave. Or run for one of the *Dawnbreak*'s starfighters, so close in reach in their cradles. I knew, though, that I wouldn't get far enough, or very far at all. So I'd waited with Toris and Kuma as Admiral Halgard's medical crew checked us and the other passengers, then we followed those passengers through the airlock and to the admiral and her guards. Ahead of us, I saw Halgard shaking hands and patting arms of many grateful passengers, offering the occasional smile that wrinkled the corners of her eyes. As we approached, that smile faded.

She must have already given her soldiers their orders, because they silently stepped up with metal mag-cuffs in their hands. Pushing down my instincts, my analysis of their weak points and the myriad ways I could overpower them, I held out my arms and let them cuff me. For that moment, they were in control, and I had to continue proving that I wasn't a threat.

For now.

Halgard had jerked her head toward a corridor leading out of the hangar, and Toris and Kuma followed, both of them glancing back at me as they went.

"Thank you," I'd said. And as conflicted as I was about everything else, I meant it.

The soldiers then had led me in the opposite direction. Since then, I'd sat on the floor, back and head against the wall, waiting. I looked to the door with every sound, every footstep on the other side, every voice and crackle of the intra-ship comms. But so far, no one had entered, leaving me to listen and wonder and cringe at the dagger in my brain.

Of course, they were likely questioning Kuma and Toris first. They needed more details, a foundation to build the story upon, and to compare my own story against.

And what story would I tell? I couldn't get Ecker's voice out of my throbbing head. I couldn't stop picturing Teah in an inverted mirror to my own experience, in a bloodied and dim and dirty cell, nursing wounds of her own, her black hair a mess and her chin quivering in the way it did when she was holding back tears.

I couldn't consign her to that fate, not when my actions would actively condemn her. Ecker was using me again, forcing me to abandon my principles—*our* principles, the principles of Bastion—to accomplish his goals. What mattered more? My duty to myself and the values I stood for, or my duty to my family? That family had been the reason I joined the war effort in the first place, to protect them and preserve the freedom and prosperity and order that lay at the foundation of our lives. And for Mom. To prevent other families from experiencing the pain we had.

Maybe Ecker was right. Maybe all things had a price, and in this case, my values were the currency.

Footsteps echoed on the other side of the door, and I tensed, ready to...fight back? Comply? Then the steps moved on, and I leaned my head back against the wall with a sigh. The dagger in my brain twisted, and I cringed, gasping. The pain was escalating again, coming in a wave that threatened to black me out. Returning to Bastion would mean they could fix my mindjack. In the agony of the moment, that almost made up my mind for me. The easiest path was certainly clear, paved with the bones of more innocents.

Take a moment, that's what Mom would say. I hadn't thought of her in a while, which was odd in itself. *Think about what's in your control.* I scoffed at that, the sound echoing in the cell. I was in an enemy cell, yet still under the control of a Bastion vice admiral, and my head was in so much pain that consciousness started fraying at the edges, and it became harder to cohere any thought.

Just try.

Was there a middle ground somewhere? I wasn't a Mudbrain, that much was sure. The Pioneers left Earth for a reason, and the society they'd built was thriving. I couldn't abandon my home and my values that easily.

Maybe Ecker was taking orders from someone higher up, but they were desperate. Desperate to win the war. Desperate to protect our people. That wasn't *Bastion*, though, it was a group of people, likely contained to the military, who were going too far. I could return, convince Teah to be a witness of Ecker's plans, and force change, real change, change driven by the people.

My status as a traitor would prove quite the barrier there, but maybe Teah's witness and the witness of other pruners, other soldiers, could overcome that? I could—

I dropped my head and let out another breath. I couldn't. There was no way I'd return Bastion before Ecker captured me or shot me down. He was right: he knew how to threaten, and I knew he could back it up. Halgard likely had a spy among her officers, one who would report back to the vice admiral.

Just try.

More footsteps approached. I tensed. My cell door clicked then slid open. Admiral Halgard stood in the corridor outside, hands clasped behind her back. Two soldiers flanked her, service pistols held secured to mag-holsters on the outside of their thighs. If I moved fast enough, I could probably—

"Want to go for a walk?" Halgard asked.

"Uh…" Not the interrogation tactic I'd been expecting.

"Great." She jerked her head down the corridor then walked away. Her soldiers stayed behind. Right. Not a real question. I pushed myself to my feet and followed. "Alistella Pareides Caliday," Halgard said when I was walking beside her. She stood as tall as I was, which was saying something. Most Earthers didn't have augments like I did. "The Moonbreaker. I don't think we've ever had an Aegis pilot as a guest."

I couldn't help but snort at that. "A guest?"

Halgard raised an eyebrow, but the corner of her mouth perked up in amusement. "Oh, did we forget the chocolate on your pillow? Your complimentary slippers?" She looked back at one of the officers. "You're fired."

"Yes, ma'am."

"Toris and Kuma told me Vice Admiral Ecker threatened you. Your sister."

It wasn't phrased like a question, so I didn't say anything.

"He seems like a peach," she said as we left the brig and walked up a ramp toward another deck. Soldiers stopped to salute until Halgard passed. If this was how she talked to prisoners, how did she talk to her subordinates? She clearly still commanded respect, but how? "Well, you may be the first Aegis pilot, but you're not the first Bastionite in this situation."

"What situation?" I asked, my curiosity moving faster than my aching brain.

Halgard shrugged. "Defecting."

I stopped in the middle of the corridor. "I'm not a defector."

Halgard stopped, rolled her eyes, then jerked her head again in the direction we were headed. "Okay, yes, you look very defiant. Well done." Blushing, I followed. "My sincerest apologies if that's not your preferred term, but, at least according to the captains, you're not the traitor Bastion's making you out to be. I mean, I could have told you that. But you're a different kind of traitor. You disobeyed direct orders, then you boarded an Earther ship, disobeyed orders again, and are now in the enemy Sphere. You clearly didn't do it solely out of self-preservation or survival, otherwise you would have at least turned yourself over. Knowing your VA, you likely wouldn't have disobeyed orders in the first place. The captains said they tried to force you to follow orders anyway? Through your 'jack?"

That wasn't just a question. It was intel gathering. Earth hadn't known that Bastion could do that. *I* hadn't known that Bastion...that we could do that. If I confirmed what happened, I was going against Ecker's orders. I was putting Teah in danger. Could one of the officers behind us be Ecker's spy? Was Bastion hacked into the system? Were they listening through my malfunctioning mindjack?

"I'll take that as a yes," Halgard said.

Shit. Of course she'd take silence as a confirmation. But would Ecker consider it betrayal? Would he know? My heart rate picked up. The dagger twisted. My legs lost some of their strength, and I stumbled in the corridor.

Halgard stopped, and when she looked back at me, the apathetic flippancy on her face had shifted for a moment, softened. I don't think it was quite concern, but at the very least, maybe pity?

"Our medical team should check you out," Halgard said. "You're clearly exhausted, too, and they can help you rest. We may not have mindjack experts, but they can at least check the damage to your brain. Help with the pain."

"I..." It was like being offered water in the desert, almost irresistibly tempting. But I didn't know what was in the water. And I didn't know what other intel I could accidentally give them by allowing them into my head. "No."

Halgard frowned but nodded. "Fair enough, then let's keep going." She started walking. I sighed and followed.

We'd arrived on the next deck up and were passing viewscreens that looked convincingly like windows. They displayed the starboard exterior of the *Dawnbreak*, just like my Aegis had done. We'd turned, putting Luna on that starboard side. I could see the glass and metal tree that was Tranquility, but Mwezi was out of sight. Was Teah still there? Had she been pulled back to the *Fang*? I squinted into the distance, but I couldn't see the Bastion battlecruiser. Surely Ecker would stay close, both to maintain his hold on Mwezi—likely as reinforcements burned from Bastion—and to see what I'd do.

"If you don't feel like answering questions," Halgard continued, "I'll share some thoughts. I don't think you're the fearsome sword of Bastion your propaganda teams made you out to be. I saw footage of what happened on Phobos. I think it was an accident. A terrible accident, one that shouldn't have happened, one that's certainly on your hands, but still an accident. You didn't destroy Stickney, you didn't become the Moonbreaker, to intentionally put us terrorists in line. And I think when you were faced with a similar situation in Mwezi, you hesitated. You tried to do the right thing." She tilted her head back and forth. "Well, as right a thing as any of us can do in this war." She looked at me. "Am I at least getting warm?"

Silence would be agreement again. What did I do?

I shrugged.

"Pah," Halgard scoffed. "I'll take it. Let me assure you of something, Alis. Despite Ecker's threat, he can't touch you here. Nor will he. Like I said, defector or not, you're not the first to experience these feelings. Whether on Earth or Bastion, you join a war for the right reasons, or at least what you think are the right reasons, but then the war challenges everything. That's what war does. It flays you raw, exposes everything, pushes on your nerves and your values and your boundaries. And it takes courage to stand there as you did, flayed and exposed, and stand by what you know is right despite your home going the other direction."

"Not my home."

Halgard looked at me, eyebrows up, clearly surprised I'd said anything. "What?"

"My home isn't going the other direction. Just Ecker. His superiors." I flinched as I said it, looking around as if I'd see a Bastion-embossed camera above me. That'd slipped out, an instinctive defense more for myself than anything else.

The admiral was silent as we passed out of the corridor with the viewscreens and turned up another ramp to a higher deck. I wiped my sweaty hands on my pants. This stress definitely wasn't helping my headache. Maybe I could bargain for something small. Just a painkiller. What could they put in a painkiller? Nanotech? What could they learn from that? Just a little relief, that's all I needed. Relief and sleep. The admiral may have been acting strangely friendly for an interrogation, but there was a strategy in questioning me in that state, in that vulnerability.

We crested the ramp onto the new deck. Lines on the floor pointed to weapons stations, likely for cannons that would be used against another battlecruiser like the *Fang*, or the particle beam weapon that tore through the void. If I sabotaged those, that would win back Ecker. Imagine a defenseless battlecruiser. The *Fang* would tear it to pieces in moments. I could achieve one of the most definitive victories in months.

Except I knew that Halgard's trust was an illusion, a tactic as devious as it was different from Ecker's. I wouldn't make it past the cell block before I was knocked unconscious—or worse.

The dagger twisted.

I gasped out and stopped walking. My vision blurred at the edges, contracting and expanding like the lens of a camera, in time with my breathing. My hands were on my knees, and I stared at the floor, desperate to stay in control. Whatever happened on the *Harriet*, when Kuma said I thrashed about, certainly didn't need to happen in that corridor. I'd likely get shot.

Halgard said something, but the sound just droned without shape or meaning, at the edge of my consciousness. I was dimly aware of my breathing intensifying, spittle on my chin, my bottom jaw jutting out, hot breath hissing between my teeth.

Then the dagger stopped twisting, my vision resolved like fog clearing off a window, and I had control of my breathing again.

"Get her some—"

"No," I snapped, cutting off Halgard. I instinctively flinched, waiting for the violent response that behavior would elicit from Ecker. But no strike came. I pushed off my knees to full height, stumbled a step, and wiped my chin. "I'm fine."

"You're deluded in more way than one, that's what you are," Halgard said. She took a step closer. "Let me ask you something. Did Ecker design that mindjack? Did *he* put it in your head with the capability to one day take control of it? To rob you of the free will that Bastion so fervently claims to champion?"

I didn't answer. There was no need. I knew where she was going. I didn't need to tow her there.

"Do you think they couldn't have designed it to be removed without killing you? Or that a malfunction wouldn't cause you agony? Did Ecker and his superiors make that decision? Would have been impressive. Talk about a long game."

She...no, the mindjacks were one of the greatest innovations of the modern age. The pinnacle of communication, integration, interfacing, convenience, learning, everything.

Reciting that did little to stop the dissonance clashing in my head, like an insect trying to stop two brawling gorillas.

"Did Ecker make you increasingly reliant on the mindjack, priming you, preparing you to be used, exploited? Did—"

"I get your point."

Halgard lifted her chin, satisfied, then kept walking.

She was silent the rest of the way as we walked up one more deck and arrived at a wide door. The officers posted up on its sides as it slid open. Halgard led us in. A table flanked with chairs dominated most of the room, a holoprojector in its center. I knew a briefing room when I saw one.

Seated one on each side of the table were Toris and Kuma. They looked as confused to see me as I was to see them.

Toris immediately moved to stand up. "Look, we're not going to be part of your interrogation. We're not part of your military."

Halgard pushed down on Toris' shoulder, forcing him back into his seat. "You're on my ship, you follow my orders. And you're not here to interrogate. Alis, please sit."

I pulled up a chair at the head of the table, as far away from everyone else as possible. The thought crossed my mind to defy Halgard and insist on standing, but the walk had already tired out my exhausted body more than I'd care to admit.

"She give you anything?" Toris asked as Halgard walked around the other side of the table and started tapping into the holoprojector controls. "Hand over the Death Star plans?"

I rolled my eyes at the hundreds-year-old idiom. Halgard must not have found it amusing, either, because she didn't respond.

The holoprojector started spinning up, humming with a light vibration that rippled down the table. "Alis," Halgard said. "As I said, I know you're in an impossible situation. And your family being involved doesn't help. But I pushed you on the mindjack issue to show you that this isn't the power trip of a few

Bastion military officers." She put her hands on the table and leaned forward. "I know you're thrown off that you're not in chains against a torture rack. Every former Bastionite is. I don't want you to think it's out of kindness. We operate differently here because we believe the way to stop this war isn't through subjugation. There's enough of that to go around. Rather than force you to tell us what we need to know, which we're never really sure we can trust, I want to help you along the journey you already started yourself."

A way to stop the war. Wasn't that what we all wanted? Even Bastion? Their method was stopping the war by winning it. After all, an end wasn't enough, it had to be a lasting end, one where we were secure. Safe. Ecker had just shown in Mwezi that our security superseded the security of all others, sovereign or not.

But...that was just Ecker. It had to be just Ecker.

"It's not about subjugation," I said, my thoughts spilling out. "For Bastion. It's about security, prosperity for future generations."

"At the expense of everyone else," Toris said without turning around.

I ground my teeth together, glaring at the back of his head.

"You're starting to see it," Halgard said. "But a lifetime of brainwashing and propaganda makes that cognitive dissonance one hell of a challenge to work through." She pushed off the table and started pacing her end of the room. "Bastion is a system designed to exploit its people for the gain of those in power. It's that simple. From your mindjacks to your military to your corporate structures to your media to the stories you tell from birth. Everything is meant to keep you in check, to give you the illusion of freedom and prosperity. I could give you a thousand examples like your mindjack. You have it implanted at birth—not your choice—and then it's not just a convenience, not just an innovation, it's a requirement to participate in society. Because of that, you become as reliant on it as any muscle." She held a hand out to me. "And now you're seeing the other side, the consequences, their true purpose. We're getting reports of similar hacking throughout the Spheres. Abnormal behavior, all in Bastion's favor, all from people with mindjacks. And this moment may be the worst of it, but they've used it against you, to keep you in place, in subtler ways, too. That's just one. One example. That's why I want to help you. You're a victim. You're also a perpetrator. You've fought and killed Earthers—and your own people—in Bastion's name, and there's no excuse for that. You will face justice. But in the meantime, I can stop you from harming your people. I think you want that, too. And one day, you'll want to face justice."

There were so many places I wanted to challenge her that it was hard to pick one to start. I wouldn't argue against the horror of what Ecker had done, but it was still a broad assumption to suggest that was the mindjack's purpose from the start. It would be far from the first time humans used an otherwise harmless innovation for evil. I could also point out that Halgard, Toris, Kuma, and every other Earther on that ship were raised with equally strong biases of a different kind. They were raised—likely out of a cultural envy—believing all manner of negative things about our technology, especially mindjacks. Her opinions were as shaded as mine. Of course, even if I cared to share those feelings, I would have stayed silent.

When I didn't respond, Halgard continued, clearly not phased by my continued defiance. "All right, we'll take a different approach. Why are you fighting in the war?"

I bristled, a wave of conflicting emotions rising at the question. "That's none of your business." Then, as anger crested above the other emotions, I added, "And it's not a road you want to go down if you want my help."

"I would put money on one of two reasons," Halgard said, clearly not taking my advice. "Either because of propaganda—you were told the war machine needed you, all to restore order and security and prosperity and other buzzwords—or because of love. Love of nation, love of family, love of lover. One of the above. And for all your repeating the same old propaganda points, I think you're in this for love. Or maybe a mixture of the two. Maybe you lost someone, and you want to prevent that from happening again. That's the story of everyone else in this room."

"Don't bring us into this," Toris said.

Halgard ignored him. "This war's gone on long enough that now we've got entire generations who've lost someone. Parents. Aunts. Uncles. Siblings. They're being raised on hate, and that hate becomes a lens to experience the world. Then everything that happens just validates and doubles down on that hate. Makes Bastion's propaganda machine that much more efficient at controlling you."

"I'm not in this war because of propaganda," I said. I wouldn't let her insult all I'd sacrificed like that. "You killed my mom." Then I clamped my mouth shut. A different pressure mounted in my head, not the pain of the mindjack malfunction, but a different kind, one that clutched closed around my heart at the same time.

I expected Halgard to make some joke about winning her bet, but she surprised me yet again by nodding solemnly. "Soldier?"

"No. An innocent," I spat, wanting every word to hurt, knowing it would likely bounce off Halgard's shell. "A civilian."

Halgard nodded again. "That makes sense."

"What does."

"Why you're so against doing the same. Not all soldiers can distinguish at a certain point. On either side. You're unique in that way. So it's revenge?"

I was silent. Partially because I'd said enough already, and partially because I'd been asking myself similar questions for years. At first, I thought it was revenge. Sparked in myself from the kindling of grief, but fueled by my father. When I grew up and actually enlisted, though, those feelings evolved. The fire certainly still burned, eternal embers in the back of my mind, but around those embers I'd built the foundation of higher ideals. Similar to the ones Halgard mentioned, but she didn't need to know that. But I still had questions that a psychologist would love to unpack. Did I think winning the war would help our grief? That we could be a closer family? Did I hope...was I more comfortable with the idea of death because it'd be an escape from everything?

Like I said, a path they—and I—didn't want to go down.

"Fine. I'll stop prying," Halgard said. "And don't worry, I'm almost done trying to convince you. Whatever your reason, you're clearly starting to see that wanton killing and manipulation doesn't solve the problem. It just leads to the same fates that brought us into the war in the first place, culling the same tragedies for new families and new generations. A cycle, an ouroboros. Again, pick your metaphor. But like I said. There's another way to end it all."

"So what's this other way?" I asked, skepticism honing my tone.

"Empathy."

Before I could react, a footstep dropped on the ground behind me, and something cold slid down around my head. A metal ring. I instantly tried to stand up, but a hand held me down. Toris and Kuma stared at me, Kuma's mouth hanging open and Toris glaring at whoever was holding me down, likely one of Halgard's officers.

"Done with the act, huh?" I asked. "Done pretending you're better than us?"

"I'm just done wasting time," Halgard said. "Here and in this endless war. You're going to help me stop it, and you're going to make that choice yourself."

"I don't feel like I have much agency right now," I said through clenched teeth. "I..." And then I stopped, noticing something. It took a moment to realize what: the pain. The dagger. It was gone, pulled out of my brain.

That didn't make me feel any better.

"What are you doing?" I asked, trying to stand up again only to be forced back down. Those guys had to be augmented. I should have easily overpowered any Mudbrain, even in my weakened state. "I told you I didn't want treatment. Get out of my—"

Halgard looked genuinely surprised. "Your pain disappeared? Interesting. You're welcome, I guess. That means your 'jack must not be totally dead, just punishing you. Anyway. Empathy. It's a quality that's been gradually culled from Bastion society, like some unnatural selection. Centuries of greedy, selfish individualism, desperate competition, and fearmongering have narrowed your view like blinders on a horse." She waved her hand and shook her head. "I'm going to stop using similes. I'm getting lazy. The point is, everything, everyone is a stepping stone, to the next award, the next promotion, the next victory. To security and prosperity and order. Because for those systems to work, there has to be someone who gets stepped on and left behind, or in your case, left beneath the Shades. So you double down in othering them, pushing them into the margins and then faulting them for being there. Over time, you start to see them as less valued, or worse. You start to forget they're people. You give them names. Like Mudbrain. And you start to lose your ability to understand them. That's when things fall apart."

I scoffed, anger heating up my face. Defensiveness from Halgard's relentless, endless attacks. Frustration at the dissonance I felt, the resonance in parts of me to her words. And beneath it all a helplessness that went against everything I was supposed to be. "You think you know it all, don't you. How many have you had killed, Admiral? What about my mom? What about Rubicon Station? The *Jefferson* Massacre? Mudbrains—Earthers. You think we act superior, but your moral posturing is even worse. You're hypocrites."

"War certainly isn't fought by saints, I'll give you that," Halgard said. "But you have to remember, every life we take is in defense of our home. Yours is in defense of manufactured values, of a pride that will be Bastion's end. It all started in the Belt Rush, when our shared success became a threat. And it'll end at Bastion. I promise you that." She tapped a few commands into her console.

"That's...the Belt's ours. It's..." Something was starting to tickle the back of my mind, jumbling thoughts, dispersing them into smoke. My stomach churned, and my mouth went dry. "What...what are you doing to me?"

The lights in the room dimmed, and the holoprojector burst to life, creating a sphere in the center of the room, bathing all our faces in light. The view was shaky. Someone running. Smoke and fire dominated their view. The very ground around them burned, the earth charred, old flora smoking from burning embers.

Not flora, the path to the library. *The library where Dad sat and read to me when the birds chirped in early spring and Mom talked about how it was finally cooling down and we laughed and Nieve held my hand because she was scared of the dog that walked by.*

I shook my head, the thoughts coming as if they were my own, not totally unlike when Ecker tried to hack me. I reached up again to grab the ring on my head.

"Cuff her," Halgard commanded. All friendliness—if it had ever been that—gone. Her officers forced mag-cuffs around my wrists and connected them to my chair. I pulled with all my strength, muscles clenching and tendons pressing against my skin, but they didn't move.

In the projection, the smoke was consuming, billowing and blowing out of view to the left. The viewer looked up for a moment. A flaming mass hurtled through the sky in the distance, leaving a tail of smoke behind it as it burned through the atmosphere.

Mommy talked about this. About the people coming from the sky. They're going to kill us all. But not them. Not them not them not them not them please not them

"Stop."

Out of the smoke resolved a building, or rather, the remnants of a building. It was little more than a shell, a husk, broken and burning and

Where are they, they must have gotten out. They had to have gotten out.

I looked at Toris and Kuma, but they just had the video footage. They weren't experiencing what I was, this jumble of someone else's panicked thoughts. Not just their thoughts. Halgard's device was somehow interfacing with my mind-jack—which I thought was totally inoperable—and making me...feel. "Fear" was too small a word. "Terror" too insignificant. "Horror" just syllables. I could throw up, and my chest ached with such pain that I thought I may have been having a heart attack, a malady that my mods should have prevented.

And there, in the back of my mind, a void, deeper and more all-consuming than space itself. The closer this person came to their...to that building, the more they felt like they were sliding toward that void, scrabbling through a steep, slick, sand to get out, to get away, to hold onto the hope that

They're here. They have to be here. They—

"MOMMY!" shouted a child through the holoprojector so loud that the three of us at the table jumped. Sobs cracked their broken voice "DADDY! NIEVE!"

The stranger ran into the wreckage. It was still hot, and I felt it, my sweat glands responding as if I were really there, instantly drenching my clothes. I could smell the smoke, could feel it grasping my lungs with ghastly fingers. I coughed. Toris looked at me with some clash of concern and contempt.

The child grabbed pieces of burning wood, ignoring the pain that made me gasp and look at my hand to convince myself it wasn't real, and throwing them out of the way. They looked around frantically, so quickly that the holofeed blurred in its struggle to keep up.

"MOMMY! DADDYHEHEHE!" The second name devolved into a sob as the child fell to their knees in their burning home. My throat burned from the smoke and screaming. Then, out of the corner of their eye, the child noticed something, a charred hand, sticking out from under a beam.

No no no no no no no no then their thoughts congealed into a rush, a blur, a static, a numbness as they pushed and pulled and tossed burning wreckage until they uncovered two shapes, one smaller and one larger, husks as charred as the rest of the house.

The child screamed, a guttural, animal sound that tore at my throat. They scrambled like a mad animal, trying to move debris even as their muscles gave out and the skin peeled off their burned hands. The fire was closing in. The heat had me breathing quick, chest heaving, loud enough that Kuma glanced over in concern, then looked to Halgard, then back to the projection. He was pale, even in the light of the hologram. Maybe he was going to throw up, too.

Then, somewhere between the sobs and the scrambling, the child fell back into the void. I couldn't find words to describe that feeling. It was like something deep inside, like their soul, imploded, collapsed in on itself from too much pressure.

Then, a flash of realization.

Nieve. Nieve isn't there. Nieve. "NIEVE!"

Like a grappling hook, that modicum of hope kept the child from falling completely back into that void.

A sound to the child's left, the crackle of someone moving across the charred remains. The child tore their gaze from their parents. Nieve was holding her arm, the soot dying her blonde hair gray. She was sobbing, the tears running trails down her dirty cheeks. The child scrambled away from the flames, shock keeping them from feeling the pain, and pulled their sister into their arms.

Behind, their home burned, and a numbness settled into the child, one that I felt, too.

Then it stopped. The hologram, in a snap, reverted to plain white light, and the end of the thoughts made me feel like I'd fallen into a void, too.

"Get. This. Off. Me." I said through gritted teeth. Sweat dripped from my hair down my forehead.

"That was Bastion's second mass driver attack on Earth," Halgard said. "Only a few weeks ago. Do you know what preceded it?"

I couldn't have responded if I wanted to, though I knew the answer.

"Stickney. Your heroic efforts there. This was our punishment for the death of your colony. Bastion distracted our fleet with another attack, then broke through our defenses and launched tungsten rods at innocent civilians. Defenseless cities. People who had nothing to do with Stickney, or the conflict for the Belt, people with families to protect, just like you. This was just one family amid thousands. Hundreds of thousands." She leaned forward, hands on the table and venom in her tone. "Because. Of. You."

I stared back at Halgard, still catching my breath. I was crying, but I honestly couldn't tell if they were my tears or the child's. Or both.

"I didn't...I didn't send those ships," I eventually said, my walls starting to crumble even as my rage grew. They may not like what happened when those walls came down completely. "I didn't agree with that. It was a dis..." I swallowed, cringing at the pain lingering in my throat. "A disproportionate response."

"You 'didn't. Agree.'" Halgard emphasized each of my words. "It was a 'disproportionate. Response.' And did that make you feel better? As you accepted your award and sailed for Luna? Hollow words from a hollow heart. Don't worry. We'll fill it for you." She typed into the holoprojector's console.

"No, please."

"Admiral," Kuma said, but Halgard ignored him.

"Please," I begged, embarrassed if Ecker or his spies were seeing this but unable to control it. I'd rather be starved, sliced open. I'd rather have the pain of my malfunctioning mindjack back and dialed up a hundredfold. I'd rather feel the burning of that home than that child's loss. They took something of mine on their way down, something that remained lost even as the pain from the transferred injuries faded. Another rock from an eroding cliff face, dropping into the ocean. "Please. I know loss. I lost my mother." At that thought, some of my pain transformed into anger. "And that was because of you. Let's put you in this chair. Hypocrite." I spat on the table.

Halgard smiled. The beast smiled, though it never reached her eyes. "Finally, some truth. Some emotion. I'll take that as progress. So let's follow this path a little further."

"I'll kill you," I snarled, my tongue moving faster than my mind. Then, as Halgard typed more commands in and the holoprojector spun, the rationality caught up: "Please. Please." I almost asked what they wanted from me, what I could give them to just get thrown back in my cell. But Teah. I'd have to face the pain of the one I loved most dying *because of me*, in a more direct way than even the mass driver assault. When that occurred to me, after experiencing that stranger's loss, the pain of losing Teah terrified me more than further torture. The admiral had made a mistake. So I clamped my mouth shut and glared at Halgard.

So, for Teah, I endured.

Chapter Sixteen

Toris

No one said a word for at least an hour. Shock, guilt, anger, exhaustion, all of it held our tongues to varying degrees. Kuma tried to break the silence a few times, checking on Lana, checking on me, but the conversation always evaporated as quickly as our breath in that cold storage container. In the silence, sleep almost took me, but I always shook myself out of it. Sleep would be an escape, and I couldn't escape that moment, no matter how exhausted I was.

My mind was careening down a steep, rocky path, veering from one guilt, one worry, one frustration to the next, all without prompting, a torturous flow of consciousness. I saw Cixin, smiling and laughing in the Hollows, then bleeding and still in the exact same spot. I thought about my last day with Mom and Dad, weeks before I failed them, too, the day I was too late.

After that hour, I finally looked up, if only to stop my own spiral, and looked at Lana. She sat across from me but turned away, her head resting on a crate of fish. Her tears had dried, but the area around her eyes was still swollen. She breathed in deep and stared ahead, but really stared at nothing.

"Where are you going?" I asked, my voice cracking.

Lana blinked, then she slowly turned toward me. "What?"

"Where are you headed? Are you going into Babylon? Or somewhere else?"

"Oh. I...yeah." She sniffed.

This was going about as well as Kuma's attempts. I glanced at him. He shrugged.

"'Yeah' as in Babylon?"

"Mm hm."

I bit back wondering why you'd run away from Bastion only to go to the one place on Earth most like Bastion. "Do you have family there? Friends?"

She nodded.

I sighed. That line of questioning clearly wasn't going anywhere, so I tried a more direct approach. I had to help at least someone that day.

"Look, I won't ask if you're okay, because none of us are. I'm sure your head's spinning. I'm sure you're second-guessing everything, wondering if you should have left Bastion in the first place, wondering if it was worth it. Am I getting close?"

She sniffed again, but this time she turned and looked at me. I took that as an affirmative. At least close enough to one.

"You made the right choice," I said. "Earth has its scars, and sometimes those scars are dangerous. Turns out that's the only way to get close to utopia. It needs to get bad enough that everyone's left with one choice: change course or slam into the cliff. We changed course, and we're all better for it. I promise, you'll see. You'll be happy, because here you can pursue your own path toward happiness, without all the barriers Bastion puts in your way." I paused, feeling like I was starting to wax philosophical. I smirked, thinking of early conversations with Alis. Then the smirk fell as I thought of Alis alone, guilty, in pain in Babylon. I turned my attention back to Lana. "Why did you leave?"

Lana turned away, and at first I thought she wouldn't respond, but then, in a quiet voice, she said, "Because we played God." Her voice went up in pitch a little, her eyebrows rising, too, as if she were mocking what she was saying.

"What?"

She snorted a little. "It's what people would say in the Shades, after the Iridesca Loop fell."

Kuma looked at me. I didn't look at him. Just swallowed blockage in my throat, the tightness in my chest. I didn't say anything else, just listened.

"We all knew it was Earth, but when the solar winds came and knocked out what little technology we had there, when people started getting sick, it started feeling more like divine punishment. It's what happens when you start playing with things like magnetic fields and resurrecting dead planets."

"But..." I licked my dry lips and swallowed again, choosing my words carefully. "The Battle of the Loop was ten years ago."

"The Iridesca Loop was the greatest engineering feat of humankind. It took thirty years to build, and that was with almost all of Bastion's resources going toward it. But after the war, when all the supply chains had been tied up in the conflict, it took a long time to untie them. And we had less access to the Belt than we'd had before. Almost sparked another war to get that access back." She sat up straighter, the conversation bringing some life back into her, taking her thoughts away from Hyrum and the revenants.

I'd rather be thinking about them.

"They're working on it, but it's...the damage was done, for most of us. We played God, and the Iridesca Loop was our Tower of Babel. We watched for solar flare patterns more closely than we did the weather." She shrugged. "Crops died, water sources were poisoned, and in trying to fix those issues, everything became more expensive. Food, clothes, everything. It was bad enough in the Shades, but...people lost homes, starved to death, and without protection from the sun, the radiation..." She swallowed, and I really wished I hadn't asked. "People died. Some started calling it the Graves instead. We...they couldn't afford basic treatment, much less augments. First, our son. Then my husband." I saw her eyes wet with tears. She sniffed and turned away. "I promised him I'd leave. I promised him I'd find a better life. I thought it'd be here."

Her child. Her husband. And who knew how many others. After the Battle, after the war ended, we didn't hear any reports. We'd cut ourselves off.

I didn't know. I couldn't have known.

In the back of my head, a tiny voice that I'd pushed down for ten years whispered: *But you did. And you did it anyway.*

To end the war. To prevent even more lives from being lost. They were Bastion, they'd recover more quickly than any other society, faster than we would have. It was better than what they'd done, better than orbital bombardment. The Grave—the Shades would have been glass. It ended the war. It saved Alis.

But her child...

Her husband.

"I'm so sorry," Kuma said, filling in the silence that I left in Lana's wake. "I...I lost a child, too, because of the war." I looked up at Kuma, my eyes brimming with tears. "That's the thing with war, isn't it? No matter who wins, we all lose. I'm sorry."

Lana was silent, but then she nodded and offered a small flash of a smile.

"But Toris is right," Kuma said. "It may not seem like it now, but your better life is here. All the systems that kept you under the Shades, they don't exist here." He leaned his head from side to side, reconsidering. "Except a little in Babylon, so you may want to reconsider there. You just had bad luck running into us. He's cursed." He jerked his head toward me.

"What do you mean?" Lana asked, eyebrows rising, clearly not seeing Kuma's joke for what it was.

"It's a dumb joke," I said, shooting Kuma a look. I did not need to go into it. Not then.

How could I talk about Alis, about my struggles, when...her child. Her husband.

"Well," Lana said. "Joke or not, I think you're in good company." Moving on, and clearly in a slightly better state despite the gravity of her story, Lana continued. "What's wrong with Babylon? Isn't it the New Cradle of Civilization? Everyone on Farstead—and even back home—talked about how great it was."

"You know how Bastion bragged about its prosperity and order while you starved under the Shades?" I responded with more of an edge than I intended, cutting through the cloud of guilt that was growing denser with every moment. I couldn't let it consume me. Deal with the Wolf, then deal with the guilt.

Lana stared at me with a straight face, my comment hitting too close to home.

"Sorry," I said. "It's just...it's a narrative. The founders of Babylon were convinced they had it figured out, the ideal society. When the Pioneers were shaping Bastion and the rest of Earth was moving past the ideals and systems of the past, the people of Babylon felt like they found the perfect medium. So they built Babylon around the skeleton of an older city, geoengineered the land around it, and slapped that title on it. But you know what most people call it around here? Little Bastion. I can't speak for the intentions of the founders, but the same exploitation and division and oppression that we thought Bastion took with them took root. It's run by corporations, the only ones left on Earth. Opportunists who filled in the vacuum left by the Exodus. It's got its perks, sure, but there's a darkness to that city. You'll see."

"But I thought you couldn't have corporations on Earth? Your Gaia Compact says that."

I nodded. "The Compact is a social contract more than it's a set of laws. Babylon chose not to follow it, one of maybe three or four cities on the planet that don't. They face the same consequences of any community that doesn't abide by the Compact; we don't trade with them, don't support them in really any way. They're just self-sustaining enough to make it work. Plus, they established their foothold before the Compact was really final, so they're an odd case."

"You said you have family there?" Kuma asked, nudging Lana further along.

"My husband's family, actually," she said. "I...he asked me to bring something to them." Then she went quiet and blew into her hands to warm them up.

"And after you find them? Do you plan on staying?" Kuma prodded.

Lana hesitated, mind clearly elsewhere, then nodded. "Probably. There's opportunity there. I'm an engineer, and I saw a bunch of advertisements on Farstead for work in Babylon. Seems like a good place to establish myself."

"You...I mean, that's great," Kuma said, "but you don't have to work. You could go anywhere in the world, share your skills with any community you choose. Engineers are rare these days. You could even teach. You could do a lot of good."

"And I wouldn't do good in Babylon?"

Kuma squinted and waved his hand in a so-so gesture. A puff of breath jetted out his nose.

"You'd do good for a corporation," I said. "Maybe it wouldn't be as bad as Bastion, but it wouldn't be the freedom and purpose of contributing to a community."

Lana tilted her head, frowning skeptically. "No disrespect to your experiment you've got going on, but I left Bastion because I wasn't getting compensated fairly for my work. Now you're telling me to just give it away?"

That almost got me to smile, genuinely, this conversation reminding me again of when I was getting to know Alis. "You're right, you weren't getting compensated fairly, but the problem wasn't just the money, right? That's only a tiny part of a much larger system, one designed to make you reliant on that compensation while also exploiting you so that compensation would never be enough."

"So the solution's that no one gets compensated for anything?"

Kuma shook his head. "The solution's rethinking what value means. What worth means. And why we do things in the first place. Why did you become an engineer?" He waved his hand dismissively. "Other than the money part."

"The money's a big part of it."

Kuma chuckled.

"But...it was solving problems." She released her hold on her legs and lay them flat against the floor of the freezing storage container. "When I was younger, I thought it was about taking things apart to understand how they worked, but that was just the surface. I wanted to understand how they solved problems." She smiled a little. "My first project was finding a way to get us some cleaner water from above the Shades. I built a whole system that went straight to our apartment." Her smile fell. "Until they found and destroyed it. Got arrested for that one."

"Exactly!" Kuma exclaimed. "You were punished for innovating. You didn't follow the right channels or pay the right people, so your work wasn't seen as valuable. You didn't get paid for that—the opposite, really—but you were still smiling about it. There was worth in solving the problem, and there was worth in the purpose you found in it, right?"

Lana raised another skeptical eyebrow, but there was a slight smile on her lips. "Is everyone on Earth this philosophical?" Kuma shrugged. I nodded. "But I was still, technically, stealing. I was diverting water that others were paying for in other parts of the city."

"Did they still get water?" I asked.

"Well, yeah."

"And clean water's essential. So why are their lives worth more than yours just because they can afford the clean water?"

Lana opened her mouth, then she closed it again. "Look, you don't have to convince me that Bastion's doing it wrong. I'm just not convinced you're doing it right. There's a spectrum to all this. You could give people access to clean water and still compensate them for the work they do."

"Sure," Kuma said. "But then power dynamics come into play. Who compensates whom? And how are those people compensated, and what incentives do they have to actually compensate fairly? It's a spiderweb of influences and powers, and we're just the," he wiggled his fingers, "little flies that get stuck in it, waiting to be eaten."

"That's dark."

"But it's what happened," I said. "It's what happened to the Earth, it's what started the Solar Gulf War, it's what's happening in Babylon, and it's what's slowly strangling Bastion. It has from the start. They're just too stubborn to let go, just like humanity was until their hands were shattered to pieces by their own faults."

"So I should just do everything for free? Give everyone the efforts of my labor? Sounds like communism to me."

I chuckled. "Good ol' Bastion propaganda machine is still going strong. Communism requires a central government to redistribute wealth. We don't have that. Political philosophers and scientists have tried to characterize," I gestured in a circle over my head, encompassing the whole Earth, "this, but they argue about the best way to go about it. Some called it anarcho-communalism—not *communism*, *communalism*—but anarchy has connotations people don't love. And it's not totally accurate. Anarchy assumes disorder, but we have order, it's just not order determined by some authoritative force. It's an order built on each other. Relying on each other. Trusting each other. Serving each other. Providing for each other."

Lana's lips were pursed, eyes a little narrowed, clearly skeptical but without anything explicit to challenge. I'd seen similar faces on most Bastionites—Alis included—it was the moment they couldn't quite deny the merits of what we'd built, but they still couldn't totally accept it, either.

"But you don't totally trust each other," Lana eventually said. "Babylon are your neighbors, your people. Shouldn't you care about their wellbeing, their success, even if they decide to live by different values? You said yourself it wasn't as bad as Bastion." She brushed a lock of black hair out of her face and looked at me. "I don't think you're as trusting, as selfless, as caring as you think you are. You create trust in groups by fostering distrust of other groups. Babylon. Bastion. They're still people you should care for all the same, aren't they?"

I opened my mouth, then closed it, realizing I was likely making the same face that Lana had been making only a moment before. "Now who sounds like a philosopher?"

Lana chuckled and shook her head.

"It's a good point," Kuma said with a shrug, but he couldn't offer any more rebuttal than I could.

Lana sighed and pushed herself to her feet, twisting back and forth, her back popping in a few places. She was a different person from only minutes before. I didn't love the new mixture of conflicting emotions tumbling between my mind and heart, but at least she was in a better state.

"Why are you going to Babylon? If you hate it so much." Lana eventually asked, leaning her shoulder against a container marked "Oysters."

"Huh?" I asked, pushing myself to my feet as well. "Oh, we're just making sure you get there safe." I glanced at Kuma. He stood up, too, and shrugged a shoulder. Eager to get out of that conversation, I added, "Speaking of which, how close are we?"

Kuma turned and tapped on a screen mounted on the wall. "Oh, we're almost there. Just got out of the Glassfields." He looked at Lana. "Do you want to see something cool?" He bounced his eyebrows up and down.

I rolled my eyes. "It's not cool. It's excessive."

Kuma dismissed me with a wave before gesturing for Lana to come closer. I stepped up behind them.

The screen displayed camera footage from outside the storage container we rode in. Gradually, the desert was giving way to greenery, cracked rock to grass and sagebrush to flowered shrubs. Kuma panned the cameras over, and Lana sucked in a breath.

Babylon sprouted from the desert, spires of multicolored metal, the tallest of which ran in a strip down its center. Massive advertisements projected on the sides of the buildings, in between which flitted myriad sizes and shapes of flying and hovering craft. Clusters of inflated wind turbines hung around the city, tethered to the buildings below, similar to Orilla del Angel, but so much greater in number. At the edge of the city, where the buildings tapered down in height like the foothills of a solitary mountain, was a small spaceport. While most of Earth used the much more environmentally friendly Dandelion, Babylon still launched starships from the surface. It may have been faster, but it was a waste of fuel, and much of that fuel ended up dumped in a different form into the atmosphere. As we watched, a bulky cargo carrier, likely bound for Luna, fired its thrusters and took to the sky just as a sleek corvette swept in from the heavens and fired its landing repulsors before settling down.

Just as its ancient inspiration, Babylon was flanked by two rivers, their waters shimmering in the bright sun. Trees, grassy fields, and parks lined the rivers. It was hard not to admire the beauty, the majesty, the human ingenuity and defiance in shaping that harsh desert. But that ingenuity had a price.

We passed over a bridge that crossed the New Euphrates River, and our storage container slowed down. Kuma pulled up a progress map underneath our view of the outside. He pointed to a point another mile or so ahead. "This is where we'll jump off. The traffic's slowing down because some shipments are diverting into the city, but this container's headed further inland. So we'll need to jump off closer to the platform."

Lana frowned and looked up at Kuma. "I thought you guys weren't getting off."

I glared at Kuma.

"Oh, right," he said. "I just meant that we'll make sure you get off and into the city safely."

Lana stared up at Kuma, then looked at me, then back to Kuma before saying, "You guys are shit liars."

"It's true," I said. "Plus, we need to find another way back. I'm not going back in this." I looked around the container as I blew out a puffy breath. "And we need to get some incident reports out, let people know to take extra precaution for revenants, and to...to let the other passengers' families know what happened."

"Ah," Lana said, the weight of that experience returning as she looked down at the ground. "I...what do you even say? Has anyone died on your watch before?"

I opened my mouth, but the sigh that came out carried no words.

"Yes," Kuma answered for the both of us.

"Do you know where your husband's family lives?" I asked to quickly change the subject.

"Maybe? I was hoping to find a way to contact them." She frowned, realizing something. "How do you all communicate without mindjacks? Don't tell me you still use the internet or phones or something."

"We have local networks," Kuma said. "Something just relegated to communities, sometimes to regions. We don't really trust global networks or connectivity. Again, got burned too many times. Babylon has a network for the city, though. We can help you find your family."

I opened my mouth to protest, but before I could, Lana spoke: "No, that's..." She avoided our eyes, turning to look out at the city instead. "It's something I should do alone." I felt a twang of guilt, wondering if she sensed my urgency, but I understood if she wanted to be alone. We should have respected that.

"Don't worry," Kuma said. "We're not going to intrude. The least we can do is make sure you get there safely." He cringed. "More safely than we got you here. We know the city."

"I appreciate that," Lana said. She took a deep breath and stuck her shaking hand in her pocket. "But I need to do it alone. I need to be alone. I'll be alone afterward; it's good for me to learn to navigate, uh, all this."

"You don't have to be alone. Afterward, I mean."

"Kuma," I said, gentle warning in my tone. I knew where he was going.

"There's plenty of room in Orilla," he continued as if I hadn't said a word. Not that he listened, anyway. He put his hands up. "Just a thought. No pressure. We know this is a lot."

I was about to respond, but before I could, Kuma looked at me and kept going. "We'll at least help you find your way. That's *all*." He raised his eyebrows at me as he emphasized that last word. "I'll send the reports on the way in. And, Toris, you can start looking for...our way home. We're going to do it smart, right?" He widened his eyes in a way that made him look like he was on just the edge of insanity.

"Right," I grumbled. I doubted it'd be long before Carivant and his lackeys were on our tail. I may not have had a chance to do something stupid. But I didn't need to say that.

"Is that okay with you?" Kuma asked, looking at Lana.

She sniffed, and I thought she may have been on the verge of tears. But then she blinked, set her jaw, and turned to us. "Yeah. Yeah, if you can show me the way. Thank you."

And as much as I loved Kuma for his drive to both back me up and help Lana, there was no way I was waiting for either of them if I got a lead on Alis. We'd already taken too long getting to Babylon. I was ready to burst out of that container like a racer off the starting line and tear down the city to find her. Before the Wolf got her hurt. Or worse.

So, for now, all Kuma needed was "Right."

The container rolled to a stop. Kuma glanced at the progress map. "Close enough. Are you ready?" he asked Lana with a soft smile.

"Ready to get out of this freezer? Hell yes. To get lost in that city, no."

"It's not as scary as he makes it sound," Kuma said. Then, after a second thought, he tilted his head and added, "Let's just stick together."

Kuma pulled down on the lever beside the container doors, and they slid open, blinding us with bright sunlight and warmth. Fog puffed out of the container into the air outside. As the light resolved into reality, I saw a few people on the nearby boarding platform staring at us with confusion.

We'd stopped a few rows of vehicles away from the boarding platform, so we hopped down and wound our way through the jammed traffic to the stone platform's steps. Kuma nodded to the people staring at us, frost evaporating to mist off our bodies.

A road ran parallel to a maglev line that led under stone and metal arches toward the city. It rose like a mountain, its spires blocking out the sun, vehicles flying around the buildings like flies over a carcass. The ground rumbled as a starship took off from the spaceport. The air had a strange cocktail of smells, ozone from the port, water from the rivers, and the perfume of the flowers. It'd grown since the last time I'd been there, a predator with a few extra scars, another layer of muscle.

Alis was in there. I could feel it in a way I couldn't explain.

"I'm almost there," I whispered, hoping that, somewhere in that steelscape, Alis could feel me, too.

CHAPTER SEVENTEEN

ALIS

(Twelve years earlier)

I SHOULD HAVE RETURNED to Ecker.

I understood why there wasn't any blood in the *Dawnbreak*'s cell. Admiral Halgard didn't need to resort to beating anyone. Their empathy torture was far worse. In the three days following the first time they synced that evil machine to my mindjack, I'd felt families burn and die. I'd died myself once or twice.

And the empathy wasn't always related to death, no. War was full of a tapestry of losses, Halgard had said. So she put me through the loss of security and personal safety as I experienced a woman on the conquered Horizon Dawn station falling victim to a pair of its male conquerors. I found myself scrubbing my skin raw without realizing it in the restroom afterward. I experienced the slow suffering of starvation and the mental unraveling, the emotional cascade that followed. I had my children taken away from me, took beatings for existing in the wrong place at the wrong time, and felt the sanity-strangling of PTSD after somehow escaping three separate orbital bombardments—and wishing I'd been caught in the last. I learned each victim had carried a mindjack, their entire lived experience translated into data and shoved into my head. Into my soul.

The joke was on Halgard, though, because every experience, every attempt at forcing me to feel empathy, only made me want to slap that device on her head and make her feel it all until she was drooling in the chair. She didn't need to prove there was darkness to war, that there were terrible people who'd found their way into the military. But as I shouted at Halgard two sessions before, she was only showing me a curated selection. I could pull similar experiences from Bastionites suffering at the hands and weapons of Earthers. I was sure of that. War was a key that unlocked the deepest, darkest, most deranged aspects of humanity. Of course I wanted to weep at the suffering of the people whose memories I experienced—and I frequently did, in the quiet of my cell and in the dark of ship-night. Of course I would prevent all of it if I could, on both sides. But Bastion was still my home, and Halgard hadn't yet convinced me otherwise. If anything, she'd convinced me that this war needed to end more than ever, but that I certainly didn't want her to be the victor.

So did that mean I followed Ecker's orders? Saved Teah and ended the war, ended all this suffering, at the same time?

If Halgard pushed me any further, I might just break. And she'd be the one picking shrapnel out of her ship.

On the fourth day, when I woke up, I screamed. *I was in Officer Logan's quarters on Horizon Dawn, but I didn't remember getting there. Again. My dress was torn, my head still swimming. I looked for a clock and...*

The room was empty. I was in my cell in the *Dawnbreak*. Wiping a tear from my cheek, I pushed myself to my feet. My hands quivered, so I clenched them into fists. The dagger twisted in my brain, making me stagger until my shoulder knocked into the wall. Halgard's empathy torture made the malfunctioning mindjack pain subside for a time, but when the pain returned, it was worse. I blacked out again the day before, and when I came to, my knuckles were bloody and split, and the cell door was spattered with that blood.

I'd take the pain. I'd take the blackouts. I'd take the bloody knuckles and all of it. The pain Halgard was inflicting on me was deeper and...comprehensive. It pulled on every seam, plucked at every fear and instinct. As torture, it was masterful, a technology Ecker would kill—kill *many*, probably—to acquire. After all, it was working. In the moments between reliving those memories, my brain was in survival mode, thinking through every path to escape further torture. One route was capitulation, Halgard's ultimate aim as much as she pontificated on the end of the war and my journey toward redemption. The other was paved by Ecker and his threat-offer. That route was slower, more perilous, and hazy. I didn't know how I would sabotage the operation and get out alive. Then again, while Halgard's path seemed shorter and clearer, the destination was hazier than the route. My life would become an unknown unlike anything I'd yet experienced. My home, my family, my career, everything, gone.

With a shaky breath, I closed my eyes and stopped that spiral before I spun into panic. I took another breath. Held it. Let it out slowly. Repeated. Then, I repeated it again. The dagger in my brain didn't totally still, but the twisting slowed.

I was a soldier. I was an Aegis pilot of Bastion. I was a daughter of Mars, a descendant of the great Pioneers. The greatest of humanity. I was no Earther, no Mudbrain, despite what Halgard tried to convince me. But...I wasn't Ecker, either. I was walking my own path. A new path. I was trained to walk new paths and find novel solutions, so I needed to start doing that. Act instead of only being acted upon.

To act, I needed more information, about both the paths forking before me.

Footsteps sounded on the other side, and for half a moment, *I was on the coastal Martian city of Port Crimson, the shadow of Olympus Mons stretching through the windows, as booted footsteps ground on the concrete outside. Pruners. They'd finally found out about Leon. My boy. My poor boy. An Earther by blood, no matter how hard I worked to change everything else. I'd hired someone, spent most of my savings, to change Bastion's records, but it clearly hadn't been enough.*

They'd come for him. But I'd die before they took him.

Then, I was back on the *Dawnbreak*, sweating as the door slid open to Halgard's officers.

This day would be different.

Toris and Kuma were in the room with Admiral Halgard. They'd been absent the last couple days. I wasn't sure why they'd been there in the first place, nor why they'd be there for that session. Halgard certainly had something up her crisp uniform sleeve.

All three of them looked at me as I entered, and I felt a strange satisfaction as both Kuma and Toris cringed at the sight of me. I'd seen myself in the mirror the night before, and I surely only looked worse after another sleepless night. The bags under my eyes were heavy and shaded, and I'd lost weight, sucking my cheeks in just enough to be noticeable. Good. Let them pity me. I could use that.

I would have to, I'd have to use anything I could, to find this middle path.

I took my seat before the guards could shove me in.

"Good morning, Alis," Halgard said, absent any of the levity and nonchalance in her demeanor when I first met her. I highly doubted my torture was weighing on her withered soul. I must have been taking too long. Wearing her patience thin. Good. Another tool to use to carve a new path.

"Morning, Admiral," I said, summoning a closed-lip smile and tilting my head. I'm sure I looked like the picture of sanity. "I saw Farstead out the starboard viewscreens on the way here. Are you taking me home? This is quite the taxi service. You could have just given me to Ecker and spared the fuel." In truth, seeing the glint of Farstead in the darkness gave me a quickening of anxiety. That meant we were nearly out of Earth's Sphere. And we weren't alone, either. Out that same window, I'd seen the bulk of three more battlecruisers and a few other smaller ships, all headed toward Bastion. That was an aggressive move, one that Ecker surely would have noticed. I needed to know what Halgard was planning, because if she was doing something rash, Ecker may, too. He may have assumed I'd given up valuable information, putting Teah in immediate danger.

"Believe it or not," Halgard said. "You aren't the center of my attention, and the moments I waste here could be spent saving lives. The war goes on, and both our peoples die."

I frowned and tilted my head the other way. "Oh, I'm so sorry for wasting your time."

Toris scoffed. "I don't think your torture's doing much good, Admiral."

"It's not torture," Halgard said, folding her arms and pinching the sleeve of her uniform. "It's reprogramming." She sniffed, and I could see her composure fraying nearly as much as mine.

Kuma frowned and held up a finger. "That feels like something Nazis would have said. Did Nazis say that?" He shivered. "Feels gross in the same way, Admiral."

Halgard worked her jaw back and forth and scowled between the two pilots. "Unlike her," she jerked her head in my direction, "you two are not military assets. So shut up before I shoot you out of an airlock." Even I knew she wouldn't do that, but her tone was enough to quiet the captains.

"Hi, military asset here," I said. "Talking object with a question. What do you want from me? You want to end the war. So do I. You want to make me see that I'm more like you than my own people. You want me to see all the things Bastion's done—which, by the way, I'm sure your own military could hold a match to if the cameras were on them. You want me to empathize with you and your people more than my own. I get all that. You've made your point. But what do you *want*? You're clearly mounting an offensive, so what are you using *me* for?"

"Using..." Halgard started, eyes narrowing. Then she chuckled with anything but humor. "You think I'm using you, like Ecker did, like Bastion has been doing to all of you since birth. What'd you call me? A hypocrite. No, you're *still* missing the point. I'm giving you a chance to understand and to *choose* to help us—and in the end, help your people, too."

"And if I don't choose to help you? How far does the superior Earthers' grace go?"

Halgard closed her eyes and breathed deep, and I saw my mother in that exasperation and that attempt at patience. Something softened in me, then. "I have faith in you, Alis. I trust that you'll make the right decision." Then she nodded behind me, clearly done with the conversation, and I felt the cold metal ring drop around my head. I almost laughed. Toris rolled his eyes.

"Admiral, did you have to teach yourself to talk out of your ass, or was it a talent you always had?" Toris asked. "Seriously. You say you trust her and then just go back to the same old torture?"

"This isn't the same," Halgard said, tapping buttons on the holoprojector's control console. Something in her voice made me go cold. My carving a path didn't get me very far, but some distance was better than none. I knew Halgard and her fleet were running out of time. Or, more than likely, that I was running out of time. I knew they were mounting some kind of offensive. I knew I was an asset, of value, and that gave me leverage. And I knew that Halgard was on the verge of breaking, too. Maybe, as much as I hated to admit it, it shook Halgard to do what she was doing to me. Not that it made me loathe her any less. That, layered with the pressure she was likely under from her leaders and the other burdens the war had lain on her, was eroding her strength. The wind carving away at the rock. I could use that.

Halgard's device connected to my mindjack, and the dagger stopped twisting in my brain. My bottom jaw started chattering, some involuntary reflex against what was coming. I almost begged, but I bit my tongue instead.

The lights in the room dimmed as Toris shook his head, Kuma sighed, and the holoprojector lit up. A cityscape dominated the image, a place not totally unlike Bastion, but lit up with more holograms, more advertisements, more excess.

Babylon, the phantom mental signals said to my brain. Babylon. A relatively new city on Earth, built on the bones of an old one. They called it the New Cradle of Civilization, a laughable title to any Bastionite, all of whom knew what true civilization looked like.

The view turned from the sprawling cityscape, viewed from a balcony, toward a huge, sleek tower, tiered and columned with a mixture of modern architecture and ancient. Then the view panned down from the building to—

"No," Toris said, pushing back his seat and standing up. "No. You won't do this."

Kuma looked like he was about to throw up. He gripped the arms of his chair with white knuckles.

I looked back to the projection, where Toris and Kuma looked back at me.

They were younger, but not by much, both dressed in matching green and black-trimmed jumpsuits. They were surrounded by people in the same attire, a half-circle beside and behind them, all of them facing a man dressed in a sharp black suit with a high collar—the fashion of the time. He had black hair cut close to his head and slicked back. Unlike Toris and Kuma, he was flanked by a handful of armed guards, the couple closest to him dressed in less-expensive suits and the others dressed in armor complete with smooth masks that made them look more like androids than people. In fact, they reminded me of the *Sanguine Lycan*.

Whoever's mind I was in stood closer to the group surrounding Toris and Kuma. They looked back out toward the city once more, and as their emotions weaved into my own, I realized they weren't admiring the cityscape.

They were afraid.

Are we safe here? Will they get us? Should I go home, too?

"Come on Kuma," Present-Toris said, shoving back his chair and standing up. "You're not going to torture us, too."

Halgard sighed and pressed a button, pausing the projection.

Kuma swallowed, then pushed against the tabletop to stand. He looked at Halgard, eyes just wide enough that his irises were completely surrounded by pink. The man was on the verge of tears. And on the verge of strangling Halgard, by the looks of it.

"You will sit," Halgard said. "You are on my ship. You will follow my orders. We're still following the old laws, Orius. Your Compact doesn't constrain me, yet." The guards took that as a cue to step forward. Light spilled into the room as the door opened and more guards slipped in, shuffling around the table. Toris and Kuma looked at each other, then simultaneously slowly sat down.

"Good luck getting any help from us now," Toris growled through clenched teeth. Help? What help had she asked them for? Were they involved in the upcoming operation? Then he turned to his friend. "You don't have to watch this, Kuma."

The other captain was silent, eyes fixed on the projection.

"I told you we don't have time to play games," Halgard said, her voice losing some of the strength it commanded just a moment before. "I'm sorry to do this, captains, but if Alis isn't swayed yet, maybe she will be when she can empathize with the good men who saved her life, and who risked theirs for her. All for this better world, this better solar system, that we're all fighting for."

Toris shook his head, nostrils flared, clearly not swayed by the Admiral's compliment, nor her reasoning.

I kept my mouth shut, unsure what I'd say as emotions clashed behind my tongue. Halgard wasn't wrong, Mudbrains as they were, I deeply appreciated what Toris and Kuma had done for me. That couldn't distort what I needed to do, though, where I needed to go on my own path. Thank God I wasn't in one of their heads, at least.

Halgard resumed the projection.

"We need to get them out of there!" Past-Toris shouted, taking a step forward, urging the suited man's bodyguards to step forward as a mirror. "We *can* get them out of there!"

The man clasped his hands behind his back. "We will allow the military to do its job. We won't interfere. And we won't risk Genesis Gardens assets in a warzone. All interstate flights are grounded."

"That warzone is our *HOME!*" Toris shouted the last word, the volume honed by a mix of rage and fear and sadness that made me shiver. I looked over to Present-Toris, who was half-turned away from the projection but unable to take his eyes off it, jaw muscles flexing beneath his cheeks.

He's right, thought the brain I shared, whoever it was. And whoever it was, they certainly had some relationship with Toris and Kuma. I saw flashes of memories: laughing over sushi, leaning against a balcony at night with drinks in hand, the lights of the city below and about. I didn't get the impression that the person was from Toris' home; no, home was certainly Babylon. But, all the same, this person agreed with Toris, and they felt frustration rising to eclipse the fear, a frustration kindled long before by unsafe and unfair working conditions, slavery of a different kind.

Carivant. That was the man in the suit, the one Toris was yelling at. Arturo Srinivasan Carivant. CEO of the megacorporation Genesis Gardens.

They hated Carivant. And not just the mind melding with mine, but more than half those gathered around Toris and Kuma. They were a fuse burning down, sparked by one act of mistreatment or another. And if they exploded, those guards wouldn't be enough.

"I understand your concern," Carivant said in an apathetic tone that displayed how very little he actually cared about that concern. "You are more than welcome to go through the proper channels to request the remainder of the week off and travel home after your shifts are complete."

The person in my mind scoffed, shaking their head. That request process was intentionally long and cumbersome, and it required a sacrifice of more work time later on. Orilla del Angel was in danger at that moment. Hours later...who knew what would be left to return to.

I realized then what moment I was living. The timeline fit. In Bastion, the leadership had called it Operation Golden Herring. The operation featured two distractions: one in space that drew away some of Earth's fleet and the fire of its orbital defenses, and another in the form of a ground invasion. The space battle was meant to appear as the distraction for that ground invasion, but that invasion was covering up another operation that, as far as I knew, Earth still didn't know about. While Bastion infantry and air support forces engaged with the Mudbrains, a handful of special infiltration teams sabotaged a base and stole valuable intel on troop and ship movements. If I remembered right, a team of pruners also joined the operation to slip into nearby communities, disguised as refugees or even Earther soldiers. It was a complex operation, dubbed "Golden" Herring instead of "Red" because Bastion saw it as such a beneficial opportunity with a tapestry of possible victories. If the invasion went well, we could gain a foothold on land—which we did, until we had to retreat a year later. If the space battle went well, we'd thin their fleet. Even the distractions had strategic value. Therefore, "Golden" Herring. Teah had always thought it was a stupid name.

And landfall started near the middle of a region once known as California, where an inlet to a sea there offered easier infiltration to several strategic targets. One of which, evidently, happened to be Toris' and Kuma's home.

Bastion still celebrated that victory two years later.

Past-Toris stared at this Carivant, head tilted slightly forward, chest rising and falling with angry-but-controlled breaths. Kuma stood beside him, hands clenched into fists at his side.

If they rush them, the person in my head thought, *I'll rush them, too. I will. They'd only stun us. They wouldn't kill us. They wouldn't kill us.*

I can do this. I can stand up to them.

But neither Toris nor Kuma attacked. Kuma only leaned toward Toris and whispered something. Then Toris nodded.

"Understood," Past-Toris said, but slowly, as if he was forcing a stone through a sieve, enunciating the syllables in a staccato. Then he spun and disappeared into the crowd of employees behind him. Kuma followed.

Carivant watched them go, eyes narrowing, clearly not satisfied. After a moment, he glanced around the surrounding crowd and said: "Everyone present will have the last hour of pay docked for wasting time. You may not make it up with overtime." Then he spun on his heel and strode toward a door leading back into the tower. His suited goons followed him. Once they were inside, the armored guards followed, too.

The projection blurred for a moment, the memories edited. Several of the others had the same treatment. A curated experience, just for my benefit.

When the projection snapped back into focus, I was walking down a corridor behind Toris and Kuma.

"Beck, you don't have to do this," Past-Kuma said.

Beck. That was me. Becadari Giulio Godfrey.

"I do," Beck said. "You two will be looking out for your families. Someone needs to look out for you." The trio turned a corner toward one of the tower's hangar bays, Beck's cognitive map of Genesis Gardens melding with my mind. "I'm sorry, I should have just said yes last night."

A flash of a memory, Toris and Kuma proposing the very plan we were now enacting. Alibren staying quiet. Anker sighing and shaking his head. Tolman calling them idiots. Beck opening his mouth, his chest burning to act, to throw himself behind his colleagues and finally stick it to Carivant—and to this damn city as a whole. But fear held him back. That had been Carivant's mistake: his apathy toward Beck's friends had made Beck angrier than he was afraid.

"Do you think we'll make it in time?" Beck asked.

"Yes," Toris said, and Beck wished he could have that confidence.

"Has Bastion already landed? Are they—"

"Beck?" Toris asked.

"Yeah?"

"Love you for coming. Really. But the questions aren't helping right now."

Beck shut his mouth, and I felt his embarrassment. Beck was inquisitive by nature, and that inquisition was generally a symptom of his insecurity. Knowledge grounded him. Facts countered fear. Mostly.

Beck stayed quiet as the trio turned onto the wider corridor. Normally full with people, it was nearly empty, with all interstate flights grounded. The end of the corridor opened to the Genesis Gardens hangar. A breeze from the hangar's open mouth washed down the corridor, and Beck thought he smelled smoke on the air, curdling both our stomachs with fear. He almost asked the others if they thought Bastion was close, just to see, just to validate whether his concerns were reasonable or to rely on them to bolster his confidence.

But Beck kept his mouth shut.

The trio stepped into the hangar, leaving the tower's carpeted floors for the dull concrete. Most of the craft parked there were smaller cargo vessels that looked more like trucks if not for the small rotors set in wings on each side rather than wheels. Near one side were some sleeker patrol craft shaped like classic jets. They patrolled the airspace around Babylon. Near the back of the hangar were the larger ships, the ones that Beck knew Toris and Kuma were most comfortable with, and right where we were headed.

"Don't look at them," Past-Toris said.

"Don't look at who?" Beck asked, butterflies fluttering in his gut—and mine—as he looked around the hangar. "I—"

Then he saw them: security officers, dressed in their black armor with handguns on their hips and plasma rifles magnetized to their backs. They hadn't noticed the trio, yet, instead speaking with each other near the mouth of the hangar. If they did see us...Carivant must have issued an alert for at least Toris after that moment outside. He'd narrowly avoided a mutiny; he'd ensure one didn't reignite.

We stuck close to cargo crates sitting in the hangar, waiting for the battle to be over, to be carried across the world or off-planet elsewhere in the Sphere. After checking the path, Toris darted from behind a crate toward the nearest ship: a starship, an interplanetary cargo transport. It squatted on wide landing gears, a boarding ramp extending from its main airlock on its starboard side. The bulk of the ship was toward its aft, with interior cargo space above the main fusion drives, but at its bow, the ship forked into two prongs, beneath which were the ship's main rockets, running from the end of those prongs to the stern. Tucked under the prongs were more cargo compartments, and the forks themselves were intended to secure larger containers that the ship could push through space. It was a powerful craft, but not a starfighter, not a war-worthy vessel. Beck kept those concerns to himself.

Seeing the *Harriet* through my own eyes, it was obvious how much Toris and Kuma had modified the starship for their needs, upgrading the rockets with an even larger model for greater thrust, as well as more external thrusters for maneuverability. Beck certainly would have felt more secure on the up-dated version.

I glanced over to Present-Toris. His hardness had softened slightly, his jaw loose and his brows gradually inverting from anger into sadness. Kuma looked worse: like he was on the verge of being sick.

In the projection, Kuma darted from the containers to the boarding ramp. Toris was already on-board. Once Kuma made it across, Beck sidled up to the edge of the container, took a step forward, hesitating, stumbling, and knocking into the side of the container. He froze, listening. No shouts. No armored footsteps echoing toward him. So he dashed for it.

And, of course, a security officer turned the corner at that exact moment.

Ignoring the shouting officer, Beck ran up the boarding ramp and into the starship. Kuma slapped a button to the right of the opening, and the boarding ramp retracted. Then he pulled down a lever, sealing the airlock doors.

"What was that?" Toris shouted from elsewhere in the ship. Beck turned from the airlock, heart still racing, to face walls of cargo containers, secured to the floor with powerful mag-locks.

"We were spotted," Kuma called back, and Beck was grateful Kuma didn't blame it all on him. At least outwardly. On the inside he probably wished Beck had gotten shot.

I cringed and shook my head. Living with so much insecurity was painful.

Beck followed Toris around containers toward the stern and a steep set of stairs. He climbed up behind Kuma as someone banged on the airlock door below. They'd have plasma cutters. Or they'd have the override codes for the door. Or they could just shoot the ship down with Genesis Gardens' defensive cannons as they left the hangar.

Beck kept those concerns to himself, too.

At the top of the ladder was the bridge Alis knew well enough, though without the personal touches that the captains had added to make the ship their own. This bridge was sterile, corporate.

"Well," Toris said from the pilot's seat as Kuma settled into his seat on the other side, "we knew we'd run into trouble at some point. May as well get it over with."

"Do you think they'll pursue us?" Beck asked, unable to keep that question back. He did keep to himself the part about how those sleek starfighters on the other side of the hangar would catch up to them in no time. Kuma and Toris probably already knew that.

"Depends on if Carivant wants to lose more of his precious 'assets' in a war-zone," Toris said, voice dripping with sarcastic anger. "My bet is that he won't. So," he shrugged as if what he was saying wasn't totally insane, "we fly into the warzone before they can take us down."

"Ah. Yeah." And then hope Bastion didn't shoot them down, either. Beck kept that to himself.

"What can I do?" he asked instead, hoping at least that question was useful. Beck was no pilot. He'd spent most of his years at Genesis Gardens working on the docks, moving containers, tracking inventory, the real exciting stuff. The stuff that would have gone to automatons or other machines if Babylon were following where most of Earth was headed. But Babylon was only following Bastion's path, throwing all their laws and regulations behind the principle that humans must be working, must be contributing to society. Of course, contributing in the way they preferred, which generally included making the company astronomical amounts of money that Beck and Toris and Kuma and everyone else never saw, despite their long hours in shit conditions. Despite sacrificing time with family and friends. Despite staying put when only a few hundred miles away, the enemy was at the door.

"We do this part," Toris said, fingers tapping and swiping through his control screens. He flicked a series of switches, and a hum vibrated through the ship. "You get strapped in safe. You'll help us when we get to Orilla." Then he turned around, craning around the back of his pilot's chair. "Thank you for coming, Beck. It means more than you know."

"You sure you want to do this?" Kuma asked. "We wouldn't blame you if you stayed. You could be losing a lot more than your job if you come with us."

Beck almost laughed. Of all people, he didn't need to be reminded of what to be afraid of. He was already shaking, sweating, stomach twisting at the fear. But: "I'm with you," Beck said. "We should all be with you."

Kuma stared at Beck for a moment, face scrunched in...confusion? Beck couldn't tell, and he wondered if he had something on his face. But then Kuma turned back around to his console and shook his head. "You almost make me feel like we can do this, Beck. Thanks."

Beck wasn't sure how in any world Kuma got that from what he'd just said, but still, what Kuma said made Beck's gut settle and diminished the shaking...a little.

BANG BANG BANG

There was the shaking again. And the upset stomach.

The guards were shouting, but the layers of metal and insulation muffled whatever they were saying. Beck wondered why they hadn't tried cutting through yet, why they hadn't fired on the door.

"Ready on launch thrusters," Kuma said, tapping some commands onto his screen and then settling his hand on a lever at his right side.

"One second," Toris said. "I'm priming the drive. We're gonna go out of here fast. You strapped in, Beck?"

"Uh. Yeah. Mm hm." Beck grasped the sides of his chair.

The banging on the door had stopped. That didn't exactly fill Beck with peace, though. After a moment, he heard a hissing, like they had a snake down in the hold.

"Plasma cutter!" Beck cried. "They've got a cutter! They—"

"Got it, Beck," Toris said. How could he be so calm? He dragged his finger across his screen, and the vibrations throughout the ship intensified as the drive powered up. "All right, Kuma. Launch thruster burst..." he looked down at his screen, watching something Beck couldn't see, "now!"

Beck's gut stayed put as the ship exploded upwards, and he cringed, waiting for them to slam into the hangar roof. But they didn't.

"Hold on!" Toris shouted, then he shoved forward a lever at his left hand.

If Beck's gut was left on the hangar floor, his brain got left suspended in that hangar as they rocketed forward, out of the hangar and into the sunlight. In my chair on the *Dawnbreak*, I instinctively gripped the arms of the chair, feeling all the memory of that acceleration. The trio hurtled above buildings as light flashed around them, followed by concussive booms that rattled the ship. Genesis Gardens' defense cannons. They'd launched out of that hangar at close to escape velocity, so the cannons would need a few moments before they could get a true target on their ship.

Toris leaned to the left, hands on steering controls, and the ship followed, though inertia pulled Beck the direction they'd been going, pulling against his restraints. Another flash ripped through the sky followed by another explosion. Beck actually ducked that time. An alarm flashed through the cabin.

"Was that a hit?" Toris asked.

"No," Kuma said. "But close enough to fry the hull a bit."

That sounded an awful lot like a hit.

Toris leveled off the ship and threw the lever on his side even further, pushing Beck back into his seat again as more thrust fired them northwest over a glittering river and barren mountains. A flash up in the sky made Beck cringe again, but he realized that wasn't defense cannon fire, but an explosion up in space. He squinted, trying to make out details beyond the haze of the atmosphere, but all he could make out was the occasional brief flash or a sliver of a starship, some of them he'd heard to be miles long, impossible to ever enter the gravity well.

Unless, of course, they crashed there.

And some ships must have fallen into the gravity well, because as their ship gained elevation, Beck could see trails of smoke and steam plummeting toward the planet like a rain of fallen angels. He shivered. The Solar Gulf War had kept itself mostly away from the planets at the center of the Spheres, the fighting relegated to ship-to-ship battles, conflicts in the Belt—where the war had all started—or on stations. This was closer to home than Beck could remember.

"We clear?" Toris asked.

Kuma glanced over his screens. "From the cannon fire, I think so. But..." he turned and flicked a switch on the portion of the console that extended out into the bridge between the two of them. A holomap flashed to life, suspended above the console. The ship, represented by a much smaller, simpler black symbol, was following a dotted green line, the trajectory toward Orilla del Angel. Red flashed at the edge of the holomap. Something was coming. Several somethings. Beck gripped his seat tighter as—

The projection went fuzzy as the curated memories skipped ahead.

"What happened?" I asked.

"Drones," Present-Toris said, still staring at the projection, though there was nothing to actually look at. I imagined he was seeing something else. Whatever I was about to see. Kuma was glued to the projection with much the same look. Although his hands had now clenched into fists atop the table. "Not meant to shoot us down. One attached to our hull and tried to hack us. We'd severed the network connection to Genesis Gardens, so Carivant was trying to get his asset—and us—back in one piece. Kuma took care of it." He looked over at his friend, and the creases at the apex of his concerned eyebrows deepened. This memory was going to hurt both of them. And I hated Halgard all the more for it.

"Well, I appreciate the admiral only showing us the most traumatizing bits," I said, staring Halgard in the eyes. She looked away.

The projection snapped back into focus. The *Harriet-before-it-was-the-Harriet* was dropping out of the sky toward a burning city. Smoke billowed in black towers, fueled by churning, snapping flames below. To the southeast, I could see an interstate leaving the city, clogged with vehicles, an artery to safety.

And as Beck watched, a Bastion dropship fired a missile that severed the artery in a spray of concrete, metal, and bodies.

"They weren't there," Past-Toris immediately said. Of course he did. He had to reassure himself. "They wouldn't try and leave that way. They'd be smarter than to get stuck there."

Kuma didn't respond.

"You're up, Beck," Toris said. "Can you connect to the city's network?"

Finally, Beck could do something other than sit there in fear. Unlike the two pilots, Beck had a mindjack. He sent a mental command to the 'jack as easily as he'd tell his fingers to snap—the fingers on his left hand, at least; he couldn't snap with his right for some reason. That really wasn't important in the moment, though.

"Yeah," Beck said. "I'm connected. They...oh my..."

"What?" Toris snapped.

"There's a message broadcasting across the network, an emergency alert to flee on the interstate. It's branded from the city of Orilla. They were assured safe passage."

Toris slammed his hand against the console with such ferocity that Beck jerked in his seat. "Why did they believe that? Why would anyone believe that?"

"You think it was Bastion?" Beck asked.

"Of course it was Bastion," Toris said. "Herding their victims into one place. Maximum damage. Maximum terror. Makes their job easier." Then through clenched teeth he added, "If they hurt our families..."

"How can I find your families? They don't have 'jacks, do they?"

"My wife does," Kuma said. "Nadiadana Eden Abara. Contact code 5877JKQ."

Beck sent the signal through his 'jack, but it bounced back, the metaphorical fingers refusing to snap. "Couldn't reach her. The signal's cut off."

"Of course it is," Toris said. "And all those people still thought the city was telling them to leave." The captain pulled back the throttle on the main rockets, flicking a switch that brought up air brake flaps along the length of the sloping forks in front of the viewport. The spires of Orilla del Angel—a young city by most standards, created since the formation of the Corcoran Sea—churned with smoke that blew toward the ship, obscuring their view. Fortunately, that same smoke also obscured them from the Bastion soldiers. That dropship would still be nearby, and they'd surely detected another starship entering Orilla's airspace.

"Try a location ping," Kuma said. "She normally keeps hers private, but we agreed she'd open it up in an emergency. If I needed..." he trailed off as if something got stuck in his throat.

Beck nodded, sending an inquiry for Nadiadana Eden Abara's location. It bounced back. Beck swallowed, kept that to himself, and tried again. It bounced back.

What if every ping he was making, every signal that was bouncing back, alerted Bastion to him? What if they targeted the ship, and Beck in particular, to stop him? They clearly didn't want anyone making contact with those in the city.

Beck was about to give up, about to say he couldn't reach them, when Kuma turned around, a hint of tears in his eyes, and in a small voice asked, "Anything?"

So Beck tried again.

"Got it!" He looked out the viewport, though there wasn't much to see. "Northeast," he said. "This is weird. I think she's...underground? Near a school."

Toris and Kuma looked at each other, then they got to work. Toris threw back the thrust on the rockets as momentum carried them forward. He guided them around the spires of Orilla's downtown toward the suburbs of the city. Green triangles pinged on the holomap, and Beck stared at them, waiting for them to pursue, for another alert to blare through the bridge.

"Why aren't they red?" Beck asked. "Are those friendlies?"

Toris glanced over at the map, then growled, "Are you kidding...no. I swear, if I see Carivant again, I'll kill him. This is that Bastion dropship we just saw." Toris pointed to one of the green triangles as it pulled away out of the holomap's view. "The enemy's pinged as friendlies. I knew Carivant was still dealing with Bastion under the table, but he's one of them. No wonder he didn't want us heading out here. Maybe he's getting something out of it."

"Toris!" Kuma snapped. "Can we whine about Carivant later?"

Toris went quiet. Beck filled the silence: "At least that means they won't come after us, right? That's good?"

"That's good," Kuma repeated.

"Landing thrusters," Toris said as they dropped over a smoking, burning neighborhood and a wide, squat building.

"Landing thrusters," Kuma repeated, and the ship rocked as thrusters fired ahead of them to slow them down and then beneath to slow their descent as gravity took hold. The pilots were settling them in a field beside the building. The school, Beck realized. The starship touched down with a rattle, and Beck heard the familiar, rapid *chook-chook-chook* of radiator vents snapping open near the stern.

"Come on," Toris said, throwing off his restraints and hurrying past Beck to drop out of the bridge, skipping all the steps. Kuma followed as Beck fumbled with his restraints using his sweaty, shaking hands.

Beck didn't have to go. He'd helped them get to the school, helped them do something they couldn't have done on their own. He'd been there when no one else had. That was enough, wasn't it?

Below, Beck heard the airlock door beep and slide open. Then, outside, he heard the echoing rattle of plasma fire.

Gunfire that Toris and Kuma were running into. For their families. No one was running in for them.

"Shit," Beck growled as he undid his restraints.

Toris and Kuma crouched at the bottom of the boarding ramp when Beck reached them, covered by the shadow of the starship. Smoke roiled around them from a home burning nearby. Beck forced himself not to look at those flames, told himself that he didn't see a charred body on the lawn. He swallowed the vomit that came up. Toris and Kuma weren't afraid, not of the flames and the guns, at least. They were afraid of what they were going to find inside that school. Beck could have courage for them. He could do this.

The area between the field and the school looked clear, which was good for the trio, but likely not for whoever was hiding inside the building.

"Do you have weapons?" Beck asked.

"No," Kuma replied.

"Are there any on the ship?"

Toris shook his head.

"Ah."

"We'll have to borrow some," Toris said, nodding to a dark shape on the field between them and the school. A Bastion soldier. Or, rather, the corpse of one, armor burned through to their chest, rifle still in one hand.

After one last look to ensure they were clear, the trio hurried across the field, Toris scooping up the rifle on the way and setting the stock against his shoulder. They headed through an open door into the building, entering a hallway nearly as dark as the smoke-shrouded outdoors. Lights flickered along the ceiling. The hall was empty. Quiet. Outside, starship engines rumbled in the distance.

"You still have their location?" Toris asked. "Have they moved?"

Beck re-pinged Nadiadana's signal—which was each time a really strange experience to feel, the command seeming to go through my own mindjack; that was the only time I felt the dagger return while wearing the empathy torture device. "It's...fuzzier, but—"

"Do you feel her or not?" Kuma snapped, spinning on Beck with frenzy widening his eyes. "Where is she?"

The signal pinged back as Beck took a step away from Kuma. "She's still here. That way." Beck pointed toward a wall to their left. "Still underground. I don't think they've moved."

Kuma's eyelids contracted enough to reverse that crazed look. "Sorry. I'm sorry. Thank you."

Hugging the wall, the trio crept to a fork in the corridor. Toris stuck his head around it.

"Bodies," he said.

After taking a shaky breath, Beck followed the other two around the corner. The lights flickered over bloodstained floor and plasma-fire-scorched walls. Slumped beneath one of those blast marks was a young man, empty eyes staring back at Beck, his chest torn open. Past him lay a pair of women, face down, one hand still reaching out for her companion with slack fingers. Still further down the hall was another Bastion soldier, body armor cracked and half their helm blown to hell, along with that side of their head.

That was when Beck threw up.

It wasn't the first dead body he'd seen, but it was certainly the most raw form. The most violent.

"That's...Benji," Toris whispered as they passed the man sagged against the wall. "And—"

BOOM. BOOM. BOOM.

The gunfire echoed down the hallway, and like a starting gun at a race, Kuma and Toris turned in its direction and ran. Beck's instincts told him to do the exact opposite, but seeing the bodies, the unarmed, harmless bodies—in a school of all places—did what Carivant's apathy had done to a greater degree. The rage toward Bastion burned away his fear.

Kuma slowed down to grab a rifle from the dead Bastion soldier. "He's got a handgun, Beck!" Kuma called. "Grab it!" Beck did, fumbling with the holster and jerking back when the body twitched. But then he had the gun in hand, disengaging the safety and following the other two through a pair of double doors and into—

In the room on the *Dawnbreak*, Present-Kuma stood up, shoving his chair back so hard it hit the wall with a crash. The officers immediately flanked him and shoved him back into the chair with enough force that he slammed back against the wall. Halgard just stared at him, as did I, the action a surprise from the otherwise calm and collected man.

"You don't have to watch, Kuma," Toris said, voice calm and quiet and sad, so much focus on his friend they could have been the only people in the room. Then he turned to Halgard. "I hope you're enjoying yourself. Because I swear to you that I'm going to find a way to put you in that chair," he pointed to me, "until you can't do anything but drool."

Halgard could have been an android as her head slowly swiveled to Toris and she responded, "If it's after this war's won, I couldn't care less."

Kuma closed his eyes, squeezed them so tight the pain was evident.

On the projection, the trio had entered a cafeteria where a few more bodies lay, none of them alive. Smoke and dust drifted through the cafeteria from the kitchen, though there weren't any obvious signs of a fire.

BOOM. BOOM.

Toris and Kuma hurried into the kitchen with Beck close behind, finger resting by the trigger, the rest of his hand a shaky mess.

No one was in the kitchen, only cookware scattered on the ground and counters. But a wide refrigerator had been moved aside, revealing a passage behind it. A secret tunnel. A much better way to escape Bastion than the interstate. But they'd been found.

Beck followed them into the tunnel, where the lights were dimmer than the rest of the school. Ahead, the tunnel turned to the right. Beck re-pinged the signal. "They're close," he whispered. "She's still alive."

Beck waited behind the other two at the corner as Toris looked around.

"HEY!" He shouted, then rounded the corner and—*THOOM THOOM*—fired two bolts of superheated plasma. Kuma followed, and Beck heard three more rifle bursts, followed by a gunshot and a scream. He wasn't sure who screamed.

When he rounded the corner, Beck hesitated.

Two Bastion soldiers still stood. One fired as Toris took partial cover against the wall, the shot ripping through the side of Toris' shoulder before slamming into the opposite wall of the tunnel. Kuma took out that soldier as Toris shot the second, yelling in rage and pain. Beck stayed there, useless. He should have been right behind them, firing at that soldier before they could hit Toris. But when it mattered most, he'd hesitated.

An animal's roar tore him from his self-flagellation. No, not a roar, a wail, a cry. The shockwave of a breaking heart. Kuma ran to one side of the corridor where a child lay in the arms of a woman with long black hair and bloody hands.

"NO!" Toris screamed, running to the other side of the tunnel, where two other shapes lay, a man and a woman, the woman with her arms around the man, blast marks in her back.

"WHERE WERE YOU?!" the woman screamed at Kuma, her face contorting into an expression almost as animal as Kuma's cry. A primal anger, fueled by grief. "YOU SAID YOU'D PROTECT HER! YOU SAID—"

In the present, Kuma launched out of his chair, diving for the projector and slamming his fists into the glass lens, shattering it and the plastic around it. The image fuzzied as Beck heard footsteps behind them. He thought about telling Kuma and Toris, about running behind their more capable gunplay.

Instead, he turned to face the pair of Bastion soldiers as they raised their rifles in surprise. To his own surprise, Beck placed two shots in one soldier's forehead before heat exploded across his chest and—

Kuma slammed on the projector again. The screen went dark.

That didn't cut off my connection to Beck's memory, though. Like the others, I felt his death. Unlike the others, and unlike most of my experience with Becadari, though, I didn't feel fear.

And whether it was Beck's courage or my own, I'd never know, but when Halgard's officer aimed their weapon at the enraged Kuma, I dove out of my chair and hugged the large, quivering man. I pressed myself against him, cheek against his back, as something cold slammed into my own.

Everything went dark before I even hit the ground.

CHAPTER EIGHTEEN

TORIS

FIND ALIS. GET THE mithril. Get out. Kill the Wolf.

I repeated those words to myself as we rode the maglev line into Babylon, Kuma filing the crash report on a holoscreen projected from his chair to my left, and Lana sitting across from us, turned and looking out the window as we sped through the industrial districts.

That was all I needed to focus on. Ignore everything else, especially the memories, especially Carivant.

Find Alis. Get the mithril. Get out. Kill the Wolf.

It was a plan with quite a few missing details. The mithril would be one of the most valuable things in the city, and therefore one of the most closely guarded. Kuma and I assumed Alis would be on the hunt for the mithril and that our paths would converge on that hunt, more than likely at Carivant's tower. That was a big assumption. Alis had better investigative skills than anyone I knew, thanks to her Bastion soldiering days, but what if she hadn't yet sniffed out that trail? What if we were wrong and Carivant didn't even have the mithril and it belonged to one of Babylon's many other trillionaires or corporate titans?

And then, when all was said and done and we left the city for home, who would perform the operation now that Cixin was...Would the Wolf break free and prevent it? Was it that volatile? All this risk would be for nothing if we couldn't actually kill the beast.

No. There was no point worrying about that. That was a tomorrow problem. I'd been dealing with the Wolf for ten years. This was different, but I could endure the time it took to find a new bioengineer or neurosurgeon. We could endure it. Even if it meant chaining the Wolf up at Wolfhome. Just the thought of that made me shiver.

I had to focus on the danger Alis was in at that moment, both from the Wolf and the other predators slinking in Babylon's shadows.

She'd only been in the city a few hours longer than us. Maybe half a day. I'd told her about my past with Carivant and Babylon, but she'd never been to the city. She'd have less to go off than I did, which would give me a headstart in finding her.

I could start my investigation in that maglev car, like Kuma had suggested. I tapped a button in the arm of my chair, and a holoscreen flashed to life in front of me from projectors in the seat. The first page was a list of advertisements for visitors. Hotels to stay in, entertainment to check out, body augments to consider, food to eat. Brands and logos and business names flashed across the screen, giving the illusion of a great variety, endless innovation and choice. But of ten brands that I saw, I knew eight of them were owned by Carivant's organization: Genesis Gardens.

Ignoring the advertisements, I tapped on the news section, searching for anything suspicious. If Alis had tried to fly her hoverboard through the electro-magnetic disruption field at the edges of the city, she could have crashed, which would certainly make at least a minor headline. Anyone caught breaking into Genesis Gardens—if she'd gotten that far—would be an even bigger headline. The city's elite loved a chance to simultaneously frame themselves as victims and showcase the ease with which they stopped perpetrators. But there were no articles or alerts of either kind. Everything else was noise. Nova, one of Carivant's businesses, announced a new corvette starship. Punarjanman, a Genesis Gardens competitor, had made a breakthrough in synthetic organisms (a small dragon, of course, nothing could go wrong there). Oh, and the city council, dominated by representatives from Genesis Gardens and its competitors, had won a landmark lawsuit around restricting anti-corporate sentiments on Babylon's network.

So, in twelve years, nothing had changed.

I deactivated the holoscreen and leaned back in my seat. The row across from me was empty, offering a clear view through windows and at the outer edges of Babylon as we crossed from the industrial districts and into the city proper. The tram started to slow down as we reached a hub. I took a breath. The first obstacle.

We stepped off the train behind a few other passengers. The smell wasn't so fresh here, further from the rivers. It was the smell of city, of smoke and metal and food and a hint of body odor. It was familiar. One breath took me back to eating tacos with Kuma from a streetcart, to stepping out into the night after an absurdly long day of work and finding the city as alive as it was during the day, if not more so. At least, back then I thought the city had a life to it, an urgency. I could see it now in the way people hurried from one place to the next, from maglev to hovercar, from building to building. After all the years of change, both in me and in the world, I knew it wasn't life I was perceiving, but the urgency of productivity, of every minute optimized for returns, whether that was money or success or gratification. Time was a relentless whip, driving its cattle from stimulant to stressor constantly. I'd been that way, once, when there hadn't been another choice, when the rest of the world was in the process of its metamorphosis, preparing to leave Babylon and its ways behind.

At that moment, though, I felt much like the cattle, driven by a different kind of urgency.

The hub hadn't changed much in the past twelve years. If anything, it was more secure than ever, which I'd been afraid of. A few steps down from the maglev platform was a series of metal arches, elegant in design but built solely for the city's security. Inside the arch were scanners and cameras, sensors that interfaced with the entrants' mindjack or the more modern synthetic biotech that had many names but similar functions. If it couldn't read technology, it'd rely on facial scans and other detectors to search for potential risks. Weapons, illegal drugs, and, in our case, Kuma and I. That was my assumption, at least. Carivant must have put us on some watchlist after we'd left the city.

On either side of the arches were concrete walls lined with tiered fountains that curved down the sidewalk in mirror of the Euphrates and Tigris outside the city. The beauty was, like most of the design decisions in Babylon, an illusion. Those walls were meant to contain, to shepherd everyone through the arches. I chewed at the inside of my lip as I slowly followed the other tram passengers toward the arches. We should have come up with a plan beforehand. I'd been in too much of a hurry.

The only small comfort I took was that Alis likely got through without trouble. They may have tagged her scan as suspicious since she wouldn't be in their records, but she likely wasn't stopped. Babylon had to walk a fine line between drawing new people into the city and maintaining its control over the population, obviously in the name of security and order. Just like their Martian cousin.

Kuma sighed as he stepped off the train behind me, Lana close behind him. "I really hoped they'd gotten more welcoming since we were here last."

"Yeah," I said, scanning the area for any vulnerability, somewhere we could slip through unnoticed, but we were as contained as the rest of the cattle. I couldn't see any city security on the other side of the arches, but I knew they were close. We wouldn't get far. They'd have other tools nearby, too. Drones, other remote weapons.

Lana looked up at our concerned faces, looked out at the fountains and arches, then back to us, raising an eyebrow. "I don't get it. What's wrong?"

"Those arches track who comes in and who leaves the city," Kuma said.

"So?"

"Weeeee," Kuma said in a high pitch, "aren't exactly welcome here."

"Wha—"

"Don't have time," I interrupted, waving away her words.

"Of course not," Lana said with a roll of her eyes. "Then I'll just go on alone. I think that's best anyway. Can't you find a way home without going into the city? Doesn't this line go to the spaceport? They've got to have local aircraft there, especially after that..." she swallowed and shook her head. "Emergency."

Kuma looked at me, still taking my lead on how much to share.

My frustration with the whole situation won over, and I snapped: "Do you think we haven't thought of that? We know what we have to do, and you don't need to worry about it. We're going out of our way to help you, so just let. Us. Help."

Lana stared at me with a hard defiance for a moment, but then her features softened and she looked down at the ground. "Sorry."

Kuma picked up the defiance that Lana dropped, shaking his head when I met his glance.

"Come on," I said, eager to just move on. "There's no way around the arches. We'll just have to hope their facial scans are going off old photography and can't find a match. I don't see another way through, and we're wasting enough time."

I started walking ahead of them and heard Kuma whisper. "Not you, you're not wasting our time." And in a small voice, Lana replied, "Thanks."

"He's got a lot bothering him," Kuma continued, almost quiet enough that I couldn't hear. "His—"

"Kuma," I said. And he went quiet. I let out a sigh, guilt tumbling around with my frustration and exhaustion. Why did my chest constrict like that every time we veered toward the topic? Why did I want so badly for Lana to stay out of it? Was I so fragile? So cracked and crumbling that confronting the issues in direct conversation would be the tremor that finally reduced me to pieces? As I thought, there was a darker, deeper answer that rose from the shadows of my mind. Was it because, even after all my fighting with Navi, that I was afraid she was right? That I'd brought a part of Bastion back with us from Mwezi, and that it would ruin not only our lives, but other lives, too? Was it because, as much as I hated myself for even considering it, I wondered if I shouldn't have ever opened that door to a Bastionite? Even Alis? I'd been so focused on stopping the Wolf, I hadn't really considered: what if I couldn't? Even if Alis had survived the Wolf up until that point, could we survive it?

"Stop," I whispered to myself as I passed under the metal arches, head down. "Stop."

Find Alis. Get the mithril. Get out. Kill the Wolf. Focus on the mission.

We walked through the arches and didn't get stunned or shot in the face, so that was something. I did glance an armed security officer near the corner of the hub, but he didn't even look in our direction as we stepped through. I kept walking with Kuma and Lana close behind. Ahead of us was a half-circular lane, where taxis waited for arrivals from the maglev lines. That lane connected on both ends to the main streets, one that led north and one that went east. Between us and the taxis was a row of staggered ad-bots, robots of various appearances—some humanoid and some simple shapes—calling out restaurants, clubs, events, and sales in a cacophony of sound. And behind it all were the towering buildings, so tall that the street below was in perpetual shade, the sun likely only shining on it if it were directly overhead. Maglev cars zipped over the streets, and rows of hovercars flew parallel with the lanes below, but a hundred feet above. Weaving between the buildings just below them were suspended tram lines, running cars back and forth between districts.

We walked another block or so before stopping beside a small square plaza cluttered with people moving between the stores there. Lana's gaze was pulled upward, mouth hanging open just a little, her attention held so tightly that she almost ran into me, gasping as she stuttered to a stop.

"Remind you of Bastion?" I asked, hoping to make up for snapping at her a moment before. At least a little.

Lana pursed her lips. "Not really, actually. It's a bit louder than Bastion, and most of the life of the city happens above the Shades. It's...a little cleaner there, too, at least if you're not in the Shades."

I nodded, looking up the street to where a boxy machine was rolling down the sidewalk, a fanged graffiti smile on its weathered armor. "They use drones to clean up what they can," I said, nodding to the machine, "but it's hard for them to keep up with all the people. All the mess. I'm guessing Bastion still doesn't use automation?"

Lana shook her head. "Nope. Everyone plays their part. Automation kills work ethic. City cleaners are one of the most common jobs."

I nodded, then: "Do you know where your in-laws live?"

Lana's jaw clenched then, whatever lightness of that moment gone. "Yeah. Somewhere called the Esagila District. The Cherry Blossom apartments."

I looked at Kuma, who returned a look that showed me he wasn't happy with me and we'd definitely be talking about it later. I ignored it. "Cherry Blossom. That was by Siren Lane. Didn't Anker live near there?"

"Yeah, but I don't know if he's going to have anything," he glanced at Lana, "that'll help us get home."

"That's closer than anyone else, and we can get Lana to her family. That's what you wanted, right?" There was more edge to that than I intended. I breathed sharp out my nose. "That's what *we* wanted, right? We don't need Anker to help us, but we could get a clearer picture of...where things are."

Kuma nodded, clearly still frustrated.

"I'm happy to go by myself, if you want to take Lana," I said. "Anker's closest anyway. Everyone else useful was up in Merker. Happy coincidence."

"Useful?" Kuma said, raising an eyebrow. "Now who sounds like a Bastionite?"

I glared at Kuma but didn't rise to the bait. It wouldn't end well. I was fraying not just at the edges, but all the way through. Night would fall soon, and I hadn't had sleep or food. All that could wait, though.

Find Alis. Get the mithril. Get out. Kill the Wolf.

"We can take a tram to Esagila," I said, pointing up at one of the lines overhead just as a tram car zipped by. I started walking again, headed for a sign pointing between buildings to a lift system that would take us up to that level.

"Esagila," Lana said as we walked. "Merker. Tigris. Euphrates. They're really leaning into the symbolism, aren't they?"

I scoffed. "More than you know. We're in the Ishtar District right now. Everything ties back to Old Babylon, but they lean into much more...metaphorical meaning."

"Ishtar..." Lana said. "That was the gate into the city, right?"

"It was. And this district is the gateway to tomorrow, to a better future, to the evolved civilization." I exaggerated my tone. "All metaphorical, all to make them feel more important."

"What's Esagila? I haven't heard of that one."

"It was a temple," Kuma said, "to the god Marduk. You'll see his name a lot there."

"But I'm guessing it's not a religious district."

"Depends on your religion," I said. We'd rounded the corner and stepped onto rectangular platforms that were rising at a slope to the next tier of the city. A drone hung suspended to the side of the lift, projecting a hologram of an augmented reality strip club, located in the Esagila District. As if that wasn't enough, a drone shaped roughly like a prone, smiling cat hung beside it, an advertisement for Chimera, another business selling synthetic organisms.

"No, it's not," Kuma responded. "Esagila is mostly an...entertainment district. A place for escape."

"Ah, I get it," Lana said. "Religion. Opiate of the masses. Esagila has other kinds of opiates."

"Yep. Have to keep their people addicted so they stay complacent," I said. "Otherwise they may wise up and get out of here."

"Maybe they enjoy it," Lana challenged as we stepped onto the small waiting tram and took our seats. This time, Kuma decided to sit by Lana. As he sat, he let out a big sigh that I'd heard a million times. "Do you talk in anything but extremes? Do you not have entertainment in the enlightened world? Is that beneath you?" She smirked a little, and I hoped the humor meant she didn't totally hold my earlier frustration against me.

"Of course we do, but we don't have to pay for it. And we don't have to work in terrible conditions just to make the money to keep doing the things we love. Big difference."

Lana leaned her head back and forth, considering, as the tram lurched forward. Then she got distracted by the view outside the window, the towering buildings around us, the vibrant holo-ads projected by drones along the tram's path, the hovercraft traffic above us, casting shadows like clouds over everything below. There was wonder on her face, but as I watched, it crumbled, her mouth closing and eyes slowly turning downward, the awe collapsing into sadness. It must have reminded her of home. Maybe her family.

As she thought about her family, I couldn't help looking everywhere for mine. On the walk over, I'd stared at every passerby, every distant shopper, every loner huddled in a corner. And on the tram, I kept looking up and down the aisles, despite already looking over every passenger several times. I hoped to see that copper hair above a seat, to catch those gold-flecked green eyes staring at me from a shadow, to find her. I was close, I could feel it, but something about the proximity only made me more anxious. What if I didn't find her, but the Wolf instead? What did we do after? What—

Breathe. Find Alis. Find the mithril. Get out. Kill the Wolf.

"So what'd you do?" Lana asked, quickly, anxiously, as if she were trying to fill the silence.

"Hm?" Kuma asked.

"You said you weren't welcome here. What'd you do?"

"Stole a ship."

Kuma didn't even glance at me that time. Guess he was done taking my lead on that one. But...I had no right to be frustrated about that. Our escape from Babylon was as much his story as mine.

"A ship?" Lana frowned, then her mouth dropped open in realization. "Not the *Harriet!*"

"Technically, we took Cargo Hauler GG9487F," Kuma said with a shrug.

"You...how...why?" she looked between us, glancing up and down. "You don't exactly seem like the thieving type. And isn't that against your Compact?" She aimed that one at me, eyebrows rising in playful mockery.

"You mean our Compact?" I shot back. "The one *you* signed? First off, that was before the Compact. And second, it wouldn't count. Babylon doesn't participate in that contract."

Lana scoffed. "So you can do whatever you want to them? That feels very morally problematic."

I rolled my eyes, tired of justifying and explaining our principles to someone who clearly still had too much Bastion in her. "Trust me, it was justified." I looked at Kuma, sobered by the memories of that day, all the days leading up to it.

And this time, Kuma's hardness toward me softened. He nodded. "It was justified. And it was nothing compared to what had been stolen from us. We just happened to steal it from the guy who owns more than half this city. Arturo Srinivasan Carivant. He'll be keeping an eye out for us."

"But this was before the Compact? That's, what, ten years?"

"Twelve," I said.

"That seems like a long time to devote resources to looking for you."

"Trust us," Kuma said. "Guy holds a grudge. And he can afford to."

The tram emerged on the other side of the canyon between buildings and dropped us in a small plaza. We stepped off in front of a sign so bright it hurt. It read "Welcome to the Esagila District, the Temple to Tranquility." Surrounding the pentagonal plaza were a few hotels and a row of shops. Directly across from us was another turnout that connected to a maglev road. That went deeper into the district, between towering buildings projecting dazzling signs for what lay within. On one, a dragon breathed fire that singed the words "The Path to Purgatory" onto the screen, and below that "With our new stim suits, you'll actually feel the pain, the pleasure, the panic." Another featured a woman biting her lip, lifting her shirt to just under her breasts, then wagging her finger before the screen read "She's waiting for you at Fantasies." On the other side, a projection dominating most of a building's facade showed someone walking down a dim hallway before it collapsed, revealing armored knights charging across a muddy battlefield, then that scene faded to show the deck of a starship—one I recognized all too well—with explosions outside the broad viewport. Then text appeared on-screen saying: "Walk through the past at Vortex."

"Cherry Blossom's this way," I said, nodding to the northwest. "It's that pink light coming from a street a few blocks down."

"I..." I looked at Lana as she stared where I'd nodded. She swallowed and put a shaking hand in her pocket, just like she'd done on the train. That didn't hide how pale her skin had gone. She looked like she was staring down a revenant, not a cityscape. "I can probably find my way from here."

"Are you all right?" Kuma asked. Then he shook his head. "Stupid question. Of course you're not. How can we help?" I swayed from foot to foot, itching to get going.

"We can start going in that direction, they're both that—" I shut up when Kuma shot me a look.

Lana glanced toward me but otherwise ignored what I'd said. "You've done enough. I don't think it was good for me to be alone."

"I know how that is," Kuma said. "I lost my...my daughter. And, man do those demons try to claw their way in any chance they get." He stuck out his hand, "but if you'd like to go the rest of the way on your own, we'll respect that, too."

Lana offered a half-smile and shook his hand. "Thank you." Then she turned to me. I summoned what friendly smile I could in my present anxiety and held out my hand, too. "Thank you for going out of your way for me. I hope you...find your way home." She said the last phrase with a hint of suspicion.

"And I hope you find a home here," I said, and anxious to go as I was, I meant it. "I'm sorry for your loss. I hope this gives you some closure."

She swallowed and looked away. "Me, too."

Then Lana turned, throwing one more smile at Kuma, and headed off toward the pink light of Cherry Blossom. We gave her some distance then started walking, taking a different angle toward a closer street, Anker's street, a block or so over from where Lana was headed.

"You going to tell me what's pissing you off, or are you just going to glare at me all night?" I asked without turning around to Kuma.

Kuma snorted. "You know I love you, brother. But you're being about as cold as that fish freezer. I know you're thinking about Alis, but damn. Alis can take care of herself, Lana is a fresh wound walking around a new world."

"And we got her where she needed to go, didn't we? We helped her. She didn't want us butting in anymore."

"How many times did I say things like that when I lost Mele? And how many times did you butt in?"

I clenched my jaw, that blow hitting too close to home. We'd shared our grief in those days, sometimes in silence on the shores of the Corcoran Sea. Sometimes in tearful, deep conversation, and sometimes in yelling that inevitably ended up with something broken.

"It's our fault, Tor," Kuma said, a little quieter. "Her life, her loss. It's because of us."

"No, it's because of Bastion," I said without turning around. We'd crossed the small plaza and were almost to Anker's street. A drone flew over bearing a Genesis Gardens logo, a minimalist Earth framed by two trees. As soon as I saw it, I looked down. Was it following us? Carivant would have drones all over the city. Just seeing one wasn't a reason to panic, but still, my heart rate picked up. If he found us before we found Alis. If he stopped me...

He wouldn't stop me. Not again. Never again.

"We didn't build the Shades. Bastion did," I continued. "We didn't oppress the poor into a state of such vulnerability. We didn't force Lana and her family to stay there. She could have left just like Alis did."

"That is not even remotely the same—"

I finally stopped and spun in the middle of the sidewalk, nearly causing a pair of Babylonians to crash into me. I ignored the insults they threw back as they rounded the corner onto Anker's street.

"I don't care, Kuma! Right now, I do not care. All I care about is finding Alis. And killing the Wolf. I haven't slept in over a day, I'm starving, I'm terrified, and yes, I know a lot of this shit is my fault. I brought Cixin here. I brought Lana here. I brought the Wolf here! But I can't change that now. What I can do is find Alis, kill the Wolf, and get the hell out of here. Then I'll deal with the guilt and the rest of the shit you're throwing at me. Okay? But can it wait five fucking minutes?"

Kuma opened his mouth, closed it, and let his words escape as jets out of his nostrils. Then, just before I turned back around, he said, "We're caught in a cycle, brother, and I'm done dragging people along with us. I don't want to go around again."

"Then we're on the same page," I snapped. "Because that's the whole reason I'm here, Kuma. You think *you're* done with cycles? I've been fending off a bloodthirsty alter ego of the love of my life for ten years. Trust me, we're ending it."

"I don't think it's that simple."

"And, like I said, I don't care."

I spun back around and steamed around the corner, almost knocking into another Babylonian. I honestly didn't expect Kuma to follow, but out of the corner of my eye, I saw him coming a moment later. My stomach clenched at how I'd treated him, but I stood by what I said, if not *how* I'd said it. There were more important things to worry about. And if he left, it didn't matter. I'd planned to do this on my own anyway.

Find Alis. Get the mithril. Get out. Kill the Wolf.

My cognitive map of the city was hazy, but when I looked halfway down the block, it snapped back into clarity. Nestled between much newer buildings was a restaurant with a flickering sign. That little old place had some of the best Japanese food in the city, definitely in the district. I couldn't have counted the times we'd met there after absurdly long shifts to share sushi and drink warm sake until the pains and stresses from the day were a little more numb. It was in that restaurant that we'd told our colleagues—our friends—about our plan. And it was there that every one of them tried to turn us from that path, rejecting our ask for support and, in the end, freedom. We'd complained around those tables, peeling coating off with anxious fingers, for years, but then, when it mattered most, when there was actually an opportunity to find justice and build a better life, the fear got to them. That was the last time we saw Anker or Alibren or Tolman or any of them. Except Beck. I wondered if Anker would react with the same fear at seeing us again.

We walked past the restaurant, and I couldn't help taking a deep breath of those salty scents. Maybe, when this was all over, I could take Alis there. Maybe not everything in Babylon was bad.

Anker's apartment building was next to the restaurant. At least, that's where he'd lived twelve years before. It was unlikely he'd moved, though. In Babylon, unless you were overflowing with cash, you generally stayed where you could find a roof to sleep under. A few other colleagues had even stayed at Anker's when they'd lost their apartments because the landlords suddenly exploded their rent. If Anker wasn't there, we'd try Tolman next. He'd be a few blocks north, on the edge of the Gardens District.

The door to the apartment building was unlocked—fortunately, a few more hours and it would have been locked for the night. We stood in silence, Kuma's arms folded, as we rode the elevator up to the sixteenth floor. I should have apologized, I knew that, but it could wait until after Anker. After we had our next lead. Or better: a way into Genesis Gardens' headquarters, where I assumed the mithril was stored.

The elevator doors slid open, and a wave of cigarette smoke, alcohol, and stale food washed over us. Haze hung in the air, music shaking the walls from one apartment, laughter coming from another. Again, sounds and scents I once took for the vibrancy of the city, the eclectic layers of life. Now it made me want for the hillside by our home in Orilla and the fresh scent of the sea.

We passed an apartment with its door open, a couple reclined against each other on a worn, stained couch, both staring in different directions with the distant expression of someone lost in a mindjack. A holoscreen flashed the day's news at them, illuminating their faces in the otherwise dark room.

The next apartment was Anker's. I took a deep breath and knocked in the center of the door, where the paint was worn from decades of knocking, no small part of that from my own knuckles.

No one answered immediately, but just when I was raising my hand to knock again, a lock clicked behind the door.

"Come in," came a scratchy voice on the other side. A voice I'd know anywhere.

I opened the door. The apartment was much like I remembered it, a small sitting area with a couch—one of them new since my time—and a holopro-jector. Behind the sitting area was a kitchen, and beside the food printer stood Ankerlund Morera Gordon. He still wore the pants of his Genesis Gardens uniform but otherwise only a simple white t-shirt. The pinky and ring finger of his right hand were metal, and he was nearly bald, his buzzed brown hair much more receded since last I saw him. He'd grown a mustache, too.

Despite my exhaustion, despite all I was feeling, I couldn't help but smile at the familiar face.

"Hey, Anker."

And Anker's face couldn't be more opposite.

His nostrils flared and lip curled in almost a snarl. "What the hell are you doing here?" He stalked past us, carrying with him a cloud of body odor, and slammed the door.

I swallowed, the little hope I had starting to curdle. "We—"

"I should kick you out right now. I should..." Anker stopped in front of me, conflict knitting his brows together in concern even as the almost-snarl remained on the lower half of his face. "What the hell are you doing here?" he repeated.

This already wasn't going how I'd hoped, and those hopes weren't ever very high. But based on this reaction, I highly doubted immediately asking for help would go well.

"Are you all right?" I asked instead.

The concern on Anker's face collapsed into a glare and a sarcastic "HA! All right?" He stalked back to the kitchen, pressing a button to tell the whirring food printer to pause. His finger lingered there, his back still toward us and his shoulders slumped. "I thought you were done with this place," he said, still turned away. "Done with us." Finally he pivoted toward us, leaning back against his counter. "So what righteous mission are you on now? What do you want? 'S the only reason you'd come back."

"I...did something happen?" Anker, like the rest of our friends, hadn't been angry when Kuma and I had left, so I didn't understand where this hostility was coming from. Had he gotten bitter over the rough years, regretting that he hadn't come with us? "You're more than welcome to come with us." I pointed back toward the door, hoping that would help. But I regretted following that theory thread as soon as Anker's bottom jaw jutted out, and he shook his head as if I'd just insulted his mother.

"Yeah, something happened," Anker said. "You left. You stole Carivant's ship. You got Beck *killed*, Toris. And then you weren't here to face the consequences, so guess who was?"

Anker may as well have stuck his hand in my gut, squeezed, and twisted. It's what his words felt like, anyway. "Did they come after you? Anker, I'm sorry. I...we—"

"Us? Yeah, they came after us, questioned us, suspected us. They beat Alibren. But no, not just us. Everyone in Genesis Gardens took the burden of *your* consequences. Hell, everyone in Babylon. You know how influential Carivant is. Got the laws changed. Tighter surveillance, removal of payment regulations and time constraints. Unions got crushed. They used what you two," he pointed his two metal fingers at us, "did as proof that the corporations were taking on more risk in this 'era,'" he spread his arms in an exaggerated wave, "and that with the benefits they were offering to our blossoming society, they needed to be protected. Prioritized. The chains removed to do what they felt best." He shrugged. "You gave them the reason they needed, because when those chains broke, the billions of dollars of corporate greed and speed came after us, running us down." He took a step toward us, his face red. We'd opened a door of anger and resentment ten years shut and holding back something that only became more rotten with time.

"Tolman's dead. Crushed in an accident because of those pesky regulations going away. Alibren's under so much stress and anxiety that she got addicted to a lovely cocktail of narcotics. She's been to rehab twice." Each revelation was another twist to my gut. "My pay got cut in half, and I work twice as much." Twist. "So, yeah, something happened, Toris. But you got what you were looking for, didn't you? The Compact. I'm sure Orilla's a paradise now, isn't it? Is that why you're here? To liberate us all?" His chest heaved up and down, his jaw still jutting out.

I held up my hands. "Anker, I'm sorry. I know that...that doesn't make up for anything, but you know us well enough to know that's the last thing we wanted. It definitely didn't...go as we planned. But I really mean it, you're welcome to leave with us. They can't make you stay." I looked up to Kuma for support, but he had his eyes closed and a frown on his face. It was his guilty face, and behind it he was processing what to say, what to do, slower to speak than I was.

And I could hear what he'd say to me later. Another person suffering because of our actions. Just like Lana. Just like Cixin.

Twist.

We were wasting time. Find Alis. Get the mithril. Get out.

But...this cycle.

"Ten years, and you haven't changed," Anker snapped. "It just doesn't compute for you that some people may be happy here. If not happy, at least satisfied. If not satisfied, it's still home. You had a family, a foundation to run away to. Our foundations are here. And our friends. Some people are willing to stay, to try to make things better in their own ways. Even if you don't think they should. But you act like everyone should see everything through your eyes. Well, now, because of that, we're less happy. Because of you."

"Kuma didn't have a family to return to, actually," I snapped. He'd gone too far. "And my sister was the only one left when I got there. Thanks to Carivant. So it wasn't all paradise."

"Tor," Kuma said, warning in his voice.

Anker's glare softened, and I saw a little of my old friend, not the enemy I'd created. He looked at Kuma, the expression softening further, glaring eyebrows inverting. "Mele?"

Kuma closed his eyes and nodded.

Anker sighed, hung his head, then walked over and wrapped his arms around Kuma. "I'm sorry, brother." He patted Kuma's back. "I'm so sorry." Then he stepped back, Kuma turning to wipe away a tear on his cheek, and embraced me, too. That brought tears to my own eyes, and I squeezed my old friend tight.

"I'm sorry all of that happened," I said. "We..." I trailed off, knowing there was nothing I could say to make it better.

"Me, too, brother," he said.

After a final squeeze, Anker stepped back and wiped his own eyes. "Well. Why are you here?" The edge was softer, but it was still there. We wouldn't win back ten years of resentment that quickly. At least he still had the good heart that had won me over as his friend all those years before. That may have been all we needed.

"We're looking for someone," I said, unsure of how much to share. What if something went wrong—again—and Carivant came to Anker for information? It may have been a case of the less he knew, the better. "New to the city. A woman. Bastionite. She may have gone straight for Genesis Gardens. Has anyone broken in? Any incidents in the past day?"

Anker frowned. Then he shook his head. "Not that I heard." Maybe that should have made me feel better, but part of me hoped she Alis—or the Wolf—was sitting in a cell somewhere. At least then she'd be in one spot. "Don't know why a Bastionite would need to break in, though. More likely that Carivant would roll out the red carpet. Why? You in the bounty hunting business now or something? Who are they?"

"Someone important," I said. "What do you mean roll out the red carpet? I know Carivant always did a little dealing with Bastion under the table, but..."

"Not so under the table anymore," Anker said, folding his arms. "Considers them partners now. In the name of innovation and all that. He's also got some philanthropic angle about it, helping rebuild their magnetic field, helping families in the Shades, and all that."

My mouth went dry. If Carivant was benefiting from a closer relationship with Bastion, that only put Alis in more danger. We didn't know if the signal beaming to her mindjack from Mars was intentional or a phantom, but even if it was unintentional, I doubted that ten years had done anything to cool the grudge Bastion would hold against her. Compound that with her connection to me and...it wasn't good.

"We're also looking for mithril," I said, moving on before I spiraled too far. "Carivant's stash of it they were always bragging about in the media. I know that would have been a better question for Tolman, since he was managing vault movements, but..." I couldn't believe Tolman was gone. I could still see his huge hands fumbling with chopsticks as he tried to eat sushi. All of us laughing. One more—

Focus.

"That I can answer for you," Anker said. "Mithril's gone."

Twist. I set my hand on the armchair nearest the entryway to steady myself. "All of it?"

"Far as I know. They sold it to some Lunese corporation. Most of it, at least. The rest went to some secret project. Tolman had mentioned diverting what was left to a subsidiary."

"Outside the city?" Kuma asked.

"No," Anker said. "Still in the tower. Don't know where it went, though. Lots of rumors about it. Some people said it went to the Vault, others into the black market, others said weapons. No one knows."

I took a breath, finding some strength in my legs again. Even if Carivant had smelted and forged the mithril into something else, we may have been able to still find a use for it. This was a hiccup, but maybe not as bad as I initially thought.

"All right," I said. "Know of any bioengineers? Neurospecialists, ideally?"

"Independent? No. Some new laws a few years back prohibited bioengineering except from certain authorized organizations. All corporate-owned, of course. You may be able to find someone on the black market, but..." he cringed, "doesn't sound like you'd want to go that route. Neurospecialists? What have you two gotten yourselves into?"

I sighed and shook my head. "Brother, we could talk all night and barely cover half of it. Okay. Last question. You always knew the best ways into the Tower. You got one for us?"

Anker raised his eyebrows. "Like, tonight?"

"Like tonight."

"Did you hear what I just said to you? They cracked down on everything after your last stunt. Every way in and out is locked down. Only way in is with a mindjack sync, and you sure ain't borrowing mine."

"Anker, if you'd let me—"

"Let you convince me to join some other crusade? After how well the last one turned out? Hell no. Did you hear anything I said?" He shook his head with another huff. "Look, it's good to see you guys. If you're ever in town other than to ask me to risk my life, we'll get some sushi." He put his hands on his hips, and I took that as a signal to leave.

But there had to be more. I needed a way in. I needed some kind of lead. This diversion, this waste of time, had turned into nothing but another guilt trip. I couldn't even take comfort in the fact that Alis at the very least hadn't been in some widely publicized accident or violent failed break-in. After all, just because Anker hadn't yet heard anything didn't mean nothing had happened. I was where I'd started, and I could scream. No, I was further back. The mithril would be harder to get, now, and we had zero leads on any bioengineers who could finally kill the Wolf even if we managed to find the precious metal.

Couldn't find Alis. Couldn't get the mithril. But I wouldn't leave until I had both.

So, keeping my words in for fear my frustration would hurt Anker more than he already was, I turned toward the door.

But then Kuma spoke. "It's good to see you, too, Anker. I'm sorry we showed up like this. I'd kill to get everyone together for sushi again." He licked his lips, clearly hesitant. "One more question, then we're out. Cherry Blossom apartments. You had family there, right? We want to check in on a...friend there."

I slowly turned back around, glancing up at Kuma. His lips rolled inward, and he rubbed them back and forth in trademark concern.

"Cherry Blossom hasn't been there in six years."

Kuma tilted his head. "But we saw the light from—"

"Yeah, they repurposed that," Anker said. "Punarjanman bought it, brought in a few subsidiaries. Biggest one's a deathwalk, I think."

Kuma nodded, slowly, but his eyes were distant.

Great. I sensed another detour coming.

"Our offer stands, Anker," I said, as eager to get us out of there as Anker was. "You want out, you call Orilla." I tried not to show the cringe I felt on the inside, wondering if I'd have a place in Orilla del Angel after all this.

"Good luck on your crusade," Anker said as we opened the door and he turned back to his food printer with a dismissive wave. "Try not to get anyone killed this time."

CHAPTER NINETEEN

ALIS

(Twelve years earlier)

WHEN I WOKE UP, I was back in my cell. I groaned as I rolled over in my bed, my entire body aching from the extremely rude shock that Halgard's officer gave me. Spasming was not kind to muscles. I wasn't sure how long I'd been unconscious, but judging by the drool staining half my pillow, it had been a while.

"Ah," I gasped as the dagger in my head returned with my consciousness. The pain throbbed, as if the dagger were not just twisting, but jerking up and down at the same time. I imagined the malfunctioning mindjack wasn't a fan of the volts shot through my body, either.

Then, lingering in the back of my mind like a bad dream, were Beck's memories. They felt like my memories, as if I'd been the one shot, the one to feel such fear only to find bravery in the end. I'd died for my friends alongside Beck. I shook my head—which didn't help the mindjack pain—as if that could jar the memory loose and send it tumbling out. I barely knew Toris and Kuma, as grateful as I was to them.

And even then, outside the moment, I wasn't totally sure if I had leaped to defend Kuma, or if Beck had. I genuinely couldn't tell. And I hated that.

To sum up, I was a mess.

As I'd slept, the *Dawnbreak* and its surrounding fleet had certainly made it at the very least to the interspheric border, if not into Bastion territory. Whatever Admiral Halgard's plan, it was in motion, which meant she'd only get increasingly desperate to win my help. Her movements wouldn't go unnoticed by Vice Admiral Ecker and his superiors, either, which only chopped down my timeline on that side, too. Maybe Ecker had already given up on me. Maybe Teah was already...

No. I couldn't tumble down that spiral. My mind was becoming unmoored enough as it was. I was a soldier; I had to focus on my mission: find my path. Although, it felt like that path was becoming more like a tunnel between two clashing mountains, and the end of the tunnel was collapsing.

I heard voices and footsteps on the other side of the door, and I knew one of those mountains was there. Another boulder tumbled to obstruct what little light I could see.

But when the door slid open, it wasn't Admiral Halgard or her officers standing there. It was Toris.

"You taking visitors?"

I didn't respond or bother standing up as he entered the cell and the door sealed shut behind him.

"Are you all right?" Toris asked, sliding his back against the wall as he sat opposite me. There were only a couple feet separating us. Too close. I itched to move to a corner of the room and give myself more space, but my aching body convinced me not to.

"Grand," I said with as forced a smile I could muster.

He bit at the inside of his cheek—a tic I'd seen him do on multiple occasions—and nodded. "Sorry. Stupid question."

"Halgard send you?" I asked, tilting my head, then cringing as the dagger twisted with the motion. "You the good cop?"

Toris scoffed. "You really think I'm going to do anything she asks me after that? No, I wanted to check on you. Kuma would have, too, but they've confined him to his cabin. He—we both, really—wanted to thank you. I don't think either of us would have ever expected a Bastionite to rush to our protection."

"Yeah, well, it was only partly me. I think. Beck was in there, too."

Toris frowned. "What? Really?"

"Whatever that device does, it interfaces with my mindjack as seamlessly as my mindjack interfaces with my brain. How it's doing it while my 'jack is malfunctioning, I don't know. So, yeah, I had Beck on the brain. I felt how much he wanted to help you, how much courage he finally felt when he charged my...those...the soldiers." I looked down, unable to hold eye contact as I thought back to what I'd seen. "What happened after?"

Toris hesitated, and I knew I probably shouldn't have asked, but I'd shared Beck's last moments with him. I was invested. "Beck killed one of them, like you saw," he eventually said. "The gunshot gave us enough warning. That soldier was dead as soon as they poked their head around the corner. And then Kuma just kept firing and...well, it's probably a good thing you didn't see what happened after."

"Who...who did you lose?" I asked, finally looking up at him. He'd been looking at me but glanced away when our eyes locked, up at the corner of the cell behind me. "Sorry," I added. "I shouldn't make you..."

"It's fine," Toris said. "My parents. My mom was actually Mele's—Kuma's daughter—teacher."

"Who was the woman with them? Was she your..."

"No. My sister. Navi. She and my dad had rushed to the school when the invasion forces were dropping through the atmosphere. Navi was actually the one who'd taken out that soldier in the hallway, the one Beck took the weapon from."

After a moment of silence, I said: "I'm sorry." The words were inadequate, a thimble trying to hold a lake. And I wasn't even sure what I was apologizing for. I could relate to losing family, I could empathize with that grief, that hole. But was I apologizing for Bastion, too? For what my military, my people, had done solely as a distraction?

"You said you lost your mom, too," Toris said, not acknowledging the apology at all. I probably wouldn't have, either. "You said it was because of us. Because of Earth. Was it in battle?"

Was he trying to get intelligence? Was he lying about resisting Halgard? That seemed unlikely given his reaction in the conference room, but I couldn't know for sure. Kuma may have been in more trouble than he let on, and Halgard could have offered mercy for getting more out of me. It's what Ecker would have done.

Toris certainly wasn't a Bastionite, though. He didn't seem like a great Earther, either, at least not as far as deferring to his superiors and respecting their command went. Maybe that was just a symptom of their devolution as a society.

I swallowed and looked down at my hands. He'd shared more with me than I deserved, and for some reason I couldn't explain, I *wanted* to share with him, too. Maybe I was vulnerable because of the torture, maybe I felt like I owed him for all he'd done for me. Maybe I was just very, very alone. In so many ways.

"Not in battle, no," I eventually said. "It was early in the war, when most of the fighting was happening in the Belt. She was working at an outpost there. When it passed into Earth's Sphere, an armada was waiting. They nuked the asteroid. She was far enough under the surface that she wasn't too physically hurt, but the radiation got to her. It was bad. Even with her augments, even with our medicine, it wasn't enough."

"Radiation?" Toris scowled. "Fusion bombs don't have fallout like—"

"They weren't fusion bombs. Earth still used fission atomics in space combat because the radiation was an added bonus." I tilted my head. "See what I was saying in there? War makes monsters of us all."

Toris wisely avoided taking that bait and simply nodded. "I'm sorry about your mom."

Just like when I said it, that wasn't nearly enough, but it didn't have to be. Nothing could fill that void. It sat deep within me, hard edges crusted around it, rings of thorns facing outward. No one could ever say enough, but trying still mattered, especially from someone who'd lost their family to someone just like me.

How many Torises had I created after Stickney?

And how many more would I create if I returned to Ecker with intel? Even if it saved Teah.

I couldn't argue against the logic, but I still didn't know if I could pay the price. The Trolley Problem had been taken to a whole other level. Save thousands, maybe millions, by ending the war, but send the trolley careening toward my sister. The little girl that I'd held in the dark corner of my room as we both cried after visiting Mom that final time. The little girl who'd tried again and again to be an Aegis pilot like me, who studied more than I ever had, despite lacking whatever it was that enabled the sync.

The little girl who may have become something else without me realizing it. Did that change things? If she had willingly enacted the plan to manipulate Mwezi's vote and dominate their mindjacks, was she even the sister I knew anymore? I should have paid more attention. I should have—

"You okay?" Toris asked.

I shook my head, not realizing I'd zoned out, staring at the corner of my cell beside Toris. "Sorry. Just..."

"I wouldn't know what to do, either," he said.

"What?"

"We heard what your vice admiral said. The situation he put you in. Yesterday I may have said we wouldn't dare make that threat to our own people, but after what Halgard just did to Kuma and I, I wouldn't be surprised if her boundaries stretched that far."

"How'd you know that's what I was thinking?"

He shrugged, a small smile tugging at his lips and a twinkle in his green eyes. "We were talking about our families, and if I were in here, that threat would be all

I was thinking about. I'm also pretty familiar with the 'holy-shit-what-do-I-do' stare."

I searched between Toris' eyes for a moment, tilting my head.

"What?" he asked.

"Well, apparently, you can read my mind, so you guess."

He scoffed, clearly thinking I was joking.

"I'm serious," I said, raising my eyebrows. "Guess."

He leaned forward, resting his elbows on his knees, eyes narrowing but still sporting the hint of a playful smile. "You're not sure if you can trust me. If you should. If I'm trying to get close to you to get something for Halgard." He tilted his head a little to match my angle. "Or maybe you're thinking of how you could use me to get out of here, to find a way out of your..." he hesitated. "Predicament."

"Predicament," I snorted. Understatement of the day.

"How'd I do?"

I frowned and leaned back against the wall. "Close. Not bad. Except for the part about using you. I know what it feels like to be used, to be a pawn on the board of people more powerful than us. And I think you've been used enough by your own people, just like me. I wouldn't do that to you. Mudbrain or not." He chuckled and shook his head at that.

Then his smile dropped, like clouds shrouding the moon in the middle of night. "I shouldn't have let it get that far. I shouldn't have even let it start, really. I guess I just can't relate to how deeply 'jacks are a part of your mind. That's not an excuse, though. Does it...does it stay with you? The things she put in there?"

I clenched my teeth, trauma-induced rage bubbling up to smother what little lightness I'd been feeling in that moment. I knew Toris couldn't have done more. Halgard would have knocked him unconscious and dragged him drooling out of the room as she had with me. Still, I couldn't help but channel some of that anger toward him, as if he represented Halgard and Earth just by being born there. I knew that wasn't justified. I didn't care.

"Stay with me?" I asked with an edge. "The 'things' she put in there were the memories and sensory experiences of people who suffered every shade of trauma. It doesn't just stay with me, it's a part of me. As if they were my own memories. Do you know the nightmares I've had for the past few days? Do you know that when I hear footsteps outside that door, I can't help but wonder if it's my rapist returning? When I catch a hint of smoke, I think of finding my family crushed under their burning home?" Toris was staring at me, eyebrows scrunched in concern. "And when I look at you, I feel Beck's pity and fear, and I feel a bullet slamming into my face."

At that last jab, Toris finally looked down. That was too far. It was difficult enough for him to remember that terrible day at Halgard's hands, but to throw the death of his friend in his face...

"Sorry," I said, my boiling rage simmering down. "Sorry. I...I'm a mess. And I'm pissed. And I'm torn and terrified. If Halgard wanted me to feel empathy, she's going to be sorely disappointed, because all I want to do is smash her under my Aegis." If it wasn't blown to pieces, at least.

"Then what are you going to do?" Toris asked, looking up with a defiance in his features, a strength in his expression and fire in his eyes.

"What?" I asked, recoiling a little at the sudden change in him.

"What are you going to do about it?" he repeated. "How are you going to make sure what happens next is because of you? Not because someone ordered you or manipulated you or reprogrammed you, but because you wanted it. Because you knew it was right."

"You're not going to try and convince me to help Halgard? To win the war?"

"I don't think those are the same question. Despite being an Earther, war has reverted Halgard, like it does to everyone. In the end, she's like every other general. Her ends justify her means. We all experienced that today." He held up his hands in preemptive defensiveness. "Some more than others, of course. So, no, I don't think her answer is the only one."

"You don't sound like a very good soldier."

"That's because I'm not one," Toris snapped, though I knew his aggression wasn't directed at me. "Halgard may be fighting for Earth, but she represents the kind of outdated systems that we're trying to move beyond. The kind of systems that will end with this war."

"Systems? You mean military? Defense forces?" I asked, narrowing my eyes as my tone became more skeptical. It sounded not just idealist, but also dangerously naive.

Toris shook his head. "Hierarchies that give people the power to manipulate and use others, to determine the worth of the majority against the interests of the powerful few."

"That's incredibly vague." I said, trying not to smile a little.

Toris caught it and rolled his eyes, hiding away his own smile. "You're asking me to sum up a planet-wide movement in a sentence." He waved his hand in front of his face as if shooing away something foul smelling. "But that's not what I'm here for. I'm not Halgard. I'm not convincing you to come to our side. Because that's the point. It's not about sides or Spheres or which color shackles you'd rather wear."

I narrowed my eyes. "You have a plan. You know something."

Toris smirked. "Now who's reading minds?"

"What is it?" I asked, leaning forward.

He shook his head. "I told you, I'm not going to be Halgard. I want to know what your path is and whether we can..." he looked upward and leaned his head back and forth, looking for the words. "Whether we can walk it together. Halgard's torture may not have worked—and I'm glad it didn't; that would only encourage her—but what *did* feeling all that do to you? And what are you doing next?"

I swallowed and leaned my head back against the cell wall. It wasn't as if I hadn't been asking myself that final question since Ecker sent that message. But I hadn't asked the former. I'd resisted learning anything from that torture and from the poor people whose memory Halgard had manipulated to change my mind. Taking anything productive from that torture would validate Halgard's approach, and I refused to let that happen.

Talking to Toris, however, was starting to spark connections I wouldn't have made alone. Halgard had gotten it wrong. She thought empathy with those who I...who Bastion...

No. Who I. She thought empathy with those whom I harmed—and those similar to the ones I harmed—would get me to transfer my allegiance. She thought I'd feel such empathy for their side that I'd turn against my people. But it wasn't that simple. Empathy had done more.

I'd been finding what little strength I could muster in my identity as a soldier. But that wasn't where the strength came from. I wasn't strong because I was a soldier. I was a soldier because of propaganda and stories, sure, but also because of what happened to my mom. Those stories may have distorted the truth, but the principles they resonated with were my own. And while part of my becoming a soldier was revenge, it was much more so because I wanted to contribute to a world where children didn't lose mothers because of atomics. Where we had security.

What I'd gotten wrong was thinking that security was defined by where our Sphere began and ended.

Empathy had done more. Halgard got it wrong. I wasn't a soldier, not like Ecker and Halgard. Maybe I wasn't...maybe I wasn't even a Bastionite anymore.

I certainly wasn't an Earther, despite the torture. I was Alistella Pareides Caliday, ambitious daughter and sister, conflicted warrior, survivor, traitor. I was the Moonbreaker, because I needed to own that. I needed to be accountable to that. For Monalua and everyone else who'd fallen that day.

Setting my jaw, I lowered my head to look at Toris. But before I opened my mouth to speak, his mouth pulled up into a smirk.

"What?"

"That look. That determination. I saw it in there with Halgard. You look like you could punch your way out of this cell, take command of the ship, and no one would stop you."

"And you think it's wise to make fun of me?" I said with a slight smirk of my own.

"Oh, I'm not making fun. It's just rare that you see that. I'm smiling because I can't wait to see what you're going to do."

"What if I answer your question, and it's not what you like? What if I told you I wanted to return to Ecker and give up anything I have to save my sister? Would you be as satisfied then?"

"I don't need to worry about that. If that was your plan, you would have done it already. And I know Halgard didn't break you. She made something stronger. No." He paused and looked me up and down. "*You* made something stronger."

I took a breath and stared at him for a moment. Toris was right. I'd been swimming in uncertainty since Stickney, and everything else that had happened were only currents that pulled me into deeper, more violent water. But now, despite the dagger in my head and the memories that weren't my own, I was above the water. I hadn't found solid ground—yet—but I was treading water, my face to the air, my muscles strong.

"I want to end the war," I said, finally answering Toris' question. "Not win the war. For either Bastion or Earth. I want to end it. For everyone Halgard put in my head and for everyone who she and your military put through the same hell. For my mom. And I want to save my sister. No..." I hesitated as Toris had a moment before, my mouth moving faster than my mind. "I want to know if my sister wants to be saved. But I don't know how to do either."

Toris was full-on smiling by the time I stopped. "That's what I thought. Kuma wasn't so sure, for the record. I love telling him he's wrong."

"Great, you're right. Congratulations. Now, will you tell me your plan?"

"No."

"I...what? After all that? You're not going to tell me?"

"Can't risk it. But I will tell you Halgard's. I'll have to be quick, though, in case she's listening." He pointed up at the ceiling, and while I'd never been able to find a microphone, there was likely one tucked away somewhere. And if it were true, Toris was taking risks just by being there, much less with what he'd said.

"Fine," I said. "Let's hear it."

"You saw we passed Farstead a day ago. We're well in Bastion territory, and a fleet's moving to intercept, but it's smaller."

"How did we make it so far?" I asked, curiosity overcoming the need to rush.

Toris smirked again, and I was on the border between finding the expression annoying and liking it. "Luna joined the war."

"What?!"

He nodded excitedly. "The Colonial Council knew that Bastion wouldn't stop with Mwezi. They saw what happened in the colony as an aggressive move against the entire moon."

I leaned back against the wall, jaw hanging open. Of course the other colonies of Luna would feel that way, they'd been arguing as much about Bastion presence for years. But to actually act on it?

"Halgard made it sound like the fighting around the moon is intense, with Bastion sending reinforcements to back up your vice admiral."

I nodded along with Toris' explanation, emotions conflicting inside. On one hand, I felt a massive relief that Ecker was preoccupied with Luna. I felt that mountain back away, leaving a wider, brighter opening at the end of my path. On the other hand, I was worried for Teah. Was she in the middle of that warzone? Would Ecker deploy her into a combat situation—which pruner's typically weren't prepared for—as punishment?

"They've noticed our approach, of course," Toris said, "but we've caught them with their pants down."

"Still," I said, "Halgard can't mean to conquer Bastion. The fleet's absence lets us get close to Mars, but short of glassing the surface..." My mouth went dry. "Please tell me she's not..."

Toris' smile dropped, and he bit at the inside of his lip again. "Just Bastion. Just the city."

I finally pushed myself to my feet. "Just Bastion?! Just the city?! That's millions of lives! That's..." Father. Mom's resting place. "That...that monster. She puts memories in my head of orbital bombardments as she goes to do the same thing? Worse?" I shook my head, talking more to myself than Toris. "No. There's no way she'll succeed. They have contingencies."

"And I'm sure Halgard does, too," Toris said, standing up himself. For a moment, we were way too close, only a few inches apart, his breath warm on my face, the bags under his tired eyes more pronounced. Then we stepped away in unison, he closer to the door and I to the back corner of the cell. "But, like I said, we have a plan. I'm with you. Bastion killed my family, but this...this isn't who we should be. We'll just be entering an endless cycle of violence and retaliation. You're right. We have to end the war, not win it."

"Okay," I shrugged, energized by adrenaline, "so, that's all you can tell me? You came here just to tell me something that I can do absolutely nothing with as we sail to burn down my home?"

I expected another smirk—and if he had, I really may have slapped him—but his face softened. "No, that's not the only reason I came down here. Protecting Kuma means more than you know, regardless of how much of that moment was you and how much was...Beck. And I wanted to know if that was a fluke, or if you can help us end the war. I'm sorry. I know it's asking a lot for you to trust a couple of Earthers, but I think we're more alike than you—"

"I do."

"Sorry?"

"I do trust you," I said, folding my arms as if that could protect me in the vulnerable position I was putting myself into. That had slipped out more quickly than intended, but I didn't take it back. I meant it. Toris and Kuma had risked their lives for me, their enemy, and through that torture I'd seen in even greater measure the kind of people they were. The least I could do was offer my trust in that situation. I quite literally had nothing to lose by it. "I don't think Halgard will agree, though. I think she's much more interested in winning the war. Despite bathing in the blood of innocents for the rest of her days." I hoped the admiral heard that one.

"Won't be the first time the admiral and I have disagreed," Toris said with another shrug. "It won't matter, either. She needs our help."

I had more questions, more doubts, more worries, but...trust. "I'll be waiting. Kicking back in my suite."

"Ha!" Toris turned toward the door.

"Wait." He turned half-around, hand still in a fist ready to knock on the door for the guards to let him out. "Thank you," I said. "Thank you for talking to me. And thank you for trusting me, too. Despite...everything."

He smiled, not a smirk, but a true, gentle smile that stretched to the corners of his eyes. It was bright and soft and warm. "I can't wait to see what you do," repeating his earlier words with a quiet verging on wonder. And then he left, the door sealing shut behind him. I stared at that door for a few moments after he left, feeling lighter than when he'd entered.

I felt lighter, at least until I thought about Halgard's plans. We were burning hard for Mars on a mission of utter destruction. I had no idea what the fleet looked like, but even a few battlecruisers equipped with the *Dawnbreak*'s particle beam could melt Bastion in seconds from low orbit. They'd struggle to get that close, but Halgard would have plans. They could have been preparing this for years, and I could give them critical intel. Planetary defense wasn't my expertise, but anyone in Bastion's military could recite the general capabilities and placements. Or maybe she had something else in mind for me, infiltration or sabotage. No wonder she was desperate to get me to comply.

And while I trusted Toris and understood why I had to stay in the dark on his plan, the uncertainty didn't help my anxiety. What if that plan failed? I needed to warn Father somehow, just in case, tell him to get out of the city. Maybe that was my path; maybe I could get intel to Bastion so they could evacuate the city. I'd win over their trust and save Teah, but then I could still follow Toris' plan to end the war. Unless that intel enabled Bastion to totally decimate Halgard and her fleet...I doubted that Toris' plan would allow for that.

I needed to talk to Teah. She would see reason as I had, I was sure of it. She would understand why I'd done what I'd done, and she'd help me end the war. We could have someone on the inside.

But was I willing to risk the entire mission on how well I knew my sister? I never thought she'd become a pruner, never thought she'd stand behind as egregious a violation of our principles as what happened in Mwezi. However, Ecker could have been lying that she knew the plan, just to drive in that wedge of doubt.

The only way to set everything straight was to talk to my sister. She'd listen. She looked up to me—too much, really. If I could have someone on the inside...that would change everything, whether she was deployed on Luna or burning back to support Bastion. It was worth the risk. I could control how much she knew.

Contacting Teah, however, was a problem in itself. If Ecker had an agent on-board, I had no idea who it was, and I doubted they'd reveal themselves to me except to maybe slit my throat in my sleep if I decided to help Halgard. My only option was the one thing Halgard couldn't take away from me: my mindjack. I hadn't tried connecting to it since right after I de-synced from my Aegis, and even the thought of that pain made my stomach turn. It was like considering kickboxing with my femur sticking out of my thigh. There was also the risk that as soon as I activated it, I'd connect with Bastion's network, and Ecker could try to control me again. Hopefully he'd be distracted enough with the Lunar conflict that he wouldn't notice in the time it took to speak to my sister.

Either way, in my mind, I didn't have a choice. I wasn't going to do anything unless I gave Teah the same chance I now had: redemption and a better future.

So I sat on my bed, put my back against the wall, placed my blanket in my mouth, and bit down. Then, grasping my sheets, I tapped into my 'jack.

The dagger twisted, then it shoved its way through the other side of my skull. I growled into my blanket, squeezing my sheets until my nails were digging through the fabric and into my palms. Still, I pressed on, I kicked at my opponent with my shattered femur. Again.

And again.

And again.

And—

The pain evaporated. The dagger pulled free. The femur locked back into place. My mind expanded, connected to the network. Ignoring the backlog of notifications, I reached out to compose my message to Teah as easily as sending a signal to tell my fingers to snap.

When those mental fingers snapped, my head cleaved in two.

It wasn't just a dagger, this time. It felt like a claymore split me down the middle, and my connection to the mindjack went dead. I screamed into the blanket, the pain pulling me toward unconsciousness. I couldn't feel the bed, nor the blanket, couldn't even tell if my eyes were open.

I screamed, and—

Then I wasn't in the cell anymore. I was in a different cell, as Idia, locked inside and waiting for the Bastion soldiers to return.

This time, I would be ready. I searched the rooms for a gun but only found a locked safe. The rest of the apartment turned up nothing of use. I could hit him with a book? Maybe a bottle? No. The kitchen. It was little more than a corner of the living room, near the door, and I already knew it didn't have many essentials.

But it did have a knife.

The edge was a little dull—the soldier threw it across the room and almost hit me the other day when it kept smashing tomatoes rather than slicing them—but that point was still sharp. Sharp enough to stab. Sharp enough to kill. I may not have been strong enough to push the soldier off, to keep his arms away, but I was strong enough for this.

I had a few minutes before he'd return, but the adrenaline was already burning through my veins as I stood in the center of the apartment, knife held in an under-hand grip and half-raised, as if I were about to stab the phantom in front of me. I knew I looked a little like a phantom myself, eyes wide, dress torn, pale and gaunt, bags under my eyes. He'd expect me to cover it all with makeup before he arrived. Before he—

I screamed, ran into the bedroom, and slammed the blade into the mattress. That mattress. It may as well have been a bed of thorns, a sheet of jagged glass. Just touching it with my off-hand made me recoil, but I kept stabbing. And at least that knife was sharp enough to puncture the fabric, to rip through it as I ground my teeth and growled sounds less-than-human. He'd made me this. Unlocked a primal fear that had festered into rage. Now I'd make him afraid. And I'd ensure that I was never afraid again.

A ding at the door. The sound of his mindjack syncing to the lock and the door disengaging.

The door hissed open and instinctive fear strangled my heart as I knelt atop the massacred mattress in the next room over. Did I go to him, hiding the knife behind my back? No, he'd see I'd been crying. He'd touch me, feigning concern. Or he'd ignore that I was clearly upset and comment on my lack of makeup. No.

I backed up off the bed and pressed myself against the wall, squeezing the hilt of the knife tight. I'd go for the neck; his thick uniform covered everything else, and he'd take off his high-collared jacket as soon as he walked in the door.

He let out a frustrated sigh before I heard him slam the kitchen drawers closed. I'd left them open when I'd searched them. His footsteps came closer.

"Can't close a fucking drawer, can…" he trailed off as he came closer to the open doorway and saw the destroyed mattress. I held my breath on the other side of the threshold, beside the doorframe. His boot crossed over, and I roared, spinning and driving the blade toward his neck. He recoiled, eyes widening as the tip of the knife cut a red line just shy of his Adam's apple.

The surprise quickly collapsed into rage, and his face contorted into an animal even lesser than I. He grabbed for my arms—like he always did—but I was ready. I stepped away and swiped at his face, slicing into his cheek as he tried to sidestep. With a yell, he dove under my arm, tackling me onto the ground. I held onto that knife, though, and slammed it through his uniform and into his side as he cried out. Faster than I could react, he grabbed the arm holding the knife and held it down, then he crashed his forehead into my nose. Stars burst in my vision and pain erupted across my face, blood instantly rushing down over my mouth. But adrenaline kept me sharp, and as he snarled at me I spit blood into his eyes. That gave me an instant of surprise to drive my knee up into his balls. With another yell, his limbs instinctively contracted. I shoved him off me, pushing him over as he tried to regain control, scrabbling at the ground with his hands. Still on the ground, I stabbed the blade through his hand, wrenched it out in a spray of blood, and then punched it into his neck.

He finally fell, collapsing with his bleeding hand to his neck, breath wheezing through the hole. Tears ran down his face, his eyes somewhere between anger and betrayal. Betrayal. As if there were any loyalty to lose in the first place.

I...

That wasn't real. That wasn't how the memory had gone before, during the empathy torture.

And I wasn't Idia. I wasn't in that apartment. I was—

Reality snapped back into place.

And I stood above a different bloody scene.

I was standing in the corridor outside my cell, and my two guards lay in spreading pools of blood at my feet, the red breaking around my feet and rippling like water around a cliff. In my hand I held a jagged piece of metal. Where had it come from? A glance back into my cell told me it was part of my bedframe. I had no idea how I'd torn it off.

I tasted metal and touched my lip, then my nose. It wasn't broken—likely thanks to my augments—but I'd definitely been hit there.

Idina's memory...it had somehow bled into reality, triggered by my malfunctioning mindjack. I...

I ran.

Halfway down the brig's corridor, I realized my boots were leaving bloody footprints. So I pressed myself against the wall and pulled them off, the metal floor cool against my feet even with socks on. The next corridor was empty, and I crept down it, no doubt under the careful watch of security cameras. That just meant I had to be faster than Halgard. With every turn, I was careful to put more distance between myself and the higher decks the admiral seemed to frequent. If I could make it to the hangar, I could find a way out. If I ran into anyone—

Footsteps. I froze at the corner of the corridor, viewscreen on the other side displaying the void of space and the silver and white slivers of other starships.

I couldn't hear any more footsteps. Had they turned down another corridor? I peeked around the edge of the wall.

Admiral Halgard grabbed me by the face and shoved me backward.

Surprised, I stumbled backward until I hit the other side of the corridor. Halgard was already on top of me. With a snarl on her lips, she whipped her right fist into my cheek. The force sent me to the ground. Before I could get up, Halgard grabbed me by the hair and slammed my face into the ground. My vision flashed, and the pain in my head spiked.

Still holding onto my hair, Halgard leaned close to me, her hot breath on my face.

"You killed two good men. I've treated you with what honor I can offer, leaving you with your agency, and you repay me with blood. Fine. If you want to be reminded of what it'd be like if you were in Bastion's captivity, I'm happy to oblige." She squeezed my hair tighter, and I hissed in pain. "You'll do what we need, and you'll be grateful for the chance. And if you think it was hard before, I've been using that machine like a scalpel. Now it'll be a hammer. And you deserve worse than that. Now get up."

She wrenched me to my feet by my hair, forcing me to cry out again. A pair of her soldiers stepped up, one grabbing me by the arm as the other slapped cuffs on me. Then Halgard shoved me by my shoulder against the wall. Her face was flushed and her eyes wild, her mouth still in a half-snarl.

"I didn't do it," I said, accidentally spitting fresh blood from my nose in her mouth. "I mean...I didn't...it was...I want to help. I want to end the war. I..." Anything. I'd say anything to stay out of that chair. That torture was breaking something inside me, weaving into the damage to my mindjack in a way I didn't understand, and that I couldn't let get worse. "My sister. I was—"

"Your sister?" Halgard snapped before taking a step closer, and it wasn't satisfaction in her face. Nor was it pity. It was disgust. "Your sister's dead. Ecker killed her. Her own commanding officer. The man you're trying to get back to. The world that used you and that you're *still* trying to save.

"You won't be trying soon."

Chapter Twenty

Toris

"Leave it alone, Kuma," I said as we walked down the hallway from Anker's room to the elevator. I had to get ahead of the next detour. We were further behind than I'd hoped, and Alis—and the Wolf—were still out there, likely closing in on Genesis Gardens and the many threats that awaited her there.

"Toris, listen to me," Kuma said, but I stepped into the elevator and punched the button for the lobby. Kuma barely made it in before the doors creaked closed, one of them stuck at an angle so I could see a sliver of the shaft as we descended.

"We got Lana here," I said. "We need to respect her choices."

"Even if it's a deathwalk?"

"She probably just has the wrong information. She was in the Shades, Kuma, who knows how long it's been since she heard where her in-laws were living. She'll find them. And, yes, even if it's a deathwalk and she knows it, we should respect that choice." The elevator doors slid open, and we stepped out into the lobby. Night had fully fallen outside, neon colors flashing through the dark windows.

"She was acting weird, Toris, and she has no one else to be there for her."

We stepped out onto the street, where the whines of vehicles, the bass of music, and the din of thousands of voices washed over us. "How do you know if she was acting weird? We don't know her. We can't be there for everyone, and we need to find the person who does need us."

"I know you're worried about Alis," Kuma said behind me as I started walking north. "I am, too. But she's smart. She's capable. She won't just throw herself into danger. Lana may be in danger right now, and we can do something about it."

"Then go do something about it," I said without turning around. Something deep within me cringed at my own response, but it was deep for a reason. I pushed it down again.

"Will you," Kuma grabbed me by the shoulder and pushed me against the wall of the apartment building, "LISTEN TO ME?" Sometimes I forgot how much taller Kuma was, and he seemed to tower in that moment, a dark silhouette against the neon lights of the city behind him. His face contorted in a harsh glare, but despite what his brows did, those eyes weren't angry. They were sad. Scared.

I tried to keep my voice calm, even though my hands were shaken by instinct, adrenaline making my heart race. "We don't have time for this, Kuma. We wasted enough already coming to Anker. I should have...we should have just gone straight for the tower. I don't need another lecture. I need to find Alis. I need to kill the Wolf and break this cycle."

Kuma's breath was hot on my face, his chest expanding and contracting with his own adrenaline. After a moment of staring at me, he shook his head then poked me in the sternum. "You're blind, brother. And I've been blind, too. You're dismissing everything Anker said because he didn't tell you what you wanted to know, but I think it's the opposite. The universe keeps slapping us in the face with what we need to know, what we need to do. And you keep ignoring it."

I sighed and looked down at Kuma's finger, still pressing into my chest. "What are you talking about?"

Kuma took a step back, dropping his hand. "You're fixated on the Wolf and its cycle while we've been caught in another. For years. Since before Alis. We're not...we're not thinking about the consequences, Tor. I..." He took a breath, put his hands on his hips, and looked up the street, searching for the words. "We can't just fly these people out of harm and drop them off. We're no better than a taxi service. These people need more than that. I think...I know we've been helping people for all these years because of what happened to Mele, to your parents, and we've said it's for those people, but I think a lot of it is for us, too. To make us feel better. And I don't know about you, but..." his face instantly softened and pity shattered my walls, too. "I don't know about you, but that void sure ain't filled. If we really mean to help these people, which we've put ourselves in a position to do, then we need to really do that. We need to be accountable for what happens *after* we pull them out of the hellholes they've been in. We didn't do that with Beck. He died. We clearly didn't think about it when we made everything worse for Anker and everyone else here. We didn't do it enough at the Battle of the Loop. We should have—"

"That was different," I interrupted, holding up a finger.

"Stop doing that! You cut off anyone who brings it up. The good and the bad, Tor! Lana's in the circumstance she is because of us, because we didn't think enough about the consequences, because we condemned people who were already beaten down to greater misery and death. And now we can do something about it."

"And what do we do?" I snapped, part of me knowing he was right and the other part prickly with guilt. "Do we build a new life for them? Find the perfect community for every person? Be their therapist? We're two people, Kuma. And we've damn well saved our share."

"We can do more," Kuma said. "We can stop doing what we see as good for ourselves and do what people actually need. And I think Lana needs us. Alis..." He hesitated, taking another breath, the kind of breath old friends take before they cross a line.

"What. 'Alis' what."

"Alis needs that, too."

"What the hell does that mean?"

"You're desperate to kill the Wolf. Fixated on it. But have you thought about what she needs?"

"She needs the Wolf dead. We wouldn't be here if she hadn't flown here herself to make it happen."

"She'd do anything for you."

"Are you saying I wouldn't? Kuma—"

"How can you expect Navi...how can you expect any community to accept her—all of her—if you don't?"

Kuma may as well have slapped me, may as well have stuck a dagger where he'd poked me in the chest. My body reacted as if he had, hand clenching into a fist, arm itching to swing. A desperate impulse to do something, anything, to stop the pain those words inflicted.

"That was too far," Kuma said, hanging his head. "I'm sorry. I just...I can't do it anymore. I don't have all the answers. I don't know what the solution is. But I know we need to do more. We need to be more. And we need to start now, before more people get hurt."

"Then go."

Kuma looked up. "Toris, I'm not going to leave you to face Carivant and his lackeys on your own. Lana's right around the corner. I'm not asking you to choose between her and Alis. I'm asking to help both of them."

"If Alis isn't the priority, then that is a choice. And I can't make that choice. Please, Kuma, go. I..." I needed to get away from him. I needed to be alone. I was wasting time. "Just go."

"Brother, I..."

"Don't." I glanced at Kuma's face for an instant to see tears in his eyes. I couldn't hold that gaze for long.

Kuma sighed, that wide chest rising and falling. "I'm sorry." He started walking away, and I unglued myself from the wall he'd pushed me into. But then Kuma stopped a few steps away. "Wait. No." He didn't turn around. "I'm sorry I hurt you. I love you, brother. And I love Alis. But I stand by what I said. We can do more. We can be better. I'll find you after I talk to Lana. Don't do anything too stupid without me." Then he walked away, and I felt something snap between us, the cords of our connection fraying and a few of them breaking altogether.

I watched him turn the corner toward where the Cherry Blossom apartments had once been, the pink glow of its apparently repurposed light shining in the dark around the block. People passed us, paying no mind to the shouting and shoving, well trained by the streets. Above, another cat-shaped drone from Chimera turned down the same street Kuma had.

Emotions clashed with such intensity that I couldn't move. I wasn't blind, I'd been feeling the same guilt as Kuma, even if I hadn't made the same realizations on how to resolve that guilt. But he'd taken what had been a crevice, a crack in my conscience, and blown it open and blown it deep. He didn't know what he was talking about. Of course I accepted Alis. I loved her. I'd been living with her for nearly ten years. I...

I love you, despite the Wolf.

I'd wondered why she looked so sad when I said that. What I'd said wrong.

But how could I accept the Wolf? How could she? There was no way. That was just Kuma's opinion. And in sharing that opinion and then leaving me behind, he'd betrayed me in a way I'd never felt. It hurt as much as Navi's exile, somehow. I'd always felt like I was a decision or two away from losing Navi, ever since Mom and Dad died. She'd disagreed with me going off with Kuma to rescue refugees. She'd slapped me when I returned from the Battle of the Loop. And of course she'd never accepted Alis in ten long years.

How can you expect any community to accept her—all of her—if you don't?

Kuma didn't understand. Just like I didn't understand what it was like to lose a child. I'd never given him advice on how to get through that harrowing challenge, and he had no right to tell me how to help Alis.

With a frustrated huff, I started down the street, past the corner that Kuma had turned down without looking, despite a gravity—that frayed connection to my friend—pulling me that way.

I'd deal with that later. I'd mend those frays, and I'd pitch in to help Lana. I'd build a room in the back of our house in Orilla if I had to. All after Alis was safe. All after the Wolf...

All after the Wolf was dead.

That was still the goal, wasn't it? That was what I—what we needed.

That was right.

So why did something feel wrong?

I ignored that feeling, walking down the street and reorienting around what we'd learned from Anker. Security was tighter than it'd been before at Genesis Gardens, and it was a fortress back when we worked there. I didn't even have the mindjack that offered access. There was always blowing down a door, but that seemed like the last resort.

Then there was the issue of the mithril. Anker said it'd been recast in some secret project. That was certainly a hurdle, but we didn't need much to create a Faraday Shield. We could hopefully scrape enough together and hope that the properties of the mithril hadn't been diluted in any way. We'd need a bioengineer to perform the procedure, but of all the issues, that seemed like the easiest to solve. We wouldn't have money to hire someone in Babylon, but surely there was someone else on the planet offering such services.

None of that mattered if I didn't have Alis safe and sound. She knew about Carivant, knew about our history, and it wouldn't have been difficult to find her way to Genesis Gardens, but she'd hit a wall trying to get in. Kuma was right on one front: Alis knew what she was doing. She'd take it slow, being much less reckless than I was, examining the situation and exploring possible solutions. It wasn't Alis I was worried about. It was the Wolf. If the cycle was now unpredictable somehow, then the monster could emerge at any time, endangering Alis and drawing Carivant's many eyes. I turned a corner and started heading east, out of the Esagila District and into the Ishtar District, the core around which Babylon revolved. The buildings changed, entertainment left for the most part back in Esagila, replaced by even taller towers of myriad designs, as if the architects of each were each competing for accolades. I passed one building constructed from the remains of a pair of starships, the old airlock and boarding ramp functioning as the door and thrusters transformed into pillars that held up the second boxy ship, which was standing vertical, its tapering bow pointing at the sky. Beside that was a tower shaped like an hourglass, with each half of the hourglass a spiral of its own, the outside of the spiral lined with a lift track so elevator passengers could get a dizzying view of the city as they climbed and descended.

Those were just teasers, though. I reached the end of that block and turned the corner into the true core of Babylon, the heart of the Ishtar District. Once known as "the Strip," the bones of that old street had been repurposed into a perfect representation of the excesses of the New Cradle of Civilization. A maglev street ran down the center of the way, lined on both sides by narrow rivers. Those rivers were flanked by hedges and trees, between which stood proud statues fifteen to twenty feet tall. They depicted great thinkers throughout history, from Galileo and Michaelangelo to Marie Curie and Rosalind Franklin. Closer to me I spotted a new addition to the lineup, one that hadn't been there when we'd made our escape ten years ago. Adeline Gesdin, a brilliant astrophysicist and engineer who'd died only a few years before. The thrusters on the *Harriet* were originally Gesdin designs, as were the great Gesdin ramjets being outfitted on interstellar exploration vessels.

Behind the statues were the towers of Babylon's corporations. Each of them an impressive feat of engineering and architecture—and each of them a symbol of the excess of the city's elite, while just a few streets down, people starved. One tower was split in half, the top half floating and slowly rotating on powerful magnets fifteen feet above the building below it. A transparent lift tube ran through the center. Several of the towers took after the city's namesake, designed like depictions of the Hanging Gardens of Babylon, tiers of blue stone held by rectangular columns, waterfalls cascading between the levels. There was Punarjanman's headquarters, a tower of white stone carved and painted with intricate geometric patterns, topped with a dome and a spire that made it the second-largest building in the city.

The largest building, of course, was Carivant's tower, the headquarters of Genesis Gardens. It stood at the end of the street, everything pointed toward it. It was a microcosm of the entire city, the modern mixed with the ancient. Black glass dominated most of the circular facade, with round Roman pillars surrounding its circumference. Winding up and around the tower was a serpent of white stone in the center of which was a vibrant garden. Flowers, shrubs, and even small trees sprouted from the garden, and in the night, lights shined on those colors. On each side of that white stone stripe were golden strips that shined even in the darkness. Inside the building, there was a stylized depiction of the tower beside the words: "Out of darkness, light. Out of darkness, life." It was a magnificent building, even I had to admit that. I'd stood there, jaw slack, for minutes the first time I saw it, almost honored to have landed a job there.

That didn't last too long.

My eyes went quickly to the open hangar from which Kuma, Beck, and I had escaped so long ago. Its mouth faced away from the street, the functional elements of the building hidden to preserve the aesthetic, but I knew where it was, about halfway up the tower, flanked by defense cannons. Could we get in that way? The hangar generally stayed open—at least, it had twelve years before; Anker couldn't have been clearer that things had changed. Plus, we'd only narrowly managed to get out back then. Getting past those defenses would be much more difficult.

I stood in the shadows, taking a deep breath and putting my hands on my hips. Then I blinked, trying to eliminate the coronas appearing around all the lights seen through my tired eyes. That minor perception snapped my attention to everything else my body needed. My stomach grumbled. My muscles ached. I was going on almost 48 hours without sleep and through a couple traumatizing experiences. How would I break into Genesis Gardens in that state?

Maybe I should have turned back. Found Kuma. Slept for a few hours somewhere before coming up with an actual plan. That's what Alis would do. Take it slow. Play it smart.

The Wolf wouldn't do that, though. If the Wolf had control, it wouldn't rest. And if it had somehow had enough consciousness to intentionally go after Cixin, somehow perceiving him as a threat, then who was to say whether it wouldn't do something similar in Babylon. It was unpredictable now. Maybe it'd even find a way to hurt Alis.

I couldn't stop. I couldn't rest. I couldn't waste time. So I started walking toward the tower.

Then, a pair of shapes flew out of Genesis Gardens' hangar. They were small, little more than reflections in the night for a moment. But as they came closer and the bright street illuminated them better, their details snapped into focus, and I stopped walking.

Cats. Drones shaped like cats. From Chimera.

Or, apparently, from Carivant. I'd noticed the first shortly after we'd entered the city. Another had flown down the same street as Kuma. In any other circumstance, I'd call it a coincidence, but to see those emerging from Genesis Gardens' tower, coming right for me, I highly doubted they were only the advertising they appeared to be. That was Carivant's expertise: surveillance you'd never recognize, manipulation you'd rarely perceive, not until you were exactly where he wanted you, giving exactly what he wanted you to give.

If I was right, Kuma and Lana were in danger. After all, I doubted those drones were only equipped with surveillance. I should have warned them.

But Alis...

It could have just been a coincidence. It could have been paranoia. Maybe they really were just Chimera advertisements, and they were just another Genesis Gardens subsidiary, and the marketing team was sending extra drones to a...lab-grown-pets-enthusiast extravaganza?

I clenched my hands into fists, feeling pulled in opposite directions, like a planet held between two opposing stars. Alis was my priority. Alis came first. Alis was in danger, too.

We can do more. We can be better.

Babylonians on the sidewalk shouldered past me, some so engrossed in their mindjack or conversation that I may as well have been a pole in the concrete, while others shot me angry looks.

Alis needed me.

Kuma and Lana did, too.

There was a difference. Kuma and Lana were in Babylon because of me. In *danger* because of me.

We need to be accountable for what happens after.

I yelled, all my frustration needing to get out somehow, and spun back the way I'd come.

Kuma was right. He usually was, and I usually hated it.

Turning away from Genesis Gardens almost physically hurt, Alis' gravity pulling me back that way, threatening to draw and quarter my soul.

"I'm coming," I whispered.

There was no time to waste. The drone could already be on Kuma and Lana, and I was a few blocks away.

I glanced around until I found a small parking lot off the main road. I dashed toward it, across a bridge over the river and between the towering statues. I spotted exactly what I needed: a sleek hoverboard, parked in a stall beside several others. Just seeing it made me miss my own, a charred husk with our aircraft in the desert.

After taking a look to make sure its owner wasn't nearby, I pulled it from its stall, the charge indicator going dark as it left the plate. I carried the board around the stall, where the bulk of it would cover me from the street. The hoverboard was a newer model, copper and blue, slimmer and sleeker than my model, tapering to a point on the front with trapezoidal notches on both sides of the center. I searched for a panel near the footpads and tapped the one I found.

"Dammit," I hissed when it didn't open. Boards had gotten more secure, likely linked to the owner's mindjack. I had to stomp on my control panel to keep it closed.

I propped the board against the back of the stall and pulled out my solarblade. I extended it to a small dagger's length, the magnetic clips snapping into place before the turquoise plasma ignited, following a tight loop around the small magnetic field. A quick slice took off the panel covering the hoverboard's manual reset controls. A small holopanel immediately projected out of the opening, a spinning circle indicating that the board was searching for its mindjack connection.

Fortunately, it wasn't my first time severing mindjack connections; we'd spent years doing it after the war. After all, these boards weren't manufactured with those connections in place, so I just had to take the board back to its factory settings. I held three fingers on the screen in a vaguely triangular shape, and the spinning wheel disappeared, replaced by a question: "Reset Starstreak hoverboard?" I tapped "Yes," and new words replaced the old: "Confirm via mindjack."

I growled again, not even a curse forming from the sound that time. Fine. If the security protocols were that layered, I'd do it the old-fashioned way. With my solarblade, I cut away another panel of sleek copper and blue metal, uncovering more wiring resting atop the air intake and all connected to the superconductor toward the back of the board. I sliced through the silver wire I was looking for, and the holoscreen went blank. There wasn't much time. Severing the mindjack connection would have alerted the board's owner.

"Come on. Come on. Come *on*."

The screen shut off.

"Come on!"

Then it popped back on with the words "Congratulations on your new Starstreak hoverboard! Please select connection method:" and two options "Mindjack" and "Mag-boots."

I tapped the second, slid the board onto the ground, and stepped onto the footpads. The screen displayed a loading loop for a moment before there was a click and my boots magnetized to the board.

After I disengaged my solarblade and clipped the hilt back onto my belt, I shoved my weight down on the board. My feet sank an inch or so as the board vibrated to life, sucking in air from the sleek intake near its pointed front. The board rose off the ground a few feet, white lights flashing to life along its length, automatically detecting the dark around us.

With one more look at Genesis Gardens—and the approaching Chimera drones—I leaned backward with my front foot while pressing down with the toes of my back foot. The board shot forward and upward, blasting up a cloud of dirt and grass beside the parking lot. I crouched, ducking my head as I flew under a floating holo-ad, then threw the board forward, leaning backward to bank around the corner I'd just come from. I pressed harder with the toes of my back foot, and the board vibrated for an instant before rocketing ahead. Wind whipped my face, and my clothes snapped around me.

I was a good hundred feet above the street below, higher than the Chimera drone had been. I banked around another corner, so close to a building that I reached out, fingers skimming the stone, then pushed off for every little bit of momentum once I was over the next street. I looked behind me, searching for the other two Chimera drones, but I didn't see them.

Neon signs and holograms became vibrant blurs as I tore through the air between buildings, reentering the Esagila District. I banked around one more corner and spotted what had once been Cherry Blossom Apartments down the block, casting its pink light down the entire street. The dark building was the same, with four deep-brown pillars rising equidistant from each other to the roof where they blossomed into vibrant glowing leaves made of pink neon light, a canopy that extended another thirty feet into the sky. The new business had modified the blossoming canopy to include the silhouette of a person walking along a path through the leaves. Below the man, scrawled in looping white light, were the words "Peace's Path."

And turning around the side of the building was the Chimera drone, pink light reflecting off its white shell. The hologram flickering through the various modifications to the cat shut off as the drone entered the shadows on the side of the building and slipped from my view.

I pressed my accelerator as far as it would go, crouching deeper to reduce my drag as the board burst forward with even greater speed. The street below, with its pedestrians and entertainers and advertisements, became a river of distorted light, my eyes watering at the speed. I really should have brought my goggles.

At the last second as I passed beneath the pink canopy of lighted leaves, I pressed down with the heel of my back foot and decelerated, then banked around the same alley that the Chimera drone had. The building on my right was old brick and plaster, but Peace's Path to the left had holo-displays in place of windows, depicting scenes from across the world. The rolling dunes of a sandy desert below me. Ahead, a beach with water crystal blue lapping at its shore. The projections were duller on my side, and semi-transparent, allowing a view of the hallways inside.

I sped between the buildings, much slower than before, but fast enough that when the board scraped against Peace's Path's neighbor, I threw up sparks. Down the alley, just a few floors down from the roof, I saw two shapes, sitting with their backs to the projection of a forest behind them. I'd know that man on the left anywhere.

And between me and them, was the Chimera drone, dark and quiet, somehow slinking as quietly as the animal it emulated. It was hovering, slowly pivoting to face Kuma and Lana.

"KUMA!" I shouted, unaware of what the drone would actually try and do.

I wouldn't give it the chance. I accelerated again, pulling out my solarblade and tapping the button until the magnetic clips snapping into place were double my height. The metal scraped on the building to my right, at least until I ignited the blade in a spray of blue fire that cut into the wall and left a smoldering serpent in my wake.

The Chimera drone spun toward me, the eyes of the cat sliding aside to reveal barrels that glowed with purple light.

But it wasn't fast enough. At the last moment before I would have collided with the machine, I shoved my weight backwards, flipping upside down and hurtling over the drone, my arm outstretched with twelve feet of churning plasma at its end. Assisted by my momentum, the solarblade sliced clean through the drone as if it were paper, bursting with small explosions and dropping to the alley below as I decelerated, spun upright, and deactivated the solarblade. The magnetic clips slid back into the hilt as I caught my breath, hovering above the alley and the drone's smoking, burning wreckage.

Now we were well and truly in trouble.

I guided the hoverboard through the windowless wall, shivering as I passed through the static of the holoprojection. Kuma and Lana stood on the other side of the projection, Kuma's arm covering Lana, both of them wearing similar expressions of surprise.

"We...we need to get out of here," I said through labored, adrenaline-laced breaths as I jerked my ankles toward each other. The board shut down, and I settled onto the ground.

"What's going on?"

"Cat..." I said, pointing out the window before putting my hands on my knees to catch my breath. "The Chimera drones. They've been following us." I had to pause to take another breath. "Saw one follow you, then some come out of Carivant's hangar. That's when..." Another breath. "It clicked."

"And you came back?" Kuma asked, much more in that question than he actually vocalized.

I spread my arms as I stood upright. I thought my presence and the smoking hulk outside were pretty obvious indicators.

But I knew what he meant, so I dropped my arms and took a step closer. "I'm sorry, Kuma." Then I turned to Lana. "And I'm sorry I wasn't here, too. I should have been."

Lana sniffed. The skin around her eyes was red and swollen from crying. "Kuma told me. Well, he told me a little. I'm sorry about what you've been through. What you're going through."

The defensive creature in me stirred and bristled, wondering how much he'd talked about the Battle of the Loop, how he'd talked about Alis. But I pushed it away. "Thank you. I appreciate that. Are you doing...will you...are you going to be okay?" The words tumbled out, feeling wrong, too weak to address the weight of what Lana was experiencing. I glanced behind her, where a holoprojection on the wall displayed what happened throughout Peace's Path. Deathwalks. The screen showed a somber man taking a drink provided by the establishment before stepping into an augmented reality space. The man walked through a beachfront city—his hometown, it indicated—before seeing and holding old loved ones. He transitioned to walking on a pier that stretched out over the ocean. As he walked, he never made it any closer to the end of the pier. Instead, a white light gradually filled the screen.

It certainly wasn't the worst way to go, I understood that better than most. But that didn't change my belief that many of the people who took a deathwalk, especially those living in Babylon, didn't at the very least need someone to tell them they were loved. Someone to show them that they had worth beyond their job, beyond their relationship to someone else, beyond...

The more I thought about it, the more I hated that I hadn't been that someone for Lana. At least Kuma had.

"I...I don't know," Lana said, looking at the ground. "I don't know what's left for me to live for, but I...there has to be something. Kuma didn't even have to pull me out. I couldn't even go in. Every time I tried, I just saw my son's smile, heard his encouragement and...Sorry. It's hard to put into words." Then she straightened up and pushed a strand of black hair behind her ear. "But I do know I want to help you." She looked over at the projection of the forest, where a bird took flight from the canopy. Behind it, I could barely make out the plume of smoke from the destroyed drone. How long before Genesis Gardens came looking into it? How long did we have? "We can talk more about my problems when we can take a breath. Didn't you say we have to get out of here?"

"Yeah," I said. "But I should warn you, it's not safe. You already saw what could happen." I jerked my head toward the wreckage.

"Well, they already saw me come in with you guys, so I don't think it matters whether I'm with you or not.""Fair point," Kuma said with a satisfied frown. "Plus, Toris," his mouth twitched before spreading into a smile, "Lana's not just an engineer. She's a bioengineer."

I took a breath that felt like the first true dose of oxygen I'd taken since we entered the city. The tightness in my chest let up, like just a hint of sun in the shades of the sky after a long night. "You are?"

Lana smiled and nodded. "I am." She shrugged. "It's not that impressive. That's where we all thought the money was made. It wasn't."

"I...That's a lifesaver." I didn't know what to say. That was one problem solved, taking us one step closer to the end of all this. We couldn't waste time taking the next.

We...I'd started thinking in "we." I couldn't do it alone. I hadn't done any of it alone, but maybe if I actively stopped trying to, I'd get further. We'd get further. Together.

"We need to get off the street," I said. "Lay low for a bit, at least until they lose our scent. When we passed through the gates, you didn't give them any access to your mindjack, right?" I asked Lana. They were already tracking us; we didn't need that layer of surveillance.

"No, of course not."

"And you trust your security? I don't think the corporations here care too much about asking for permission."

"I trust it, yeah."

"All right," I said. "Then welcome to the team. Let's get out of here."

They started down the hallway as I reached down and grabbed the board. When I stood up, though, I didn't move.

"Wait."

Both of them stopped.

"I'm glad you're still with us, Lana. Thank you for wanting to help." Then I turned to Kuma, and I was surprised when tears came to my eyes. "And thanks for not giving up on me, brother."

Kuma didn't say anything, instead stepping toward me and consuming me in a bear hug. I squeezed my friend tight, letting a tear fall down my cheek. He slapped my back as he pulled away.

"All right," I said with a sniff. "*Now* let's get out of here."

***

The Old Spot was just as we'd left it twelve years before, other than another layer of dirt and grime. It was near the edge of the Gardens District, on a rooftop tucked between humming heating and cooling units and behind a wall that stuck up from the rooftop higher relative to other buildings. With machines handling the maintenance of the HVAC units and with our spot facing away from where anyone from the street or another building could see, I guess I shouldn't have been surprised it'd stayed hidden.

Our pair of foldable chairs were sun-bleached, blue turned white, and falling apart even more than when we'd sat in them on quiet nights after a long shift. The din of the city was far suppressed here, with a view looking over the outer suburban ring of Babylon and the Tigris River at its edge. Beyond Babylon's manicured experience was the unforgiving desert. As harsh as it was, it too had its own beauty in its rolling, desolate hills and, in the distance, the ridges of small mountains. If winds had blown through that day, we'd even get a view of the stars clear enough to remind us of home.

"We had to live near our workplace in Bastion, too," Lana said from between Kuma and I as we stood in front of our worn-down chairs, leaning on our elbows and looking over that view. "Expected to be of service at any time, day or night. Why didn't your families move here with you?"

"Genesis Gardens would only pay for us," I said. "Well, not even pay, subsidize. They'd only help secure an apartment—which is almost impossible here, by the way—for employees. We couldn't afford to stay and work in Orilla, but our families couldn't afford to come here with us." I sighed, remembering sitting before the view of the desert longing for home. I patted Kuma on the back, knowing he was remembering, too, and that his remembering would be far more painful than mine. He'd hated missing Mele growing up. He'd talked about how every day that passed felt like a year. It was almost enough to drive him to get a mindjack just to see the videos recorded in Nadia's memory. I think he would have if we'd stayed any longer.

"Do you think we're clear?" Lana asked, leaning further over the edge of the building to look for Chimera drones below.

"I think so," I said. "There aren't..." I swayed a little, dizzy and disoriented, exhaustion taking a tighter hold. "There aren't any cameras up here. At least, there weren't ten years ago. We were probably caught on one at some point on the way here, but that's a lot of ground for Carivant to search, and I'm sure there's restrictions on what resources he can deploy where. Much of the Gardens is actually owned by Punarjanman, and they don't tend to play nice with Carivant. We'll want to set up a watch, though, just in case."

Kuma looked around Lana to me, one eyebrow raised. "You're actually going to rest?"

"I don't think I have a choice," I sighed. "And it kills me, but standing in front of the tower again, seeing those drones come out...It's going to be hard enough to get in rested. We've done enough today. And you're right. Alis will take her time."

But what if the Wolf didn't?

I shook the thought out of my head. There was nothing I could do about that. I had to trust Alis. She'd take precautions, especially after Cixin.

"I'm proud of you, brother. We'll find her," Kuma said, stepping around Lana to slap then grasp my shoulder. "The plan's going to work."

Calling it a "plan" may have been a bit of a stretch, but it was more of a plan than I would have come up with on my own. We'd generated it as we crept through alleys and hugged the shadows on our way to the Old Spot. It was risky. It depended on factors out of our control, but if all went well, we could get out of Babylon with Alis and on our way to the end of all these cycles.

I'd come to the city on a quest for vengeance. Revenge for ten years of struggle and pain and sleepless nights. Revenge for a constant burden that afflicted the woman I loved. Revenge for Cixin's death. Killing the Wolf was the priority, and I told myself that it was for both of us. I still believed that, despite the dissonance I was experiencing, but I'd so quickly convinced myself that focusing on killing the Wolf was what Alis would want, too, without actually thinking about Alis. Kuma was right. I was stuck in a cycle.

Find Alis. Get the mithril. Get out.

No. That was wrong. I was wrong.

Find Alis. Help Alis.

Whatever that meant, whether that was killing the Wolf or...something else. Alis would be reeling, hating herself *and* the Wolf for what had happened to Cixin. She was in an intimidating city alone with great odds against her. She didn't need me to come in guns blazing with mithril in hand.

First, she just needed me.

That was the center of our plan. Find Alis. Help Alis. Everything else would be a bonus.

"Thank you," I said, the three of us turning to face each other. Luna was almost directly overhead, casting light over our rooftop, across the glittering Tigris, and onto the barren desert below. "You're both doing more than anyone should ever ask. I'll owe you forever."

"I thought you all stopped dealing in transactional relationships," Lana said with a teasing half-smile.

"Look who's sounding more like an Earther already," I said with a smile of my own. The expression felt strange, pulling at muscles that hadn't seen much work in the past couple days. "You're right. It's not transactional. Just mutual. When this is over, we've got your back, Lana. Both of us. I'm sorry again that I didn't from the start."

Lana waved a hand, shooing away my umpteenth apology. "Love can give us a narrow lens sometimes. I understand. Trust me."

"And you and me," I said to Kuma, "we'll end more than just the Wolf's cycle. We'll do better. We'll be better. I already have some ideas."

Kuma's smile spread across his face, wrinkling the corners of his eyes. "Damn right we will."

"Do we put our hands in the middle now?" Lana asked.

"Nope," Kuma said, then he spread his arms wide. "It's night night, time for a family hug, sister."

Lana cringed, raising her shoulders, but still she smiled as Kuma pulled the three of us into a group hug.

"You guys stink," Lana said, her voice muffled between us.

"Toris sweats when he has to confront his feelings," Kuma said as we pulled apart.

"That's true."

"I'll take first watch," Kuma said. "Our luxury hotel beds are ready for our guests." He sashayed around our old worn chairs, sweeping his arm around them as if they were prizes on a game show.

Lacking the energy to insist I take the first watch, I settled into my old chair—the one on the left—my body sinking into it as the old metal creaked and the fabric cracked.

I leaned the chair back and stared up at the stars, up at Luna with its bulbous colonies spider-webbed across its surface. And for the first time in not just those couple days, but for the first time in ten years, I could perceive the way forward. It was a way forward not just for Alis and I, but for me, past the guilt and shame and irresponsibility I'd held onto.

That hope quieted my mind enough that I must have fallen asleep as soon as I closed my eyes, a single thought on repeat:

Find Alis. Help Alis.

Chapter Twenty-One

Alis

(Twelve years earlier)

"YOU'RE LYING!" I SCREAMED for the third time, spit flying onto the table as Halgard's officers secured me to my chair. It took three of them this time. I'd broken one of their noses in my thrashing as we entered the torture chamber once more.

"Gag her," Halgard said as she unbuttoned her uniform jacket and pulled it off. An officer shoved some fabric in my mouth—despite my best attempt to seal my lips shut—and tied it around the back of my head.

The admiral tossed her jacket onto a chair and rolled up the sleeves of her black undershirt. The bags under her eyes were deeper than even the day before. I genuinely hoped the guilt of sailing on my home with the intent of destroying it was eating her alive. That and the guilt of lying to me to get what she wanted.

Teah wasn't dead. Halgard was desperate. She'd do anything at that point to get either information or loyalty out of me. She'd get neither.

"I don't need to lie to you, Caliday," Halgard said, leaning forward and putting her hands on the table. "Your people give me everything I need. Ecker was no exception."

I shook my head, groaning a "No," into the gag. It was a lie. I knew it was a lie. So why were tears coming to my eyes? Why was my heart collapsing into a black hole? Like it knew.

Halgard typed some commands into her holotable, and I flinched, expecting the mindjack machine to slide over my head. But it never came. Instead, the hologram lit up with an image of a small room of dark metal that I'd recognize anywhere. The *Fang*.

"No no no no no," I moaned into the gag.

Ecker stepped into the frame. He'd shed his vice admiral's cap, the *Fang*'s lights reflecting off his bald head. His bottom jaw jutted out in a kind of snarl as he stepped backward and wrenched something with him.

Teah.

Ecker had her black hair snarled in his fist. She was on her knees, her pruner's uniform ripped, her arms bound behind her back. She was crying, and that alone awakened my sisterly instincts to dive through the hologram and rip Ecker's throat out.

"*Say it*," Ecker growled, shaking Teah. She squeezed her eyes shut and hissed in a breath at the pain.

"*You...you chose them over me, Alis,*" Teah said, glancing back toward Ecker. And suddenly she wasn't an eighteen-year-old soldier of the Bastion military. She was five, hair a tangle, wide eyes wet with tears as she held a broken bracelet in her little hand. An heirloom from our mom that I'd taken, accidentally broken, and put back. *You broke it*, she'd whimpered.

The black hole pulsed, pulling more of me inside.

"*Keep going,*" Ecker said.

"Please." I cried into the gag. But Halgard just watched the hologram with the same disgust she'd had on her face in the hallway.

"*You've killed me.*" Teah sobbed, spittle drooping from her bottom lip. Teah never cried like this. Ecker had broken her down.

No...I had.

"*Why?*" Teah whispered, barely more than a breath. And I knew that part wasn't rehearsed, wasn't something Ecker had told her to say. Behind that question I could see the same betrayal that I felt when I saw her standing behind Mwezi's governor, after Ecker had told me my sister's part in the upending of all our principles.

I sank into my chair, physically collapsing forward as the black hole contracted and wrenched more of me inside it.

"*I gave you more of a chance than you deserved, Caliday. It should be you here, rotted as you are, instead of your loyal sister. She told me we'd have to hack your mindjack, you know. She—*"

"*No,*" Teah pleaded. "*I—*"

Ecker grasped her hair tighter and pulled her almost off her knees as she gasped. "*Quiet,*" he hissed. "*She knew the rot inside you would keep you from doing what needed to be done to win this war. To secure our future. She was right. And now she pays the price for your betrayal.*"

Teah opened her mouth, ready to plead again, but then I saw her strength return, and she closed her mouth, took a breath through her nose, and stared at the camera. Stared at me. I'd seen that face before, that control, after Mom had passed. It was a mannerism she'd adopted from my father, and it'd always bothered me. Was I weaker for being unable to just bottle up all my pain like that?

Because in that moment, as before, I did not show the silent composure that Teah did. I screamed into my gag even as my throat felt like it was ripping open, even as the dagger pounded into my brain again and again and again and again and again.

"Laniteah Aurora Caliday," Ecker said, the enunciation of each of Teah's names like a knife plunging into me and twisting. "For the crimes of your sister against the Free World of Bastion, you are sentenced to death. Thank you for your service."

In a single motion, Ecker shoved Teah forward with one hand as he unholstered his plasma pistol with the other and fired into the back of her head.

I screamed into the gag, my entire body vibrating with the source of it.

Teah's death was instant, a mercy, if there was any in that nightmare. I could barely see the image through my tear-shrouded eyes as the light left her eyes and she dropped forward out of view, smoke rising from the back of her head.

I screamed again, heaving my body against my restraints, as if I could dive into the hologram—and back in time—to save Teah. To kill Ecker. Or to fail, and let him kill me, too. Let him end this.

"*Your father will receive communications regarding your sister's death, Caliday,*" Ecker said as he holstered his gun. "*We'll ensure he knows that she died at your hands, killed in action by the Traitor herself.*" He came closer, taking a step over some part of the body that I couldn't see. The body. Teah's body. Teah. "*You'd better hope that you die in combat, or that Earthers throw you out an airlock when they're done with you, because this?*" He pointed down toward Teah. "*This is just the beginning of your accountability. The Spheres will know the price that Bastionites pay for betrayal.*" Then, after a look off-camera, the hologram froze, Ecker's face stuck in a kind of half-snarl, a tendril of smoke still rising from...

"When." I finally said into the gag, glaring over the table at Halgard. She stared at me for a moment before nodding to an officer, who pulled down the gag. "When?" I repeated. "When did they send this?"

"Three days ago."

Three days. My sister had been dead for three days.

The pieces fell into place, and the resulting picture was everything I'd feared when Toris told me Halgard's plan. "When they noticed us sailing for Mars. When Luna started fighting back. He assumed I'd given you something. That you wouldn't make such an aggressive move unless you knew more than you should have." My eyes narrowed. "You did that intentionally. You used his threat against both him and me. And Teah." Then, through clenched teeth as fresh, angry tears came: "You killed my sister."

Halgard sighed and shook her head. "I consider myself a patient person, Caliday, but I'm starting to get sick of repeating the same shit to you to try and break through your..." she waved a tired hand as she searched for the word. "Your brainwashing. Your denial. You just watched your vice admiral kill your sister. You can blame me, and you can blame our actions, but it does nothing to change the *truth*," she slapped the table as she said that last word, "that you are nothing but a tool to be used. Your life means nothing to them. Your family's life."

I scoffed, the angry tears starting to dry, giving way to pure apathy. "And it means something to you? As you sail to burn God knows how many families to ashes?"

Halgard's head fell. "Toris. I'm going to launch that asshole out of an airlock."

"Asshole? The asshole who saved my life? The asshole who understands that glassing a city makes you no better than your enemy?" I leaned forward, getting as close as I could to Halgard. "You love to hurl blame at whoever's convenient, and you can bet that I'm going to find a way to kill Ecker for what he's done, but you're both in the wrong. I want this war to end, but not this way."

Halgard chewed at the inside of her cheek as she stared at me with narrowed eyes. Then she walked around the table toward me. "All right. I've given this a fair shake. I've given you a chance to choose the better side. But I don't have time to wait around any more. So I'm going to give you one more choice." She stopped at the end of the table, just a few feet away from me, and leaned back against the table as she folded her arms. "Here are your options. One, you choose to help me end this war and prevent further loss of both our peoples in a final, decisive blow. Option two: I put that empathy device back on your head and turn it on 'reverse.' I remove any empathy you feel for your family, your people, and I put in your brain the desire to help me, to help us." She frowned and tilted her head. "That seems like the safer option to me, anyway. And I really should do it as punishment, as justice, for killing my guards, but I also know messing with your brain too much may wipe out what I need." She shrugged. "Pros and cons."

I stared at her for a moment, jaw slack, half expecting her to be joking. But of course she wasn't. "You call that a choice? Either way, my people die. Either way, I lose the only family I have left. And either way, what'll stop me from coming back to seek justice against you? It's a cycle. One that you won't stop with this."

Halgard scowled at me for a moment, then she leaned closer and tilted her head, exposing her neck to me. "You want to come back for justice, I'll give it to you. You can take it. Right here," she leaned back and swiped her thumb across her jugular. Then her shoulders slumped, and I knew she wasn't speaking out of bravado, but total exhaustion. "This war...it's gone on too long. Entire generations lost to it. You and I both know that; it's taken our lives, too. You're right, it is a cycle, one that started with the Belt Crisis and that we've fed with assault after assault, propaganda after propaganda, subterfuge after..." she waved her hand, dismissing the rest of her point. "And maybe a new cycle will rise out of this, but we have to put a stop to this one and hope that we all learn from our mistakes. If I have to face justice for that, I'll do it proudly."

"I..." I looked away. I couldn't help her. I stood by what I'd discovered: we needed to end the war, not just win it. For the sake of *both* Earth and Bastion. That was my path, the way between the crushing mountains.

Toris had a plan. I had to trust him, young and vulnerable as the trust between us was. And in order to enact his plan, I had to give Halgard what she wanted. Because as much as she was acting as if she were the one in control, as if she were the one constraining my choices, I had something she needed. In giving her what she wanted, I'd get greater control over the situation. I'd make my own choices.

I wouldn't be used again.

"Fine," I said. "I'll do it. Keep that thing away from me. If I'm going to do this, I deserve to feel everything." None of that was a lie. A deep part of me, the bones quivering under the gravity of the black hole, considered wiping out that empathy out of defensive instinct. I could remove this pain. I could forget Teah's betrayed face. I wouldn't care about what my father thought about my decision, about whether my mother would be disappointed or proud. It'd be easier.

But then all the memories would become hollow, all the good, all the foundation that made me who I was. Mom with her arm around my shoulders while she held Teah on her other side, looking up at the infinite stars and bright Earth shining in the void, then saying, "You see all those stars? There are billions more out there. And you know what? I love you more than all the stars in the sky." Teah and I at Mom's bedside as she held my hand and stroked Teah's hair while she said, "Take care of each other, and take care of anyone who needs it. You'll have so many choices that come down to one thing: making someone else's life easier or harder. Always choose to make it easier. Life's hard enough." It was one of the many simple truths she taught us, in terms we kids could understand, especially as she tried to pack a lifetime of wisdom into a few short months. After she died, there were moments where I may have accepted Halgard's offer to wipe out all feeling toward her just to feel some relief, but now those moments were treasures, and the pain a dull ache, one that would never disappear but that I'd accept to retain the beauty of the rest. I knew one day I'd feel the same about Teah.

One day. And until then, I had to do my best to be what we both should have been all along.

Plus, I needed that feeling to fuel the justice I'd rain down on Ecker one day.

"What am I doing?" I asked.

Halgard folded her arms and stared at me for a moment, and I could see the calculations behind her eyes as she searched mine. She needed me, but she trusted me as little as I trusted her. If I hadn't killed those guards, maybe it could have been different, maybe I could have built an artificial trust.

The guilt for that ate away at me, too. Those officers may have been Mudbrains, and who knew what they'd done under Halgard's orders, but...I had enough blood on my hands. I didn't even understand what had happened, how I'd overpowered them. Halgard didn't, either.

Finally, Halgard stood up and walked back around the table. "I need two things from you," she said. "Intel and cooperation on a simple mission. I know Toris talked to you about what he knows, and I'm assuming that's what sparked the rage to kill my officers."

"No, that's not—"

"I don't know what he's up to," Halgard said as if I hadn't spoken, "but we're ensuring he won't cause any problems."

"Wait. No. What does that—"

"We have a rudimentary understanding of Bastion's orbital defenses, but our intel is sparse, and we need you to fill in our gaps. We have a better picture of Bastion's fleet positions, but you'll be expected to refresh us there as well. Then, you'll accompany the *Harriet* on a mission ahead of our fleet to remove the one obstacle to our weapons: the Iridesca Loop."

"The Loop isn't a shield."

"For particle beams, it may as well be. Not much can stop a particle beam, which is why we're taking that route over projectiles or other mass objects that Bastion could easily destroy. But a powerful magnetic field could throw off the beam's trajectory. The broader field generated around the planet isn't enough to disrupt our aim, especially from low orbit, but if Bastion manages to position the Loop itself in our way, that field is much stronger at its source. Since the Loop's mithril plating keeps us from just blowing it to hell, preventing that obstacle will be your role."

The admiral expected me to remove the one obstacle in the way of glassing my home? Killing my family? She was expecting me to watch from orbit while it all burned? I...

I waited. I was patient. I was in control.

"How?"

Halgard tapped a button at the end of the table, and the holoprojector hummed to life, something in the mechanism clicking in a way it wasn't before Kuma smashed it. The image that generated was choppy, too, like staring through a broken window. Still, I could make out the shape: the red planet, Mars. Bastion. My heart ached at the sight, at the beauty, the green climbing up Olympus Mons' slopes toward its snow-capped summit. The brilliant blue of the Mar Borealis and the sprawling cityscape of Bastion itself. When Halgard was done, it would be a charred husk, the greatest of human ingenuity snuffed out.

Patience.

Halgard pressed another button, and a thin metal ring appeared around the planet, tilted and slowly rotating. The Iridesca Loop. As part of the terraforming process, the Pioneers built the greatest feat of human engineering: a planetary magnetic field generator. Without a magnetic field, the sun's solar winds would strip away the weak atmosphere as it had done eons before. Bastion's atmosphere was stronger now, but all of the Pioneers' terraforming efforts couldn't restart the dynamo at the planet's core, and so the artificial magnetic field remained, a shield from the vicious winds and radiation of space.

"The *Harriet* still retains its Bastion signature, which will allow it to slip past enemy ships as you head toward the Loop. I'm going to send a strike team with you aboard the *Harriet*." A green triangle flew, trailing a dotted line behind it, toward a boxy bulge on the Loop. "You'll dock with the Loop's control module and get the strike team inside to take command. You may have to react to any countermeasures the enemy's put into place, maybe even moving the Loop itself. By the time that's complete, we'll ensure we're in position to execute the rest of the plan."

The plan. To burn away a civilization, to reduce parents to ashes before their children's eyes. It'd have ripple effects across the planet as well. The colonies on the frontier and even the more established cities would struggle with feeding and sustaining their people without Bastion.

I could work with this, though. I'd be with Toris. We could work together to find a way out. An accompanying strike team was certainly a constraint, but we could find a way through it. In having me help her execute her plan, Halgard was giving me the power to disrupt it. Already I had an idea percolating between the stabs of pain from the mindjack dagger.

I didn't want Halgard to perceive any of that confidence, though. I needed her to see me as weak. Afraid. I needed her to trust me at least enough to fulfill my end of this bargain. "My mindjack's malfunctioning, and even if it works, I don't know if I'll be able to get us into the Loop's systems. Ecker had to have locked me out."

"That could be," Halgard responded. "But we'll have specialists on the team that can help you get into the system and breach any locked doors. Your knowledge of the Loop's defenses, design, and systems, even if it's rudimentary, is far better than ours."

I stared at the map with a contemplative scowl. "What if Bastion's fleet tracks our trajectory back to the *Dawnbreak*? A signature won't matter then."

"The captains have a device—an illegal device, but I'm looking past that for now—that modifies their trajectory data, and you'll take a roundabout approach to give you a more realistic vector."

They'd thought of everything. Maybe not so mudbrained after all. I wanted to ask more, wanted to understand their fleet and how the Bastion fleet was split between the homeworld and Luna, all to better gauge Halgard's survivability. But I knew she wouldn't give it to me, and pushing it would only be more suspicious.

"And let me make something clear, Alis," Halgard said, shutting off the projector. "I'm giving you a chance here. I mean that. We could take the risk of running this mission without you. It may take longer, it may result in more casualties, but we would try. I'm giving you a chance to atone for the deaths you've caused and the horrors you've propagated in this war. I'm giving you a chance to do more for humanity. And I'm sorry for your sister, genuinely. But you must know: your second chance is secondary. The mission comes first. If you so much as sneeze suspiciously, my team will either cuff you again or shoot you on the spot. And trust me, you won't get far before they do."

"Oh, I wasn't assuming they were my escorts," I said with a scoff. Then, worried I'd start hinting toward my plans, I added: "Ecker killed my sister. You may have tortured me—and you'll pay for that one day—but he represents something worse. He always talked about a rot, how it spread from person to person and threatened Bastion's foundations. I know that he's that rot, and he's not the only one. There are people in that city who don't deserve what you're doing to them—and you'll face justice for that, too—but Ecker's rot can't spread, either. He can't win the war. You don't have to trust me, but you can know that."

Halgard stared at me for a moment before giving a satisfied nod. Most of that was the truth, anyway. The rest was that Halgard's hypocrisy was just as rotten, and that I'd ensure she didn't win, either.

"Take off her cuffs," Halgard said, pointing toward me with her chin. The officers flanking me leaned over and released the restraints. "I'll escort you to the briefing room, where you'll give us what intel you can. Then we'll rendezvous with Captain Orius."

I stood up and frowned, rubbing my wrists. "What about Kuma?" My stomach twisted. Were they punishing him further for his outburst? If she was...

"I don't know what Toris is up to," Halgard said. Of course she'd been listening to our conversation. Good thing Toris had been careful about how deep into the details he'd gone. "But I can't trust him not to screw this up. So until the battle's over and the war is won, Kuma will remain aboard the *Dawnbreak*."

Oh, no. "Does he know about this?"

"Not yet," Halgard said as she stepped around the table and started walking toward me.

"He'll love that. It'll really inspire him to be loyal to you."

Halgard stopped in front of me and straightened her shoulders. "As you've seen yourself, I don't care about loyalty right now. I care about compliance. Obedience. We'll worry about the rest when the war is over."

I nodded, biting back a few retorts about how similar that sounded to a Bastionite officer. Behind those retorts, I was thinking through how missing Kuma could disrupt Toris' plan. It certainly complicated my fledgling idea.

Halgard moved to walk past me, then stopped and turned back. Her demeanor had lost the strength it just had. All that remained was that sadness, that exhaustion, that I kept catching hints of. "I have one more question. Why did you kill those men? And why did you do it so..." She clenched her jaw and took a breath. "Despite what you may assume, they weren't just good soldiers, they were good people. With families."

"I..." I thought about lying, but I didn't need to in this circumstance. "You may not believe me, but I don't know how I did that. I don't know why. I lost consciousness, and I got stuck in one of those memories, from the empathy device. But it was different. That time, Idina fought back. I had no reason to hurt those men, and..." I hesitated, but I wasn't going to bear the weight of that guilt alone, not when: "You did something to me, to my mind, to my 'jack. That's why those men died."

The admiral stared at me, eyes widening a little, expression hardening, for long enough that I thought she'd either yell at me or spit in my face. But then she deflated, seeming to shrink an inch or two, and looked away. After a moment, she swallowed and started walking, gesturing for us to follow, a hunch to her shoulders as if she carried a great weight.

I felt pity for the woman for a split-second, but then I dismissed it. She didn't deserve my empathy.

Before following her and her officers outside the room, outside that torture chamber, I took one last look at that chair and that smashed projector, and I could nearly see Teah there, on her knees, her hair in Ecker's clenched fist.

If all went well, hopefully, both leaders would receive their dues, and that room would be nothing more than shards of metal and glass tumbling in the void.

Chapter Twenty-Two

Toris

We left the Old Place before the sun was up.

Looking down at the city, you would never have known anyone went to sleep, but the quiet land that the Old Place looked over was just stirring with pinpricks of lights in suburban windows, and the desert was turning from black to gray with the rising sun.

I didn't sleep for more than four hours, and when I first woke up, my body ached so much that I thought for a moment I wouldn't be able to move. But after I groaned my way out of the chair and creaked as I stood, I could feel how even those few hours resharpened my senses.

That would be the day. We'd find Alis. We'd give her the help she needed. If the plan worked, at least.

After the three of us left the Old Place, we split up, just for the moment. The longer we traveled together in the city, the more likely Carivant would pick up our trail again. I'd strapped the stolen hoverboard to my back using some of the worn fabric of the Old Place's chairs. It wouldn't hold for too long, but hopefully long enough.

My first stop was to a city terminal. Most of the citizens didn't rely on such old means of communication, but those without mindjacks—and therefore, generally, those without money—had to rely on them. The closest one to the Old Place was in the corner of a run-down bar on the edge of the Esagila District. I had to wipe a coat of dust and grease off the glass to see it properly, the technology so old that it didn't even rely on holo-tech. Once it finally booted up and connected to the city's network, I sent a signal to the Dandelion.

Then, I sent a much more difficult message to Orilla del Angel. Hopefully whoever was on communications duty would be paying attention. And hopefully that message wasn't too little, too late. But I trusted Navi, and she deserved better than I'd given her.

I'd been careful in my message, knowing that Carivant likely had AI crawling communications for anything suspicious, and anything going to or from Orilla would have a blazing red flag. Fortunately, Navi would be able to interpret the code I wrote in. If she even got the message.

She'd get it. The plan would work.

Find Alis. Help Alis.

After logging off the terminal, I stepped past a few of the bar's swaying clientèle and out onto the street. The sun was up, and the sidewalk was crowded with employees headed for work. Like a river's current, the largest group of people flowed toward the Ishtar District, where most of the corporations had their offices. I joined that flow, falling in between a group of sharply dressed people all speaking to someone through their 'jacks. Without being too obvious, I kept my eyes on the sky, searching for Chimera drones. We hadn't seen any all morning, but knowing Carivant, he'd likely started relying on a different form of surveillance after I'd destroyed the drone the night before. He could be watching us through anything. I wouldn't even put it past him to hijack mindjacks to find us. But that would take time. So we had to move fast.

At the next intersection, I followed a smaller flow of people heading up to the tram station. It was standing room only as the tram left its stop and sped through the canyons of buildings. As we passed the Ishtar District, I stared down the road at Carivant's tower as I had the night before, feeling much more confident than I had then. I half-expected to see barricades around the tower and security forces buzzing like insects around the skyscraper, but it looked like a typical morning, heavy traffic of both pedestrians and vehicles headed for another long day at Genesis Gardens. I didn't let that lull me into complacency, though. Carivant had to be on alert. He'd be watching for us.

That was why we wouldn't use the front door.

After a few stops, the tram sped out of downtown toward the edge of the city, curving north toward the spaceport. I watched out the window as a bulky, bulbous starship fired its landing thrusters with a flare of light and a roar that sent vibrations through the tram.

We slid into the terminal, and I followed the flow into the wide corridors lined with shops and the same flashy, holographic ads that shined from the buildings downtown. The view gave me a flashback to Farstead, to Cixin and Lana.

We had to give Cixin something better than vengeance. We had to end the cycle.

Security for outbound flights was far lighter than passengers who had just touched down and were heading into the city, where I would have been scanned and checked. It was even easier as a pilot. All I had to do was provide my starship's credentials, which would sync up to the Dandelion's records and prove that my ship was on its way.

It was still entirely possible—even likely—that Carivant was tapped into the spaceport's surveillance and that he'd get an alert that we'd passed through here, but I had to hope that we'd get lost in the shuffle of thousands of travelers, and that Carivant's attention would be focused deeper in the city.

I stood on the moving floor as it carried me through the port, watching the sky out the window. There. A flash of sunlight on metal quickly resolving into the *Harriet* as it dropped out of the atmosphere, leaving a white trail behind it. The moving floor split at a junction, and I stepped onto another narrower path that would take me to my terminal. I glanced backward, down past other pilots and passengers behind me to where Kuma and Lana stood. Kuma'd donned a cap and some sunglasses. Lana had her long black hair up under a beanie. I lost sight of them for a moment as the moving path descended into an underground tunnel. Outside the window, the *Harriet*'s thrusters fired above its designated landing pad.

The tunnel took me underneath the spaceport, then sloped up and stopped at a pair of glass doors. On the other side was the *Harriet*, steam still sloughing off its underbelly from its atmospheric entry.

"I thought you couldn't land your ship in the atmosphere," Lana said as she and Kuma arrived at the terminal. "Gases and the environment and all that." She waved her hand as if "all that" didn't involve rescuing our planet—and therefore, our species—from certain death. "Are you telling me we could have just landed on the ground instead of riding that elevator down for days?"

"It's a loophole in the Compact," I said, cringing even as I said it. Lana was right; we shouldn't have been bringing our ship in. "The communities that participate don't have spaceports. Babylon does." She raised her eyebrow, and I added, "I'm not proud of it, okay? But it's our only way in."

Lana held her skeptical expression for a moment, even narrowing her eyes before suddenly smiling and winking. "I just like making you uncomfortable. You make it too easy." She slapped my shoulder as she walked by, and the glass doors onto the landing pad slid open.

Kuma followed her and glanced at me over his sunglasses. "You really do."

After one last look around for lingering drones, we headed up the boarding ramp and through the airlock, and I took a deep breath of the familiar recycled air. Before heading up to the bridge, I set the stolen hoverboard down and opened a small closet near the stern. Inside were mine and Kuma's old uniforms: dark green jumpsuits with black trim across the chest and down the arms and legs. On the back was Genesis Gardens' logo. There were a few spares behind the well-worn suits Kuma and I had worn. I grabbed the smallest I could find and tossed it to Lana.

It occurred to me as I put on my old uniform—grunting as I had to pull it over places that were much tighter than before—that they may have updated the uniforms in the past ten years, and that my old one could stick out. I zipped it up anyway. There was nothing much I could do about it. If I got into the tower and the uniforms were updated, I knew where to grab a replacement.

On the bridge, Lana settled into the seat behind mine—Alis' seat. I set my jaw as I sat in my chair and swiveled to face my controls. We would leave that tower with her. We had to.

"Setting the Cloak," I said, tapping commands into my system as Kuma began pre-flight prep.

"I don't like how this uniform is judging me," Kuma said, pulling at the belly of his jumpsuit and adjusting where it hugged his thighs.

"They must have shrunk in that closet. Gone stiff. Something like that."

Kuma chuckled. "That's it."

The Cloak was our nickname for a system we'd had installed after taking the *Harriet* to Orilla. We'd likely never have made it that far if Bastion hadn't registered the ship as one of theirs, and we wanted to use that to our advantage—not just against Bastion. The Cloak interfaced with other detection systems and adapted our signature and even our trajectory data to whatever we needed, so we could hide in plain sight. It'd been an illegal piece of technology back in the pre-Compact days, but we'd managed to convince some Bastionite revolutionaries on Horizon Dawn to install it.

"We are now a Genesis Gardens cargo ship," I said. "Sorry, girl," I added, patting the console.

Thanks to the Cloak, the *Harriet* had regained a signature as just another transport vessel, coming in from Luna. The trajectory data would prove that, the Cloak having erased the system logs showing that the *Harriet* had dropped in from the Dandelion, and even fabricating other logs showing the ship making other stops throughout the Sphere.

"Here we go," I whispered as I engaged the underbelly thrusters. With a roar, the *Harriet* lifted off the ground, and I guided it toward the spaceport's launch lane.

After a slim, pointed starcraft zipped up into the blue sky, I eased the thrust open and blasted out of the spaceport, rising high above Babylon before easing back on the thrust and beginning a wide loop that would take me back toward Genesis Gardens.

"You doing okay back there?" I yelled over the roar of the air outside. Out of the corner of my eye, I could see Lana clinging onto the seat with white-knuckled hands, her eyes squeezed shut.

"Yeah, I'm just realizing that I don't think I like flying."

"Seeing a revenant rip through an aircraft will do that to you," Kuma said.

I glanced back again as Lana pried one eye open, the other still squeezed shut. Then they both spread wide in wonder.

We were banking back toward the city, bringing our view nearly perpendicular with the ground. The metal spires of Babylon in all their eclectic colors speared the sky on our starboard side. The serpentine Tigris and Euphrates rivers glittered like currents of diamonds as they flanked the city, slithering toward the horizon. Beyond the city, the desert stretched on, dwarfing the city that must have seemed nearly as massive as Bastion to Lana. Wasteland as it was, there was still beauty in the squat mountains and the sloping expanses between, portions of it spiderwebbed with more Glassfields.

"Okay, maybe it's not so bad," Lana said.

We leveled out the *Harriet* as we began our approach to the city. There was Carivant's tower, above its neighbors, a titan among giants.

After double-checking the Cloak to ensure it was active, I took a deep breath and looked over to Kuma, who nodded. "Sending landing request to Genesis Gardens." The building's automatic systems would handle the request, but if they detected anything suspicious, staff would get involved. Then I'd be in trouble.

Kuma engaged our air-brake flaps, not taking my eyes off the screen, where it read *Request pending* with a circle rotating below it.

An alarm dinged as we officially re-entered Babylonian airspace. Green holographic lines lit up the viewport, showing designated flight lanes. I nudged the *Harriet* to port to stay in the sloping lane that dropped down to Genesis Gardens.

The screen changed: *Request processing*.

I held my breath and re-checked the Cloak. Kuma fired a pair of bow thrusters to slow us down further. The mouth of the hangar was open in the side of the tower, and while they may have been concealed, I knew flanking that hangar were anti-aircraft cannons that could chew through the *Harriet* in seconds. I'd entered that hangar hundreds of times, but after the last time I left it, that open mouth may as well have been bristling with fangs and dripping with blood.

Request on hold.

"On hold?" Lana said, craning around my shoulder to see the screen. "What does that mean?"

I wiped my sweaty hands on my pants as a ding rang throughout the bridge. Mind racing, I answered the hail.

"Starship 84JTZ, this is Genesis Gardens Hangar Control. We don't have you on either our pickup or drop-off schedules. Please provide reason for request."

This was okay. We were fine. We'd anticipated that this could happen. After all, the Cloak could mask our signature and manipulate our flight logs, but it wasn't able to hack into other systems and change their files.

"Apologies, Hangar Control," I responded, keeping my voice as level as possible. "We have a possible fuel leak and thought it'd be better to check it here than crash on our way west."

Kuma gave me an approving frown and an emphatic thumbs up.

The screen still read *Request on hold* as we approached the tower. We were going slowly enough that we could maneuver around it, but if we didn't get permission soon, we'd—

Request approved.

I let out my breath as Hangar Control reconnected: "You've got permission to land, 84. And we've contacted a repair crew. You'll—"

"Oh, that's not necessary," I interrupted, cringing as I did. "We…we have an engineer on board." I gave an awkward chuckle. "Just give us the berth, and we'll get out of your hair as fast as we can." We had to prevent anyone from getting too close to the ship, especially close enough to log into its systems to conduct repairs. They'd realize in seconds how we'd retrofitted it. The Cloak could only go so far.

"All right," Hangar Control responded after a moment. "You can dock at Berth 7, but we'll need you out of here in three hours to make room for another arrival."

"Three hours," I repeated. "You've got it. Thank you." I cut the connection.

Kuma slowed us down to almost a crawl and started firing steam thrusters as we entered the hangar, hovering over smaller transport craft. Once we reached the rear of the hangar, he spun us around and dropped us into Berth 7 beside other ships that looked mostly like the *Harriet*. Their engines were smaller and they lacked the battle-scarring our trusty craft had seen, but it was close enough to blend in against any but the most scrutinizing eye.

"Step one, done. Not so bad," I said as I powered down the ship and unbuckled my restraints.

"Okay," Lana said, standing up and bouncing on her feet. "I guess I'm up."

"And you're still comfortable doing this?" I asked. "I know we're asking a lot."

"You know, the more you ask me that, the less comfortable I get."

"Sorry. Thank you. I...thank you." Then I pulled her in for a hug. Her surprised arms hung in the air for a moment before patting me on the back. "I'm glad you're still here," I said as I pulled away. Lana had been avoiding talking about almost taking that Deathwalk, but at that mention, her eyes welled with tears. "And not just because you're kind of a central part of this plan," I added a smirk to make sure she knew I was joking. Mostly joking. "I'm glad you're here. And we're going to help you get that life you deserve. The one your family would want for you."

Lana sniffed, blinked the tears away, and nodded.

I patted her on the shoulder and pulled away. Kuma handed her the small, scorched metal box that was key to the next phase of the plan. "There will be a map on the wall right outside the hangar. The surveillance center was two floors up and to the south. They may have moved it, though. We'll stay in touch."

"On it. You said this place was more like Bastion than anywhere on Earth." She shrugged. "If I fit in anywhere, it'll be here."

We followed Lana down to the passenger cabin and activated the airlock. I held up a finger as it slid open to the hangar, half-expecting crew waiting, but there was no one. The smell of grease and ozone hit me with a familiar comfort that surprised me. Genesis Gardens may have had terrible work conditions, but the one place I found some brief moment of peace was in that hangar. And the only time I half-enjoyed my job was when I left gravity behind as those cargo transports would lift off.

"You're clear," I said. Lana stepped past and headed down the ramp. "Good luck."

Lana gave me an emphatic thumbs up that was clearly mimicking Kuma's earlier encouragement, then she left. I stood there for a moment, staring out into the hangar as a small, boxy transport settled down, wondering how I ever thought I could have done this on my own.

When I turned around, Kuma was still staring out the airlock, a look on his face that I'd recognize anywhere, but that I hadn't seen in years. When he finally noticed me smirking at him with raised eyebrows, he said, "What? She has a nice smile."

"A nice smile, huh?" We stepped back inside as I sealed the airlock.

"And a good heart," he said more quietly as he followed me back up to the bridge.

"Look at you, living your own *To the Moon* plot line," I said.

Kuma chuckled. "If her husband turned out to be alive, and she ran into him in the hallway right now, then maybe."

We settled back into our chairs on the bridge, and I put in the contact code for Lana's mindjack. "How do you think she's doing? Really."

Kuma folded his arms and looked out the viewport. Beside us, the *Harriet*'s sister rumbled before taking off. "Better than yesterday, but by how much? I don't know. She's hard to read. She opened up to me last night, but it always felt like she was staying at the surface."

"She's been through a lot," I said. "She's probably scared of going deeper."

"Yeah. But I think she meant what she said. She wants to be more for her kid. She didn't want to give up like that, now that she has a chance for a better life." He glanced over at the hologram on his console of Mele dancing. He smiled, and tears shimmered in his eyes. "I get that. I think she wants it, too, though. Not just for her son. And that's the only way it'll stick."

I nodded along. "I'm glad she had you, brother. I'm—"

Kuma held up his hand. "You've said sorry enough, Tor. I get it. She gets it. Now let's find Alis."

I took a breath and looked down at my console. We'd established a connection with Lana's mindjack.

"Lana, you there?"

Silence, for a moment, then: *"Mm hm."* She hummed it quietly. There must have been people around.

"Everything all right?"

"Mm hm." Then: *"Sorry, people in the elevator. Almost to the surveillance center."*

I rubbed my hands together beneath the console, elbows on my knees, face only inches from the screen. Neither Kuma nor I liked the idea of Lana in there alone, at risk of more danger, as if we hadn't put her through enough.

"*Yeah, it's locked down,*" Lana said after another couple minutes. "*No passcode, either. Must be 'jack-locked. Or facial recognition. Going old-fashioned.*" Through her feed we heard her knock on the door then a hiss as it slid open.

"*Hi. Hello. Yeah, I'm from engineering. I was sent up to sync this drone's data.*" She'd be showing whoever stood on the other side of that door the scorched box we'd lifted from the drone I'd destroyed the night before.

"*We can do that for you,*" said the voice on the other side.

"*I appreciate it, but it's damaged, so I may need to tinker with it to get a clean sync. I really don't mind.*"

A pause, then: "*All right.*"

A screen flashed open on my console, and the words *I'm in* appeared. She wouldn't be able to speak while she was in the center, so her 'jack was translating thoughts into text.

I looked over at Kuma, who was rolling his bottom lip around between his thumb and forefinger, eyes a little wide. Everything was going smooth so far, but there were still so many unknowns. We couldn't be sure if, in tracking us, Genesis Gardens had put Lana on their watchlist as well. If they had, she likely would have already been apprehended by security, but there was no way to be sure.

You were right, said the words on-screen after a few tense minutes. *The system has an alert if any cameras in the building detect your faces. Along with orders to stun you immediately and permission to shoot you if you don't comply. I think I can deactivate it, but I don't know how long it'll be before someone notices.*

"We just need a little time," I said.

All right. One minute.

We both stood while we waited, and I pulled at the tightness of my jumpsuit around my legs, then checked in the pocket for the hilt of my solarblade.

"Could be an old alert," Kuma said.

"What?" I asked, my mind hardly in the moment.

"The alert on our faces. It could be from ten years ago. Our faces may not have even tripped it. And we may not be on Carivant's mind right now. The drones could have been following us because of an automated process. He may not even know we're here. We'll be okay."

"You saying that for you or me?"

"Both. And for Lana."

"Yeah."

Okay, you should be clear, said Lana on the screen. *Let's just hope you don't run into any old lovers.* I chuckled, glancing at Kuma as he laughed and shook his head, thinking like me back to his *To the Stars* joke. *Hurry down. I've got good news and bad. I'll let you in.*

Good news and bad. That was all right. I could deal with that. I'd really been only expecting bad news.

"On our way," I said.

Kuma and I disconnected from Lana and powered down the ship except for a few systems that would allow us to power her up quickly for a fast exit. I also swiped in some commands that would divert power to the airlock for another surprise if anyone tried to break into the ship.

We sealed the airlock behind us, triggering the defense mechanisms I'd engaged. I leaned closer to the door until I heard the faint hum indicating the defenses were active. We stuck near the back of the hangar as we wound between containers and transports on our way to the door. No one had accosted us as we left the hangar and stepped into the hallway. The few crew we did see were consumed with their work. And, from what I could tell, none of them looked familiar.

The hallways were mostly empty as we made our way to the elevator and up to two floors. A woman in a suit joined us in the elevator but only paid us a disinterested glance when she entered. I still couldn't help but feel exposed, as if I were wearing a sign on my jumpsuit that said "Yes, I'm that Toris, the one that stole a starship worth billions and got a colleague killed." All it took was one face to recognize us. And whether Kuma was right and Carivant was actively searching for us, he certainly wouldn't give up a chance to apprehend us when he learned we were in his building. The entire city was his domain, but this tower was his fortress and keep. He had to maintain control, such was the fragile state of oppressive systems. If he found us...

Deep breath. Focus. Find Alis. Help Alis.

The elevator doors opened just as my head was getting light from holding my breath. We left the woman behind with a courteous nod and headed down the hall. I hadn't been to this floor much, but it looked much the same as the rest of the building: black metal walls and marbled floors, with holo-images projected on the walls to look like windows. Those holograms reminded me of the Deathwalk place the night before, which summoned a comparison so ironic I almost laughed.

We rounded a corner and saw Lana sticking her head out of a doorway. "Hurry," she whispered when we reached her. The surveillance center was a dark, circular room with a huge holomap in the center that displayed all of Babylon. Lights of different colors moved through the city, some up in the air—I assumed those were drones—and some slower on the ground. The rest of the center was full of control consoles and holoscreens, the vast majority of them completing tasks automatically, an AI likely handling most of the work. There were only a few staff members on the other side of the room, all of them huddled around a console, not paying us any mind as we entered. Just in case, Kuma and I crouched so we were mostly hidden behind the room's consoles and definitely concealed behind the holomap.

Lana led us to a console near the back of the room, where she had a holoscreen pulled up.

Alis was on it.

Everything else in the room disappeared, gravity itself reorienting around that screen. She'd traded the bloody pajamas that she'd been wearing when she fled Orilla to a billowy cream shirt, black pants, and brown boots, a simple outfit that would fit in with the fashion of the time. Her hair was tied up, a few strands dropping to frame her face. She looked unharmed, though the bags under her eyes were heavy.

"This was yesterday morning," Lana whispered. "It looks like they tagged her pretty quickly."

"Tagged her? What do you mean?"

"They know who she is. Somehow." Lana swiped over to another screen, where Alis was on her knees, hands behind her head, a pair of armored Genesis Gardens security officers standing over her. Gravity increased and I leaned closer to the screen, looking for blood or bruises, but she still looked unharmed. She didn't even look like she'd put up a fight. Alis was a Bastionite soldier, an Aegis pilot. Those officers wouldn't have stood a chance if she really tried. The only way I'd survived against the Wolf was because it never fought with the control and power Alis had.

"I think she let herself get arrested," I said. "I think she let herself get caught." I couldn't help but smile as I shook my head. "It was her only way in. She knew we'd come for her."

"Actually," Lana said, "I don't think she was interested in waiting." She swiped to another screen that showed an empty cell and flashing lights. "She escaped not an hour ago. Also," she looked up at Kuma, "not important, but since when do corporate buildings have cells?"

"Welcome to Babylon," I said, then: "She escaped? She escaped. She's okay. Do you know where she is? Where she's headed?"

"The center's tapped into the security chatter," Lana whispered, glancing up at the other staff members, who were still gathered at the other end of the room.

"They think she's headed somewhere called 'the Vault?'" I searched it on the map and—"

"I know where it is," I said, backing away from the screen. "Can you watch out for me? Clear the way ahead somehow?"

Lana smiled and nodded. "Yeah, I can do that. It looks like they're all chasing her from the east, where the cells are. If you come in from the north or west, you should be clear." Her smile dropped. "But this Vault seems really secure. I don't think I can get you in from here. I'd need extra permissions."

I patted my modified solarblade in my pocket. "I'm not worried about that." I looked up to Kuma. "Can you stay with her? They may catch on to what she's doing."

He nodded.

"Thank you," I said to Lana, hope fluttering in my chest. "Thank you so much."

"Of course," she winked, and I backed out of the room, keeping an eye on the staff on the other side. Maybe they were helping the security forces chasing Alis.

I had to move fast.

Ignoring attempts at subtlety, I ran back down the hallway to the elevator and hit the button for the second basement level. The Vault was below that, but the main elevator didn't go down there. I'd have to take a staircase. As the elevator descended, stopping occasionally for passengers that would get off only a floor or two later, I bounced from foot to foot, unable to contain the clash of hope and anxiety. Alis was there. She was only a few floors away, and I could almost feel it, that source of gravity that I'd perceived only a little through the holoscreen. But she'd have a small army behind her, and she must have had Carivant's attention by then. Whether he knew about her relation to me, I had no idea, but if he was still working with Bastion, he likely had records that they were still looking for their Moonbreaker. Their traitor. Carivant wouldn't surrender a chance to make money out of that situation.

After a few agonizing minutes, the elevator opened to a low-ceilinged hallway lined with storage rooms. I wound through the halls, slowing down only when I heard footsteps and summoning a friendly smile and greeting for the few staff that I passed. None of them gave me a second look. It wasn't all too rare for someone from the hangar crew to be down there, looking for a spare part or a tool.

At the end of one hallway, I ducked into a room that looked like all the others. Inside it hummed cooling systems for some of the adjacent server rooms, but at the back was an old metal door that opened into a stairwell. It creaked as I opened it, and I paused before descending, listening for footsteps or whispers. But it was quiet. Either the security forces really were focusing their approach to the east and north, or Lana had diverted them.

I leaped the last few steps at the bottom, grunting as my knees reminded me I wasn't young enough to be doing that. Ahead of me was a door with a camera and a scanner beside it. Inside that scanner would be a mindjack link as well. I didn't need any of that.

I pulled out my solarblade and engaged the electromagnetic clips to form into the length of a shortsword. While this door may have looked unassuming, it was thicker than it appeared, designed to withstand the cut of a standard-issue solarblade or other would-be infiltration tools. But there wasn't much that my modified blade couldn't cut through.

With a flick, the plasma erupted around the magnetic field, spraying light in the small space. I took a breath and stuck the blade in the crevice where the door met its frame, then I swiped it down, feeling barely any resistance as the plasma sheared through the locks within. Then—

Alarms blasted around me, making me jerk. I should have expected that. Gone was our subterfuge, but that didn't matter. Alis was on the other side of that door, and she'd have the attention of the security forces.

Unless they assumed it was her cutting through that door and came my way.

I grabbed the door's handle and pulled. It didn't budge. I must have cut through it; smoke was billowing out from the smoldering metal within. The locks must have surrounded the door. It was the Vault, after all, and—

BANG!

That was the door slamming open on the floor above. Booted footsteps rattled down the stairs toward me.

"Shit shit shit," I hissed as I sliced through the top of the door.

BOOM BOOM BOOM BOOM! They'd hit the landing just above my head.

I sliced through the bottom of the door, acrid smoke filling that small space, then tried the door again. It moved, but it was heavy, too heavy to move with one hand. I disengaged my solarblade and dropped it into my pocket—which made me feel naked as armed officers descended the stairs behind me—and heaved at the door with both hands. Just when I thought my strength had reached its limits, the door came toward me. I squeezed through the crack, catching a glimpse of the first masked officers turning the corner of the stairs.

Abandoning the door, I ran down the half-circle foyer on the other side, dashing down the hallway past laboratories and sealed warehouses. The Vault was more than what it sounded. Carivant did keep spoils down there—valuable keepsakes from the Old Earth and the like—but it was also Genesis Gardens' secluded research-and-development division. The Vault held not just possessions, but Carivant's secrets. And not only secrets that would give competitors an edge over him, but secrets that would likely have his employees in open revolt. Kuma and I had once rescued from a Bastion-occupied station a chemist who'd worked in the Vault, designing bio-weapons that Bastion used in the war. Conspiracies about the Vault abounded at Genesis Gardens, but anyone who could actually confirm or deny the truth of those rumors was bound to secrecy and cut off from others, housed in the Gardens District and gifted an exorbitant lifestyle.

"Alis!" I yelled as I turned down another hallway. "ALIS!" I wound down a few more hallways, passing no one, doing what I could to move east, toward where Lana said Alis would enter the Vault. Down one hall, I—

I slid to a stop. To my left, down a wide corridor, a door was open. All the other doors had been sealed, their secrets behind them. Not only was it open, but gravity too pulled in that direction.

Once I was through the door, I eased it shut behind me, then I turned around.

I was in a warehouse, an advanced warehouse, equipped with cranes and other equipment installed into tracks along the walls and ceiling.

And in the center of the warehouse, hung by cranes and other apparatuses with arms wide and head hung as if on a crucifix, was the *Sanguine Lycan*.

I'd only seen images of Alis' fearsome fifty-foot Aegis, its elongated limbs and smooth face with narrow lines of light running down each side, sharp fins like exaggerated wolf's ears. But Alis herself had seen the top half of her Aegis destroyed in Mwezi by the defense forces she'd refused to kill.

Now I knew where Carivant's mithril had gone.

The *Sanguine Lycan*'s legs were the original blood-red of Alis' Aegis. But from the ribs up, the titanic humanoid machine was a deep midnight blue, the color of plated, treated mithril. Anker's intel had been right; Carivant had used up his mithril stores to create...that.

But why?

I crept forward into the warehouse, which was mostly dark other than a few spotlights illuminating the *Lycan*. I couldn't help but shiver, feeling like I'd gone further past the basement and stumbled into a corner of Hell, stepping into the shadow of a slumbering demon.

"Alis?" I hissed. "Alis?"

A shuffle on the other end of the room. Fear of the demon fading away, I spun to the sound.

And a different fear took its place as a trio of officers stepped around the *Lycan's* kneeling leg.

THOOM THOOM THOOM

Light flashed as plasma bolts punched through the air. Toward me. I dove behind a nearby crane arm, a bolt boiling into the concrete where I'd just been standing.

"COME OUT WITH YOUR HANDS UP!" The officer's mechanically enhanced voice echoed through the warehouse. "YOU ARE—"

His words dissolved into a guttural gasp. I spun around, peeking out from behind the crane. The officer in the lead dropped, grasping at something impaled into his neck. A shadow rolled around his body, swiping up the officer's rifle before rising to one knee and slamming plasma bolts into the chests of the other two officers. Before the shadow stood, I knew who it was.

An angel had descended into that hell.

I ran. I dove out from behind the crane and dashed across that warehouse, leaping over cables and cords. Alis turned and dropped the rifle. She smiled, and the sun rose on my long night, the storm ceased and the winds stilled.

I swept her up into a hug, crying into her shoulder as she cried into mine. I breathed in her smell as if it were oxygen and I'd been deep in the sea. It hadn't even been two days, but it may as well have been a year.

Alis' happy tears and gasps of relief quickly devolved into sobs that racked her body, weakening her so much that I had to catch her under her arms. Her head fell into my chest, and I knew her well enough to recognize that her relief at seeing me had also revived her guilt.

I stroked her hair as I dropped to my knees, holding her as she followed me there. When she pulled away, I wiped the tears from her swollen eyes. We stared at each other, both of us having so much to say that we didn't know where to start.

"I'm—" We both said at the same time.

"Sorry," I said, unable to keep myself from chuckling. It didn't matter that officers were closing in on us, that we were in the shadow of a Bastion Aegis, that we still had to get to safety. My joy and relief were bursting at the seams. "You first."

"Cixin...I..." she took a deep breath to control the sobs. "'Sorry' isn't enough. I can't even say sorry to him. I...I'm sorry I ran. That was...I just couldn't..." I pulled her back in for another hug as she gave up trying to form that storm of thoughts into words.

"It wasn't you," I said. "It was—"

Alis shoved me away with such force that I fell backward, catching myself on one hand.

"It was me," Alis snapped. "It's always me. We can call it the Wolf, we can try to separate it to make ourselves feel better, but it's *my* hands that have his blood on them. *I'm* the one who's broken."

"You're not—"

"No. I can't. It's getting worse. I turned again when I was in the city. I'd locked myself away first, so no one got hurt, but...I can't take the chance. You have to leave. I...I'll make you leave."

"Alis, please. We'll do this together. The mithril's right here," I said, gesturing to the Aegis towering above us. "I have a bioengineer with us. One of the people we brought from Farstead. She can help. We can end this. We can kill it." Seeing Alis there, defeated and in such pain, the vengeance returned. This would be the end. I'd show Alis that it wasn't her. That we could get through it. Together.

"The Wolf dies today."

Chapter Twenty-Three

Alis

(Twelve years earlier)

"Then I won't fly," Toris said, standing with his arms folded before the door to the *Dawnbreak*'s hangar. "We're not going to play your game, Halgard. I thought we'd made that obvious."

"Frustratingly so," Halgard said with a sigh. Behind her stood the strike team, dressed in white and blue armor, that would accompany us on the *Harriet* to take command of the Iridesca Loop.

So that Admiral Halgard could burn my home to the ground.

"As I've said far too many times these past couple days," Halgard continued, "I don't have time to deal with your self-centeredness. You're welcome to try and go liberate Kuma, but I guarantee you won't make it a single step. We have a war to win here, Toris, and our chances are better than they've ever been. Direct all your anger toward me, I don't care, you'll be second in line behind Commander Caliday. But think of your people. Think of your home. Think of why you left Earth and started helping people in the first place. Kuma will be safer here than on your ship. Trust me."

Not if my plan went well, he wouldn't. But Toris and I would figure that out. I couldn't let Kuma get hurt.

Toris' jaw ground back and forth as he stared down the admiral, but we both knew this was a battle he wouldn't win. As much as he loathed the idea, we had to play the game in order to maneuver the outcome we wanted. Of course there would be a hiccup like this. Hopefully that's all we had to deal with.

"This is the last time," Toris said, holding up a finger. "If your gambit fails, if we lose, we're done. And when this is all over, *you're* done. The New World has no place for the way you lead. You're little better than Bastion."

"You're repeating yourself, Toris," Halgard said with a slight tilt to her head. "And you're not saying anything that hasn't crossed my own mind over and over again. I said it to Caliday and I'll say it to you: when this is over, I'll face any and all accountability for my actions. But first, we win the war."

"You say that like it excuses you," Toris said. "Like you're better for saying you'll face accountability, like it reduces the horrors down to minor nightmares."

Halgard stared at Toris for a moment before nodding with a frown, the kind of face that told us she heard him, but she didn't much care. Instead, she moved on, having no time to argue: "Willing or not, I appreciate you flying this mission, Toris. I respect what you've done in this war, how you've directed the pain of what happened to you. I truly am sorry for making you experience it again, for what little that's worth to you." Toris didn't argue, but he didn't thank the admiral, either. To my surprise, I believed her. Like Toris said, it didn't make anything better, but I could tell that respect was genuine.

"As I said, you'll be working with some of my best," Halgard said. "They'll protect you with their lives, and they'll ensure you accomplish this mission." She stared at me, and I could feel the threat implied in those words. "Commander Godwin will be leading the team. He's my voice on this mission. And my ears." She patted the shoulder of the man beside her. He had buzzed blond hair, broken by a broad scar that ran across the side of his head. "Wait for our clearance to disembark. We'll stay in close contact with you. Good luck." She clasped her hands behind her back, gave us both a weary look, then nodded, turned, and walked back down the corridor. When she passed the strike team, I watched her shoulders slump, the performance over, the weight returning.

Toris watched her leave for a moment, hands clenching into fists, then spreading wide as he bit at the inside of his cheek. I understood the instincts he was pushing against, the urge to try, knowing that Halgard's warning was true: those soldiers wouldn't let him get one step toward the admiral.

"Thank you for having us aboard, Captain Orius," Commander Godwin said. "Shall we?"

Toris' eyes moved to Godwin. "After you," he said, his mouth moving as little as possible, the rest of his face like stone.

Godwin gave him a gracious nod and passed the two of us, the rest of the strike team following him through the airlock and onto the ship.

I opened my mouth to say something, but before I could, Toris spun on me, a fire in his eyes, and growled, "Let's end this war."

***

Toris and I didn't have a chance to discuss our plans before Commander Godwin joined us on the bridge. Despite Toris insisting that we didn't need supervision, Godwin took the seat that I'd occupied before, with me taking Kuma's spot in the co-pilot's seat. As I'd sat down, I stared at the hologram of Kuma's dancing daughter.

We're doing this for you, I thought.

We'd sat mostly in an uncomfortable silence since boarding, with minimal communication between Toris and I as we prepared for disembarkation. Every so often, the *Harriet* quivered as the *Dawnbreak* engaged in battle. I felt blind, sitting in that ship as a battle raged just outside the hangar. I was used to knowing the tactics and plans, to having a constant feed into my 'jack, to having all the inputs from my Aegis. Without that information, I felt vulnerable, despite the layers of metal protecting us. Toris was working on connecting to the *Dawnbreak*'s network so we could feed their data into the *Harriet*'s systems and at least get an accurate picture on our holomap. So far, we had nothing.

After almost a half-hour of waiting, anticipating, listening, and cringing whenever the dagger twisted in my brain, Godwin broke the awkward silence: "The admiral intends to demand a surrender first."

"What?" I asked, turning around.

Godwin rolled his jaw back and forth, clearly questioning whether he should say more. Then he leaned forward, setting his elbows on his knees. "The mission's contingent on whether or not the Bastion government surrenders. Admiral Halgard is confident that between this battle and combat around Luna, we'll have forced Bastion into a position where they'll accept that."

I scoffed. "Then even after twenty years of fighting Bastion, you still don't understand them."

Godwin shrugged. "We'll see. I understand this is a...difficult mission for you to participate in. I can only imagine what would be going through my own head. So I think it's important that you know we're Plan B."

Toris shook his head but didn't turn around. "This shouldn't be a plan at all. Millions of innocent people will suffer for the decision their leaders make. There are other ways to end this war. Don't make it sound like we should thank Halgard just because she's willing to wait until after Bastion says "hell no" before we burn them off the planet."

Godwin let a breath out of his nose and leaned back in his chair. "This war has to end. If we have to be the ones to bear the burden of whatever that means, so be it. It ends today. All the loss. All the pain. After today, we rebuild, all of us." He pointedly looked at me in the end, as if I represented all of Bastion, who I doubted would ever be able to rebuild, at least in this generation. I held my tongue on that, as well as on making the same counter I'd directed at Halgard: that winning the war wouldn't end this cycle. That if they succeeded, Bastion would come back for blood as soon as they had the chance. There was no point, and I didn't care to convince anyone. It was wasted breath.

Finally, a notification dinged through the bridge, and I turned back to the control console. I wanted to get this over with. I'd rather be out in the field than sitting and waiting in that coffin.

"We're connected," I said, then streamed the data to our holomap and flicked the switch on the console between us. The spherical hologram burst into existence. It was dominated by another sphere: Mars. Bastion. Home. My heart became a stone.

The rest of the map was a mess: green triangles pointing toward the planet indicated the Earther fleet, which was much larger and more intimidating than I'd anticipated. They'd obviously been able to spare resources on this assault with Luna's own fleets joining the fight in that arena. A smaller, more spread-out assortment of red triangles, pointed away from the planet toward their enemy, indicated the Bastion fleet. They were clearly maneuvering to intercept the incoming Earther ships, clustering especially over the sprawling city of Bastion, forming a shield of metal thorns. Surrounding the planet like a halo was a ring shining blue on the map: the Iridesca Loop.

"*Harriet*," said a voice over our channel with the *Dawnbreak*. It wasn't Halgard. "*Our fighters will be launching in thirty seconds. We'll give you clearance to disembark once the enemy's distracted by them and we've adjusted our angle. We want to reduce the chances of them noticing you exit the hangar.*"

"Copy, *Dawnbreak*," Toris said. Vibrations shook the ship. We looked to our port, where the giant teeth of the hangar doors were opening to the void of space. Sunlight reflected off bright Bastion, and I couldn't help but admire its beauty as I had on the way to Stickney, when all this started. A storm was rolling in from the Mar Borealis, breaking around the Tharsis Montes and heading toward Bastion, its sprawling cityscape visible even from that great distance, climbing up the foothills of massive Olympus Mons. I could picture the grasslands south of the city blowing with waves of wind, moving like an ocean of its own ahead of the storm.

Was Father down there? Had he fled to another city? Or maybe back to Al-Havini Station, where he'd grown up? Did he...know about Teah? Did he know about me?

I shook my head. I couldn't go down that path. Not at that moment. I'd be more lost than I already was, useless to this mission, and therefore to him and everyone else down there.

I would end the war. No one would win.

On the other side of the hangar, pilots rushed to their starfighters, clamped in rows, all of them shaped roughly like daggers, the wings a crossguard and the rest of the body the blade. Earther ships were known for being faster than Bastion's, but they gave up some firepower. That left the two sides relatively balanced, and tactics had to account for the differences. At a distance, Bastion starfighters were more dangerous, but once Earther ships got close, they'd cut right through and be difficult to track. Halgard would have accounted for this and likely waited until the cruisers were at an optimal distance before deploying. That or she'd done something to ensure her fighters got closer to Bastion's ships before they could respond.

At thirty seconds, alarms sounded in the hangar and lights flashed. The first row of fighters released from their clamps, burst forward in the zero-G with a steam blast, then launched out of the hangar, the flashes from their engines like clusters of tiny suns. Each row followed the last until most of the hangar was empty. It was best practice to keep a squadron behind to launch and protect the battlecruiser if necessary. I watched the tiny suns as they rocketed toward the Bastion fleet, then as the *Dawnbreak* fired a volley of missiles and a storm of lasers to disrupt whatever starfighters had deployed from Bastion's own cruisers. Once the fighters were clear, the *Dawnbreak* banked to their starboard, both to cover the vulnerable point of the hangar and to give us additional cover on our launch.

"Harriet," said the officer over the speakers, *"prepare to disembark."*

Toris flipped a pair of switches and swiped some commands into his control screen. "You'll have control of the thrusters. All you need to do is give us a burst on the starboard side, thrusters two and three. Nothing fancy."

"Got it." I'd performed far more advanced maneuvers in my Aegis, and in a few starships before that. It was strange to operate a starcraft without being synced to my 'jack, like moving a finger using the fingers of the other hand, but I could do it.

"*We're drawing combatants away from your flight path*," said the officer. "*You should have a clear shot to the control module. Remember, once you launch, we can't actively protect you, or we'll blow your cover. Good luck.*"

Toris pressed the button that opened communication to the passenger cabin below. "We're preparing to disembark. Make sure you're strapped in." Then he turned to me. "Ready?" I could tell by the look in his eyes that he was asking if I was ready for much more than engaging the steam thrusters.

"Ready."

"Harriet, *you're clear to launch.*"

Toris nodded to me, and I pressed the command waiting on my screen. I jerked to starboard as the thrusters fired, launching us to port and out of the open mouth of the hangar. Toris threw the thrust lever, and I clutched the sides of my seat as we exploded forward, then immediately turned downward, skirting the belly of the *Dawnbreak* toward the stern, the light of the battlecruiser's massive engines shining mostly out of view like the sun below the horizon. Once we passed the *Dawnbreak*, we rolled—which almost made me lose the little food I'd had—and then banked to port, following a flashing line projected on the viewport. The line showed the flight path we'd put into what Toris called a "Cloak," which would mask their departure from the *Dawnbreak* and instead show enemy craft that we were heading in from Farstead.

Once we had a straight shot to the Iridesca Loop's command module, he pushed the throttle to its limit, and the *Harriet* pressed me into my seat as she accelerated. The two fleets were moving closer to each other, like the jaws of a great monster closing. Starfighters swarmed in a cloud between them, the space popping with explosions, bursts of chaff, and the flash of missile and plasma fire.

And we were flying right toward it.

Thanks to the Cloak—and the intel Halgard shared with her troops—we'd be marked as an ally of both sides. Neither would fire on us unless Bastion somehow saw through the ruse. But that didn't eliminate the threat of stray shots and the general chaos of battle. Despite Toris' and Kuma's many modifications to their cargo ship, the *Harriet* was no warcraft.

We could do this. We had to. So many lives—on multiple worlds—depended on it.

"All right," Toris said, sitting up straighter and rolling his neck. "You may want to hang on."

He placed one hand on his throttle control while the other stayed on the yoke.

"Anything you need me to do?" I asked, feeling like much more of a passenger than a co-pilot.

"Keep the thruster controls up. We may need them for quick maneuvers."

"Got it," I said. "Sorry, I know Kuma would—"

"You can do it," Toris said. He glanced at me with an encouraging half-smile. "You'll make Kuma proud."

I took a deep breath, held it for a moment, then let it out slowly as I stared at Kuma's dancing little girl. Mele. That's what they'd called her in the memories I saw. We were doing this for her, so children on neither Mars nor Earth would have to worry about the fate she faced.

"Here we go," Toris said, and we entered the battle.

It was impossible to completely avoid, but Toris pulled back slightly on the throttle and steered us to port, toward where the fighting was lighter. We'd have to realign to dock with the Loop, but we weren't too far off course. I didn't love how quickly we'd have to shed speed, though. Toris would have to—

Plasma fire burst past the viewport, missing us narrowly as an Earther starfighter pursued its enemy. It was catching up to the bulkier Bastion fighter, which flew above us close enough that we got a warning about its engines heating up our hull. We were gone by the time the Earther ship followed.

Toris banked to starboard just as a pair of missiles streaked through where we'd been a moment before, too big for a starfighter and likely fired from one of the Earther battlecruisers. Ahead, an Earther starfighter exploded in a cloud of fire and shrapnel that burst in all directions, several of them large enough to put a hole in the *Harriet*.

And we were going too fast to turn around it.

"Fire the dorsal thrusters. Now!"

I selected the right thrusters and hit the command. The thrusters on top of the ship fired and forced the ship downward so quickly that most of my body stayed where it'd been. And the dagger twisted ferociously in my head.

But the maneuver worked. Mostly. We avoided the largest pieces of debris, but smaller pieces peppered the ship as we passed through the cloud at high speed. Alarms rang until Toris flicked a switch to turn them off.

"Superficial," he said, then glanced at a screen that was flashing to his left. "Mostly."

"The cruisers are closing in," Godwin noted, staring at the holomap. He was right. The fangs of the two fleets were clamping together. I searched out the viewport to our starboard, where four Bastion battlecruisers surged toward us, cannons lighting up as they shot down any Earther starfighter that strayed too close. Like their starfighters, Bastion's battlecruisers were also bulkier than Earth's, always looking to me like an elongated and boxy molar, with what would be the roots of the tooth sticking out the stern, illuminated by their massive engines.

Something burst out from the bow of the closest cruiser, larger than a missile, shaped more like...

"They just launched an Aegis."

"For space combat?" Toris asked, searching space for the mass of metal hurtling toward the battle. "I thought they were only deployed on the ground."

"Not always," Godwin said before I could respond, a haunted tone to his voice. "They're more difficult to avoid on the ground, but they wreak their own kind of havoc in space. I...we once lost an entire frigate to one."

I decided not to ask if it had been me. I'd destroyed multiple frigates, with heavy support from the *Fang*, of course.

"And there's another," Godwin said, pointing to one of the other Bastion cruisers—and the humanoid-shaped missile flying away from it.

"And another," I added as a second Aegis launched from the first cruiser. "That'll be the maximum they'll risk here. They'll save the rest in case we break through and land on the surface."

"Three's enough," Godwin whispered.

He was right. To our starboard, the first Aegis fired thrusters throughout its armor and flipped upright. I recognized this Aegis: more slender than mine and colored a deep green with black trim. The helm was shaped like a half-diamond. The *Viridian Viper*. One of the more maneuverable of the Aegis suits, making it perfect for space combat. I'd never been in a battle with it—Aegis rarely needed to fight close to each other—but I'd met its pilot: Arastasia Livaun Talay. She was quiet, let her actions speak for her.

As she did now.

The *Viper* used its momentum to catch up to and grasp the wing of a passing Earther ship, then fired thrusters to counteract the starfighter's momentum, spun, and ripped the fighter in half. The ship exploded, and I couldn't help but cringe.

"We need to get out of here," I said as more debris peppered the ship.

"Agreed," Toris said, pushing the throttle further, even at the risk of running into something.

The other Aegis arrived to the battle. This one was built more like mine but painted royal blue with silver trim and with a sharp fin swept back from the center of its head. The *Sapphire Marlin*. I heard a story about some of the other pilots teasing the *Marlin*'s pilot, Dakarai Adabeda Singh, about the name, prior to a training exercise. At face value, "Marlin" did produce a less intimidating idea than the other predator namesakes. Apparently, during the exercise, Singh critically damaged every other Aegis and walked away unscathed. His speed, much like the predator he was named for, was unmatched.

Singh proved himself again as he didn't bother slowing down as Talay had. He shot like a missile, limbs tucked in, into the fray. A spray of smaller missiles fired from launchers in his Aegis' shoulderblades, slamming into an Earther starfighter just as it flew into the path. The *Marlin* fired thrusters that sent it into a roll and directly into the path to reach out, grab a starfighter, do a somersault with another thruster fire, and hurl the starfighter into another comrade as if it were a toy.

"Can we do anything about them?" Godwin asked. He seemed restless, his knee bouncing as he watched the battle with wide eyes. He probably would have much rather been out there, defending his people, rather than trapped with us. "Can you...distract them? Deceive them? Try to call them off?" Without turning, I knew he was talking to me. I was the asset. The insider. "Your Cloak could do that, right?" he asked Toris.

"We can't hack into their channels," Toris said as he steered us gently around a spinning, shredded hunk of a Bastion fighter. "They'd have to contact us."

"Can you give them anything?" And this time I looked at Godwin and saw the desperation in his eyes. His brothers and sisters were out there dying. And he was helpless. "Information? Tactics? Anything?"

"I gave Halgard what I could," I said. The truth was, Earth hadn't quite devised a proper countermeasure for the Aegises. The railgun on Mwezi had worked well enough against me, but that was mostly because I was in the middle of having my brain hacked. They'd tried a number of strategies: cutting off mindjack signals to disrupt the sync, using electromagnetic pulses to disable the armor, and more, but Bastion learned from every response and improved. Earth had even tried creating their own Aegises at one point, but they were far inferior. "The best they can do is overwhelm the Aegis. Look, they're doing that now."

A trio of Earther starfighters had broken off from their original pursuits and was following the *Marlin*, firing lasers that confused the Aegis' missiles, and even sent one slamming into the leg of the *Viper* in an explosion that sent that Aegis tumbling across the battlefield.

"Using their own weaponry against them," Godwin said with a satisfied nod.

"Bastion loves to show off our...their toys, so you have plenty of intel on each Aegis. That let Halgard give them some pretty specific tactics. It was...impressive," I said, shivering at giving that woman a compliment.

"What's that third one doing?" Godwin pointed at the final Aegis that had launched from the closest cruiser. It seemed disinterested in pursuing starfighters, instead carving a path through the battle and firing only when necessary. That Aegis was bulkier than the others. From our distance, it was difficult to tell which suit that was. But, squinting, I could see what it was doing, why it was behaving differently.

"See those transports behind it? Those are boarding craft. That Aegis is going straight for the battlecruisers."

Godwin sighed and sat back, wiping sweaty hands on the side of the chair. The pressure of this battle was heavy on everyone, if for different reasons. Even I—

"Harriet. Harriet, *come in.*" That wasn't the same officer who'd been hailing us. That was Halgard.

"*Harriet* copies," Toris said. A starfighter exploded above us, and the force knocked us downward, sending warnings throughout the cabin. A hand slapped into the viewport, stamping a splash of blood before careening off into space.

"*We have a problem. The* Fang *is approaching.*"

Toris and I shared a glance before I looked out the viewport, scanning the battle. None of the nearby Bastion battlecruisers were the *Fang.* And I couldn't make out anything much beyond the cloud of metal, plasma fire, chaff, and lasers. I turned instead to the holomap, which I zoomed out until...there. A cruiser marked red, just entering the Inner Sphere. It was burning hard, and it'd be at the battle soon.

Ecker was there. Would...would Teah's body still be aboard?

No. It'd be somewhere out near Luna, dropped out of an airlock and...

The dagger twisted. Focus. I couldn't think about that.

Ecker was there. That likely helped Luna's defense, but...it complicated my plan.

"*We don't think he's supposed to be here,*" Halgard said. "*Ecker's command was central to the Luna offensive, and he would have needed to leave soon after the battle began. If that's the case and he's disobeying orders either out of pride or vengeance on your part, Caliday, he may have lost Luna for Bastion. That's good news for them, but it may be bad news for us. How confident are you in your Cloak hiding your signature, Toris?*"

"Very," Toris said, "but we can't do anything about visual recognition. If he identifies us..."

I swallowed a lump in my throat. Toris was right. We may have blended in to everyone else as a Bastion-marked cargo ship in Bastion airspace, but Ecker would have tagged us back when he had me pursued all the way to the *Dawnbreak*. We'd stick out. Unless...

"Admiral," I said, "I have an idea, but it may paint a target on your ships."

"I don't know if you've noticed, Caliday, but you're on the edge of one of the largest space battles in years. Shoot."

"Have a pair of fighters pursue us. Fire some shots nearby. We need to blend in better with the battle. We need to look like a ship escaping to the Loop, not traveling there intentionally. With Ecker here...we need to blend in as much as possible."

"Not a bad idea, Caliday. Done. Your fighter escort is on its way."

Warning notifications dinged throughout the bridge as a duo of Earther starfighters dropped in behind us. A volley of harmless plasma shots lanced past our starboard side, burning bright against the backdrop of space and leaving afterimages as I blinked.

"Not bad," Toris said.

"Hopefully it's enough."

It seemed to be. We were nearing the edge of the battle, and Toris guided us upward to align with our original flight path and the Iridesca Loop's command module. One of the starfighters off our port fired, missing just close enough that we got a heat warning from the hull above our port engines.

"A little close," Toris said through gritted teeth.

"Try hailing the Loop," I said. "I have a boarding code that should work."

He did, and I figuratively crossed my fingers that the crew and its defenders had left the channel open.

After a moment, Toris looked at me and nodded.

"Iridesca Loop, this is cargo ship EX-150, requesting permission to dock. We're damaged and have valuable cargo. We won't be able to make it through atmosphere. I repeat: requesting permission to dock until the battle is over. Clearance code Zeta Caliber Nova."

I held my breath. That code would indicate that I had high military clearance. As long as they didn't ask who I was or where I got that code, we should have been fine. I watched the blinking green light on my screen, indicating the open channel.

"Cargo ship EX-150, this is Iridesca Control. We are on full lockdown. We recommend you reroute to Deimos or a darkside station." By "darkside," they meant a station currently on the far side of the planet, where we'd be safer from the battle.

"Negative, Control," I responded, sticking to the story Halgard, Toris, and I had discussed. "We're leaking fuel and won't be able to make it to either Deimos or another station. We understand your lockdown protocol, but we have extremely valuable assets aboard. I'm repeating, clearance code Zeta Caliber—"

"ALIS!"

Toris screamed just as a hulking something came at us from starboard at full speed. I only saw it for an instant out of the corner of my eye before one of the Earther starfighters exploding sent us careening in a spiral. I clenched the arms of my seat and tried to lean against the spin—a lesson I'd learned in my last voyage on the *Harriet*.

"Thrusters, Alis!" Toris yelled. "Thrusters!"

Still cringing against the spin as my vision contracted and my stomach lurched, I fired all the portside thrusters to counteract the spin.

"Aegis," Toris said through his heavy breathing. "It was...an Aegis. The green one."

"The *Viper*," I said. Better than the *Marlin*. "They're probably defending us, going after the—"

As a cruel response, the *Harriet* lurched, the sudden halt of acceleration slamming us against our restraints so hard that something cracked in my neck.

"It's got us!" Toris yelled. "Alis, how do we get out of this?"

"We won't get out of it by yelling at me!" I yelled back, perfectly understanding that he wasn't yelling at me, but needing even just a second to get my thoughts together. The *Viper* had us. We must have been made. Ecker knew we were there, and he likely assumed I was aboard. And I doubted he only alerted the *Viper*. Getting into the control module would likely be even more difficult, too.

"You don't have any weapons on this thing?!" Godwin yelled from his seat.

Toris ignored the officer and threw the throttle forward. The *Harriet* pulsed forward, shearing from the Aegis' grip with a terrible sound of tearing metal that echoed through the ship and set off a flurry of alarms. I fired thrusters to align us once again with—

We swiveled starboard as the *Viper* caught us again. Alarms screamed and the ship vibrated as a sound worse than the shearing tore through the starcraft, accompanied by the steady hum of a plasma cutter.

Toris glanced up at the screens to his right. "They're *tearing off* our starboard engine! Alis! How do we kill this thing?"

The dagger twisted in my head, but I fought back the blurring of my vision. I couldn't let whatever had happened on the *Dawnbreak* happen here. We had to get to the module. This had to end. And I was the one who knew Aegises best.

The terrible shearing and plasma cutting ceased, and Toris pulled back the throttle. We didn't need another spiral.

"*The vice admiral wants you alive, traitor.*" That was Talay's voice, somehow broadcast through the ship. "*But he never said anything about whole.*"

Coming from the *Viper*, especially acting on Ecker's orders, that was no idle threat.

"She's already damaged," I said, thinking out loud. "From the *Marlin*. Her left leg. That'll slow her down and hamper her maneuverability. And its a vulnerability." I opened the channel back to the *Dawnbreak*. "Admiral! We need support. The *Viper's* going to try and tow us in. I have an idea, but we'll need someone to light a fuse." Then I turned to Toris as the plasma-cutter shearing began on the portside. "You could jettison containers; can you jettison your engines as well?"

Toris cringed as he answered: "Yes."

"Fuel containers attached?"

Toris sighed. "Yes."

"Admiral," I continued, "while the *Viper* is cutting into the *Harriet* to immobilize it, it has several points open: the mechanism in the arm where the blade exits, as well as vents in its chest and back to radiate heat. It'd be hard to hit with individual shots, and its anti-missile systems would catch those, but..." I trailed off, looking at Toris.

"But an engine-sized bomb would do the trick." He let out a heavy breath.

I looked at him with true sympathy. This ship was his and Kuma's life. "I'm sorry. We can end this."

He searched my eyes for a moment before nodding. "You ready to light that fuse, Admiral?"

"*You have a trio incoming. I'll patch them in. On your signal.*"

"She's fifty percent through," Toris said, glancing up at the screen.

"Wait," I said. "Don't jettison yet. We need to orient so the explosion sends us toward the Iridesca."

Toris nodded as I fired thrusters at full strength to pivot us around so we were in between the *Viper* and the Loop. Talay gripped us tighter, but we were in a better position than before, the Loop on our starboard side, close enough that we could maneuver into position to dock.

As long as the engine's explosion didn't catch us, too. At least then Ecker wouldn't be able to take me in alive. Even that would be a small victory.

"Eighty percent," Toris said.

"Let's go to ninety," I said. "The longer the plasma blades burn, the wider the radiators need to open to vent out the heat."

"You owe me two new engines after this, Caliday," Toris said, but there was that teasing half-smile on his face.

"You got it," I said. "Ecker can take it out of my paycheck."

Toris let out a short scoff, but neither of us could muster any more humor than that. "Eighty-eight," Toris said. "Eighty-nine."

"Jettison!"

Toris threw a heavy switch on his left, and we jerked to starboard as the force of the jettison nudged us away from the *Viper*.

The Earther starfighters swooped in above us. I fired our port thrusters at full power to give us as much distance as possible.

The *Viper* shoved the engine away. A shower of plasma fire rained on the rocket.

And a new star blossomed in the void as the engine exploded.

The light blinded us an instant before the shockwave threw us away like a dandelion seed blown by a god. Alarms blasted as the ship spun, but I did my best to right her. We'd lost a few thrusters in the explosion, but we eventually wobbled into something approximating a straight flight path. Out the port side, the shrapnel of the *Viridian Viper* expanded in a cloud, its mostly intact half-diamond head spinning off toward the approaching Earther fleet.

"*Are you alive in there*, Harriet?" asked Halgard.

"Barely," Toris responded.

"*Good. Well done, Caliday. Happy to have you on our side.*"

I cringed as the comment hit more like an insult than a compliment.

"*Now finish the mission. Let's win this war. Having the* Fang *in play here helps Luna's chances but hurts ours. It's all riding on you.*"

"We'll accomplish the mission, sir," Godwin said. I rolled my eyes out of his view.

"*We don't know the extent of your blown cover,*" Halgard continued. "*So we'll do our best to cover you while you're inside the module.*"

Neither Toris or I expressed any gratitude, so after a moment of awkward silence, Godwin said, "Thank you, sir."

We didn't bother hailing the Loop again as we maneuvered toward its dock. Fortunately, it didn't have any external defenses; Bastion had relied on the planetary defense fleet for that.

"I'm going to check on the squad," Godwin said as he removed his restraints and stood. "Good work out there, you two."

Both Toris and I watched as Godwin left the bridge, both of us still catching our breath.

Then both of us tried to speak at the same time in something that sounded like "Iknowsorrywhattoaboutdoyourship."

"Sorry, you first," Toris said.

"Ugh, I feel like I've been holding my breath with him in here," I said. "Your plan. What was your plan? Quick."

"The Loop. They're worried it can disrupt their particle beams. So, we make their fears come true and use the Loop to redirect the beams, but we redirect it into the Loop to destroy it. We'll save the city, but we'll disrupt Bastion's infrastructure enough to still handicap them."

I frowned, surprised at how close our plans were.

"What? Is that bad?"

"No, it's good. That was an impressed frown."

"I can't tell with you, sometimes."

I chuckled. "My mom would say the same thing. But it may not work. The Loop is covered in mithril plating, which is why Halgard isn't just firing on it to take it out of the game. I don't know if particle beams will destroy it. Plus, destroying the Loop will harm the innocents in the city, too. But my plan is closer than I thought it'd be. We need to go further if we want to end the war. With that plan, the Earther fleet could just recharge and fire again, but that time without Bastion having any defenses. We can't let that happen. We're going to use the magnetic field to redirect the beams."

"But we're going to destroy the fleet, and we're going to end this war."

Chapter Twenty-Four
Toris

I swiped the plasma rifle from one of the fallen security officers and slung it around my back. "We'll have more company soon," I said. "I tripped an alarm that got security on my tail. They would have heard the shots."

When Alis didn't respond, I turned to her. She was standing below her old Aegis, staring up at it. In the *Sanguine Lycan*'s state, on its knees, arms spread wide, head bowed, it almost looked like the machine was staring back at her. The spotlights on the Aegis shined on Alis, casting a long shadow behind her, and my relief clashed with my anxiety. I'd found her. Now I needed to help her. Now I needed to kill the Wolf. We needed to kill it.

"I may be able to cut off some of the mithril plating with my 'blade," I said, adjusting the rifle on my shoulder and stepping next to her. "Then we can rendezvous with Kuma and Lana. Get all this over with. Alis?" Cold fear gripped at my heart. "Alis? Are you—"

"Tor, I'm fine. I'm here, don't worry," she finally turned toward me with a soft smile. "Sorry, it's just...weird." She looked back at the *Lycan*. "Why would they reconstruct this? How did they even salvage the legs? Bastion's picky about what they leave behind on a battlefield. They would have taken this off Mwezi's streets right away."

"Carivant probably bought it," I said with a shrug. "He collects. It makes him feel important."

"Yeah," Alis said in a tone that clearly showed she didn't agree. "But the cost to repair it? Especially with mithril plating?"

"I don't think you understand how much this guy will pay to make a statement, my love," I said.

"Maybe. But what's the statement? And is it his? Or Bastion's?"

That sent a chill up my spine. "What do you mean?"

She stared at the *Lycan* for a moment longer before shaking her head. "Nothing. One problem at a time." She turned to me with a glitter in those beautiful eyes. "I have an idea. I think—"

Shouts. In the corridors outside. No, not right outside. Still distant but closing in.

"I know we need to hurry," Alis said. "You can carve off the plating while I...try something." Before waiting for me to answer, Alis ran for the scaffolding that stacked up the Aegis' right side. Narrow stairs ascended the layers of metal.

"Wait," I hissed, looking back at the doors to the warehouse before following. "What are you doing?"

"All of this started when I de-synced from the *Lycan*. What if it just needs to be reset? What if that's all it takes?"

"Uh, because that seems like a really bad idea. What if it immediately reconnects you with Bastion and they try to dominate you again? De-syncing was the only thing that stopped them taking control. It's probably the only thing that's keeping you from completely becoming the Wolf." I shivered at the thought of what that would be like.

"Cixin said it was possible that I was experiencing some kind of phantom signal, the domination signal looped over and over precisely *because* I de-synced the way I did. We haven't totally ruled that out. I have to at least try. And then we can still use the mithril plating to create a Faraday Shield to keep Bastion out. Plus, we wouldn't have to worry about Carivant's security if we have an Aegis on our side, and we'd be taking it out of his control. I doubt someone like Carivant only wants this for a collection. He's looking to make a profit, and I don't want this to end up with whoever's paying. Orilla probably wouldn't mind having it, either."

We'd climbed up past the Aegis' hips. Up above, a dim light spilled out of an opening in the ribcage. At the mention of Orilla, I paused on the step, wondering if I should mention that we may not have been able to return there at all.

Alis turned back, saw me hesitate, then took a few steps down to stand on the one ahead of me. She took my face in her hands, and I closed my eyes at her touch, like the kiss of sunrise after a cold night.

"Trust me," she said, probably assuming my hesitation was worry about her syncing with the *Lycan*. Not quite, but certainly still relevant. "I can sync with the Aegis without connecting to Bastion's network." I opened my eyes and stared into hers, the spotlights catching the gold flecks in her irises. "I love you. Thank you for coming to me. Thank you for not giving up on me, even after…" Her eyebrows pressed together for a moment before she steeled herself. "Thank you."

I kissed her palm as she pulled her hands off my face. Find Alis. Help Alis. We were going to kill the Wolf because nothing would help Alis more, but I couldn't let my worry and fear keep her from ending this the way she wanted to. The monster was living in her head, after all. And I could never let her think she didn't have my trust, that she didn't have all of me.

"I trust you. Always. Let's try it."

We climbed to the opening in the ribcage. The armor around the opening was the red of the original *Lycan*, but halfway across the chest, the red met dark-blue mithril, which plated the left side of the chest, both arms, and the head. As Alis entered the Aegis, I paused for a moment, staring up at the drooping head, feeling like it was staring right back.

I followed Alis into the Aegis' cockpit. The space was small, dominated by the reclining seat, set into a pod in the floor, and the screens and controls around it. Like the outside, the cockpit was bisected, the bottom half red and the top half navy.

"This is original," Alis whispered, crouching behind the seat and running a hand along the material. She looked up at me, and I could see emotions clashing on her face. So much had happened in this cockpit. This was where Alis had done things she'd forever regret, and where she'd made the first decision that would set her on her own path. In those eyes, though, above it all, I saw the determination that I'd fallen in love with years before.

"Let's do it," I said.

Alis took a breath, then she slid down into the seat. "When I start this up," she said, "they're probably going to come running."

"Well, they're bringing guns to a big-ass-robot fight."

Alis chuckled and shook her head. Then, with a solemn tone, she said: "I've never done this without my sync suit. Teah made…" She swallowed. "And I can't connect on my end because of the malfunction. So I'll have to try it through the Aegis." She looked up and back at me. "Ready?"

"Been ready for ten years."

I meant it to lighten the mood, but the little light on Alis' face darkened instead, and she turned back to her instruments.

Find Alis. Help Alis.

With a twist in my gut, I had a feeling I wasn't doing the latter.

Outside the warehouse, shouts echoed. They were getting closer. Well, that wouldn't matter soon. Like Alis said, Carivant himself would likely know when his little project lit up.

"Here we go," Alis said. She flicked a pair of switches, and the holoscreens activated around her, most of them dark. A couple nearest her showed basic systems and diagnostics. Alis pressed another button, and the entire Aegis vibrated as its engine drives kicked on. The holoscreens that had been dark lit up with camera views of the warehouse outside the machine. One of the screens flashed with a warning: a group of unidentified potential hostiles were incoming.

"Okay," Alis said, "attempting to sync...now." But even as she said it, her hand hesitated above the screen in front of her. I crouched down beside her, kissed her forehead, and put my hand on her shoulder.

"You're not alone. You don't have to do any of this alone. I'm here, no matter what happens. Wolf or no Wolf." She looked up at me with tears in her eyes.

"It's hurt for so long," she said. "In so many ways. What if this makes it worse?"

I pushed aside my fears mirroring those concerns and instead said, "You asked me to trust you. I do. It's not even a question. Now you need to trust yourself."

Alis swiped a tear away and gave me a half-smile. That smile gave way to a sniff and a determined nod before she pressed the command on her screen. A rotating circle dominated the screen as the Aegis attempted to connect.

"Feel anything?" I asked.

Alis shook her head, gaze glued to the screen.

A warning flashed on another screen just before I heard the warehouse doors slam open below. We were out of time. Through the Aegis' camera view, we watched as the squad that had followed me down filtered in through the open door, rifles against their shoulders, and took cover behind crates and equipment. They were being careful, likely unsure of how much control we had over the Aegis. I wouldn't run against that machine guns blazing, either. That was good. That would buy us a few moments.

"YOU'RE TRESPASSING WITHIN TOP-SECRET GENESIS GARDENS PROPERTY," shouted an electronically enhanced voice, "DESIGNATED A CAPITAL OFFENSE BY BABYLONIAN LAW."

A capital offense. Of course it was.

"EVACUATE THE AEGIS IMMEDIATELY, OR WE WILL REMOVE YOU BY FORCE, DEAD OR ALIVE."

"Alis," I said, "do you—"

I stopped short as I looked down. Alis' eyes were no longer looking at the screen. They were wide, almost unnaturally so, staring out at nothing. It was an expression I knew well. For ten years that look coincided with the rise of Mars in the sky.

"Alis?" I backed away until my back hit the wall of the cockpit—which wasn't far enough from the Wolf. "Are..."

What did I do? Run away? Right into the rifle fire of the officers waiting below? I couldn't fight off the Wolf in that cockpit. I—

"Toris," Alis whispered. "Wait."

And then the words that stole the breath from my lungs and unclenched an anxiety I'd been bearing for ten years: "It's working."

I cried. I fell to my knees, forgot everything outside that cockpit, and clasped Alis' hand.

"It's working," she whispered again, tears coming to her own eyes. Gradually, she closed her eyes, losing that eerie expression that must have had more to do with connecting with her mindjack than necessarily with the Wolf. "I...the dagger...my head." She opened her eyes and stared at me, a smile breaking across her face that put all the views I'd seen in my life to shame. "It's gone."

The circle on her screen stopped spinning, and green letters scrawled across the screen: *Sync successful. Welcome back, Pilot Caliday.*

"Welcome back, indeed," I said, returning Alis' smile.

"YOU HAVE 30 SECONDS TO EVACUATE THE AEGIS!"

Right. We were being threatened with death. Rifles were trained on us. None of this mattered if we couldn't get out of Carivant's tower.

"I love you," I said, pressing my forehead against Alis'. "Let's go home."

"Yes, please," Alis said with a relieved laugh. I backed away from her to let her do her work. She settled deeper into her seat, and her fingers danced across the controls, inputting commands, warming up systems and—

ACCESS DENIED

The red letters flashed across most of her screens.

"Dammit," Alis hissed through clenched teeth. She tried a few more commands, and the only response was another ACCESS DENIED.

"What does that mean?" I asked. "The sync worked!"

"The sync worked," Alis repeated, "but Carivant's locked the systems. It's like...a computer can connect to a network before you log into it. I can't do anything."

"Okay." I bit at my lip, thoughts frantic. We'd won. We'd won our battle with the Wolf. We had to get out of here. "Could you contact Kuma and Lana? They're here in the building. Maybe—"

Alis shook her head.

"Then we have to fight our way out," I said, accepting the inevitable. "But if you de-sync..."

"I'll de-sync properly," Alis said. "That was the problem before. I should be okay." I could tell by the way she swallowed that she was more hopeful than confident, but it wasn't as if we had a choice. "Oh!" she exclaimed, her eyes lighting up. "I have an idea. We may not be able to use the *Lycan*, but we can still use it."

"I have no idea what you just said."

"We need to get those officers a little closer, but we need them behind their cover. They can't reach the scaffolding."

"So you need me to shoot at them."

"More or less."

I spun the plasma rifle from behind my back and into my hands. "You know I'm not a great shot."

"You don't have to be. I'll handle the hard part." Alis brought up the sync screen in front of her once more. "Here goes nothing." She tapped a command and immediately cringed, one eye on the screen as the wheel spun once more. A moment later: *De-sync successful.*

I looked at Alis. She opened both eyes and glanced around without moving her head.

"I think I'm okay."

I released the breath I'd been holding in a burst that blew over Alis' face. She recoiled, then she laughed as I said, "Sorry."

She patted my cheek as she pulled herself out of the cockpit seat by bars above her head. "Let's get out of here."

I nodded and clicked the safety off my rifle.

Alis took her own rifle in hand. "Can you cover me?"

"Always," I said.

I spun around the opening to the cockpit in the *Lycan*'s ribcage and fired a few shots toward the back of the warehouse, where most of the officers had taken cover. A few of them shouted as my shots pounded into the concrete floor and the metal wall, leaving smoldering marks. I scanned the rest of the warehouse and noticed that one of the officers had gotten closer, moving between cover almost to the scaffolding. Holding down the trigger, I peppered the crate they hid behind with shots until they were forced to pull back, diving back behind one of the crane bases holding up the *Lycan*'s arm. The crate I'd been firing on was melting from the shots, the holes glowing red and spilling smoke.

Behind me, Alis fired, but not at the officers. Her shots slammed into the crane arm holding up the Aegis' arm.

Ahhh. Use the Aegis when we couldn't use the Aegis. I'd missed her mind so much.

"Ow!" Alis hissed after firing so many shots that her gun overheated, steam venting out from the barrel as its cooling systems kicked in. But it'd worked, the plasma bolts had eaten through the metal crane enough that the weight of the Aegis was pulling it down, the remaining metal shearing as we listed forward and to the right.

"Shit," Alis said. Her gun was still cooling, and we needed to hit the other side to make the Aegis fall at least somewhat evenly.

"I got it!" I ran through the tilting cockpit, losing my footing once, and threw down the switch that opened the opposite door. From inside the cockpit, I fired, lighting up that crane arm. Below, the officers were shouting things I couldn't make out. Just as my rifle was beeping that it was about to overheat, that side of the Aegis started pulling, the rest of the arm snapping with the weight.

"The bars!" Alis called over the grating sound of shearing metal. We ran to the center of the cockpit and grabbed onto the bars Alis had used to pull herself out of the seat. I followed Alis' lead in looping my feet into bars bolted to the floor, too, both of us facing the front of the cockpit. The crane arms snapped almost at the same time with two cracks of thunder, and we fell.

I cried out and squeezed my eyes shut as my head and stomach tried to stay where they'd been an instant before. We slammed into the ground—both of us barely holding on as our bodies tried to follow—with an even louder thunder and other crashes outside as we pulled over more apparatuses with us. The officers shouted, some of them at a pitch that meant they were very hurt. Dust and smoke billowed into the cockpit from outside.

Pulling out our feet first, we let gravity swing us down so we were standing on what had been the front of the cockpit, where the holoscreens had projected.

"Good...plan," I said with a smile, still catching my breath.

She shrugged. "Half a plan. We still need to get the rest of the way out of here."

"Kuma and Lana should be watching. They've got our backs. We can do this."

Alis gave me a determined nod and climbed up onto what had been the cockpit's side wall as she made her way to the exit. There, she leaned back against what had been the floor and pulled her rifle up to her shoulder. Every time she did that, I could feel the familiarity of the stance, the soldier, the Moonbreaker, settling in.

"RETREAT!" someone shouted. "FALL—"

THOOM THOOM

Alis fired twice, and the voice fell silent. Then she dropped out of the cockpit. I climbed out and followed.

We'd certainly made a mess of the place. The *Sanguine Lycan* was sprawled on the ground, right arm smashing piles of crates—and an officer that had been hiding behind it; their legs stuck out at an awkward angle, and I had to look away. Its head reached almost to the doors I'd entered from, and the officer Alis had just shot lay there. On the left side, we'd pulled down most of the crane apparatus with that arm, bringing cables and jagged metal down over that half of the warehouse as well.

"I think we're clear," Alis said, taking a few steps forward but keeping her rifle up. "But we—"

THOOM THOOM THOOM THOOM

Magenta light exploded through the dust as bolts fired from our right. Alis and I both dropped back, but one of the bolts clipped Alis' left arm, and she cried out.

"ALIS!" I shouted and pulled her toward me, further toward the Aegis' armpit, where we'd have more cover. That squad must have entered from the other door, where Alis had come through.

"I'm fine. I'm fine," she growled through clenched teeth. Her shirt sleeve smoked, and I caught an acrid whiff of burned flesh beneath. "We have to—"

THOOM THOOM THOOM THOOM

Shots peppered the Aegis around us. We dropped down to a squat and slid closer to the armpit of the Aegis. We could try and dive back into the cockpit, but we'd be exposed as the squad rounded the arm, putting themselves between us and the exit.

There were too many. We were trapped. I could have screamed. I could have cried. We were so close. *SO CLOSE.* We'd found each other again. The Wolf was dead. But that didn't matter, since we were about to join it.

I looked over at Alis, and I could see in her eyes that she was thinking the same thing. She tilted her head and gave me a smile, bringing the sun into that dusty room once more, even as her eyes watered from the pain in her arm.

"I love you," she said.

"I love *you*," I said. "We're going to get out of this. We're going home."

Alis chuckled, that kind of chuckle she gave me when I was being unrealistic, when I was dreaming. "I've got you," she said, "and I've got this," she jerked her head toward the *Lycan*'s arm. "I've got both my homes right here. Pretty fitting."

"That's not—"

More shots cut me off, slamming into the Aegis to my left. I scooted in closer to Alis, firing wildly, the officers only dim silhouettes in the dust. A shot sliced through the side of my calf, and I yelled out. A shot punched the armor above me, the heat so close I smelled singed hair, and I knew that was it. This was the end. I dropped the rifle and covered as much as Alis as I could. Blazing heat, like a miniature star, hit the back of my shoulder. I screamed, closing in tighter around Alis as she pushed at me to get off. But I refused.

"TORIS!" she screamed. "PLEASE—"

THOOM. THOOM. THOOM. THOOM.

I squeezed my eyes shut, but the shots never hit. They even sounded different, staccato, more precise than the shots of either us or the officers.

"Tor," Alis whispered.

Taking in a hissing breath of pain, I moved off Alis and turned, looking back toward where the officers had been silhouetted in the dust. They were all gone, save for one, who dropped as we watched, a tendril of smoke rising from their shadow.

Behind them, the door to the warehouse was open, and a shape moved through it. Slender, with long hair.

"Lana!" I yelled out, struggling to my feet on my injured leg. Alis followed, moving to my other side and putting her uninjured arm around my back. We stumbled forward as the dust settled and the smoke began to dissipate. Lana walked toward us, rifle still in hand.

"Thank God," I said as we came closer, relief surging along with a cluster of questions. "How are you such a good shot? Where's Kuma? We—"

Alis stopped.

More air was blowing in from the corridor and the open doors, moving the dust. Lana stopped, and something was different about her. Gone was the sad, uncertain woman. She stood up straighter, her jaw was set, and her eyes were focused. Hard. Cold.

I looked to Alis, who'd lost all the color in her face. Her mouth hung open and her eyes were wide, lining with tears as her chin began to shake. She looked like she was staring down a nightmare.

When she spoke, her voice was small, barely more than a breath. And that breath carried one word that bore the weight of a decade of guilt, regret, and pain:

"Teah?"

CHAPTER TWENTY-FIVE

ALIS

(Twelve years earlier)

"You two stay put until we're clear," Godwin said as he checked his plasma rifle.

"We'll do a lot more good with weapons," I said, still working out how exactly we'd overpower the strike team in order to redirect the particle beams back at their ships.

"Pft," Godwin said. "Nice try. You're critical to this mission, Commander Caliday, but this armor isn't that thick," he knocked on his helmet. "You stay behind until we give you the all-clear. Then you'll win us this war, and you can play with all the weapons you want."

I rolled my eyes but didn't argue further. There wasn't time for that. We'd just have to find another way. I could likely put in the commands without them realizing, but we'd be shot immediately.

As long as both Ecker and Halgard faced their justice, I could deal with that.

"We're locked in," Toris said as a solid *THUNK* echoed through the ship.

"They'll have sealed the airlock," I said. Godwin opened his mouth, but I continued and answered the question I knew was coming. "Codes won't break through that, except for maybe some mindjack magic. And I," now it was my turn to tap my own temple, "am a bit hampered there."

Godwin clicked the safety off his rifle. "Old-fashioned battering ram it is." He turned to leave the bridge, then he paused. "Good flying there, Captain. And good thinking, Caliday. I'm glad you're both on our side."

"Oh, the pleasure's ours," Toris said, rolling his eyes at me.

Godwin nodded and descended the stairs. Again, as he left, I felt like I could breathe.

Toris immediately turned to me. "What about Kuma? I...understand your plan, but I can't..."

293

"I know. There's been enough collateral damage. Kuma can't be a part of that. Can you get a message to him?"

"Past Halgard? Who would immediately have her team turn on us once they had a hint of your plan?"

"Well, I wasn't suggesting we tell him to duck and cover because we're going to blow up the fleet, Toris."

He shook his head. "Right. Sorry. This is all…"

"Too much."

"Yeah. Too much."

Below, Godwin was giving orders to his team. They were preparing to breach the airlock.

Toris was listening, too, and ran a hand through his hair, then clutched it with a white-knuckled fist. "If they damage my ship…"

"If they damage your ship, it won't be any worse than what the *Viper* did to it."

He let go of his hair and turned to me. "Yeah, speaking of that, not to sound ungrateful that we're alive or anything, but how are we going to get out of this without our engines?"

"Toris," I said with a shrug and a sigh. "I don't know if—"

Ding ding ding. That was the hail notification. Toris spun toward his console. "It's the *Dawnbreak*." He pressed a button beside his screen.

"*Toris? You there?*" Kuma. Toris and I shared a relieved smile.

"Kuma. Thank God," Toris said, hanging his head and dropping his shoulders as if he'd let go of a great burden. "Are you all right?"

"*For now. The ship's been boarded. Halgard's people are holding their own, but I don't know how long that'll last. My guards were called off to fight, so I snuck out and found this comms terminal. How are you two?*"

"Eh," Toris responded. "We—"

BOOM

The ship shook, and Godwin shouted orders below. The unmistakable sound of plasma fire followed.

"*What was that?*"

"Halgard's team breaching the Loop," Toris said. "We're fine. A little handicapped. Got thrown around by an Aegis a bit. But we're alive."

"*And the plan? What do you think, Alis?*"

"I think it's a start," I said, glancing at Toris, whom I still wasn't convinced was totally behind it. "But we can do more. I want to use the Loop to cripple the Earther fleet."

A pause, then: "*Huh. You can do that?*"

"I think so. It might not be the most precise maneuver, but we can strengthen, expand, and adjust the direction of the magnetic field to redirect the particle beams."

Another pause. Kuma clearly chewed on his thoughts more than his co-captain. "*A lot of people will die.*"

"And even more so if we don't do this. At least, this way, the only casualties are the people who signed up for this."

"*What about the Bastion fleet? That just sets them up to punch back, doesn't it?*"

I shifted weight from foot to foot, trying to shake a discomfort that no fidgeting would dismiss. Kuma was...he was right, but I wasn't sure I could turn those beams on our fleet...their fleet. Ecker was one thing, but most of the ships were there defending their homes.

"I don't think so," I eventually responded. "Halgard's already pretty handily winning this battle. Between that and Luna, Bastion won't have a fleet to do much of anything with. I don't think they'll be fighting back anytime soon."

"*Maybe not. But we could be prolonging the inevitable. Destroying the fleets doesn't guarantee an end to the war, does it? Don't we need a...treaty or something? An agreement?*" He sighed, the sound crackling through the speakers. "*We're way out of our purview here. What do you think, Tor?*"

"I think you're right," Toris said. "We're way out of our league. But we're here, and we have an opportunity. The Spheres need a fresh start. All of us. We know we can't let Halgard even attempt to win like this, or the world we're trying to build will just keep getting crushed by the old, broken hypocrisies. The rest of the world, the Gaia Council, they'd agree. They can come in and clean up the mess. Make the treaties. Make it official. No one...no one has to even know we were on the Loop. Bastion tried to defend themselves. And it went wrong. I do still think we should destroy the Loop, too. From the inside. Dealing with that will keep Bastion down longer."

I tilted my head, considering. "I don't know...destroying the Loop wouldn't be like blowing up a power plant. Without the magnetic field, innocent people could suffer. Plus, I don't even know how we'd do that. The beams will follow the field produced by the Loop. We can't direct it back at us."

"*All right. I'm with you both. But I'd rather not be on this matchbox when it lights up. Any ideas?*"

Toris looked at me, as if I'd have some immediate solution. I raised my eyebrows at him in a way that told him I didn't.

He chewed at the inside of his cheek then eventually said: "The reserve starfighters in the hangar. Grab one of those and we can rendezvous..." he looked over to me. "Somewhere?"

Somewhere. We couldn't initially get far on the *Harriet*, and we'd need somewhere to lay low for a moment as the battle simmered down after...everything. Where could we...

"Phobos," I said, ignoring the pit in my stomach that opened at the thought of returning to that place. "Stickney. There won't be any Bastion resources there."

"*Stickney it is.*"

Toris was staring at me with a conflict of concern and...frustration? Resentment? I wouldn't blame him. That was where I'd become the Moonbreaker, where thousands of innocents had died.

I'd do them justice that day.

"Safe travels, brother," Toris said.

"*You, too. And Alis?*"

I shook my head to remove the memory of Monalua that kept playing over and over, standing defiant in the shadow of my Aegis. "Yeah?"

"*Thank you for standing up for this Mudbrain. I owe you.*"

"Just get out of there safely, and we'll call it even."

"*Deal. Good luck, you two. Kuma, out.*"

The transmission ended, but Toris stayed there, leaning over the console, taking deep breaths. I took a step closer and reached out with a reassuring hand, but then I hesitated, as if getting touched by the Moonbreaker may physically hurt him.

"He'll be all right."

"Will he?" Toris asked. "You just said that what we're trying to do won't be precise. What if we..."

"We won't. Phobos is on the other side of the planet for the next few hours. He'll be out of the way."

"He better be." He turned to me, and he had tears in his eyes. "I've lost enough, Alis."

"I know." I wished I could say more, to promise him, give him solid assurances. But I wasn't even sure we'd make it out ourselves. Kuma probably did have the better chances.

Below, the plasma fire had gone quiet. Smoke wafted up into the bridge, carrying with it the acrid stench of burnt metal.

"Caliday! Orius! We're clear!"

Toris and I looked at each other. Then he said: "Let's end this."

I followed him down through the smoke and into the passenger cabin, coughing as the haze thickened. As we rounded the corner, we found the source of most of that smoke: a cluster of plasma-fire marks burned with a dim light. Toris stopped to inspect them, a kind of growl escaping through clenched teeth. Most of the damage appeared superficial, but a couple had pierced through enough hull to destroy some wiring.

Toris sighed. "Any chance we can postpone your plan until Halgard pays for this?"

I patted him on the shoulder, and we both turned to face Godwin, who stood at the airlock. Most of his strike team had entered the Loop, with a couple remaining behind to drag one of their comrades from the airlock tunnel into the *Harriet*. It looked like that was the only casualty on Godwin's side. The rest of the corpses in the tunnel and on its other side wore the black armor of Bastionite soldiers.

"We were expecting more resistance," Godwin said, removing his helmet and wiping sweat from his forehead. "Any chance there's more inside?"

"In the control room? Maybe." I responded. "But there's never been more than a minimal force on the Loop. The planetary defense fleet was meant to be the main line of protection. There's not much room to house a larger force, anyway."

"Lucky us," Godwin said, turning sad eyes on his fallen soldier. "I'm sure that'll change after today."

"Then let's make sure we don't have to come back," I said, and while I was absolutely trying to maintain Godwin's trust for the moment, I meant it, too.

Godwin replaced his helm and waved for us to follow. We stepped through the haze and over the bodies—Toris pointedly trying not to look at them—and onto the Iridesca Loop. Space was minimal, with our heads nearly touching the silver-metal ceiling and the corridor barely wide enough for two people to walk side-by-side. The Loop was as efficient as possible, with the vast majority of it reserved for its core function: running electrical currents through massive superconducting magnets—enhanced with mithril from the Belt—to generate a magnetic field for the planet. Most of the Loop had no space for people; maintenance generally happened from the outside via spacewalk or with machines.

Ahead, Godwin signaled for us to stop. To our right and left were open doors that led into tiny quarters, smaller even than I'd had on the *Fang*. They had a bed, small cabinets built into the bulkhead, and a toilet that folded down from the wall to take up the only standing room.

"Alis," Toris whispered, and gestured to the quarters on his right. A wrist holocomm was still projecting a woman's head, turned toward the wall and lying sideways on the bed.

"G? Are you still there? What's going on?"

I closed my eyes, wishing I could close my ears as easily. I saw flashes of memories. Olli finding his parents. Kuma...those left behind. One of those soldiers we'd just stepped over in the corridor was probably checking in on their family. I could imagine them whispering assurances, making promises, and then grabbing their rifle as we docked with the Loop. The enemy at the door.

"G?" Even in that one syllable, I could hear her voice becoming more desperate. *"Please answer me! Are you there?! Are you—"*

Should I have said something? Given her some piece of mind that "G" had done their duty? Before I could come to a decision, Godwin reached past Toris to press a button that closed the door to the room, entombing the woman and her cries.

Toris looked at me with a set jaw.

"We end this," I said.

Godwin waved us forward as he followed the rest of his team, all of them holding their rifles set against their shoulders. I could barely see past them, but after a few minutes of creeping forward, I could see through the clustered helmets that we'd reached the end of the corridor.

"Control room door is sealed," said one of the soldiers at the front.

"Precision infiltration on this one," Godwin said. "We don't want to blow it in case we damage something we need to use."

Fresh smoke billowed down the hallway as the strike team used plasma cutters to slice through the door's locks. There was a grinding noise as they manually heaved the door into the bulkhead. A sliver of light shined through the smoke before:

THOOM THOOM THOOM THOOM

Toris and I ducked as plasma bolts surged through the gap in the door. One of the shots clipped the pauldron of Godwin's armor, and I heard another soldier cry out before dropping to their knee, the other leg smoking. The shots were haphazard, but no less dangerous.

"Drone!" Godwin shouted.

Ahead, one of the strike team pulled a machine barely larger than my hand from where it was clipped to his belt and pressed some commands into a projected holoscreen.

"Wait!" I said. Half the strike team turned back to me, including the one holding the drone. Godwin turned last, and even with his helmet on, I could sense his exasperation in his stance. "That may just be civilians."

"Armed civilians," Godwin said. "And we don't have time to negotiate. The fleet will be in position in a few minutes."

"Can we at least—"

"Drone!" Godwin yelled, louder this time, the speaker in his helm crackling.

The soldier tossed the drone into the air. It zipped through the gap at a speed so fast it became a blur. Shouts echoed on the other side of the door, then more plasma fire, then silence.

"Proceed!" Godwin commanded. The soldiers rolled the door aside without any issue and filed inside with Toris and I at the rear.

Vents whirred, pulling smoke out of the air that rose from holes pocked into the bulkhead—and into the bodies. Only two of them were soldiers, dispatched with clean shots through the helm. The rest were dressed in blue jumpsuits, likely engineers and administrators. Innocents doing nothing more than maintaining critical infrastructure even while a battle raged around them.

"Move the bodies," Godwin said. "Give us some space."

The strike team went to work as Toris and I waited just inside the control room. The captain looked like he may throw up, and I wouldn't be far behind. The acrid stench trapped in that enclosed space was stomach-rending.

"Caliday," Godwin said. "You're up. They locked us out of the system, and we can't battering-ram through this one." He stood behind one of two rows of consoles. Ahead of the consoles, projected on the bulkhead, were holoprojections that looked almost like viewports to the outside—save for one that crackled with static, the projector smoking from an errant plasma-fire blast that had likely been meant for the drone. The screens showed that Godwin was right: Halgard's fleet had gained ground, closing in on the planet. Bastion certainly wasn't giving up, though, and the *Fang* likely helped.

"Why don't they just use the particle beams on the fleet first?" I asked.

Godwin looked at me, then up to the screens. "The admiral doesn't want to reveal our hand too early. Bastion intel knows the *Dawnbreak* has the new beam weapon—since they used it to rescue you—but they don't know our other cruisers are equipped with it as well. They're also better used on stationary or slower targets. So while we could cripple their cruisers, their starfighters would be able to target the weapons while they recharge, reducing our chances of do-ing...meaningful damage to the capital."

Meaningful damage to the capital. A euphemism for complete destruction for hundreds of miles, a scorch mark that Olympus Mons would bear forever, as if the sun itself touched down on the surface.

I held my tongue. I had a job to do.

I stepped up to the control console. As Godwin had said, the staff had locked control of the system. An approved mindjack sync would unlock it, or a clearance code known only by a relative few. Fortunately, as an Aegis pilot who needed to operate in a versatile array of situations, I was part of that few. Good for Halgard.

Zeta Caliber Nova. The clearance code I'd tried to use to get us onboard in the first place. I typed it into the screen and waited, leaning against the panel, face close to the surface, as the system read the code.

Then: "We're in."

Godwin slapped his hands together, a single, victorious clap. "Good. Check their activity logs. Have they manipulated the system in any way that could shield the city? I'll update the admiral."

I started swiping through screens, thinking fast. The final moments of the Solar Gulf War, whether I succeeded or not, were minutes away. Twenty years of war and centuries longer of simmering conflict all leading to this. I glanced up at one of the screens on the bulkhead, which displayed the planet below, with Bastion in the center. My home. Should I not defend it? Pave the way for a resurgence and a true victory? Purge the rot from myself and return to my father, my only remaining family, a hero?

No. I shook my head. Those were the thoughts of another me, one whose killing blow still ached in my brain. That was the Aegis pilot of Bastion.

Then, was that also who resisted firing on the defense fleet?

Because while I'd justified earlier that these were people defending their home, they were also the same ships and soldiers who, on different assignments, had burned down hospitals, had torn through communities on that same homeworld on suspicion of Earther conspiracy, the rot. Who had taken Idina captive. Who had killed Olli's parents. Who had shot Mele beneath her school.

"Report, Caliday!" Godwin yelled.

I had to play this right. I needed to be in control of the Loop when Halgard fired, right where I was. But I had to lie. The engineers seemed completely ignorant of incoming particle beam attack; their activity log showed no defensive maneuvers, just standard operation.

"Halgard was right," I said. "They must be suspecting an attack. They've increased the current through the Loop, making the field stronger. And they've positioned the Loop directly over the city for increased defense." I needed an excuse to maneuver the Loop. The screen before me was showing the field around the entire planet, including the field lines the magnetic forces followed. We needed a better angle so the beams—which would follow those lines—would pierce the oncoming fleet.

Godwin let out a sigh. "Thank God we're here. Get us out of the way and reduce the field's strength."

"Yes, sir," I said, and got to work. "Toris, can you give me a hand?" I gestured to a console beside mine. "I'm going to worry about the field's strength. I need you to use the Loop's thrusters to maneuver us to the position I sent to that console. Can you do that?" I met his eyes and gave him the smallest nod.

"You've got it."

The Loop lurched as Toris nudged us into position. Behind us, Godwin's troops returned from searching the rest of the module. I tried to eavesdrop on if they'd found anything, something I could use to get them out of the module. Instead, they swarmed behind us, watching the battle through the screens, rifles down but still in their anxious hands. We wouldn't make it far.

A notification rang through the room. A hail. I didn't press anything to accept it, but a voice came over the speakers anyway. A voice I hoped I'd never hear again. But of course I would, in the end.

"*What are you doing on the Loop, Caliday?*" Vice Admiral Ecker asked.

"Cut him off!" Godwin shouted, and his soldiers rushed for consoles to try and figure it out. I could have killed the signal from my controls...but I didn't.

"*Do they want to use it to ram our ships? Turn off the magnetic field?*"

"I want that signal down NOW! Caliday, don't listen to him."

"*It's not too late, Caliday,*" Ecker said. I wasn't sure if he could hear Godwin. "*This is the last stand. It will be our triumphant victory. And from here we'll return in righteous vengeance to Luna and to Earth. We'll show our old home what forging out into the cosmos forged us into. And there we'll forge the prosperity and peace we've forged here. That home is our heritage, too. Your heritage. Come home.*"

Now I knew Ecker was really desperate. I wasn't surprised that he'd lie like they were on the brink of victory. But trying to win me over again? His words had the opposite effect: the same narratives that had once inspired me now made me cringe. It was the same shiny, contrived shell, hiding the rusted core of humankind's age-old flaws: greed, arrogance, and egocentrism.

"*You're not one of them,*" Ecker continued. "*No matter what they told you. You're an Aegis pilot of Bastion. The Moonbreaker. The—*"

"You're right," I said, and he must have been able to hear us, because he stopped. "I'm not one of them. But a world where breaking a colony is an honor isn't a world I'm part of, either. You won't use me anymore, Ecker.

"This is for Teah."

Then I cut the communication.

And I made my decision.

"Bastion refused surrender. We're priming to fire!" Godwin called, staring up at the screens. The Earther ships, which dominated our view now, were directly over Bastion, obscuring the city from sight. The ships were close to the Loop. And a magnetic field was always strongest at its source.

Toris and I glanced at each other.

Light bloomed from beneath the battlecruisers.

And I maxed out the Loop's strength.

The beams fired, white light rending the void, like the heavens were tearing open. Then the charged particles immediately followed the field lines, spiraling away from the planet in a blinding array that reminded me strangely of the petals of a flower.

Those spiraling beams lanced through the Earther ships first. I heard a sharp gasp from Toris beside me and an angry yell from Godwin behind. The beams punched through the starships, layers of metal and shielding, as if they were paper, leaving only glowing rings as they sliced through the moving vessel.

"What is this?!" Godwin shouted. I didn't look at him. "Traitor!"

I heard, as if from a greater distance, the commander raising his rifle. Then, much closer, I heard a *THOOM*. But I didn't fall.

Toris shouted something. More shouts followed, but I couldn't move.

I could only watch as the beams spiraled around the Loop and pierced the *Fang* straight through the bridge, a killing blow. Explosions peppered in staccato behind the bridge as the beam cut through the rest of the ship and emerged out the other side.

Justice. For Teah. For Monalua and Stickney.

And yet, I couldn't help but feel that I'd been lanced through, too.

CHAPTER TWENTY-SIX
TORIS

LANITEAH AURORA CALIDAY.

She was...

"You..." Alis could only get the single word out. She swallowed and took a step forward. I hadn't seen her so shaken since the Battle of the Loop. This may have been worse. "Ecker. He killed you."

"That what they told you?" Teah seemed far less affected by seeing her sister than Alis, but she wasn't as apathetic as she was trying to appear. Every few moments, the mask of her cold expression would crack, and she'd cringe, as if seeing Alis caused physical pain.

"Halgard...they...we had a transmission from the *Fang*. Ecker...he..."

"Vice Admiral Ecker died a *hero*," Teah snapped that last word like a whip. "I didn't believe them when I heard you were the one on the Loop. I didn't believe that you would have helped them, despite Ecker trying to convince me ever since Mwezi. I was on that ship, Alis. You turned those particle beams on me."

"No, I...we ended the war. You were..."

I clasped Alis' hand and squeezed. I knew she was seeing what I was: those beams of brilliant light, like we'd fired the sun itself into those fleets. The burden of that day had been heavy enough, and now...

"Ecker saved me," Teah continued. "He let me take his escape pod from the bridge after the beam cut the *Fang* in half. The explosion took out one of my pod's engines and crippled the drag flaps. I crashed into the Tharsis Montes. I almost died there, too." She grabbed at the skin on her forearm and tore, ripping off the flesh to reveal a metal limb beneath. "My arm got pinned, almost taken off. I had to do the rest of the work."

"Teah...I'm sorry," Alis said, the shock finally giving way to sobs. "I'm so sorry. They told me...I shouldn't have believed them. I'm so sorry. I..."

"SHUT UP!" Teah screamed, then she immediately regained her composure, though her chest was rising and falling more intensely. "You don't get that. You don't deserve to apologize. Those words mean less than shit in the drain, Alis."

"So...it was all a lie?" I asked, barely recovering from my own shock; and the searing pain from the plasma shots didn't help. Kuma and I had foregone finding Alis to help her. "The Shades, your husband? Your child? Everything?"

"You'd like that, wouldn't you? If I'd made all that up? But no. I may not have had a family there, but after the Loop fell, the solar winds came. They started tearing the atmosphere to shreds, along with our atoms. Most people sheltered indoors, but that didn't prevent the inevitable, just slowed it down. The Shades were almost emptied within three years. Anyone left shuffled around like zombies, skin dead and black, sloughing off, their faces gaunt and their mouths hanging open, desperate for food that they wouldn't vomit up in a mess of blood." Then she turned to Alis. "But it wasn't just people in the Shades who suffered. No, Father did, too. He died like Mom, Alis. Radiation. You remember how she suffered? How we'd hear her in the middle of the night sobbing in pain, trying to hide it from us while her insides fell apart? It was worse for him. And who did he have to sob to? To scream to? Not Mom. Not you.

"The war ended for you. You got your Gaia Compact. You made a home in your paradise. And I brought hell back to you."

"What do you want?" I asked after a glance at Alis told me she was still struggling to find the words as tears streamed down her cheeks. "You were a pruner. What are you here to do? There aren't any governments to topple. No electorates to manipulate."

Teah smiled, but it lacked any humor. It was the smile of the conqueror, the victorious, the knowing. "No, but that's not where we got the name 'pruner,' is it?" She shook her head. "That's not how this is going to go. I'm not here to answer your questions. I'm here to hurt you. Both of you. I'm here for justice."

"Where's Kuma." I said in almost a whisper as fear settled into my bones. She could call it justice, but she was here on a quest for revenge, maybe more, if she was still part of Bastion's military.

The mask cracked again, not in quite the same cringe of pain, but with her eyebrows pressing together for the quickest instant. Almost in...regret?

"He helped you. He was there for you, even if they were all lies. And he had nothing to do with the Loop. Where. Is. He."

The mask froze into place again, and Teah raised her chin slightly. "I'd worry more about yourselves right now." Then she lowered her chin almost to her chest and stared at Alis, who'd gone quiet. In my hand, hers had gone slack.

"No." I let go and stepped in front of Alis, shaking her by the shoulders, as if that had ever made any difference. "Alis! I'm right here! Please." All the hope from her successful sync with the *Lycan* went up like a puff of smoke. And I fell apart. "Please. No. Stay with me. Don't do this. Don't..." I trailed off as the clarity of rationality shocked through the panic. Slowly, I turned away from Alis—dangerous as I knew that was—to Teah.

"You," I said with firm, cold malice. Tears cooled on my cheeks. "There's no phantom signal. Alis isn't broken. It's you." Teah tilted her head, and her jaw clenched beneath her cheeks. "When we were on the other side of the sun, you couldn't reach her. Only when we were aligned with Mars." I took a step toward her, toward the architect of all our pain, the sole barrier keeping us from the paradise she mocked Alis for, the one we'd fought and bled for. "She wasn't getting worse when she turned the other night. The Wolf wasn't getting smarter. It was you. We brought you back here from Farstead, and *you* turned her. *You* made her kill Cixin. I...Why? Why would...No." I stared down this woman who we'd trusted, who we'd protected, who we pitied and thought we saved. For ten years she'd tortured us. For ten years she'd tried to force her sister to kill me. Then she lost her patience and decided to finish the job. "I don't need to know. I don't care." I raised my plasma rifle and set the stock against my shoulder.

Teah was the source of the cycle. And I was ending it.

I set my finger on the trigger and—

A hand seized my bicep and spun me around. I squeezed the trigger, but the shot went askew, slamming into the wall of the warehouse.

Alis—no, the Wolf grabbed me by the throat and jumped on me, throwing me to the ground with her augmented strength. I cried out as my injured shoulder rubbed into the floor. The Wolf pressed her other hand over my windpipe and squeezed with both. I gasped, desperate, pulling at her arms with all the power I could muster.

"Please," I wheezed. "Alis, please."

Teah walked up behind Alis, a silhouette against the lights on the ceiling behind her as my vision pulsed between clarity and cloudiness.

"I'm not *making* her do anything," Teah said, squatting down beside her sister. "Whatever she did at Mwezi prevented Bastion from totally hacking her, but we figured out that we could strongarm our way into activating her 'jack, and that was all it took. It flipped a switch. We could see through her eyes. We could see you. It took a few years to realize *she* wasn't seeing you, though."

I knew that. We'd always assumed that the Wolf was a combined result of the attempted hack, the resulting malfunctioning 'jack, and the empathy torture that Halgard put her through. Alis had told me that every time the Wolf took control, she experienced those memories again, but a version where she took control, where those poor people who'd suffered at the hands of Bastion became their rage and pain and channeled both into righting the wrongs done to them. It just so happened that I always took the place of the Bastionite who'd wronged them, just like the soldiers she'd killed the first time she turned.

Alis squeezed tighter, her eyes wide and shaking with that hate. Spit splashed my face through her clenched teeth.

My vision faltered, everything going dark for a moment. I had to hold on. I had to get out of this. For both of us. I couldn't leave Alis in Teah's control. And I couldn't let the Wolf win, not when we were so close.

So I focused, and I kept pulling on Alis' arms and staring into her eyes, hoping some part of her would break through.

"We found out we could nudge her mind," Teah continued, "stimulate her subconscious in ways that affected what she saw, which memory we tapped into. I don't know what technology those Mudbrains used to get them into her head, but they opened the door for us. Without those memories, the worst we could give her was a headache. With those, we could tap into raw emotion, and we could pull those memories up from the depth of her subconscious. When she killed Cixin, she was convinced he was the pilot who'd dropped the bombs on her parents. When she killed him, that little boy finally had his revenge. But we have to be careful." She stroked Alis' hair, but then she pulled her hand away as if she'd touched a hot stove. Her eyes darted to me to see if I'd noticed. I pretended not to. That wasn't difficult as I gasped for breath. "We didn't give her catharsis. That would have been mercy. Every time she came close to overcoming you, or when she killed Cixin, we'd rewind the memory, and she'd feel that pain all over again. She'd remember how powerless she was."

"For someone who..." I trailed off my whispering as I used what little breath I had, "said they weren't going to share their plan, you're gloating a lot."

My head swam, the room spinning with Alis at the center and Teah over her shoulder, chuckling. "I've told you none of my plan, nor am I gloating. I want you to understand." She leaned closer, and any of the humor from a moment ago had dissipated. "Because when you understand, you'll suffer. That's my goal, Toris, and it has been from the moment I met you."

Of course it was. Everything about Lana's story was designed to make both Kuma and I feel guilt. She pressed on our guilt over the Iridesca Loop with her fabricated history. We were supposed to put her misery on us, which we had. The Deathwalk was the pinnacle of that: we'd created such an unbearable life that she'd leave it behind. And we'd bear the burden of it. If Kuma hadn't found her, if I hadn't shown up, Teah would have left and continued her plan. She was a pruner indeed, a master of manipulation.

She wouldn't manipulate us anymore.

I couldn't wait any longer. My vision was little more than a pinprick, focused on the Wolf's snarl. I was going to die, and who knew what would happen to Alis after.

"Sorry, my love," I whispered, then with what little strength I had, I squeezed her upper arm, right over the plasma rifle injury she'd taken earlier.

The Wolf hissed and jerked away from me, finally letting go of my neck. I pushed myself back with my hands and feet, cringing as my own injuries in my calf and shoulder burst with pain. Then I launched to my feet just as Alis dove for me. I dodged, nearly collapsing with a cry as I put weight on my injured calf. Why didn't I bring the device Navi had given me during the last cycle? I could have disabled the Wolf without hurting Alis. I'd been in too quick a rush after Cixin.

"Alis," I rasped, still catching my breath. She was rolling her head back and forth as she stalked in a circle around me. "Please. This is all Teah. We can put a stop to all of it, but you need to break through. I don't want to hurt you. Please don't make me..."

I trailed off. Take us out of the warehouse and we may as well have been at Wolfhome, surrounded by mountains, Mars high in the sky.

I couldn't do this the same way. Alis deserved better. Teah may have fabricated most of our experiences of the past couple days, but Kuma's call for us to take accountability and be more was genuine. If anything, it was more so. Teah was a result of Alis' choices, of Admiral Halgard's, of mine.

It was time to end the cycles.

"I'm not going to hurt you," I said, putting up defensive hands, palms toward the Wolf. Toward Alis.

No. I wasn't talking to Alis. But I also wasn't fighting the Wolf. I'd started thinking that way as a shield—one to protect me more than Alis. I was standing against the child from the first memory, who only thought of himself as Olli. I was in the doorframe before Idina in chambers that weren't her own. I was staring down Beck as he overcame his fears and stood for his friends.

And every time I fought, even if it was in self-defense, I fulfilled the role of the Bastionite in the memory. I became their greatest fear, the source of their hate. And by extension, I made it all worse for Alis, who felt it all.

"Idia?" I asked. Alis didn't respond. No, that wasn't right. There were subtle differences to how Alis behaved when she embodied those different memories. "Olli?" No, not him. The way she moved, with a slight hunch to her shoulders, that anxious look in her eyes, was familiar.

Oh. Of course. Teah was certainly fulfilling her goals that day.

"Beck."

Alis stopped. Her eyes went a little wider.

"Beck." Tears came to my eyes, surprising me. "Beck, it's me. The..." Alis was seeing that memory, that day. If Teah could influence it, maybe I could, too. "The soldiers are gone. You got them."

Alis blinked, then she hissed in a pained breath as she squeezed her eyes shut and clutched at her head.

"No," she said, still hunched over in agony. "You're lying."

"I'm not lying. If I were one of the soldiers, would I know your name? I'm Toris." I paused as a tear rolled down my cheek. "But I also haven't been the friend that you deserved. I...thank you for following us, for helping us, for risking everything to help two desperate people. And I'm sorry. For years, I..." I took a few steps closer. Alis stayed still, but her head slowly moved back the closer I came, her eyes still a little wide, as if she couldn't believe what she was seeing. I didn't know what "Beck" had been seeing before. Maybe I'd been shot in that twisted memory. Maybe he was seeing me rise from the dead. It didn't matter. This was already more progress than we'd ever had.

"For years I told myself that you made your choice. That you overcame your fears and that was a victory for you." I didn't want to explicitly mention Beck's death, unless that would throw off the memory; but I also needed to talk down that primal rage, the hate that fueled the Wolf. To do that, I needed to be more, like Kuma said. "I told myself all that to avoid feeling the pain and the guilt. You made your choice, but we never should have brought you into that situation. We should have done more to protect you. We should have remembered you better afterward. I'm sorry for all of it. Thank you, Beck. You're a hero."

With shaking hands, I took one more step and wrapped my arms around Alis. Slowly, so Beck wouldn't take it as an attack, so whatever Alis was perceiving wouldn't warp in that strange hybrid consciousness.

"You're safe," I whispered, to both Alis and Beck. "Bastion's gone. You're safe."

Alis suddenly went stiff, the Wolf's hackles rising. I braced, waiting for the strike, but I held on.

Then, slowly, Alis' arms rose around me. I closed my eyes. She could break my neck with that augmented strength—though, if she was still experiencing Beck's memories, he wouldn't know how to do that.

But Alis' arms stopped halfway up my back, and a whisper with a sound sweeter than wind through leaves brushed my ear: "It's gone. Tor. It worked."

I pulled away, crying again, this time in more relief than pain, and Alis and I held onto each other's arms. "Are you okay?" I asked. "Is it really…"

"Yeah, I…" she shook her head. "My head still hurts. Whatever Teah did ruined whatever the sync fixed. But, the Wolf's gone. For now. Did I hurt you?" She looked me up and down, then she noticed what must have been bruises around my neck. She leaned toward them before recoiling as if she'd been slapped. "Toris, I'm so sorry, I—"

"It's okay. I'm okay." I pulled her in and kissed her head, taking a deep breath of the sweet scent of her hair. "We're okay." But we couldn't waste time. So even though moving away from her felt like trying to pull apart supermagnets, I stepped back, still holding her hands. "It's all her. She's been the one bringing the Wolf out of you. If we can stop her, we can stop all of this."

"My family…" she whispered. The pain in her voice broke me anew, and I forced myself to slow down. Teah had turned her just after battering her with guilt. "My father…we knew there'd be a price, but…she's in pain, Toris. Her circumstance is our doing." When I opened my mouth, she held up a finger. "Whether our actions were right or wrong. Regardless of what she's done."

"Alis, I understand, but she's tortured us for years. She made you kill an innocent man. She's hardly justified in—"

"I know. And she'll answer to me for that." The look she gave me was that pure determination. That steel and fire. "But we're going to make this right. We're going to end the war, not just win it."

Those words. Suddenly I was sitting across from her in that little cell on the *Dawnbreak*, all those years ago. And my stomach twisted with disappointment that, despite everything, I still hadn't embraced all the nuances of that principle.

I nodded and squeezed her hands. "Then let's end it."

Alis returned my nod and looked past me, then she scowled. I turned.

Teah was gone.

I'd lost track of her when all my focus was on Alis and the Wolf. She wouldn't have gone far. We were her prey. But maybe her mission went beyond us. Maybe—

Light exploded behind us, and we both spun as the air filled with a low, ascending hum, the unmistakable sound of motors warming up.

The *Sanguine Lycan* lived.

"No," Alis whispered. "That's impossible. She can't..." but she trailed off as the Aegis' massive head, which had been lying like a corpse before us, turned and rose off the ground. Its right arm rose, then its hand clenched into a fist that punched the ground, cracking the concrete and shaking the entire warehouse. The *Lycan* stared down at us from its hands and knees, the red light running down the sides of its helm washing us in the color of blood.

Then the *Lycan* rose, hydraulics and servos whirring, a fifty-foot-tall metal titan. As it stood, its gaze never left us, even when it reached its full height.

"*This is for Mom,*" said Teah through the *Lycan*'s speakers, "*and for Dad. For everyone. You may have stopped fighting, but I never will.*

"*This is for Bastion.*"

Chapter Twenty-Seven

Toris

THE *SANGUINE LYCAN* STARED us down, the red light running down its face illuminating the smoke drifting through the warehouse.

"She...she could never sync," Alis said. "She tried for years. This shouldn't be possible. That doesn't just...change."

"*So much has changed, Alis,*" Teah's voice echoed from the *Lycan*'s speakers. "*But you still haven't. You can't reconcile why the world would work any differently than you think it would.*"

"What do you want, Teah?" Alis asked. "You want the Aegis? Is that your mission? Bastion wouldn't send you here just for me. That's personal."

That would make sense. An Aegis made (half) of mithril, and one of their own to begin with. Bastion would certainly deploy the resources to get it back. And maybe there was something genetic there, something that would predispose Teah to be able to sync with the machine. Alis was right, though, it should have been impossible.

Teah was silent. We should have been dead already. She could smash us beneath the Aegis' feet, swat us against the wall, evaporate us in a spray of gunfire. Did Bastion want us alive? Or was she hesitating?

Alis suddenly cringed, grabbing at the side of her head.

"Alis, what—"

"She's trying again," Alis growled. "But...it's not working. It just...hurts."

"Is it gone? The Wolf?"

"No. I can feel it." She let go of her head and looked up at the Aegis, hands forming into fists. "She's going to help us kill it, Tor. I'm not leaving here like this, not when the cause is right in front of us." She turned to me, and behind that determination, I could see the lingering pain. "And then we're going to try and help her."

"I love you," I said. "But I don't think she's too keen on getting help."

Alis cringed again. "YOU CAN STOP THAT, NOW!" she yelled up at the Aegis. "If you want us dead, you're going to have to do it yourself. I'm not doing it for you anymore, T. Or you can get out of that thing, and we can talk."

In response, Teah lifted an arm, pointing the Aegis' fist at us, and plasma-gun barrels extended out of the armor. I stepped in front of Alis, realizing how absolutely pointless that would be. The *Lycan's* guns were more like cannons, their barrels longer than I was tall.

Alis gently pushed me out of the way and took a step *closer* to the cannons that could evaporate us in an instant. "Teah, please. I...I was convinced you were gone. If I'd thought there was even a chance you were alive, I would have done anything. I would have combed through every inch of Bastion. We were both played, by both sides, for that entire war, and—"

"EVACUATE THE AEGIS, NOW!"

I jerked, instinctively ducking, as more armored Genesis Gardens soldiers pounded into the warehouse, leveling their rifles at the *Lycan*. I grabbed Alis and pulled us behind a stack of containers that would at least hide us from the newcomers.

"Maybe let's get her out of the Aegis and *then* talk to her," I suggested. Alis bit at her bottom lip for a moment, narrowing her eyes, then shrugged and nodded, as if it were the best of a bunch of bad options, rather than the only one that wouldn't have us staring down a cannon.

"*THIS AEGIS IS BASTION PROPERTY,*" Teah shouted, her voice magnified.

"Please!" shouted a voice that instantly simmered my blood. "We can renegotiate the terms of our agreement!" I peeked around the edge of the containers, and sure enough, there was Arturo Srinivasan Carivant, dressed in the same kind of suit he'd been in ten years ago, when I'd seriously considered throwing him off the tower. He must have been using augments—of course he was—because at this point I looked older than him, despite the time.

"*THESE ARE THE NEW TERMS,*" Teah responded, and I couldn't help but feel just a little satisfaction that karma was catching up to Carivant. "*WE ARE RECLAIMING OUR STOLEN PROPERTY. BE GRATEFUL WE AREN'T SEEKING FURTHER RESTITUTION.*"

"Are you *smiling*?" Alis asked.

"Just a little."

"The mithril on that Aegis is worth more than most of the wealth in this city combined," Carivant said, taking a step closer with his hands up before him. "We repaired it in hopes that it would regain its symbolism, that it could represent Bastion's resurgence to glory."

Resurgence to glory. That was enough to make me shiver. But I knew Carivant, as always, was aggrandizing. Bastion was devoting all its resources to preserving its people, to repairing its magnetic field. It likely didn't have the wealth to spare, especially enough wealth to pay for the Aegis. So they sent a pruner to take it back.

"*BASTION NEVER LOST ITS GLORY, LITTLE MAN,*" Teah said, and I was very conflicted about my emotions toward her at that moment. It didn't help that in that defiant tone, I heard notes of Alis. "*MOVE. NOW.*"

Carivant sniffed and straightened his suit jacket. "Your government requisitioned us to make this repair. If you neglect to uphold your terms on the contract, we will be forced to enforce its execution on less favorable terms."

At that, the Aegis bent over, slowly, servos whirring and steam jetting out from between its armor plates. It placed its hands on the sides of Carivant and his agents and brought its head only feet from Carivant. The *Lycan* looked almost like it was preparing to run a race, its feet bent at the toes behind it. Steam jetted out around the Aegis' helm, tumbling over Carivant and making him flinch. Even we felt the heat from it.

Alis nudged me, then nodded toward one of the doors at the back of the warehouse, behind the *Lycan*. In the darkness, with steam filling the space and the killer machine a helpful distraction, we could get out of there.

Looking back toward Carivant and Teah, I followed Alis along the edge. We moved behind the *Lycan*'s feet, dodging around torn metal from when we had dropped the Aegis.

"*When were you intending to inform us that you had the Moonbreaker in your custody?*" Teah asked, and Alis froze, a hand on the door.

"We...it's only been a day. She attempted to break into our property. Moonbreaker or not, we were well within our rights to detain and question her. So I wouldn't try to make that false equivalence. You're about to sever a very lucrative partnership. And I can assure you that you won't get very far."

That certainly wasn't an empty threat, and Teah knew it. She'd seen the starfighters in the hangar. And while she may have been able to sync with the *Lycan*, she wasn't the masterful pilot that Alis had been. She'd surely prepared for this, but simulations would never compare to that first real combat scenario.

Great. If we were going to catch her, we'd have to fight through Carivant's forces, too. It would have been inevitable. There wasn't exactly a subtle way to extract an Aegis.

"This partnership is built on lies. We know about Luna, Carivant."

Alis and I looked at each other with wide eyes. Carivant had played both sides of the war. Honestly, I was most surprised that he supported Earth at all.

"Why don't you evacuate the Aegis," Carivant said, his voice quieter, "and we can have a—"

The *Lycan*'s head snapped forward, sending Carivant flying backward with a *crack* that echoed through the warehouse. Immediately, his soldiers started firing, but Teah swatted them away with a hand, launching them into the walls like they were children's toys. Alarms blasted through the warehouse.

The *Lycan's* head snapped around, looking over its shoulder straight at us. And in that stance, it truly embodied the Wolf.

Then it lunged.

The Aegis leapt, spinning in midair to face us, shaking the entire warehouse. Alis and I pushed through the doors into the Vault and ran, sprinting down the hall as a giant fist slammed through the doors. Then the larger garage door behind it—likely used for moving the larger pieces of the Aegis for assembly—buckled once before being thrown across the hallway, through a wall, and into a laboratory with an explosion that washed us with heat.

We rounded the corner and ran up a set of stairs. Teah wouldn't be able to get far in this hallway, and she'd have to abandon us once Genesis Gardens mustered their full forces.

"She's going...to have to run soon," I said through gasps of breath as I limped my injured leg as fast as it would go. "We have the *Harriet* in the hangar. And...Kuma. We gotta find Kuma."

"You remember the last time we tried to fight an Aegis with the *Harriet*? And we won't have zero-Gs to use to our advantage this time. Teah may have come here alone, but she could have assets in space, at least at the Spheric border. She can't leave atmosphere. We'll do better on boards. It'll be harder to hit us, and I can try and get into the cockpit."

We reached the next floor, and I followed Alis as she wove through the hallways. Below, an explosion rocked the stairwell. I couldn't tell if that was Teah pursuing or if Carivant's forces had—

The center of the floor exploded in the middle of a laboratory to our right as a churning red plasma blade emerged, attached to the Aegis' forearm as it pushed upward like a demon crawling out of Hell. The glass around the lab shattered as the blade retracted and the arm pushed the hole open wider. The *Lycan's* helm followed, molten metal sizzling as it rolled down the mithril. The red light running in lines down its face shined through the smoke and steam, staring right at us.

"This way!" Alis yelled, and we ran—

Right around the corner into a squad of security forces. They jerked in surprise as much as we did, raising their plasma rifles as they looked us up and down. The two of us and the group of them were frozen, Alis and I keeping our hands up in surrender. We couldn't shoot our way through them, but we were very clearly the less important threat, and dealing with us would just waste time.

"Carrol! Delaney!" yelled the armored officer in the lead. "Detain them. The rest of you, with me!" Most of the squad ran around the corner, toward the crashing sounds of Teah climbing up to this level. How long would she pursue us before she ran?

The two officers who'd remained behind kept their rifles on us as one stepped closer. "Drop the rifles, turn around, and put your hands on your head. NOW!" His voice made me cringe, magnified through the sleek, black helmet.

"We're not with the Bastionite," I said. "We can—"

"QUIET!" The soldier took an aggressive step toward me, shoving his rifle in my face. Intimidating, but the wrong move. His motion put him in the perfect path for Alis to shove his rifle up and in the same motion put her in between me and the officer, while also using that officer as a shield against the second behind him. I lifted my plasma rifle under Alis' arm and fired point blank into the officer's side. He yelled out as the superheated plasma tore through his armor and a few inches of flesh. That took his strength away, so Alis shoved him toward the other officer while raising her rifle to take a clean shot at the second officer's chest just as they pushed their comrade out of the way.

We ran past them, winding around a few hallways, until Alis slid to a stop. Behind us, plasma shots fired and yells echoed through the halls. Then the entire floor vibrated.

"My board and other things are just a couple floors up, near here," Alis said. "There's an elevator if they haven't shut it down. You go find Kuma, and I'll meet you at the *Harriet*. She can get us close to Teah. We can use boards from there.""I'm not leaving you," I said. "When your sister is—"

Alis grabbed both my arms and pulled me close enough that our torsos were pressing against each other. "I love you. I'll be fine. Most people won't recognize me. We can't waste time, and we need to make sure Kuma's all right."

I hated it, but I saw her logic.

"Fine," I said with an exaggerated roll of my eyes.

Alis smiled and kissed me on my cheek, a blossom of warmth. "Just get the ship warm. This is almost over, Tor, one way or the other."

"I pick the way where we both survive and leave the Wolf behind."

Alis' smile slipped. "Me, too." Then she pulled away, and I leaned toward her, my source of gravity, before realizing what I was doing. "Good luck," she said with a wink, then she rounded the corner.

I ached to follow her. What if Teah managed to turn her again? What if she got caught and outnumbered? She was clearly more capable than I was, but...

Find Alis. Help Alis.

I'd found her, and we were on our way to helping her. Catching Teah was the next step.

So I followed my orders and ran for the elevator. Behind me, another explosion rocked the tower.

Chapter Twenty-Eight
Toris

Kuma was fine.

When I slid to a stop outside the surveillance center, the door slid open, and we mirrored each other's shocked expressions.

"You're—"

"Yeah, I'm fine. You look like hell, though."

"But Teah...I mean Lana...she's not Lana, she's Alis' sister—"

"I know. I watched it all."

"She didn't...hurt you?"

"No, she said you two were compromised, that she had to go help you, and I had to stay there to keep an eye out. I tried to go instead, but she said that her 'jack would help her get access that I couldn't. I saw everything."

I frowned. The pieces weren't fitting together. "She didn't hurt you," was all I could repeat.

"No. Tor, she's clearly a mess, but..."

"Nope. No. Look, you've been right about a lot of things lately, brother, but don't tell me that the woman trying to get Alis to kill me for ten years is 'not that bad.'"

Kuma pursed his lips like he very much wanted to say that and more, but he clearly—and wisely—decided it was a topic for another time. "Where's Alis?"

"Meeting us at the hangar with her board." I jerked my head down the hall, and Kuma followed me as we started for the hangar. "Teah's going to try and escape with the Aegis. Alis thinks she's aiming to rendezvous with more Bastionites in space. We can't let her get that far. You saw what happened. She controls the Wolf. So we need her to finally end this."

"How's Alis doing?"

"She's..." I hadn't asked how she was doing. I mean, we were trying not to get killed or caught, but...no, that was a stupid excuse.

Find Alis. Help Alis.

317

And I was still screwing it up.

"She's in shock. You know we thought Teah was dead. Halgard showed her." Frustration boiled up at everything that admiral had done. "It must have been just another ploy to get Alis on her side. The connection to her mindjack must have gone two ways, and they pulled memories from her. Twisted them. Just to get what they wanted." I let an angry breath out through my nose.

"Didn't exactly work out for Halgard, though, did it?"

"No. It didn't."

The hangar was far more chaotic than when we'd left it, and no one paid us mind. Pilots rushed past us. On the other side of the hangar, a pair of starfighters lifted off and roared out to stop the *Lycan*. She must have taken to the skies.

"Do you think Lana...Teah actually covered our tracks? Cut off the warnings we'd set off?" I asked as we wound past the smaller cargo transports and headed back toward the *Harriet*.

"She did. I checked after she took off the mask. You got them on your tail when you broke into the Vault, but no, she held to her word. Probably because if we got caught, she couldn't have gotten to the Aegis."

"That doesn't make sense. She went in first. She could have just gone down to the *Lycan* and left us hanging."

"Maybe. You cut into the Vault, though. Maybe she wasn't lying when she said she couldn't hack her way in. That was the way she followed to get to you two."

"Right. And...I think she wanted us together. I think she wanted to turn Alis on me. You heard her. She wants us to suffer. It's all she's ever wanted. Still think we should give her a chance?"

Kuma didn't answer as we rounded some crates and faced the *Harriet*. Undisturbed. The Cloak had done its job. A deeper scan would have revealed it, but the tower had a few distractions to deal with since we'd arrived. I pressed a button hidden on the hull to the left of the airlock to disarm the traps we'd laid there, then we hurried inside just as another pair of starfighters left the hangar. Kuma ran through the cabin as I rushed to grab our first aid kit and apply ointment to our injuries, hissing as the cool medicine touched my shoulder wound.

"Let's warm her up," I said once we'd climbed up to the bridge and kicked on the engines. I pulled up the holomap, too. The starfighters were red triangles coming around back toward the city. A yellow square—since the system didn't know how to mark it—was on the right side of the Genesis Gardens tower. As we watched, it lifted off, darting down the street toward the edge of the city. It was staying low, between the buildings. A good tactical move in most civilian environments, but Teah likely didn't anticipate that Carivant would absolutely order his people to shoot down that Aegis at any cost, regardless of the casualty count. The mithril on that machine was more valuable than I could fathom. It was the kind of value that started the Solar Gulf War in the first place.

"Go!" shouted Alis' voice down in the passenger cabin, and I breathed an audible sigh of relief that she was safe, that she was close. "Go, go, go," she repeated as she climbed up onto the bridge.

"You got it, sister," Kuma said, and he fired thrusters that got us up in the air.

"Good to see you, brother," Alis pat Kuma on the shoulder as I eased us forward. When I pushed the throttle forward, Alis grasped onto Kuma's chair and the holomap console to keep herself stable. I cringed as we passed the defense cannons and exited the hangar, but they didn't fire on us. The Cloak was still working. Still, we'd start to draw suspicion as our cargo ship entered a combat situation beside starfighters. By then, it wouldn't matter.

I eased us around, following the path the starfighters had, guiding us back toward the city. Smoke rose from a hole in the side of Genesis Gardens, only a few floors up from the ground. The Vault had been a few levels below-ground, so Teah must have found the first opportunity to get outside.

The holomap showed the *Lycan* flying down a street in the Gardens district, to the east of the tower. Starfighters were in pursuit, but they were one less. Teah had already taken one down.

"Get us on top of her," Alis said. "We need to disable her rockets. Right now she's staying in cover, but she'll eventually make a break for space. Once she really tries, we won't be able to keep up. We have to knock her down before that. Tor, did you bring your solarblade?"

"You know it. It's how I got into the Vault."

"Good. That'll sabotage the rockets." She shook her head. "I can't believe that thing's flying again. I can't believe it's here."

"I'm sorry," I said. "I know it's hard to see it again. But we'll make sure Bastion doesn't get it. And we'll take care of the Wolf. We're here for you this time."

"I know." She stared out the viewport, chewing on her bottom lip as we flew parallel to the *Lycan*'s street. The Aegis was up ahead, flying only twenty or so feet above the ground, the power of its rockets blowing dust, cars, drones, and other machines out of the way in its wake. The starfighters flew behind it, launching volleys of plasma fire that the Aegis would roll to avoid. A particularly heavy, coordinated spray forced Teah to fire thrusters on the *Lycan*'s chest and bank a hard turn down another street. Two of the four starfighters made the maneuver, one tried but ended up missing and was forced to continue down the street, gaining altitude to make a turn. The fourth fighter realized it was going to miss the turn, overcorrected, and slammed into a skyscraper with a violent explosion. Doubtless that Carivant would blame those deaths on Bastion.

Was history repeating itself? I shivered to think that we were in the shadow of something much greater. Much more terrible.

"We have to get her out of the city," I said. "She clearly doesn't care about collateral damage."

"She'll leave the city herself," Alis said. "She's just trying to shake the fighters. We need to get above her." Kuma tapped some commands into his console, and a flight path flashed up on the viewport, making the calculations to get us over Teah. "As long as she's in the city, we can catch up to her. And it'll drain her fuel. I don't know how much training she's gone through, but Aegises don't carry much fuel. They're designed to stay on the ground or close to their cruiser for easy refueling. If she burns it all in the city, she won't get far in space."

"Can we cut her fuel lines?" I asked. "Might be easier than destroying her rockets; and that sounds like less of a chance of an explosion."

"You can try. Less of the lines are exposed than the rocket, once she's engaged it. But that's a good idea."

I pushed forward the throttle and followed the system's flight path as Teah turned down another street, diverted by one of the Genesis Gardens starfighters.

"Almost there," Alis said. "Come on, Tor."

"You got this, Kuma?"

"I'll do what I can," Kuma said. "Here." He pulled a pair of earpieces from beside him. We'd be able to connect with the *Harriet* using those. "Good luck, brother."

"Thanks, brother." I patted his shoulder and followed Alis out of the bridge, pausing to hold tight to the ladder as the ship vibrated from a patch of turbulence. Once in the passenger cabin, I pulled off the Genesis Gardens jumpsuit and retrieved my stolen board and a pair of goggles.

"What's that?" Alis asked as she grabbed her board.

"Oh. Right. I lost my board when we crashed outside the Glassfields."

"You crashed?!"

"Yeah. Because of a revenant. Now that I think about it, Teah could have contributed to that, too. It's been a long couple days."

She closed her eyes, sighed, and shook her head. "I'm so sorry. I shouldn't have...I wasn't thinking right, and I thought I could just..." She opened her eyes and stared into mine. "I'm sorry, Tor. For...so much."

I grabbed her by the waist with one hand, the board in the other, and pulled her in for a kiss. The rumble of the ship disappeared, and the fear dissipated. It was just the two of us, and the universe shifted its orbit to put us at the center.

"Let's finish this," I said, my forehead still pressed against hers. Then I hit the airlock button, overrode the warning that said we were moving at too high a speed to disembark, and stepped onto my board.

"You're over the Lycan. *Good luck, you two."*

The airlock slid open to a roar of air that pulled at us.

And we let the sky take hold.

We dove out of the airlock, Alis first, my stomach turning and head spinning as my body tried to orient itself. The buildings were rising to meet us, the jagged teeth of a great beast. Two starfighters roared by beneath us, pursuing the *Sanguine Lycan* just ahead.

Almost in perfect sync, Alis and I swung ourselves upright and engaged our boards, shooting forward at full speed. The wind shrieked in my ears, and I pulled the goggles down over my eyes, blinking quickly to dispel the dryness.

We tore past buildings in a blur, catching up to the starfighters, then passing over them, both of us squatting down and leaning forward to create as little wind resistance as possible. Alis was right: in the city, the great machines below us had to hold back, sacrificing speed for the other advantages Teah had between the buildings. We had no such limits.

The *Lycan* banked around another corner, using its chest thrusters in the same move as earlier. Both of the starfighters missed the turn this time, shooting down the other street and ascending to turn. Alis and I leaned backwards, throwing the boards up to easily bank the corner, closing our distance on Teah.

A flash of light burst in my upper periphery just before the *Lycan* rolled to the side, firing thrusters to move more quickly, and a cannon blast screamed by beneath us, slamming into something down the street. A barricade stood on the street ahead, including a pair of tanks.

Teah's roll sent her scraping against the side of a building, sending up sparks. She leaned into that, firing her thrusters again to swing her vertical, where she shoved the Aegis' hands into the building, shattering glass and shearing metal. She dug the *Lycan*'s toes in a few floors down, hanging there for a moment like a gargantuan spider before she *launched* herself upward. The floors of the building collapsed from the force as she engaged the larger rockets in the Aegis' back and legs and shot into the sky.

Alis and I pursued, pushing our boards harder and harder. We leaned back, shooting toward the sky, our boards inches from the building Teah had used as a launchpad.

"*COME ON!*" Alis shouted, her determined yell crackling through my earpiece.

We rocketed above the building, leaving the city behind as Teah spiraled into the sky, leaving trails of smoke and steam in her wake. We wound around those trails as we ascended, mirrors of each other. Alis raised her plasma rifle and fired, but the shots missed, sailing higher until they disappeared. She growled in frustration. We were so close, but it still felt like this chance was slipping through our fingers. Teah was simply faster, gradually pulling further ahead as her rockets took her toward space—and whatever rendezvous awaited her there.

I pushed down with my toes, forcing the board to draw in more air and accelerate to its limits. We were passing through thin clouds now, soaking the two of us. Before long, we'd start losing oxygen. We were running out of time.

Something rushed past me at such a speed that I spun away as it slammed into the *Lycan*. A missile. I looked back and below as I regained my speed. The remaining three starfighters were on our tails. If we couldn't keep up with Teah, they could, especially in the open air. Smoke and fire streaked from the Aegis, the missile finding its mark somewhere on the *Lycan's* thigh. It slowed Teah down, and we gained some distance on her lead. Then another missile screamed past and exploded against the *Lycan's* mithril shoulder. That one only left a scorch mark, but it sent Teah into a somersault that shed more speed. She fired thrusters across the armor to right herself again.

"*Would they kill her rather than let her escape?*" Alis shouted through the rush of wind.

I didn't need to give it more than a second's thought. "Yes. They'd blow up the Aegis before losing that investment to Bastion."

"*Their missiles won't be able to breach the mithril,*" Alis shouted. "*But they can batter the rest enough to take her down. We can't let them. We don't know what other contingencies Teah has. We need her to shut off the Wolf permanently. And...I can't lose anyone else, Tor. Now that she's here.*"

"Alis..."

"*I can't. I know what she's done. I've suffered from it more than anyone, but I have a chance here, to do better.*"

I didn't agree. I couldn't. Not yet. Not after everything she'd done to us. To Alis. But I kept that to myself for the moment.

"What's the plan?" I shouted. "We're closing on her. If we drop back to deal with the fighters, we risk letting Teah escape."

"But if we don't, she dies. We—"

An explosion cut Alis off. Teah must have fired something, because the giant inflated wind turbine ahead of us started belching smoke, obscuring everything—including Teah. I covered my nose and mouth with my elbow as I pushed the board upward. Gradually, the smoke cleared enough to see ahead.

Teah was gone.

"BELOW!" Alis shouted.

We flipped our boards up to make a hard turn, cringing against the Gs. The starfighters were pushing through the smoke as we had. But just as they passed through the densest part of the cloud, the *Sanguine Lycan* shot out of the burning turbine like a cannon, a massive fan blade in one hand, its plasma blade ignited on its other arm. Teah hurled the fan blade like a spear into the cockpit of one of the starfighters, then spun with a precise thruster burst and cut through the next closest starfighter with her plasma blade, sending the two halves of the fighter spinning wildly through the air until they exploded. The third starfighter emerged from the smoke unscathed—but now it was the quarry. Plates popped up from the *Lycan*'s trapezius, and a volley of small missiles launched, spiraling toward the fighter. It banked to the right and fired a flash of lasers to confuse the missiles. A few crashed into each other in explosive bursts, but most of them slammed into the fighter. Its engines sputtered, adding smoke to the cloud expanding from the damaged turbine. The machine slowed down enough that with a burst from her rockets, Teah was able to grab the fighter, spin to gain momentum using her thrusters, and hurl the machine into another nearby turbine, ending both machines in a blast that hurled Alis and I backwards.

I lost all my bearings as I tumbled backwards, my vision threatening to collapse. But I pressed down on the board's accelerator and rocketed downward for a moment before pulling myself back up and curving around the first burning turbine to continue our pursuit.

"Alis!" I yelled. "Are you all right? Where are you?" I needed to get out of that smoke. But if I went too much higher, I'd start losing air. We couldn't push this any further. Maybe Kuma could pick us up and we could at least follow Teah into orbit? We wouldn't be able to do much beyond that. Maybe it was finally time to consider putting true weapons on that ship.

"ALIS!" I shouted, then coughed violently as I inhaled the surrounding smoke. I slowed down and hovered for a moment to get my bearings before I shot off miles in the wrong direction. "AL—"

Red light glowed through the smoke, creeping closer, the smoke thinning as the *Lycan*'s head took shape, only a few feet away. In that moment, the Aegis embodied its name. I felt like I may as well have been staring down a wolf as it prowled in the shadows of a forest. I was in its domain, in its control.

And while every instinct screamed at me to flee, I realized that may have been the solution. "Is it me you want?" I shouted, knowing she could hear me in that cockpit. "You want me dead? You want Alis to suffer? If I'm gone...if I go...will you leave this alone? Will you free Alis from the Wolf and let her live the life she wants?" The *Lycan* hovered close enough that I could see my muddied reflection in the mithril. The Aegis lurched a little, the damaged rocket in its thigh sputtering with flame and smoke. "Because I'd do it. I'd go. You can have the Aegis and me. You can—"

"*No. You. Can't!*" Alis shouted. Then she shot through the smoke, opening a shaft of light like a divine messenger, leapt from her hoverboard, and landed on the *Lycan*'s ribcage, straddling the entrance to the cockpit with her mag-boots. "*Tor, blade!*"

Shaking away the awe Alis inspired, I shot toward her just as Teah swiped for me with a giant hand. The Aegis spun, but I followed, pulling the solarblade hilt from my belt, twisting myself horizontal, and holding it out toward Alis' outstretched hand.

"I love you," I said as our fingers brushed, too quiet to hear in the wind, but she read my lips and smiled brighter than that divine shaft of light.

I flew by as she ignited the solarblade and plunged it through the slanted metal of the cockpit door. Teah reached the Aegis' arm around to grab her sister, but I shot into the way, twisting just in time to whip the hand away using the momentum I'd generated. I flew around the body as Alis dropped into the cockpit through the still-smoldering hole she'd created.

"*Put it down, Teah. Desync. Let's just talk.*"

Muddled through the microphone on Alis' earpiece, I heard Teah say: "*You're ten years too late for that.*"

Then she engaged the *Lycan*'s rockets and launched through the smoke toward space.

"*What are you doing?*" Alis shouted. They'd lose oxygen soon, even if the armor tried to compensate, thanks to the breach Alis had created.

"Alis! Pull her out! Desync her!" It was the only way. Alis wouldn't be able to take manual control as long as Teah was synced. But she could disrupt the connection, just as she'd done when Ecker had tried to dominate her mind. When the Wolf was born.

"Teah, please. I'm sorry."

I pressed the accelerator as far as it would go, shooting out of the smoke and into the cold, clear sky. The smoke from the *Lycan*'s damaged rocket streamed beside me. Thanks to the wound, I was able to catch up, climbing up past the Aegis' other thigh rocket, welcoming the heat from it as we continued deeper into sub-zero temperatures.

"Kuma, you still with us?" I shouted.

"Beneath you."

I looked down, where the *Harriet* emerged from the smoke.

"We may need support."

"You've got it. And may need it soon. More Genesis Gardens ships on their way."

"Teah, please. More fighters are coming. You won't outrun them. This isn't worth your life."

Teah said something I couldn't hear, but it didn't matter. I was close. I'd pull her out myself if I had to. Of course Alis would hesitate to do that to her sister. I wouldn't. I'd do it for her.

I was level with the hole in the cockpit door. Alis was standing there, ignited solarblade still in hand like she knew she should use it but couldn't. I twisted inside the Aegis, grabbing onto the cooling rim of Alis' damage, then killed the hoverboard. The *Lycan*'s acceleration slammed me into the floor of the cockpit, but I disengaged my boots and hopped to my feet, then re-engaged the boots.

"Toris, wait!" Alis shouted as I stalked toward Teah, who reclined in the cockpit chair wearing a white and red-trimmed sync suit, a cord plugged into the helm at the base of the neck. If she got up to confront us, she'd have to desync. If she wanted to maintain control of the Aegis, there wasn't much she could do other than watch.

Good.

"Alis, please, just give me the blade. You don't have to do it. I will."

The *Lycan* twisted, and though my mag-boots kept me upright, the Gs nearly knocked me out. Alis cried out, grabbing at her head, where the damage to her 'jack would make any head pain worse.

Enough. I'd had enough. Sister or not, this Bastionite monster wouldn't harm Alis anymore.

I didn't need the blade. I dove and wrapped Teah in a headlock, grabbing at the sync cord with my other hand.

"TORIS, NO!"

Teah jerked her head back, trying to hit me in the face, but she just slammed her helm into my shoulder—which still hurt enough to make me cry out.

"Take us down. Now." I growled beside the helm. "Or I give you the same suffering you put your sister through. You want to talk about justice?" I tightened my headlock, even though the armor was likely protecting her throat enough for the move to do little else than hinder her movement. "That's justice."

Teah pulled at my arm with one hand while the other reached for one of the plasma rifles she'd taken from the Genesis Gardens security forces. Alis stepped forward and sliced it in two with the solarblade before Teah could even lift it up.

"Desync, Teah." Alis glanced up at the screens above us. "You're leaking fuel. You won't make it far enough. More fighters are coming. Please."

I tightened my grip on the cord, ready to pull. I'd wait, but only for a few seconds.

Teah made the faceplate of her helm retract, revealing her sweaty face, strands of black hair stuck to her forehead. She was flushed and getting redder. Maybe I was putting on enough pressure to do some damage.

"You can kill me," she hissed. "You can torture me. You can break my mind. But nothing will fix you, Alis. The Faraday Shield won't be the silver bullet you think it is. Our signal just allowed us to nudge you how we wanted. To *experiment* on you." She spat that verb, as if she wanted Alis to know she was less than human, nothing more than a lab rat. "Your 'Wolf' lives in your head, thanks to your betrayal and to whatever the Mudbrains did to you. That last cycle?" She started chuckling, the laugh of the desperate and broken, and I couldn't help it, I tightened my headlock as much as I could until her chuckle devolved into a cough. "Before you came to Farstead? We didn't initiate that one. Your own mind did. The Wolf will live as long as you do. Nothing I do, nothing you try and force me to do, will change that."

The spark of hope in my chest sputtered. I'd stopped the Wolf. Or, at the very least I'd forced it to slink away back into the shadows. There had to be a way to make that permanent. We couldn't—

"Then the Wolf lives," Alis said.

"*What?*" I snapped. "How could you...why..."

"You want to make me suffer, Teah. And I understand why. But I'll take that burden. I'll face those consequences, if you come back with me. Talk to me. Because no matter how much I suffer, you'll never fill that void. Let me help you."

Teah hesitated. I saw it in her eyes. In the way the glaring lines of her face softened as she stared up at her sister.

But it could all be an act. She'd manipulated Kuma and I. Alis could help her, and I could help Alis.

"We'll help you after you help Alis," I said. "Or I pull this cord out right now. You think you're hurting now? You have no idea what you've put your sister through. You—"

"Toris."

I looked up at Alis, and I could feel the snarl my face had twisted into without intention. She recoiled a little, subtly, her head jerking back just slightly, her eyes widening.

As if she were the one staring down the Wolf.

Find Alis. Help Alis.

Help Alis.

I was still trying to help her my way. I wanted to end her suffering for both of us, not just her.

But this was her battle. Her family. And she deserved to end it her way.

Still fighting against a part of me, my own Wolf, I let go of the sync cord. I released Teah and pushed myself to my feet, clenching my hands into fists so tight it hurt. Adrenaline and fear and pain and doubt all surged through me with nowhere to go. But I looked at Alis, and I trusted her. With all of me.

"Thank you," she whispered, tears wetting her eyes. Then to Teah: "Put it down, Teah. I'm here. You don't have to do it alone anymore. And I'm sorry you had to for so long."

Teah's glare returned, but with it came tears that mirrored her sister's. "You—"

"*Toris!*" Kuma shouted. "*Missiles—*"

The cockpit exploded.

327

CHAPTER TWENTY–NINE
TORIS

"ALIS!"

The explosion swallowed my scream, the force more powerful than the magnets in our boots keeping us on the floor. As the *Sanguine Lycan* tumbled, I flew toward the wall opposite the cockpit opening, slamming into the ribcage on that side.

And Alis fell through the door.

Ignoring Teah and the firestorm and the dangers waiting outside, I shoved off that wall, grabbed my floating hoverboard, and launched into the sky. For a moment, I was diving through smoke, board in front of me, the heat of flames washing over me from beneath. The Genesis Gardens starfighters must have hit the Aegis' other thigh rockets.

"Kuma!" I shouted. "Alis got knocked out of the Aegis. She doesn't have a board. I—"

"*I've got eyes on her. But I don't have a way to catch her at that speed, Tor.*"

"I know! Just keep an eye on her, knock anything out of her way. I'll get her." I dropped out of the smoke, my stomach turning at the sight of the city rising to meet us, its spires like stalagmites at the bottom of a cliff.

Alis dropped, limbs limp above her, back toward the ground. I was too far away to tell for sure, but she looked unconscious. Hopefully not worse. I hadn't seen if she'd hit—or been hit by—anything as she fell out of the Aegis.

Please please please please please

I pulled my legs toward my chest and brought the hoverboard beneath my feet. My boots latched in, and I kicked the accelerator to full power, crouching as I rocketed toward Alis. She hurtled past another wind turbine, arm slapping the inflated side and rotating her so she faced the ground and her back faced me.

To our left, the Genesis Gardens starfighters flew past, their passing buffeting both of us just before another explosion burst above. The fighters' disturbance sent Alis tumbling away, and I followed.

Two more explosions punched the air above us, but I didn't turn around. To our right was the *Harriet,* making a wide turn to catch up to us. In the distance, another ship was approaching, little more than an insect approaching the edges of the city. It was larger than a starfighter, but not by much. Another Genesis Gardens craft, maybe? Just what we needed.

"ALIS!" I shouted again, pushing the accelerator down so hard that my toes hurt. I was gaining on her, but as we got closer to the city, the air became more cluttered. Holographic advertisements flashed banners across the sky. Drones buzzed, some large and some small, carrying cargo, projecting more advertisements, or pointing cameras up at the chase happening above the city. The wind turbines and hovering solar panels also clustered together closer to the skyline.

And Alis was headed straight for it all.

"Kuma! We may need to tow or knock some of this shit out of the way. I don't think she's conscious!"

"I'm almost to your position. Had to make a turn and shed some speed. But Tor, we have help! Navi...TOR! LOOK OUT!"

I looked around, searching for threats, but didn't see anything. But then I noticed a roar behind me, deeper than the roar of the air rushing by. I risked looking back—

And stared right into the face of the *Sanguine Lycan*, a trail of fire and smoke churning around it. The Aegis' arm was outstretched toward me, mithril fingers reaching.

I pressed on the accelerator, but I was already pushing the board to its limits. Then I lurched as Teah grabbed the back edge of my board. Roaring in my own way as my head swiveled from Alis to the Aegis drawing me closer, I ignited my solarblade and swung at the *Lycan*'s fingers. But the plasma just scorched the surface, and the magnetic clips bounced off, one of the few substances resistant to the superheated blade. I swung again anyway, then again and again, each swing as useless as the last. I hazarded a glance back downward at Alis, who hurtled past a drone so closely that I hissed in a breath.

"KUMA! I NEED YOU! I NEED..." I didn't know what I needed, what anyone could do. Tears stung my eyes as defeat encased my heart. Teah may as well have just ended it. She...

Why hadn't she ended it? She could have easily shot me and Alis both from much further away. Was she just trying to prevent me from saving Alis? To make us suffer? She could bail at any point; she'd have to, soon, especially if her directional thrusters were damaged. The mithril could take the hits, but not the already-severely-damaged bottom half of the armor.

The Aegis squeezed the back of my board, smashing one of the two small engines beneath.

I ground my teeth together and stopped that defeat before the parasite could consume me. Our suffering would end. Or, at the very least, Teah would direct it no longer.

With my board stuck and handicapped, the *Lycan* started falling faster than I was, its fingers still holding on as the rest of the weight pushed me along ahead of it. I could disengage from the board and jump, but I wouldn't fall fast enough to catch up to Alis.

I killed the board's power to prevent it from pulling itself apart in an attempt to escape the Aegis. Then I swiped my solarblade through my own hoverboard, around where the Aegis' fingers were smashing it.

I dropped, the molten metal of the board spitting acrid smoke into my face. With a flick of my heel, I reactivated the board.

It didn't work.

I'd been careful not to sever the superconductor sitting behind the engines, and I should have still had one functioning engine. I tried again.

The engine sputtered to life. I pressed on the accelerator.

And a giant hand eclipsed the sun. I threw my weight backwards, pivoting away from the hand. This time, Teah was losing patience. The *Lycan's* massive solarblade extended from above its wrist, the heat of it washing over me and singing the ends of my hairs. I pressed the accelerator to its limits, but I wouldn't get far enough.

The Aegis brought its arm toward me and—

BABOOM

Something slammed into the *Lycan's* side, knocking her off course. Then another, sending her fully tumbling away from me. They weren't missiles. The explosions were too small, and the sound was too...dense. Like the Aegis was getting hit by something heavy and slower, but still fast enough to disrupt it.

The *Harriet* rocketed over us, launching another of our hotboxes at the Aegis. It slammed into the *Sanguine Lycan's* torso, just under the mithril, throwing it into a giant holo-ad projector. That explosion was anything but small.

I cheered, throwing my fist up in the air toward Kuma as he started making his turn back toward us. It wasn't lost on me that we'd pulled that same trick on that first day. The day we met Alis.

"*Toris.*"

Her voice was quiet in my earpiece, almost lost in the roar of the wind around her.

I crouched and spiraled downward, realigning with Alis from where Teah had thrown me off. The accelerator cracked from the pressure I was forcing on it.

She was too far. Teah had slown me down too much.

Alis was dropping straight for a large, stationary drone, black solar panels on its top, reflecting the sunlight so that Alis seemed wrapped in a halo.

I screamed, shredding my throat as I forced all the energy out of my desperate soul. I wasn't going to catch her.

I'd failed.

And I could only watch.

The world slowed down, Alis staring up at me, hair slapping her face, as the solar panel rose too fast to catch her, the halo constricting.

"Alis." I said through a sob, too quiet for anyone to hear.

She met my eyes. She smiled. Alistella Pareides Caliday. Moonbreaker. Traitor. Hero. My heart and my life. Even in the end, leaving me racing to catch up in every way.

"I love you."

Alis mouthed it back: "I love you."

She closed her eyes.

CHAPTER THIRTY

ALIS

(Twelve years earlier)

I SHOVED MYSELF AWAY from the console as if it had burned me. But I'd only burned myself...and everything around me. My shaking hands rose to cover my horror-stricken mouth as explosions bloomed like blossoming flowers across the void. Bastion's ships—the vast majority of them, at least—fell apart along glowing molten wounds. Below the Loop, Earth's ships suffered even greater damage, hulking hunks of their great battlecruisers drifting in a cloud of debris. The particle beams had faded, the great display of divine power harnessed by humankind was so bright that it'd left an afterimage on all the screens.

The plan worked. We'd...the war would be over with both fleets crippled...Teah had been avenged, and Bastion was safe, along with its millions of citizens.

That rationality did little to calm the way my stomach twisted at the sight of thousands of bodies—and parts of bodies—tumbling through space away from their cruisers, consigned to their graves.

I'd made that decision for all of them. I should have warned them. I should have given them a chance to surrender.

But then the Earthers never would have fired their beams and...

Maybe the fleets would have destroyed each other anyway?

Or Earth would have used its beams on the opposing ships first before turning them on the city, and it all would have been lost anyway.

But—

"ALIS! GET DOWN!"

Toris wrenched my arm down as a plasma round flashed through where I'd just been standing and slammed into the bulkhead behind me. I blinked, shaking myself out of that spiral, but still unable to shake the numbness that'd iced over my entire body. We were crouching behind the second row of control consoles. Someone was firing at us.

Godwin. It was Commander Godwin and his soldiers. He'd shouted something when I'd...when the particle beams had fired. It was only seconds before, but it was still *before.*

Following another volley of shots, Toris rose from his crouch and returned fire. Someone yelled. In pain.

So much pain.

I cringed as the dagger twisted in my head and my vision constricted for a moment. Not now. I couldn't allow whatever I'd done to those soldiers to happen then. I could hurt Toris, who'd already risked enough.

The constriction faded while the pain lingered.

"Alis, hey," Toris said, crouching beside me again. "Are you...no, that's a stupid question. We're going to get out of here. But they're going to flank us, and they're blocking the only way back to the ship. Any ideas?"

I stared into his eyes, mouth moving but no words coming out. "I...I'm sorry. I..."

He clenched his jaw but nodded. Then he put his hand on my shoulder, and in my cold shock, it was like holding a fire close to my skin. Not close enough to burn, but enough to warm. "It's all right. We'll get out of here."

Another round of plasma fire peppered the bulkhead above us, at a different angle. Halgard's soldiers were on the move. One of them peeked around the curved row of consoles, and Toris forced him back under cover. None of his shots hit anything but the far wall, though.

"Take them down!" Godwin shouted. "You traitors! After every chance the admiral gave you. After...Oh, God. What have you done?" His tone spiraled from rage into genuine pain. I may have even caught the hint of tears near the end. He must have looked out at the screens, at the remains of his fleet, his temporary home—and the coffins of his found family.

"You were going murder hundreds of millions of innocents, Godwin!" Toris shouted. "Even Bastion never went that far."

"We could have won," Godwin said, his tone and volume sounding almost like he was talking more to himself. "We could have ended this."

"We did," Toris said, and he sounded anything but victorious. But he looked at me and nodded. "We ended it. The slate's clean. And now we can build something better."

Now I could be something better.

And I didn't want anyone else to die.

"We don't have to do this, Godwin!" I yelled, finally finding my voice. "No one else has to get hurt. We'll leave, and you can hail someone to get you."

"Hail *who*?" Godwin snapped. Shock had worn down the composure of the calm, in-control commander.

"There will be evacuees. Shuttles." Saying it did little to convince even me. "I...I know it hurts. No one has to know the mission failed. They'll think Bastion did this, and...it went wrong. Backfired."

"Bastion *did* do this. You're no better than the rest of the demons. Everything the admiral did was for *nothing*. You can never change, and your city—no, all of you—should be wiped off the face of the universe. You—"

"Commander!"

I didn't understand why a soldier was shouting at Godwin—until the commander stepped out of cover and faced us, holding his rifle with shaking hands, his helm off and tears streaming down his face.

Talking would do little good. I'd tried.

For an instant, I wondered if I should just sit there. Let him shoot me. Face my justice. Let it all end with the war.

But I heard Toris in my head: "*We can build something better.*"

I'd destroyed enough. I wanted to be part of that.

I dove just as Godwin fired, the shot lancing past my back, searing through the clothing and burying in the floor where I'd been sitting. Toris fired back as he scurried backward, hitting Godwin in the shoulder. The commander's armor took most of the hit, but it did push him back a few steps. I rolled to the side, trying to move around the first row of the consoles for cover. But Godwin fired again, this time hitting me square in the back of the shoulder. And I didn't have armor to protect me.

Plasma shots may not have immediately bled like old bullets did, but they unleashed an entirely different kind of agony. The heat left a crater in the flesh, burning through skin and muscle and sometimes bone. The plasma instantly cauterized the skin where it hit, and that heat rippled throughout the body, boiling the blood around the wound and spiking body temperature.

So when Godwin's shot struck, the force threw me to the ground, and the pain was like being stabbed with a flaming spear. The pain burned across my shoulder as the crater spread, and I screamed, clawing at the ground and arcing my back in agony. The smoke of my own burned flesh stung my nostrils. Sweat dripped off my face and hands, making my clothes stick to me as my body tried to cool off. My head swam, which only made the dagger in my head twist and shove deeper.

I cried out again as I forced myself to turn and face Godwin with tears blurring my vision. I wouldn't die with my back turned. He'd have to see my face—and remember it. I grasped control of my heavy, panicked breathing and stared him down as he raised his rifle.

"STOP! MOVE OR SHOOT AND WE ALL DIE!" Toris was standing, holding his finger millimeters above one of the control screens, the one he'd been using to maneuver the Loop. Another soldier had stepped around the side of the row, flanking us. I had no idea what Toris was doing, or if he was just bluffing, but it was looking like we wouldn't have a chance to build much of anything. The wreckage out there would be my only mark on the cold universe. That and the hollow shell of Stickney.

"Walk away, Godwin," Toris said. "Your squad doesn't have to die for this."

I leaned my back against that first row of consoles, gasping as the cool metal touched my wound. Godwin still had his gun on me, but his gaze jerked manically from me to Toris. I could see the calculations happening behind his eyes. Were our deaths worth it? For the justice of it all? Could he or one of his soldiers shoot Toris before he did whatever he had planned?

I still wondered if he could do anything. If he was bluffing. But when I looked over to the captain, he was looking at me, eyebrows inverted and an apology in his gaze. Then I remembered his plan: to destroy the Loop. Disrupt Bastion's infrastructure to keep them from retaliating against Earth anytime soon. We didn't know what the consequences would be, but many would suffer. The Loop was our...was Bastion's shield against the harsh universe. Without it...

And with it, they would surely strike back against Earth, mustering every-thing they could to make their enemies suffer. To burn away the rot. To make innocents suffer, because the perpetrators against them were floating among the wreckage here.

Except for me, of course.

Whatever the consequences, I could see that, despite the acknowledgment and apology in his expression, Toris had made up his mind. Just as I'd thought of Teah as I turned the Loop on my own people, he was seeing his parents. He was seeing Kuma and Mele.

"Step away. Now." Godwin still had his rifle barrel pointed at me, but it was quivering.

"Drop your weapons," Toris said, voice calm but firm. "Back away. Or this is it. Be better than the admiral, Godwin. We were all desperate for this war to be over.

Now it is. You can go home. We can all go home. And we can make that home better. Please."

Godwin's face softened for a moment, and I wondered what home he pictured in his head. I had to instantly stop thinking about mine. I was close enough to losing my composure without seeing Father alone, staring up at the starbursts of the destroyed fleets, wondering where his daughters were.

Defeated, but safe.

The commander shoved his gun forward once more, but his face didn't reflect the same conviction. "You're just trying to avoid responsibility. Justice. You have the blood of thousands on your hands. You..."

"Commander..." one of the other soldiers said from near the back of the room. "Sir. Earth lost enough today. We—"

"COWARDS!" Godwin shouted, glancing back only for an instant toward the back of his squad. The man truly didn't know what to do. "Enough! We do the duty no one else can. If we let these traitors go free, then we failed our families, and all the families who lost someone today. Because of *them*." At "them," he swung his plasma rifle toward Toris and fired. Toris ducked, pressing the screen as he did.

The control module lurched, tilting and knocking everyone off their feet. Godwin slid down past me and the first row of consoles to hit the bulkhead on the other side.

"Come on!" Toris said, helping me to my feet and up the now-sloping floor toward the corridor.

"Fire! Kill them!" Godwin shouted, lifting his own rifle and firing.

But the module lurched again, and a series of explosions rattled the entire Loop, making the plasma shots go awry, peppering the bulkheads around us. One lanced past Toris, burning through the leg of his pants and singing the skin.

"Run!" Toris said as we reached the corridor. I ground my teeth against the pain in my shoulder and dashed toward the airlock, over the bodies of the Bastion soldiers and the open door where the hologram of the woman was gone. The module rattled again...

And started to move.

We were drifting, and the gravity created by the Loop's regular rotation was gone. My stomach turned as we lifted off the floor, my hair wafting around me as if underwater. Toris fired a burst of shots for cover as we reached the airlock door and pulled ourselves into the *Harriet,* past the body of Godwin's soldier. Toris gently eased him out into the module, then he pulled the lever to seal the airlock.

"They'll be okay," he said as he floated past through the passenger cabin. I followed. "Someone will come get them."

"So you were half-bluffing," I said, cringing as I grabbed onto the ladder into the bridge with my right arm and stretched my wound. "What..." Part of me didn't want to know. But I had to. "What did you do?"

"Overrode the AI and used the thrusters on each of the Loop's modules to fire at full power in opposite directions of each other. Sheared the sections apart."

Those were the explosions we'd heard. The Iridesca Loop was destroyed...Bastion could repair it, but it would take years. And in the meantime...people would suffer. There was no avoiding that, and a part of me, the part of me that ached to go home, seethed with a hot anger that Toris had made that decision for an entire planet.

Had I done anything different?

We floated through the bridge, and I took my seat behind Toris' chair. A light flashed on the console. Above it, through the viewport, the cylindrical modules of the Iridesca Loop floated through space. Most of them spun in a blur, their thrusters still firing. A pair collided with each other in an explosion that expelled a spray of debris, joining the wreckage of the decimated fleets.

Toris settled in and pressed a button beside the flashing light.

"Kuma? Kuma, is that you?"

"*Toris, thank God. Please tell me you're not on the Loop.*"

"We're fine. Detaching now."

There was a hollow *thunk* as we let go of the control module, and a thruster burst sent us away. Debris rattled against the hull like rain.

"*I'm almost to Stickney.*" Kuma's voice was quiet, his words clipped, haunted by what he'd seen.

"We'll meet you there," Toris said.

A pause. Then: "*Is it over?*"

Toris glanced back toward me. "For better or worse. Yes, it's over."

***

Stickney was a scar.

Phobos wasn't much to look at in the first place, but Stickney's destruction had left a horrible mark, a black sun, its corona expanding away from the shattered shell that had once been the colony domes. I'd later learned that the anti-starcraft rounds that had penetrated the colony had also caused the violent collapse of the fusion reactors powering the domes. That collapse, in the end, was the cause of this total destruction. The reactors should have been better protected, but in building the colony, Bastion had opted for speed and cost efficiency. We shared the blame for Stickney's death.

Settled in the wreckage of the old spaceport was the sleek shape of an Earther starfighter. Toris brought us down beside it, orienting the thrusters to slow our descent. The journey to Phobos had been slow without the *Harriet*'s primary rockets, but the combined power of the thrusters and Phobos' orbit toward us made the journey only a few hours long.

Quick as that was for space travel, with each hour I found myself sinking further into myself, under the shadow of a churning storm of conflicting feelings and doubts. We'd maneuvered out of the bulk of the debris cloud, but I eventually had to close my eyes to avoid seeing the iced bodies float by. Was one of those Teah? I should have found a way on to the *Fang*, found a way to get her body back. To at least give Father that burial. I'd given Teah her justice, but was that enough?

We touched down on the moon, facing the broken dome only a few yards from where I'd stood in the *Sanguine Lycan*, my sinister helm reflected in the dark glass and metal.

Toris stood and left the bridge without a word. We'd traveled in silence. I didn't sense any tension, any anger from the captain. I think neither of us knew what to say.

Below, I heard the whine of the airlock cycling, the clanking of the door opening, then the slap of the two men embracing. I sat there, unmoving, as the captains returned to the bridge. Kuma was wearing an Earther military jumpsuit, a helmet in his hand that'd allowed him to traverse the space between his fighter and the *Harriet*. He acknowledged me with a nod and what little smile he could muster before setting the helmet on the ground and settling into his seat. Toris sat down in his, swiveling so we were all facing each other.

We were silent for a while, long enough that I started looking up into the space above Stickney, wondering when ships from the surface would decide to brave the battlefield. We'd need to be gone before they reached us.

"They killed my sister," I eventually said, the sound strange after that heavy silence. And strange for altogether more painful reasons. I knew it didn't matter to say, but I felt like I had to explain why I'd turned the Loop on my own people.

"Ecker did. Three days ago. When the fleet started moving toward Bastion. And I knew that even if we stopped Halgard from destroying the city, they'd return to Earth. They'd be more desperate. More angry. And more sisters would die." I glanced up at Toris and Kuma. "More daughters. More mothers and fathers. It had to end. Both ways."

"I'm sorry you had to do that," Toris said, still looking at the ground. "You shouldn't have had to make that choice. But...you don't have to carry the burden of it alone. We'll help you."

"Damn right," Kuma added with a sniff. At the mention of daughters, I'd seen tears instantly wet his eyes.

I scoffed. "I appreciate the offer implied there, but I don't think anyone on Earth would be particularly interested in the Moonbreaker being their neighbor."

"It's a different Earth," Toris said. "And it'll be especially different with the war over. That was all that was propping up the last institutions keeping the world from becoming what most of us were already living. The last economies and governments will topple, and we'll adapt to a new life: one where we support and serve one another rather than fear and exploit each other. Where we live with peace and purpose."

"Sounds too easy."

Kuma chuckled. "Oh, it's not. But that's the heart of it. And it's taken centuries to get here." He shrugged. "It may be hard at first. I wouldn't exactly lead with your resume when you introduce yourself. But if we're going to truly live by our words, by the Compact we'll all be signing, then there needs to be a place for everyone."

Toris leaned forward, and I looked up to meet his eyes. I almost recoiled, so intently were they staring into me. "*Especially* for those who gave up their own home to save it," Toris said, and those words sank into my heart. That's what I'd done. I'd done it for all of them, flawed as they were. Because they at least deserved the chance to be better, to live without the war sharpening them into that hateful and hypocritical society. "And who saved ours. You're a hero, Alis."

I looked away, partly because I didn't know what to say—and calling me a hero had very much replaced that assurance with discomfort—and partly because I couldn't hold that gaze any longer. The sun shone off what little remained of the glass of Stickney's dome, where all this had started. With Monalua and her people standing defiant.

The people of Stickney made their home in that harsh environment because they didn't quite have a place anywhere else. Not down on the planet in Bastion, who had ostracized them. And not from Earth, who was little more than an ancestor, their family and other loved ones abandoning that rock for another. They'd tried to build something in Stickney that they couldn't find elsewhere. They may have planted their roots in Bastion's Sphere, but they couldn't assimilate to it. They'd brought their own cultures and values with them. They weren't spreading rot. They were resilient. They were committed. They stood for each other, and in front of each other when the enemy—when I—came knocking.

"That's what I want to build," I said without looking away from the viewport. Toris and Kuma both looked up at me. I didn't mean to say that out loud, but my conviction was strong enough that I couldn't hold it back. "I want to build a place that the people here could have called home. A place for people who have been pushed out of other homes, who aren't sure of their place, who just want to live without submitting themselves to a power that'll do nothing more than use them." I looked at Toris, who had on that sly, sideways smile, as if that's exactly what he'd hoped I'd say.

"You can't build something like that here," I said. "I hope that changes one day, but it won't right now. Can we really build it on Earth?"

Toris' smile spread wider, from satisfaction to the sign of a deep-rooted happiness. A hope. "Yes. We can. Together."

CHAPTER THIRTY-ONE

TORIS

A SHAPE SHOT BY from the north, swooping up Alis just before impact, so close that their hoverboard scraped across the solar panels. I pulled up to follow, my board lurching beneath me as it struggled to keep up with my demands. My heart raced, but I still held my breath, the tears blurring my vision, my body still frozen in that final moment, when it should have all ended.

I slowed down as Alis' hero did. No. Her heroine.

She'd pulled her black hair back from her face. Even after only a few days without seeing her, she looked different. She looked like Mom.

Navi.

"You...I..." I stuttered as I nudged my board closer to them. Navi held Alis in her arms, who stared up at her savior with as much surprise as I did.

"Can you stand?" Navi asked. Her arms were shaking. "And don't tell Vic; she keeps saying I'm neglecting my arms."

"I...here," I said, reaching out to take Alis. I brought her into my arms, which were shaking for altogether different reasons. Her closeness bloomed spring to the winter that had frozen me over as I watched her fall. I helped her stand on the board behind me. Her mag-boots would engage, but the connection wasn't as secure as mine. Kuma would need to grab us.

But she was alive.

And Navi...

"How are you here?" I asked. "I sent a message to you, but I—"

"Toris," she said, and in her tone I could sense the weight the last couple days had placed on her, too, "we started preparing to leave as soon as we got the report that you'd crashed. It took some time to get Vic's ship from the Dandelion."

She put her hands on her hips like she was about to scold me, but her lips just folded inward as tears came to her eyes. "I thought I'd lost you. I thought I'd lost...everyone. I..." She sniffed. "I have so much I want to say. It's all I've been thinking about the last couple days. And I know this isn't the place, but

I'll start with this: I thought I was putting the community first. I thought I was living up to the Compact, to the promises we made. I've been so afraid of failing those promises and starting us on a road to becoming Bastion again. But as soon as you left with...As soon as you went to bury Cixin and find Alis, I hated myself for what I'd said. In exiling you, I was breaking the most important community. I thought...that maybe family lines dissolved in this community, that we all become a family. And that's partly true, but I was treating it more like a replacement for those connections, not an evolution of them. I...sorry, I'm rambling." She took a short breath and shook her head, and for a moment I saw the sister I'd grown up with, before she'd started bearing the pressures of the de facto leader-in-all-but-name of Orilla. "I'm sorry. I'm so sorry. I'm sorry I exiled you, but more than that, I'm sorry that I didn't help you, that I didn't do more to understand you." She turned to Alis and took another deep breath. "And Alis, I...I don't even know where to start with you, either. You've been my sister for longer than I've accepted, but I hope I can become the sister you deserve."

"Navi," I said, wishing I could bring her into a hug so tight we'd both crack something. "Thank you. I have more I need to say, too. I have my own apologies to make. But you've more than made restitution. I...you saved Alis. 'Thank you' can't contain how much gratitude I feel. I owe you everything."

"That's the point, Toris," Navi said with a soft smile as a tear ran down her cheek. "You owe me nothing." She wiped the tear away and regained her composure. "So how do we end this? Who's in the Aegis?"

All three of us turned toward the smoking wreckage of the broken ad projector, half of it still hovering as the rest fell toward the city. The *Lycan* wasn't falling with it. Was it tangled in the still-hanging wreckage? Or was it lurking in the smoke, keeping within the shadow of the treeline?

"Teah," I responded. "Alis' sister. She's the one behind all this, Nav. The Wolf. Cixin. Everything."

"Your sister?" she asked Alis. "You said she was..."

"Yeah," Alis said. "Turns out Admiral Halgard tricked me. And she's to blame for the Wolf, too."

"Of course she is," I countered, "but she's not to blame for forcing you to turn. Teah is."

"And I'm to blame for nearly killing her at the Battle of the Loop," she snapped, and I clamped my mouth shut. "*We're* to blame for leaving her alone to watch my father die. WE'RE..." she trailed off as her volume escalated. "We're the catalyst for almost everything she's gone through. Of course she made her own choices, and we'll hold her accountable for that. But we need to be accountable, too."

Her words brought me back to Kuma on the dark streets the night before. *We're no better than a taxi service. We can do more.*

We could end the cycles.

I'd pressed the button that had destroyed the Loop. Not Alis. I'd shredded the shield that kept the violent universe at bay. I'd done it for Earth. I'd done it for Alis, even if I was still figuring out my feelings for her in that moment. Regardless of all that, my decision had killed Teah's Father. Alis' father. And who knew how many more.

I hadn't understood...there had to be some price to pay...

But I shouldn't have decided for them.

"Kuma?" I asked. "Can you give us a hand?"

The *Harriet* was already circling back from its attack on the Aegis. It fired its thrusters and came to a steady hover beside us. The airlock door opened. Vic's starship—a much smaller, sleeker craft with thin wings that tapered out and back from the cockpit almost like a stingray—pulled up above the *Harriet*.

"I'll go get her," I said. "We'll bring her back to Orilla, and we'll figure all this out." Navi poorly suppressed a wince at the thought of bringing a Bastionite agent back to our haven—a haven I'd already disturbed with the ghosts of the war.

"No, I should do it," Alis said as I nudged us closer to the *Harriet*. "Let me borrow your board. She'll—"

"You should go together," Navi said. She hovered into the *Harriet* and disengaged her mag-boots from her board, then gestured with both hands from Alis to the board. "Neither of you should go in alone. We'll be your backup."

"I..." Alis started, then she stepped off my board onto the starship and hugged Navi. Navi's eyes widened, her arms rigid at her sides, before she softened and wrapped them around Alis. "Thank you," Alis said. "Thank you," she repeated as she pulled back.

"We'll be here," Navi said as Alis stepped onto the board and hopped out to hover beside me. "Don't be stupid."

I smiled and shrugged, finding the whole idea stupid anyway, however necessary it was. My board sputtered again as we accelerated away from the hovering starships toward the column of smoke. Alis jerked her head to one side, and she went one direction around the smoke while I went the other. The fact that Teah hadn't leaped out and tried to either kill or subdue us meant that she was either hiding or so badly damaged that she couldn't move.

As we rounded the smoke, we found the latter.

The *Sanguine Lycan* had fallen once more, the symbol of Bastion shattered again by the forces it felt inferior. Kuma's strike had sent the Aegis through the damaged ad projector and into one of the wind turbines. Teah had crashed through one of the turbine's walls and tangled within the blades, which were still trying to spin, biting deeper into the armor. The mithril was largely untouched, but one blade had found a weak point in the neck joint and buried itself there, causing the head to loll to one side. The bottom of the Aegis was mostly destroyed, thanks to the battering the Genesis Gardens starfighters gave it. One of the legs was completely gone, severed mid-thigh. The other was twitching, foot gone and exposed wires and hydraulics smoking beneath the armor. The Aegis' arms were tangled in the blades, protected by the mithril, but locked in place.

Alis approached first. I winced as we hovered closer, staring at the turbine blades. If one came loose...it would be an anticlimactic but no less painful way to die after all we'd been through that day.

But the blades continued struggling against the armor as we came under the shadow of the turbine's ceiling and the Aegis arm trapped above us. The entrance to the cockpit was still open, smoke wafting from within. Alis stopped at the edge of the door, peeked in, then hovered inside. I put my hand on my solarblade hilt and followed.

The cockpit sparked across its broken systems. Small fires snapped here and there, the screens all black. Even the emergency lighting flickered. The seat was empty.

Teah lay against the opposite side of the cockpit on her side, a line of blood running down her cheek from somewhere beneath her black hair. Between the crackle of the fires and the sizzle of the electricity, Alis drew in a sharp, worried breath. She dismounted from her board and ran across the cockpit, sliding to her knees before her sister.

In that moment, as much as my anger toward Teah threatened to conquer all other feelings, I loved Alis even more. Her sister had sewn misery into her life for over a decade. She had every excuse to hate Teah as I did, and yet...

Alis had seen what second chances could do. Maybe I hadn't quite learned the same lesson.

"Teah!" Alis brought her face close to Teah's, leaning her head to one side to feel for breath. "She's alive." She glanced over the cockpit. "The mag-restraints

344

must have failed. They should have held onto the sync suit." Alis leaned back and studied the injury on the side of her head. "We need to get her home. We can help her."

I took a breath, knowing that was coming. We'd be bringing not only the Wolf back to Orilla, but its master as well. Or we could remove that risk in that moment. Let her die with the *Lycan*. She'd already said we couldn't do anything to stop the Wolf. She wasn't of any use...

Use. Now who sounded like the Bastionite?

Ashamed at even the thought, I took my hand off the solarblade hilt and stepped up to Alis' side. "Kuma, can you come closer? The *Lycan* crashed into a turbine on the other side of that smoke. We're bringing aboard another...passenger."

After a pause, Kuma responded: "*Wouldn't be the first time, eh brother?*"

The smoke outside the cockpit blew away as the *Harriet*'s thrusters brought it close, sunlight reflecting off its hull into the Aegis.

"I've got her," Alis said. She crouched and brought her sister into her arms, then she stood, Teah's head rolling to lie against Alis' chest. I grabbed her board and followed. The sunlight off the hull made Alis a silhouette stepping through some divine gate as she carried Teah from the metal body that had broken them both.

Chapter Thirty-Two

Toris

The sun was beginning its descent when we arrived at Wolfhome.

The cabin lay ahead and below, looking over the forested valley and the sheer gray cliffs that framed it, towers more majestic than any of the skyscrapers of Babylon could emulate. In the distance, a waterfall spilled over one of those cliffs, the sunset splashing the waters orange and pink.

Suspended between the *Harriet*'s forks, held by the cargo ship's magnets, were the remains of the *Sanguine Lycan*. Genesis Gardens wouldn't be happy with that, and they'd likely try to hunt it down, but Alis and I agreed that we couldn't leave an Aegis with Carivant, nor allow it to get back to Bastion. The Cloak would prevent Genesis Gardens from tracking us, and Vic and Alis were going to ensure Carivant hadn't planted anything in the *Lycan* during its reconstruction that would allow them to follow us. Navi had suggested dumping the Aegis into the sea, but I wasn't so sure. That mithril could do a lot for the community. Or, on the other hand, a rebuilt Aegis on our side would be a powerful defender in the face of whatever threats came.

Kuma fired landing thrusters, and we dropped onto a stone ridge a few hundred yards from the cabin. Vic had flown ahead with Navi.

I patted Kuma on the shoulder as I stood. We hadn't spoken much on the flight home—cut down to less than an hour in a starship—both of us lost in our thoughts.

"Tor," Kuma said as I turned to leave the bridge and join Alis and the still-unconscious Teah in the cabin below. I turned as Kuma stood. "I know you probably don't want to hear it, but for all her lies, there really is something broken in Teah. Just like—"

"In Alis, I know. But we can't just make excuses based on that, Kuma. We both know that when you break, you *choose* how you build yourself up again. Look at what Alis built. There's no comparison."

"Choice is a part of it, sure, part of it's luck."

"Luck?"

"Yeah. Like the luck of a desperate woman barely making it on the last refugee ship, captained by two people who understood second chances."

"Look, I get what you're saying, but you give us too much credit. That's Alis. She almost died defying those orders at Mwezi, because she was so determined to do what was right. Maybe we helped her work through it all. We gave her a place to go. But *Alis* chose who she wanted to be. And so did Teah." I held up both hands when Kuma opened his mouth to continue. "Either way, what happens next is up to Alis, in the end. It's her sister. Her family. Whatever we do, we'll do better. I promise. I heard you last night. Really. And I'm trying."

Kuma took a breath, a short one that expanded his chest and came out his nose, the kind of breath that told me he had more to say, but he was going to let it rest. He closed his eyes and nodded. I thought back to the night before, when I'd seen Kuma and Lana-Teah sitting so close together, and that morning, when he'd watched her leave the ship. There were feelings deeper than sympathy there, and he was likely feeling a betrayal altogether different from mine.

"I'll catch up with you tonight," I said, turning to climb down from the bridge. "I have an idea. For being more. And I kind of hate it, which means you'll love it."

Kuma chuckled. "Your taxi awaits. Good luck."

***

"I'm not taking her down there," Alis said, the still-unconscious Teah in her arms. I was bent over, lifting the corner of the rug to reveal the trapdoor to the basement where we'd chained up the Wolf.

Where I'd chained up Alis.

Despite the many reasons I could think of to chain up Teah, I dropped the rug, my stomach turning.

Alis carried her sister into the bedroom and laid her down. We'd done what we could to treat her injuries while on the *Harriet*, but her injuries were extensive—and deep. The gash on her head went almost to her skull, and was likely the primary source of her comatose state. She'd also broken her arm—which Alis had splinted using a kit we kept on the ship—and sustained severe burns to which we'd applied ointment and bandages. Treating those reminded me of caring for the point-blank plasma shot Alis had taken from Commander Godwin during the Battle of the Loop.

Despite it all, Teah was alive. Her heart rate had leveled out during the flight and with the help of some painkillers. Alis couldn't tell whether the blast that had thrown her against the wall had also forcefully desynced her. We wouldn't know until Teah woke up. Then again, it would be difficult to distinguish the pain of a mindjack malfunction from her other head injury.

Alis gently closed the door to the bedroom and stood in the middle of the living room, hands on her hips, staring out the door. I'd taken a seat on the old couch, sinking into the well-used cushion but feeling anything but comfortable.

"She never tried to kill us," Alis said, still staring out the door.

"*What?*" I asked, eyes going so wide they must have been bulging out of my head. Then, at the sigh and glance from Alis, I repeated in a much gentler tone: "What? She's been trying to get you to kill me for ten years. I'm only here because none of the victims Halgard put in your mind are killers."

"I know. But not today. She could have smashed us with that Aegis. She could have crushed you rather than just your board. She could have fired missiles that took care of us both. At any time. Hell, she could have just *shot* us after she turned me, while we were distracted. She had every chance."

"You would have died if Navi hadn't caught you. And Teah would have watched. That's just one instance." I leaned my elbows on my knees and clasped my hands together. "I understand why you're thinking this. I understand why you're trying to...find explanations. And I love you for looking for the good. I do. But...you two took different paths and became different people."

"And I set her on that path. We both did. We have to take accountability, Tor."

"Yeah," I said with a sigh. "Kuma said the same thing. But it's one thing to take accountability and help people who are in greater need because of our choices—which I can get behind—and another thing entirely to dismiss what she's done. Cixin died because of her. The Wolf is her monster, and—"

"The Wolf is *MY* monster," Alis shouted, jabbing at her chest. "It's me. No matter how you try to separate the two. It's a part of me, and as much as you want to kill it, that may not happen. And," some of her anger deflated with a heavy breath, "don't look at me like that. Of course I want it dead, too. But it may not be that simple. I'm not dismissing what she's done. We're going to deal with that. She used me. She hurt me. Hurt us. Locking her up or...hurting her or whatever you want to do isn't going to change any of that. We need to get at the root problems, Tor. Then we'll worry about justice. I need you to respect that."

"I..." I held her gaze as long as I could, as intense and unstoppable as a firestorm, until I had to look away. "Of course I respect that. And I don't want to...well, no, I can't lie. Part of me does want her to feel some modicum of the pain she's caused you. That's the Wolf in *me*, I guess."

Alis stepped up to where I sat on the couch and crouched in front of me, taking my hands in hers. "I understand. This is...it's all too much. It's so complicated. That's the life we built, isn't it? And just like we did that together, for better and for worse, we'll navigate this together, too."

I smiled softly, the firestorm in Alis suddenly contracting to a crackling campfire that pushed away the chill. But then her eyes suddenly clenched shut and her hand flew to her head, fingers tangling in her hair as her knuckles went white.

"Guess she's awake," Alis said through clenched teeth.

I tensed, watching Alis, waiting for the tell-tale signs of her turn. Was it too soon? She'd only just turned that morning, and the Wolf always seemed to go into some kind of remission. But this was uncharted territory. We'd never had to worry about another turn until the next cycle, when Mars aligned with Earth.

Alis stood, still clutching at her head. "Enough," she snapped and threw open the door to the bedroom. Teah was sitting up in her bed, bandage wrapped around her head and smaller bandages covering the burns across her body. One dominated her left cheek. In her eyes blazed that same Caliday fire. "ENOUGH!" Alis grabbed her sister by the shoulders of her shirt and threw her off the bed, sending her crashing into the wall.

I shot up from the couch, but Alis held up a hand for me to stay put.

"We saved your life!" Alis shouted.

Teah crouched where she'd crumpled against the wall, one eye closed as she cringed from the injuries that must have screamed as Alis threw her. Then, with an animal roar, Teah lunged from where she crouched, springing toward her sister with her metal arm outstretched, the other still in a sling. Her shoulder slammed into Alis' gut and knocked her back onto the bed. Alis used the momentum to roll backward and toss Teah into the opposite wall.

This time, when Teah staggered to her feet, Alis was standing strong on the other side of the bed, tears rolling down her cheeks. This wasn't a fight, this was the most primal violence, the outburst of emotions so powerful, so all-consuming, that they couldn't remain trapped in the mind. Alis knew this, too. Her face had gone from angry to pitiful.

"You done?" Alis asked. "Because I am. You used me long enough. Bastion's used me long enough. You wanted me to suffer? Mission accomplished. So if you want to move toward something more productive, let's talk. Otherwise, we may as well kill each other right now. Is that what you want? Because I don't think you do."

Teah stared up at her sister, face in a half-snarl, chest heaving with angry, desperate breaths. Every few huffs, her eyes would narrow just slightly. She was trying to ride those waves of pain. It was a smart move on Alis' part; she hadn't been aimlessly violent. Teah's head injury would already hamper her ability to use her mindjack. If Alis could exacerbate that effect, she'd totally prevent Teah from drawing out the Wolf.

"Who's waiting in orbit?" Alis prodded when Teah didn't respond. "Who were you going to rendezvous with?" I frowned, surprised, as I stepped closer to the bedroom and leaned against the doorframe. That rendezvous wasn't even in the back of my mind, but I wasn't a retired soldier. Alis was thinking about the threats to our home. Her home. If there was a force up there that would come looking for Teah, we needed to know.

Teah didn't answer, her jaw clenching beneath her cheeks as she glared at Alis through fallen strands of sweaty, black hair.

"Why didn't they support you? Even a light cruiser could have picked off those starfighters from orbit. And you'd need a ship at least that size to transport the *Lycan* back to Bastion."

No answer. Not even a blink. I wasn't surprised. Teah was a pruner. Interrogating her wouldn't go far. But I had the impression this wasn't an interrogation. Alis was going somewhere.

"Maybe you were meeting on Luna?" Alis folded her arms. "Or, maybe, you weren't meeting at all."

Teah blinked.

"Because if Bastion really wanted to pull the *Lycan* out of that tower, they wouldn't have sent just one pruner. Sure, they'd want to keep it quiet, but they'd send at least a small squad. So, my guess is that you've gone rogue. You came here yourself. But why? Just to hurt us? Or was this all to prove something? Prove that you could pilot the Aegis? Become the hero I never was?"

Teah scoffed, her first reaction of the conversation, much more angry than humorous. "Of course you'd think it was about you."

"You've spent the past ten years trying to make our lives miserable," Alis said with a raised eyebrow. "I'd say it's more than fair to assume it's been about us."

"No, it's not," Teah snapped, then she went silent. But it didn't matter; Alis was breaking through. Teah may have been a pruner, but she was still a Bastionite first, and Bastionites took pride in their purpose. They were brainwashed with it since birth: to contribute to the prosperity and security of their society.

And she was still human. If anyone was going to breach her walls, of course it would be Alis, even after everything.

"Justice, then? That's what you said earlier. Justice for Bastion, for the end of the war, for...Father." Alis shook her head. "That's the propaganda answer. The Ecker answer. There's something deeper you care about. Is it revenge? You don't know what to do with all that grief, so you took it out on us?"

Teah's glare deepened. "You have no clue what I care about. Stop acting like you understand me. You don't know me, so this condescension isn't doing anything but make you look more arrogant."

Alis paused, then sighed. "You're right. I don't know you. After Mwezi, I wondered if I ever did. You enabled Ecker and the rest of the military to go against every principle we were fighting for. Were you trying to prove something? Or did you never actually believe those things? What Mom—"

"Don't."

Alis could have pushed, boring into that pressure point until Teah exploded with...anything. But, of course, she didn't. "That's why I left. I imagined Mom seeing what I'd done at Stickney. I imagined justifying it in all the ways Ecker did, and feeling like none of them would earn me anything but that silent disappointment. Then when we...when they manipulated the vote? And dominated mindjacks? I started to realize I wasn't just doing it for Mom. She'd given me the foundation—the same one she gave you—but that went against everything I wanted to stand for. That wasn't the Bastion I wanted to build." I felt the pressure of tears in my own eyes. Alis may not have shown the same emotion, but I knew that she'd wanted to say those words to Teah for a decade. She'd left most of Bastion behind, but the thought of her family thinking she was a traitor, that she cared for Earth more than them, ate at her. "I know Ecker spun his stories. I know I became the traitor he could pin everything on. He made sure to let me know that Father knew. That—"

Something softened in Teah's face. "I told him you weren't."

"What?"

"Father. I didn't want him to suffer more than he already was. I told him you died on Mwezi. That Ecker didn't want to take the responsibility of the Moonbreaker dying under his orders, so he turned you into a traitor instead. He believed me. He died thinking you were a hero. Never shut up about it. Didn't matter that I was the one there."

Something in Alis deflated. Her arms dropped and her shoulders fell, her head tilting as she looked down at her sister, who in turn looked at the floor. The pillar of sunlight streaming through the window over Teah's head was fading, the painted hues mixing into a light gray. "I know it's too little, too late, but I am sorry. If I'd known you were alive...no, even then I should have checked on Father. But I was sure I'd just make him suffer more, too. The traitor returned to disappoint her family even more. I didn't want to risk the Wolf hurting him, either. We understood it even less, then."

Teah blinked and looked around the room, more of the anger slowly fading. "I recognize this cabin. It's where you came before the planets' aligned. So you wouldn't hurt anyone, right?" Then she turned to me, and it surprised me so much that I jerked back, the frustration and betrayal simmering back up as our eyes met. "But if that was the case, why did *you* come?"

I scowled. "If you have to ask that question, then you haven't been paying very close attention. I'd never let Alis go through that alone."

"Right. You'd just chain her in the cellar?"

I snorted. "Of all people, you're sure as hell not in a place to—"

Alis placed a hand on my chest. I didn't realize I'd taken a step into the room toward Teah. Letting the rest of my retort collapse into a frustrated breath out of my nose, I backed up to the doorframe once more.

Teah cocked her head. "Aw, I see who the real dog is in this relationship."

I didn't rise to that one, instead only rolling my eyes.

"You should have stayed home," Teah said, continuing to pull on her thread. "You gave the Wolf a target, especially when you fought back. Really, we wouldn't have had much to experiment with if you weren't there. So thanks for the help." She winked in a way that reminded me too much of Alis. I shivered.

She was continuing her mission, burdening me with more guilt, trying to pull me deeper into misery. I hated how well it was working. Still, I resisted totally rising to the bait. "We didn't understand what was happening. I wasn't going to leave her alone. You don't need to tell me I could have done things differently. Whatever guilt you're trying to place on me is feathers compared to what I've put on myself."

Teah adopted a smug look that likely preempted another retort, but Alis held up a hand. "All right. We're going in circles. So was that your mission? To complete your experiments on me? And the Aegis was a bonus? Your opportunity to climb the ladder?"

Teah clamped her mouth shut again.

Alis stared at her sister, waiting for her to respond, then threw up her hands in surrender. "Fine. If you don't want to talk, then we'll bring you home empty-handed. We'll show them how you failed to secure what I'm sure was a very valuable investment. Not only that, your incompetence got that investment destroyed."

Teah's eyes widened almost imperceptibly at that. Her mouth opened slightly then closed, then opened and closed again.

Pity softened Alis' face again. "Teah." In that tone, I could tell she'd figured it out. She'd used it enough on me whenever I'd hid my feelings. "This wasn't just your opportunity, was it? You didn't come here under orders. When did they relieve you?"

Several emotions flashed across Teah's face. First, she cringed, as if Alis had jabbed one of her injuries—of course, she had, an injury deep inside, calloused but still seeping pain. Then, her anger returned, but she was glaring out into some middle distance, not directly at Alis. That anger slowly collapsed, and the mask returned, her face mostly impassive. But not totally. The mask was cracked, just like her.

"It's why you don't have a squad, or any actual way home. Was it after the Loop? You were punished for surviving?"

I ground my teeth together, some of that pity Alis felt for Teah trickling in.

At first, I didn't think Teah would respond. She just stared at nothing, but then she responded, and I knew that she had her own words she'd waited ten years to say. "My pod was damaged when the *Fang* exploded. I...thought that'd be it. The thrusters couldn't take me to Bastion, so I dropped onto the Tharsis Montes. Transmitters weren't working. When I got out of the pod, the Loop was dropping out of orbit. Like a meteor shower around the entire planet. I almost stayed on top of that mountain. The snow was ten feet deep. I just fell into it and watched one of the modules from the Loop drop onto Cresthaven." She shrugged. "Wasn't a big city. Few thousand." She glanced up at me, and it was my turn to cringe. "Most of them were artists. Trying to escape the Bastion elite. More like Earthers than Bastionites. No survivors."

I couldn't hold her gaze any longer and looked at the ground.

"I lost my hand trying to get down from the mountains." She flexed her metal hand, the one she'd torn the skin off. "And then I walked."

"You *walked*? To Bastion? That's hundreds of miles. Why didn't you call someone?"

"I tried. The networks were chaos. Everything was chaos. People turned on each other. Terrorists took it as an opportunity to seize some cities."

"Terrorists," I said, knowing exactly how this Bastionite framing worked. "You mean people tired of squirming under your boot?"

Teah shrugged. "When I got back to command, I found out they had been receiving my transmissions. They'd just ignored them. The chain of command was blown to hell. They didn't know what to do with me for a while. They kept me on base, said I couldn't go home. Couldn't see Father. They were struggling to keep the public under control. Word was getting out about Mwezi, and after that loss with the Loop...The only thing that kept me around was you." She looked up at Alis, that deep anger showing through the mask for a moment. "They wanted to keep experimenting on mindjack control. More subtle than what we did on Mwezi. Your case was especially fascinating to them, because they didn't have to be subtle. You became a totally different person. It took a while to understand what was going on." Teah waved those details away. She'd already told me. "But I understood you. Your mind. So I was an asset. Until I wasn't." Teah scratched around one of the bandages on her arm. "New administration came into power. They tried to restart the dynamo in the core. The details were top secret, but they didn't want to waste the resources on creating another Loop that *terrorists* could destroy." She jerked her head toward me when she said "terrorist." I ignored it, more because I was finally starting to accept that...maybe I was.

An entire city? How many had the Loop fallen on?

"They blamed us. They went back to the Battle of the Loop and the failure of the military of the time to defend the planet. Took attention away from their own failure with the core. I thought everyone would see through it, that my superiors wouldn't obey the orders. They did. There was a hearing. I was discharged. They used you against me," she lifted her eyebrows toward Alis. "And they've been watching me ever since. I'm a risk." She shrugged. "I keep waiting for the day they decide I'm not worth the resources, and I just don't wake up."

Alis took a step back and leaned against the opposite wall of the room. The pillar of setting sunlight that had been shining through the window was gone. Night was nearly on us.

"And all that while you had to...take care of Father."

Teah's silence was enough of an answer.

Alis stared at her for a moment, tears welling in the bottom of her eyes. Then she sniffed, blinked, and said, "You keep saying 'they.'"

"What?"

"Not 'we.' 'They.' Separate." Alis shook her head. "I started noticing it when I left. Started doing the same thing. We grew up with Bastion inextricably woven into our identity. We were all small parts of one great whole. We were building Bastion. That gave us purpose, and it was hard to imagine ourselves outside of that 'we.' Until they push us out of it. Until they lean too hard on that identity and it collapses, the same values we held to revealing what they really want: control. At any cost. We weren't building Bastion for us. They were building their Bastion—through us."

Teah's jaw was working again. She didn't want to listen, but Alis was getting through.

"So." Alis said, resuming her questioning. "This was your opportunity, just not in the way I thought. You knew about Bastion's deal with Genesis Gardens to rebuild the Aegis. You thought you could bring it back and win their trust again. Then what was our part? Just continuing the experiment? Bring more results back home?"

Teah finally looked back up at Alis, eyes narrowing, considering whether to continue her obstinance. But Alis was through the mask. "I needed him," she jerked her head toward me "to get me into Genesis Gardens. We had enough intel to know he could do it. For that, I needed a reason for him to go back there. What better reason than you?"

"And Cixin?" I asked. "How..." Then it clicked. "You needed to get me out to Farstead. To bring you back. You couldn't use any Bastion assets to get you out here. You used him. Then you killed him."

"Technically," Teah said, fake-cringing, then leaning her head toward Alis. "She did."

"He was one of you," I responded. "He was an innocent man trying to get away from the same system that betrayed you. That betrays all its people from the moment they're born. The same system that teaches you lives are meant to be used. So you used him." Now Teah couldn't hold *my* gaze. The mask cracked, and for a moment the guilt she was holding at bay seeped through.

"Why *did* you do it?" Alis asked. "And don't give me the bullshit answer. Why were you so desperate to keep serving?"

Teah licked her lips, cringed from her head pain, then she let out the deep sigh of someone carrying too heavy a weight. She opened her mouth, drawing in a breath to answer, then closed it again and released the breath in a frustrated huff.

Then she closed her eyes and answered in a quiet voice: "If I'm not a soldier, if I'm not a pilot, if I'm not even a Bastionite, then what am I? And if none of what

I did…none of it," she looked up at her sister, "was actually building the Bastion we were promised, then…" The mask fell. Tears shimmered. "What am I?"

Alis moved away from the wall toward Teah. "I want to help you find out. I felt the same way, and I had Toris and Kuma to help me. You…you have me."

"Why?" A single tear fell.

"You're my sister," Alis responded, shrugging as if it were the only, obvious answer. Then she looked down and bit her bottom lip as her own tears came. "I…when I thought Ecker killed you, it opened a pit that I've been trying to fill ever since. I haven't. And you made it worse." She snapped that last bit, releasing some of the anger she'd been holding back better than I. "You can't hide your actions behind Bastion. I don't forgive you, but I do understand you. And I want to help you." She wiped the tears off her cheeks. "Not because you deserve it, but because it's right. And because I have accountability of my own to stop running from." She looked at me. "We both do."

Be more.

After a moment of staring at each other through tear-swollen eyes, Alis got on her knees before her sister, hesitated with hands in the air as if holding an invisible box, then wrapped her arms around Teah. At first, Teah glared, though I don't think it was directed at Alis. Tears fell down her cheeks, but she didn't hug her sister back. After a moment, she lifted her head and set her chin on Alis' shoulder. The closest embrace she'd give.

Alis let go and stood, wiping her face again. She turned to me. I didn't know what she needed, what she wanted, but I knew what I needed to say, what we needed to do. I needed to stop running, too.

"We've been helping the people who choose to come back to Earth," I said, folding my arms and staring at the ground, "to become part of our community. But some can't leave. Or maybe they don't know they have that choice. We act like we're helping people, that we have such an open community, but that's only if they join us. I've still been thinking by borders, and who we help shouldn't start and stop where the Spheres do." I stepped over to where Teah sat against the wall and held out my hand. "So let's go help them. Maybe you'll help yourself along the way."

Teah stared up at my hand, then up into my eyes.

And Laniteah Aurora Caliday—soldier, pruner, broken sister—clasped my hand, and I helped her to her feet.

***

"Tor, wait."

I stopped, halfway back to the *Harriet*, its ventral lights shining on the stone beneath it. Teah was already stepping into the airlock, holding onto the hull with her unbroken arm.

Alis stood in the long grass, the rising moon bright behind her. She looked down when I met her eyes.

"I'm sorry. I thought...one way or another, this would end with the Wolf dying."

My heart sinking for her, I stepped closer, taking her hands in mine. "It's okay. We may still find an end. Maybe on Bastion—"

"No," Alis said, shaking her head vigorously. "You heard her. It's part of me. I'm broken. I'm..."

"No, you're not. I love you, and—"

"I know. I know you love me. Despite the Wolf. Despite this curse that I. Can't. Cure. How long can you live with it? How long before..."

"No." And I hated that I'd always added that condition. I understood now why she'd always cringed when I said it. I'd made her feel like something was hindering my love, something she couldn't change. No more.

I took her face in my hands and pulled her close until our foreheads were touching. Then I closed my eyes, breathed her in, and said with all my soul:

"I love you, Wolf and all."

I pulled back just enough to look her in the eyes. "And I'm so sorry it took me too long to assure you of that."

Alis searched my eyes as fresh tears glistened in hers. I felt them in my own.

Then she grabbed my face and pulled me toward her in a kiss that silenced the world, that pulled my heart toward hers like gravity, that sparked between us like something new.

And, in the end, that killed the Wolf.

CHAPTER THIRTY-THREE

TORIS

ALISTELLA PAREIDES CALIDAY—MOONBREAKER, TRAITOR, hero—crouched atop her hoverboard as she hurtled between buildings. And as I'd done in so many ways for ten years, I followed.

It'd rained the night before, leaving the air heavier and smelling like paradise, the ivy growing over the skyscrapers glistening in the morning light.

Alis banked around a corner, and I followed. We shot out of downtown and over the fields. They swayed with bounties of crops, automatons and volunteers moving among them. Children waved up at us as we passed overhead. Down the slope, the Corcoran Sea shimmered, its towers of flower-like solar panels facing the setting sun.

Home.

Alis leaned back and launched into the sky. Her board resisted for a moment before a burst of light and power launched Alis toward the shredded clouds of the night's storm. Having lost her old board in the conflict with Teah, she rode an even older board that hadn't been operable for at least five years. She and Vic had repaired it in the weeks after we returned to Orilla.

I pulled my goggles down over my eyes as we flew up through a low-hanging cloud, Alis laughing as the cold water clung to us like the grasp of a ghostly hand. Bright sunlight immediately started drying us as we ascended higher toward one of the city's many floating wind turbines. The cold bit through my clothes the higher we went. Alis didn't seem to notice at all.

Once we were just above the turbine, droplets of water still clinging to its surface, Alis pivoted and flew sideways over the turbine, brushing her fingertips across its top. I followed, my fingers tracing her path. On the other side of the turbine, we swung our boards around and shot down toward the city. We veered away from downtown, away from the core of the city and toward the field where the journey had started for me.

We'd torn down the school that had stood in that field, haunted as it was by Bastion's invasion. In its place was a monument, a statue representing what we'd lost—and the new promises we had to keep. It didn't look exactly like Mele, but she was clearly the inspiration: a little girl with a long, thick braid and a flowing dress with flower print. One hand reached for the sky, her hopeful eyes looking upward, one leg stretched behind her in a frozen dance.

Kuma stood at her feet.

We circled around the field, where the *Harriet* sat on its landing gears. Navi and Vic were waiting near the airlock, giving Kuma his space. We'd said goodbye to everyone else at the Hollows the evening before.

I hopped off my hoverboard once we were a foot off the ground and tucked it under my arm. Alis jerked her head toward Kuma as she walked toward Navi and Vic. I watched them both hug her and smiled, that small gesture feeling anything but small. The three of them had been at Wolfhome—without me—during the last cycle. Once we'd returned to Orilla and explained the situation to the rest of the community, they banded together to help Alis. Better understanding her condition enabled us to better help her.

Navi and Vic came with us to Wolfhome, where, when Mars reached its height, Alis turned. Despite the three of us being there, her anger clearly directed at me. After some prodding, we realized she was embodying Idina, but I wasn't able to talk her out of it as I had with Beck.

Instead, I left.

I was taking the shape of the man who'd traumatized Idina, so I countered the memories by removing myself from them. Leaving Alis in that state had raked me with enough anxiety that I stayed up most nights they were gone, but it apparently worked. She hadn't immediately regained full consciousness, but she at least found a quiet peace in Navi's and Vic's presence. They'd explored the valley together, told stories around fires, and ate some of Navi's impressive cooking. Alis was mostly silent, but Navi said she did smile a few times. Even laughed once. Just like I'd helped Beck's memory by giving him the closure he needed, they'd helped Idina. They'd given her friends.

"She'd be proud of you, brother," I said as I stepped up beside Kuma and reached up to put my arm around his broad shoulders. His cheeks were wet with tears, but he acknowledged my words with a smile.

"Sometimes my brain forgets she's gone. I'll hear a laugh and turn for her, or hear a song and want to call her to dance. Even after all this time. My heart never forgets, though. Sometimes I wish it would, when the crater there becomes a pit. But it's better to remember, right?"

He knew it was. He didn't need me to say that. He just needed me. "Of course it is." I squeezed his shoulder.

"Woo," Kuma huffed, wiping the tears from his face. "Sorry. Just wanted to say goodbye. You ready?"

"Hey. Why are you sorry? And we're coming back, all right?"

"Right." He straightened his shoulders, and I removed my hand with a final pat. "Thanks, brother."

"Ha! Keep all those for yourself. You helped me get Alis back, not just physically, but...you helped me be better. Thank you."

"We should just make a recording of that so you can stop saying it so much."

I chuckled as we turned away from the monument—Kuma blowing one last kiss—and walked to the ship. A breeze washed over the field, and I took a deep breath of the sea air and fresh flora. How different would Bastion's air smell?

"She already onboard?" I asked, pointing my chin at the airlock.

"Mm hm," Kuma muttered. He'd experienced his own betrayal, the kind of a deeper trust broken than I'd had with Lana. The weeks since had done little to warm the chill he felt toward her.

"You sure this is the only way you can be a hero?" Navi asked, folding her arms but wearing a soft smile.

"Pretty sure," I said with a chuckle and pulled her in for a hug. "We'll take care of each other. And, remember, we're not going to start a revolution. We're just giving the people who need it a way out." Navi had of course resisted our idea at first, but after hearing our reasoning and learning more about the consequences of our choices at the Battle of the Loop, she accepted our decision.

When I pulled away, she held onto my shoulders. "Anyone who needs a home has one here, okay?"

"Okay," I said, those few words nearly bringing me to tears. "Thank you."

Navi stared into my eyes, coming to the brink of tears of her own, then pulled me in for another, tighter hug. "I love you, Tor."

"I love you, too, Nav."

She sniffed and let go, and I turned to Vic. "Thank you for everything, Vic," I said as I hugged her, too. "Sorry you got roped into all the fun."

"Adventure's good for the soul," she said with a shrug when we pulled away. "I knew what I was signing up for." Navi took her hand, and they shared a smile.

Then Navi's smile dropped, and she summoned her serious, leader-like demeanor. "You promised a report once a week. We'll keep the channel to the *Harriet* open. If there's a gap longer than a month, we're repairing that Aegis and coming to get you."

"Heard," I said with a quick nod.

We stared at each other for an awkward moment before Navi waved toward the airlock. "All right, go on. No one needs to see me cry anymore. Go save another world."

We exchanged final hugs, and Alis and Kuma stepped through the airlock onto the ship. I followed, but then I turned and lingered. The towering sun-flower-shaped solar panels had fully unfurled, catching the sunlight burning through the torn remnants of the night's storm. Another breeze blew across the long grasses, stirring waves across the sea down the slopes.

I closed my eyes and took another breath, wishing I could capture that beauty and carry it with us across the void to a world that couldn't possibly compare.

When I opened my eyes, Navi and Vic were standing halfway behind the ship and the monument, waving. Behind them, it almost looked like Mele was waving goodbye, too.

***

Fire roared against our heat shields as we dropped through the atmosphere. When the flames dissipated, the world opened beneath us. Bastion. Swirling clouds moved over an ocean toward the continent. Near the coast was a trio of mountains. I didn't know much about Bastion's geography, but I knew those were the Tharsis Montes, where Teah had crashed after the Battle of the Loop. Northwest of the Montes stood the tallest mountain in the solar system, proud Olympus Mons. Snow capped almost half the mountain, so high it reached. At the titan's base and climbing up its foothills was the largest city I'd ever seen. If Babylon intended to be a sister to Bastion, it was certainly the little one. I'd glimpsed the city while we were on the Loop, but that didn't do it justice. I almost admired it, the efforts of the Pioneers to carve a place for humanity on that once-barren planet.

If only they hadn't nearly killed Earth on their way out.

"How are you?" I asked, glancing up at Alis where she stood behind my chair. I looked at Teah, who sat behind me, craning her neck to see as much as she could through the viewport. She didn't need her head bandages anymore, but she wore a baggy black sweater with a hood that covered where Orilla's doctors had to cut off hair.

"With what?" Alis responded. "Returning to the home that hates me? With watching only *To the Moon* for three months? With the...'jack?" It was a difficult habit to kick, referring to the Wolf. That kiss at Wolfhome had killed it for me. That connection and acceptance made me realize that separating the condition from Alis to make the struggle against it easier only created a barrier to actually helping Alis. In making a monster of the condition, which was inseparable from Alis, I'd made a monster of her, and I felt more the monster myself.

"Hey!" Kuma exclaimed. "You said you liked it!"

"I did," Alis said, patting him on the shoulder.

"Both. Home and the 'jack," I said.

"I...don't know. I thought I'd been away long enough, separated myself enough, that I'd feel...foreign coming back. But I don't." She sighed as if disappointed. "It's still home."

"And the 'jack?"

"Nothing. Pain's no worse than normal."

I wasn't sure if I should take comfort in that or not. We'd obviously deliberated about whether Alis should return at all, whether it was to great a risk to have her mindjack constantly trying to connect to the Bastion network and tripping her condition. If that wasn't happening, then the condition had bored deeper, wiring into her brain in ways deeper than we could fix with a simple Faraday Shield.

"Good," I said. Focus on the positive. She was there. All of her.

As we dropped through the highest layer of clouds toward the city, I checked the Cloak to ensure we were still displaying a Bastion signature. We were. I wasn't sure how tightly Bastion was restricting space traffic, but we didn't want to chance them firing on an Earther ship without asking questions. Instead, we'd appear to be a harmless Genesis Gardens cargo ship, traveling in from Farstead.

"It's in better shape than I thought," I said.

"What did you expect?" Teah asked with her trademark attitude. During the three months of travel, it had become no more endearing. "Did you happen to notice that hot stuff when we dropped in? That was atmosphere."

I rolled my eyes.

"It'll take a long time for the solar winds to totally strip away the atmosphere," Teah said, with far less sarcasm. "You can't see the damage they cause." Then, in a quieter voice: "Not 'till it's too late."

Kuma and I followed the flight path projected on the viewport, banking east toward the spaceport, extending flaps and fins to shed speed. The air battering the hull was the air of a new planet, air that had never touched the *Harriet*. Air I'd never breathed. I couldn't help but feel a little excited at that, at the feeling of adventure in that new air.

Lines of air traffic criss-crossed between the sleek buildings, a smoother, more uniform architecture than in Babylon. I caught massive walls of projected advertisements, but they weren't as obnoxious as in Babylon, where they constantly flashed in your face. The death throes of capitalism's last stand on Earth.

"That's the Shades," Alis pointed out the port side toward huge metal sails near the bottom of the vast majority of the skyscrapers. Beneath them was darkness with the occasional flicker of light. We'd hoped that we'd return to find the Shades gone, Bastion's plights unifying them, elite and marginalized alike. But ideology so stubborn, with roots so deep, didn't die so easily.

We'd made their difficult lives worse, and we'd driven more there because of our decisions. Now we'd be more than a taxi service. Now we'd help them. Because our community encompassed all Spheres, arms open to any willing to build a better world.

Soon we reached the massive spaceport. The concrete landing pads extended for miles, divided in zones dependent on the size of the ship. We dropped toward our assigned pad, and Kuma fired the ventral thrusters, slowing us down to a crawl until we settled onto our landing gears.

"Welcome home, Calidays," Kuma said as we shut down the engines. The sudden disappearance of the rumbling that had vibrated my bones for three months was jarring, nearly as much as the feeling of true planetary gravity pulling us down again.

And even that heaviness was little relative to the heaviness weighing down the bridge. Alis stared out at her home, the city towering over the spaceport and titanic Olympus Mons casting its shadow over what seemed the whole world. They'd betrayed her, tried to kill her, used her sister against her. And still, she returned. I couldn't imagine everything she was feeling, staring down a wolf of her own.

I stood up as Kuma and Teah descended from the bridge to grab their things. Alis remained, unable to take her eyes off the city.

"I never thought I'd come back," she said. "I certainly never thought I'd come back with you. I mean, you want to talk about wolves, we're in their den, now."

I stepped up beside her, looked out the viewport, and put my hands on my hips. "I don't know. It can't be all bad."

Alis recoiled and scowled at me as if I'd insulted her mother. "Are you sick? Did Teah do something to you?"

I chuckled. "Other than make me want to stick my head into space for a minute just to make my eardrums burst? No. There's something good here. It shaped you, after all."

Alis raised an eyebrow, but her mouth spread wide in a smile like sunrise.

"Yeah, I heard it. That was bad," I said, shaking my head. "We watched way too much of that show. I—"

Alis shut me up by leaning in and placing a gentle kiss on my frozen lips. It was light as snowflake, soft as a whisper. And she smelled like home.

"Still worked, though," I said, unable to keep the heat from rising to my cheeks and ears, even after all this time. I turned back to the viewport. "Do you really think we can make a difference here? Be more?"

"Yes. We can," she said and clasped my hand, grounding me better than gravity ever could, repeating the words I'd said to her when our journey began, their meaning truer than ever. "Together."

ACKNOWLEDGMENTS

I WAS PRETTY DISAPPOINTED in *Star Wars: The Rise of Skywalker.*

Despite that disappointment, as I think about these acknowledgments, I keep coming back to that "I am all the Jedi" line. Because while *Bastion* may be my debut, it's the twelfth novel I've written. And so, a little like Rey, this book has a little of everything that came before, all the lessons learned, the mistakes made, and even some ideas that got scrapped then to be executed better now.

And I, a little like Rey, carry with me all the support, encouragement, and advice of years past. "Thank you" isn't sufficient to communicate the depths of gratitude I have for those who have held up my dream of becoming an author, even when I was too weak or defeated to hold it up myself.

My parents, Tara and Travis Walton, and my brother, Lucas Walton, were the first to support that dream from when I would sit on our dilapidated wooden porch in middle school and write fantasy in a notebook. Thank you, Mom, Pop, and Lucas, for your support through every rejection letter, every moment of doubt, and for always being excellent alpha readers. I well and truly would not be here without you. I'm also immensely grateful to my dad, Travis, who deployed his artistic mastery in creating *Bastion's* cover, and to Lucas, who designed the internal maps and the illustrations on my website. I am in awe of your talent (and you all should be, too; support artists!)

Like Nick carrying the Keaton torch for Schmidt's mom (I really hope people get that reference), my brilliant wife and partner, Lacey Walton, has been a constant source of support, feedback, and guidance through several novels and many (more) rejections and doubts. Thank you, Lacey, for your listening ear, your endlessly empathetic heart, your patience, and for making me feel like I can do anything (and also that in order to do anything, I should probably take care of myself first). Here is where I'll also thank my angelic daughters, Bryn and Mara Walton. You girls are sunbursts on a cloudy day, an endless source of joy that burns through any funk.

I'd also like to thank my wise and supportive writing group, Rebecca Cazanave, Ranae Rudd, Micah Cozzens, Taisha Ostler, and Lindsey Owens. Your incisive feedback made this book much better, and thanks to your feedback on many past novels, you are some of the Obi-Wans and Qui-Gons who have shaped this Jedi.

Finally, as always, I thank you, the reader. Thank you for giving this story (and its writer) a chance. Thank you for your time, your mental energy, and your imagination. I hope this book has helped you imagine a brighter future, one we get to by all being a bit better.

Until next time!

THANK YOU SO MUCH FOR READING!

When you have a moment, please appease the Virtual Gods with a review on Amazon and/or Goodreads.

And sign up for my newsletter at michaelscottwalton.wixsite.com/author to keep up with what's next!

About the Author

Michael Scott Walton is a science fiction and fantasy author. Bastion is Michael's debut, but he's been writing novels since seventh grade, when he penned a 300-page fantasy in a college-ruled notebook. His professional and academic lives have also revolved around storytelling: he has a Master's degree in English—with an emphasis in writing and rhetoric—and works full-time as director of a content marketing team.

When he's not working, writing, or dreaming of stories while he really should focus on driving, you'll find Michael adventuring with his family in the mountains of Utah.